D0377076

When Your Time is Up...

EXPIRATION DATE

edited by

Nancy Kilpatrick

EDGE SCIENCE FICTION AND FANTASY PUBLISHING

AN IMPRINT OF HADES PUBLICATIONS, INC.

CALGARY

Expiration Date
Copyright © 2015

All individual contributions copyright by their respective authors.

This is a work of fiction. Names, characters, places, and
incidents are the products of the author's imagination or
are used fictitiously and are not to be construed as real.
Any resemblance to actual events, locales, organizations, or
persons, living or dead, is entirely coincidental.

Edge Science Fiction and Fantasy Publishing
An Imprint of Hades Publications Inc.
P.O. Box 1714, Calgary, Alberta, T2P 2L7, Canada

Editing by Nancy Kilpatrick
Interior design & illustrations by Janice Blaine
Cover Illustration by Jimmy Maillet

ISBN: 978-1-77053-062-1

EDGE Science Fiction and Fantasy Publishing and Hades Publications, Inc.
acknowledges the ongoing support of the Alberta Foundation for the Arts and
the Canada Council for the Arts for our publishing programme.

Conseil des arts   Canada Council
du Canada   for the Arts

Library and Archives Canada Cataloguing in Publication

Expiration date / [edited by] Nancy Kilpatrick.
Issued in print and electronic formats.
ISBN: 978-1-77053-062-1
(e-Book ISBN: 978-1-77053-063-8)

1. Science fiction, Canadian (English). 2. Short stories,
Canadian (English). 3. Canadian fiction (English)--21st century.
I. Kilpatrick, Nancy, editor of compilation

PS8323.S3E95 2014   C813'.08760806 C2013-905020-5   C2013-905021-3

FIRST EDITION
(M-20150108)
Printed in Canada
www.edgewebsite.com

TABLE OF CONTENTS

❖ ❖ ❖

INTRODUCTION

BY NANCY KILPATRICK

MODERN LIVES SEEM littered with expiration dates. Packaging tells us when: our food will go bad; we can expect appliances to cease functioning, (often around the date the warranty expires!); contracts for services like cell phones and internet finish (and sometimes we only know this after the fact!). We spend a lot of time checking to make sure we're in the good zone, that we're covered, that there's still life happening.

But as annoying as these small expiration dates are, they fade to nothing compared to the larger events, when life as we know it stops: a species that goes extinct forever; a body of water evaporates, or dies because the PH balance alters; giant icebergs break apart and glaciers melt forever, threatening the ecosystem of this planet.

And beyond this, we are plagued with gargantuan, abstract worries the media forces us to contend with that effect not only life in the present, but the threat of oblivion for future generations of humanity: when will a huge asteroid hit the Earth and change our climate irrevocably, if it hasn't already reached that stage through ozone depletion that leads to climate change? Our sun is halfway through its existence— should we start to worry about when it will burn itself out and make living in this solar system impossible?

Buried in the midst of all this worrying are the undercurrents that touch us when the news services of the world report another catastrophic flood, tsunami, hurricane, earthquake, sinkhole, tornado, pandemic, wildfire, or a man-made devastation like a leaking oil tanker; a nuclear plant meltdown; a massive annihilation through the genocide of modern warfare. These are occurrences that reset the hands of the famous Doomsday Clock closer to the midnight hour, drawing our planetary expiration date too close for comfort.

As if we mere mortals didn't have enough on our plates, from the micro to the macro in terms of expirations, we are faced with the one termination with which we are all too familiar— the up-close-and-personal end of life for each of us and for the ones we love. It's the personal that terrifies us most because it feels the most real. And despite the internet's deathclock.com where anyone can, supposedly, estimate at which age he or she will die, the reality is, no one knows the exact date and time of their departure from this mortal coil. The only guarantee we have is that it *will* happen. The fact that you were born and are reading this means your end is destined.

Death of the young is always horrifying, because the bud of youth has not yet had a chance to blossom. Death of the old is often a release from physical or mental infirmities due to aging and, while still difficult to accept, it is perhaps more understandable that the flower wilts. Terminal illness and fatal accidents are shocking and sad, but sometimes provide relief for both the dying and for those who care about them. And then there are the hale and hearty people who succumb to a sudden heart attack or stroke, an instant end to life, unexpected, leaving survivors unprepared to cope. And victims of senseless violence that shock us and cause everyone wondering: why? Human beings die in war and in peace, at home and in prison, alone and in crowds, surrounded by loved ones or enemies or strangers. Some welcome their passing, others resist the end. We may die conscious of the process or unconscious. And the exceptional Aldous Huxley took the mind-altering drug LSD on his deathbed to provide him with more insight into the experience which, sadly, he was unable to pass on to the rest of us.

For almost all of us it is shocking to contemplate: the *I* that we identify as who we are, will be no more. The philosophy that offers the balm that we are part of nature's compost heap soothes only some. It's commonly said about life: nobody gets out alive! More than one person has wondered did the God or Gods they believe will offer another crack at existence in some form, in some realm, did these deities really give enough thought to the notion of being incarnate?

Expiration Date is an anthology of brilliant stories that examine all sorts of expirings, but mainly the ones that are personal, because those are the demises that matter most to us. How people meet their end speaks volumes about who they are, who they were, and sometimes who they were not. Death is the final mirror that reflects back at us ourselves in our raw form. All the excuses and smoke-screens and other facades vanish in the face of this brutal inevitability leaving a shocking-honest visage. Such clarity has a power and honor to it that is unique.

These stories span a range of emotions. Some will make you laugh, other will make you cry. They are grim and hopeful, sad and joyous, horrifying and comforting. You can expect to be touched in some way.

Death is one of the two largest experiences we will have, equaled only by our birth, though we are usually more aware of the one ahead than of the one behind us. It's been estimated that in the roughly 50,000 years of homo Sapiens history, more than 100 billion of us have been born. The planet's population today is less than 8 billion. As far as we can tell, but for the present survivors, everyone who has ever lived has died, and we who are alive at present will join them, eventually. Expiration is a universal connection we share with all human beings, those currently living, those who have lived and will live in the future. It is what homo Sapiens have always and will always have in common and one of the major definitions of what it means to be alive. We come with an alpha and an omega stamp, an inception and an expiration date. Knowing this is what allows us to focus on what is truly important: paying attention to our best-before date and treating ourselves, each other and life in general with kindness, understanding, respect, and experiencing the awe of the miracle that we are, at this very moment, alive!

—Nancy Kilpatrick
Montreal, 2015

✜ ✜ ✜

Negotiating
Oblivion

Sorry Seems to be the Hardest Word

by Kelley Armstrong

"**LOOKS LIKE SOMEONE** made a wrong turn on her way to Yorkville," Rudy grunted as the bar door swung open, a blast of October air rushing in.

"Close the fucking—" someone began.

Then he stopped and murmured an apology that almost sounded genuine. That's what made me twist on my stool for a look. The woman did indeed look as if she'd gotten lost on her way to the fashionable shopping district. She was in her early forties, long designer coat pulled tight, knee-high boots under it, short copper hair perfectly coifed, as if the gusts outside didn't dare disturb it.

As her gaze swept Miller's, I swear every guy sat up straighter, even the ones so drunk they needed to prop themselves on their elbows to do it. Part of that was because she was an attractive woman. Mostly, though, they pulled themselves together for the same reason one had apologized— because something about her says they damn well better. A bar filled with supernaturals, half of whom look like they'd rob their grandma for beer money, and when she walked in, they straightened and squirmed like errant schoolboys.

She strode across the hardwood floor, boots clicking. I was impressed. I've never been able to manage that sound effect in here, where the sheer amount of old booze and vomit underfoot sticks to my boots with every step.

"If you're looking for the wine bar—" Rudy began.

1

"I would love the wine bar," she said. Her accent was French. France not Quebec. Old, aristocratic French. Very old. Very aristocratic. "In fact, I'm quite certain I would prefer to squat in the alley next door. It certainly seemed cleaner. However, the person I am meeting seems to be quite comfortable here. Which does not surprise me one bit."

I lifted my beer. "Hey, Cass. Found the place okay, I see?"

"No, I do not find the place 'okay,' Zoe, as I'm sure you knew when you told me to meet you here."

"Rudy? Meet Cass. Cassandra Ducharme."

Up until this moment, there'd been one guy in the bar who hadn't quailed under Cass's haughty stare. When she was insulting his bar, Rudy looked about ready to toss her out on her ass. Now he stopped, bar towel hanging from his fingers. It took him a moment to close his mouth. When he did, he winced, as if he'd shut it so fast he bit his tongue.

"Ms. Ducharme." He hurried from behind the bar and extended a beefy hand. "Rudy. Sorry about the, uh..." He waved around the bar. "The mess. We had a party last night, and I haven't quite finished cleaning the place up."

I peered about. Miller's looked exactly as it has every day for the last fifteen years. In all that time, I'd never heard Rudy apologize for it. Now, he was wiping off a stool and offering her some Cristal he "kept in the back." He kept Cristal in the back?

I could say he was tripping over himself to be nice because Cassandra Ducharme is a vampire. But so am I. The difference, as I'm sure he'd point out, is that Cass was a real vampire— the kind that other supernaturals imagine when you say the V word. Hell, even other vampires aspire to be Cassandra Ducharme. She embodies the romantic, sophistication of the stereotype with none of the broody angst. Also, she's a stone-cold bitch. Who doesn't want to be a bitch? Well, me, for one. But that's why the joke in Millers is that there are no vampires in Toronto, because Zoe Takano doesn't count.

"I don't believe we're staying," Cass said.

I opened my mouth.

"No," she said. "We aren't staying." She started for the door.

"I haven't finished my beer."

"Bring it."

"Haven't paid for it either."

She growled under her breath, stalked back to the bar and slapped down an American twenty. I mouthed for Rudy to apply the rest to my tab, but he was too busy gaping at Cass to even pick up the money— another first for Rudy. He didn't even give me shit for absconding with his glass.

"There *is* a wine bar up the road," I said as we stepped out. "And a fetish bar the other way. I'm fond of the fetish one myself."

"I'm sure you are. As I believe I tried to indicate on the phone, this is a private conversation, Zoe. We're going to your apartment."

She swept off, coat cracking behind her. I let her get twenty feet before calling, "Wrong way!"

She glowered, spun on her heel and headed back as I went to hail us a cab.

❖   ❖   ❖

If I was still using oxygen, I'm sure I'd have been holding my breath as we walked into my apartment. I'm very proud of my place. I spent two decades in Toronto before I found just the right apartment, high above the city, with an amazing view. Then I'd set about decorating it just as slowly, each piece chosen with exquisite care.

With anyone else, I'd have rested easy, knowing they'd be impressed. But Cass makes her unliving dealing in art and antiques. I consider myself something of an expert in old stuff too— I'm a thief, specializing in artifacts. Both are excellent occupations for people who've been around a few hundred years. But as confident as I am in my expertise, I'm not on Cass's level, and I watched her walking around my apartment, waiting for her to snark.

"Nice," she said, sounding surprised. "Very nice."

"Thank you." I should leave it there, but I couldn't. "Any suggestions?"

She took a slow look around. "The sake jug doesn't fit. It's a very nice piece of folk art, though. Meiji period?"

I nodded.

"I would suggest a tea kettle from the same period. I saw a beautiful tetsubin one last week. Octangular. Silver inlaid handle. I could provide you with the seller's information."

I said I'd take it. She was right about the sake jug. As much as I liked it, I'd known it didn't quite fit.

"Also," she said. "I'd get rid of the human hiding in your bathroom."

"I'm not hiding," said a voice from the hall. "I was using it. Do you want to check?"

A young woman walked out. I'd say "a teenage girl" but she hates being called that, even if, at nineteen, Brittany technically still is one. I'd forgotten she'd be here— she often used my place as a crash-pad following afternoon classes.

"Who's the vamp?" she asked as she strolled in.

"What makes you think I'm a vampire?" Cass said.

"Because I wasn't making any noise," Brittany replies. "You sensed me. Ergo, a vampire."

"Brittany's an ex-slayer," I said.

Cass turns to me, as if she's misheard. "A what?"

"Former vampire slayer. Well, she never actually got around to slaying one, but that was her plan. I dissuaded her."

Brittany gave me a look that said she might be un-dissuaded if I keep introducing her that way. It was like having your mom tell people you wanted to grow up to be a rock star or something equally ludicrous.

"She wants to join the council someday," I said. "Fight evil. I'm training her."

I braced myself for her to make some sly remark about Brittany's chances improving if she finds a new trainer. Yet she resisted, which only made me more anxious. Cass was being nice. Cass wanted something. Shit.

"Speaking of the council..." Cass said as she made herself comfortable, while managing not to inflict a single wrinkle on her outfit. "I need to speak to you about an opportunity there. Perhaps your young friend should be on her way?"

"The council?" Brittany plopped into the chair nearest Cass. "Hell, no. What's your connect..." She trailed off and her eyes rounded. "You're Cassandra Ducharme. Holy fucking shit."

"Language," I murmured.

"But this is Cassandra Ducharme," Brittany said. "A real..." She didn't finish that. Even managed to look guilty for thinking it. "You know what I mean. She's, like, the Queen of the Vampires."

"I wouldn't say that," Cass murmured.

"You are!" Brittany said. "You're the oldest one around, right?"

Cass stiffened. Brittany didn't notice and barreled on. "You must have the most amazing stories."

"I'm sure Zoe does, too."

"Sure, but none she'll tell me."

Cass hesitated, and then seemed to remember why I might not be eager to share my past with Brittany. Might not be willing to share it with anyone I actually wanted to be able to stay friends with me. Cass knew what I was like in the early days. It's just been so long that she's forgotten.

"Well, maybe they weren't that interesting," Cass said. "You know Zoe. She has two modes: stealing things and partying. Both terribly exciting in the short term, but after a hundred and fifty years? Quite dull, I'm sure. The settings may change, but Zoe Takano does not."

Brittany tensed at the insult and looked over, waiting for me to react. When I didn't, her annoyance shifted my way. Even when I was insulted in my own home, I didn't rouse myself to fight. What Brittany didn't know is that Cass was actually saving my ass with her insults— giving an excuse for me not telling those old stories.

"What do you need, Cass?" *Now that you've finished buttering me up.*

"I don't need anything. However, the council will eventually be in need of a new delegate. My term won't last much longer, as I'm sure you're aware."

"I thought delegates served for as long as they wanted," Brittany said.

That's not the term Cass meant. Her life-term was ending. Our immortality comes with an expiry date, and by all accounts, Cassandra Ducharme's had passed years ago.

"Are you asking me—?" I said.

"Of course not." Her words came out clipped, as if I was the one who reminded her she was dying. "The *council* is asking you. I thought it would be better if Aaron came, but he insisted I do it."

She muttered something uncomplimentary under her breath. She didn't mean it. If there's one person in this world that Cassandra Ducharme cares about, it's Aaron. They were lovers for over a hundred years before she betrayed him, escaping and leaving him to a Romanian mob. He spent the next century avoiding her, but rumor had it they were back together. Did he forgive her? Probably. If Cass is the bitchiest vampire you'll ever meet, Aaron is the nicest. People sometimes nominate me for that dubious honor, but if he's forgiven Cass, he gets it. Hands down.

Also, if Aaron sent Cass to ask me to sign up as his co-delegate, that can only mean one thing.

"Britt?" I said. "I think you should leave."

"Hell, no. This is just getting—"

She stopped as she saw my look. We had a five second stare-off, but she knew better than to push. I might not fight, but I don't budge either.

"I'll catch up with you tomorrow," I said. "We'll get some training in."

She hauled herself off the chair, managing to sigh the entire time. She made it to the hall, then turned to Cass.

"Are you staying long?" she asked. "In Toronto?"

"No." Cassandra paused. "But if you are interested in the council, perhaps we can speak tomorrow. Briefly. My plane leaves at noon."

"Sounds good. Sorry you aren't staying, but that's probably just as well. It's a bad time to be a vampire in Toronto. Zoe's been having trouble with some immortality questers." She looked at me. "You were going to warn Cassandra about that, right?"

"Of course."

Brittany's look called me a liar, but she only shook her head and left.

When she was gone, Cass said, "Immortality questers?"

"Wild and crazy supernaturals who want to live forever and think we can help them do it," I said. "Preferably by decapitating us, carving us up and seeing what makes us tick— and keep on ticking."

"Obviously, I know what an immortality quester is, Zoe. If you're having problems with them..."

"Nah. There are always a few in town. Every now and then they get annoying. I haven't lost my head over it yet. So, Aaron sent you here to ask me about the delegate post. He wants you to apologize, doesn't he?"

"For what?"

"Ha-ha."

She sighed. "If you mean that business back in the twenties..."

"Thirties. 1934 to be exact. Spring in Venice. A perfect time for love."

"She was human, Zoe."

"No law against that. Which didn't stop you from interfering."

"I misunderstood the situation."

"Bullshit. You didn't trust me."

She straightened. "Which was understandable, given your past—"

"Ten years. I fucked up for ten years. Then I got my head on straight, and I hadn't caused one bit of trouble in decades—"

"Given your line of work, I'd hardly say you don't cause trouble."

I glowered at her. For a vampire, stealing was about as serious as jaywalking. "I'm as clean as they come, in every way that counts, and I was back then, too. Yet you interfered. You cost me someone I cared about. Someone I loved."

"I didn't *kill* her."

"No, you just drove her away, and made sure she'd never want to speak to me again."

"It wouldn't have worked out."

"Then it wouldn't have worked out. She was in no danger. You know how I was turned."

Silence. A look passed over Cass's face. It seemed almost like compassion, but I'm sure it was a trick of the light. They say it's impossible to make someone a vampire against her will. It's not. That's what my first lover did to me, when I refused her "gift." It was a hell beyond imagining.

"Then you know I would never, *ever* do that to someone else," I said, my voice low. "I would not have told her what I was. I would never have asked her to join me. She was safe. And you interfered."

"That was a very long time ago, Zoe."

"So no apology?"

"I don't believe I owe—"

I stood. "Then find yourself another delegate. Tell Aaron I'm sorry. I'm sure he'll understand."

"This isn't about me, Zoe. The council—"

"—will be fine with one delegate. Aaron can handle it. Now, if you'll excuse me..."

I escorted her out the door.

❖ ❖ ❖

Cass was right. Agreeing to replace her on the council didn't help her. It helped Aaron, whom I liked. It helped the werewolf delegates, whom I also liked. Hell, I knew most of the council. Good people doing good work. I wasn't much of a joiner, but I wasn't exactly anti-social. I could help. I probably should. And I would, just as soon as I got my apology.

Aaron was right, too, in sending Cass here. She needed to make amends. Put her affairs in order. One could argue that

Cassandra Ducharme didn't give a shit who she'd mowed down in the last four hundred years. A cast of thousands, I was sure. But if she truly didn't care, Aaron wouldn't send her on this quest for forgiveness. So I'd get my apology, for her own good.

"Five hundred," Rudy said when I told him my plan.

I snorted a laugh.

"Six hundred, then," he said. "You keep arguing, the price keeps rising. I need my cut, Zoe."

"If I pay you six hundred, then your cut will be six hundred. Whoever you hire will work for a bottle of booze. Cheap booze, which you'll write off as spoilage. I'll give you what you'd get with a standard fifty percent cut. Two hundred and fifty."

"Three."

"Three and you wipe my tab." I counted out the money on the bar before he could argue, and then told him what I wanted.

✤ ✤ ✤

Next I called Cass up, said I felt bad about the way we left things, and asked if she'd accompany me to the opera that night. She jumped at the chance, certain it meant I was waffling. Aaron would be so much happier if she came home saying she'd secured my agreement. And she'd be so much happier if it could be accomplished without all that apologizing nonsense.

It was a lovely performance of *Fidelio*. Afterward, I took her to a wine bar— a very nice one, I might add. Together with the tickets, the evening cost me as much as I'd paid Rudy for his performance artists. But Cass was impressed. Also, a little tipsy, as we made our way along the darkened streets. Tipsy enough that she let me steer her into a "short cut" through a churchyard. She didn't even pick up the life-signs of the guy at the other end until he stepped into the moonlit gap.

"Hello, Zoe," he said. "You're a hard girl to find these days. Been thinking hard on our offer, I hope."

I wheeled. Another man slid from the shadows, blocking our retreat. When Cass turned to see him, he lifted a machete and grinned.

"Oh God," I whispered to Cass. "I am so sorry. Don't worry. I'll get us out of this."

"I'm sure you will," she said, her tone as dry as the Chardonnay we just finished. "But I think I can handle it."

"No, don't—!"

She was already striding toward the guy with the machete. "And what do you think you're going to do with that?"

"What should be done to all blood-suckers," he said. "Off with 'er head." He grinned and waved the machete, blade glinting in the moonlight. "You'll be a lot more useful when you're dead, parasite. You'll help someone for a change. A lot of someones. Once we discover the secret—"

"Oh, stuff it," she said as she stopped in front of him. "Do you really expect me to believe you're going to lop off my head *here*? In downtown Toronto? And then what? Drag my decapitated corpse to your lair?" She turned to me. "Really, Zoe? I thought you were smarter than this."

"Cass! Watch—!"

She grabbed the guy's arm as he swung the machete. She didn't even turn around to do it. Just reached back, grabbed his arm and yanked. He might have been almost twice her size, but she caught him off guard and he stumbled. She was on him in a second, teeth sinking into his neck.

"No!" the other man cried.

He raced toward his companion as Cass let the man fall to the ground.

"Oh please," she said. "Save the drama. I'm sure you know enough about vampires to realize I've merely sedated him with my saliva. I'm hardly going to drink from a man reeking of cheap whiskey. God knows what kind of hangover I'd get." She stepped toward the second man. "Now, unless you'd like the same..."

He turned and ran. Cass looked at me, shook her head and resumed walking.

❖ ❖ ❖

I had to jog to keep up with Cass. For four hundred years old, the woman can move damn fast.

"I did not set that up," I said. "I swear it. There's no way I could have told Brittany to warn you about fake immortality questers."

"No? The girl can't receive text messages on her phone?"

"You think I texted her to say that? When? You didn't mention the delegate offer until she was in the same room with us."

"Elena forewarned you." Her coat cracked like a whip in the wind, punctuating her words. "No, not Elena. If she told me she wouldn't, she'd keep her word. It was Clayton, wasn't it? The man has a grudge against me. I have no idea why."

"Um, because you hit on him… while Elena was being held captive, fighting for her life."

She wheeled, boots scraping the pavement. "Who told you that?"

"Everyone knows. But Clay wouldn't call me with tips. He doesn't much like me either. Probably because I hit on Elena."

She rolled her eyes and resumed walking.

"Okay," I said. "Clearly those two were not real immortality questers. I'm guessing someone from Rudy's is playing a prank on me. They know I've been having trouble with questers and that you're in town. Making me look bad with a *real* vampire. Ha-ha. I'll get them back. But I did think, at first, those two were the real deal, because I have been having problems."

"I'm sure you have. Your ruse has failed. Don't compound the damage by insulting my intelligence."

"But—"

"Go home, Zoe. Our evening is at an end."

❖ ❖ ❖

I'd been following Cass for five blocks, reasoning that if she really wanted to get rid of me, she'd have hopped in a cab by now. She knew I was there, keeping pace fifty feet back, working out a strategy. Also, I was calling directions, when she'd pause on a corner and try to figure out which way to turn.

We were cutting across a quiet residential street of townhouses when I noticed the car. It was black, all the lights off as it inched along the road toward us. Then it stopped.

I broke into a run and caught up to Cass.

"That car," I whispered. "I've seen it before."

She fixed me with a look. "Really, Zoe?"

"No, I'm serious. It's them. The immortality questers."

She sighed. "I cannot believe you'd honestly try this again after—"

The car shot forward, motor gunning. I grabbed the back of her coat.

"Come on! There's a walkway right—"

She pulled away and turned to continue down the sidewalk as the car raced toward us.

"You'd better warn your friends," she said. "If they lay a hand on me, they will lose it. I am not in the mood for games."

The car rear door flew open as it slowed.

10

"Cass!" I yelled. "I'm serious! This isn't me!"

A man leapt from the car. Cass ducked him easily, but a second man had swung out from the other side. He caught her from behind, wrenching her arms back.

"Zoe!" she snarled. "This isn't funny. Tell these men to unhand me or—"

The first man grabbed her legs and they threw her into the backseat. As he wrestled her in, the second man took a step toward me.

"Little Zoe Takano," he said. "What are you going to do now? Try to stop us? Or be happy we have a prize in your stead?"

I took a slow step back.

He laughed. "That's what I thought."

I could see Cass in the backseat, fighting two men as they restrained her. She looked over at me, her eyes blazing.

"I'm sorry," I mouthed. Then I turned and ran.

✛ ✛ ✛

I watched from my hiding place as the car made a right turn, sticking to the residential roads tucked deep in the heart of downtown. Once it turned the corner, I took off. I knew a shortcut, and the roads here were narrow, plagued with stop signs that would keep their progress slow.

I calculated where they'd go, coming out onto a busier street to make a speedy escape. Sure enough, the car appeared as I waited, hidden, near a stop light. They were on a side street, meaning at this time of night, the light wouldn't change until it needed to. As they idled at the red, I snuck out, popped the trunk and slipped inside.

✛ ✛ ✛

They took Cass clear out of the city to what looked like an abandoned farm house, on a chunk of property with signs warning that condos would be coming soon. Sneaking in was a breeze. Hey, I'm a thief. It's what I do. Sadly, there was nothing here worth stealing. Except Cass, and I wasn't sure she was worth it either. At least it was an easy break in.

Cass was being held in the basement with only one guard on duty. I snuck past him and found Cass, huddled dejectedly in a room, resigned to her fate... Yeah, not in this lifetime. She was on her feet, cell phone out, obviously blocked, pacing as she waited for that life-sign that would tell her someone was coming. Although the door made barely a whisper as I opened it, she spun, fangs out, eyes glittering.

She saw me and stopped. For at least five seconds, she stared.

"It's okay," I whispered. "I had nothing to do with this."

"Yes, I know," she said. "But... you came back." I knew why she was so shocked. If the situation had been reversed, she would not have come for me. She would have gotten help — she's not a monster — but she wouldn't have rescued me herself.

"I had to," I whispered. "As nice as Aaron is, he'd have hunted me to the ends of the earth if I let you die before your time. Now, there's one guard. I didn't want to disable him, in case someone noticed. I'll go do that now. Count to ten and follow."

Before I could go, she laid her hand on my arm, stopping me.

"Thank you," she said.

"Hold that thought. We're not out of here yet."

❖ ❖ ❖

The guard was easily dispatched, and the way was still clear. The only problem was the hike to civilization after we escaped, but we stayed away from the roads, so it was merely long and cold, until finally we saw lights that suggested a place where we might find a cab.

As we headed across a field to reach the lights, Cass said, "You have my apology, Zoe. I know that's important to you, so I'll give it."

"Even though you still don't think you did anything wrong?"

She glanced over, green eyes shimmering in the dark. "No, I do not. The relationship wouldn't have lasted." She turned forward again. "They say that, for vampires, this is our afterlife. If so, then that is our hell. Everyone we care about will die. If it happens often enough, you learn that the only way to protect ourselves is not to get too attached to anyone or anything."

"Even other vampires?"

"Perhaps. Everything can die."

That's why she'd betrayed Aaron. To drive him away. Obviously, it hadn't worked. Sometimes the pain of forced separation — knowing your beloved is still out there — is worse than death. I could understand her reasoning, but I didn't agree with it. Attachments are all we have. Yes, a vampire will watch their world crumple over and over, but there's always something that follows, something new and filled with promise. And the memories remain, sweet and bittersweet.

"I did what I thought was right," she said. "But you are correct that I interfered, when I should not have. I didn't trust you to handle the situation. For that, I will apologize. Sincerely."

"Thank you."

We continued on in silence. Her mission was accomplished. Both of them. She'd been forgiven and the council would have a new delegate.

Mine had been accomplished, too. I got my apology, and it only cost me three hundred bucks. Rudy's guys had done well. I'd need to buy them a round the next time they were at Miller's.

❖ ❖ ❖

KELLEY ARMSTRONG is the author of the *Cainsville* modern gothic series, *Otherworld* urban fantasy series, *Darkest Powers* & *Darkness Rising* teen paranormal and the *Blackwell Pages* middle-grade fantasy adventure trilogy (co-written with M.A. Marr). She lives in southwestern Ontario with her family.

Banshee

by Daniel Sernine
Translation by Sheryl Curtis

THE LAST TIME anyone saw Keable was in the Elsewhere Bar.

He was drinking alone, as usual, eyes roaming over the room with a distant look, as if he were contemplating a vast, changing landscape, rather than the same old Coke ads or the Gladstone clock with the green neon.

People asked me if he was a snob— "aloof" was the word that came up once or twice. No, I didn't feel he was. Not from what I saw. He gave the impression that he had nothing to say or, at least, nothing to say to *us.*

Maybe there was nothing he *could* say to us.

I believe that there were a lot of things in Keable's life that were worth telling. But, as far as he was concerned, there was no point.

There was nothing to be done for him. So we left him there, staring down into his pint of *Chasse-Galerie*, listening to the music as if there were some truth to be found there, some comfort to be expected in those tireless decibels.

We knew almost nothing — so precious little — about him.

❖ ❖ ❖

Keable lived in a small house on Orcutt Street, one of those streets near the hospital up on the hill. The shaded lawn was reasonably well maintained, the grass occasionally too long, the wooden trim in need of paint. On the ground floor — I'd been there once — a room ran lengthwise, taking up half of the house.

The walls there disappeared behind bookshelves, interrupted only by the door and the windows. Books and records shared shelves packed so tight dust had nowhere to settle.

Few people, even among those who greeted him on a daily basis, knew what Keable's profession was. He was a composer. I believe that his past successes ensured that, from time to time, he received contracts for a movie soundtrack or a TV series. He also gave violin lessons: two or three youngsters came each week to perform their scales in the large room where, in addition to his own violin, Keable kept a computer and a synthesizer— professional quality equipment, it seemed to me.

It was possible to imagine that he listened to his own tunes, through the headset of his music player, when you saw him taking a walk or running errands, but I don't think so. His collection was rather well stocked — and his opinion of himself was relatively modest — for him to prefer the music of better known bluesmen and jazzmen. He also owned a great many operas, most on vinyl.

Bernadette, his wife, had been an opera singer.

Well, in fact, although she was an opera singer, I'm not sure she was his wife.

All I know about her is that she died in her 30s— "under tragic circumstances", according to the stock phrase, as if there were comical ways of dying.

I don't doubt that during the time spent in the Elsewhere Bar — one hour each evening, two or three times a week — Keable thought about her often.

He lived in fear of hearing her again.

❖ ❖ ❖

The little I do know about their drama, about Ronald Keable and Bernadette Dupré, I got from a common friend, Brodeur.

It's all veiled and blurry now: I don't recall Brodeur's exact words and I don't know which part I imagined or dreamed, afterward, in that twilight where dreams and memories take on the same hues.

It had all happened several years earlier. They were living in North Hatley at the time and the accident occurred at Ayer's Cliff, along one of those treacherous curves where there's a cliff on one side and the lake on the other, down below. Darkness and the freezing rain joined forces against Bernadette Dupré and her little car. The singer died in a meter of icy water, crushed against the roof of her overturned Jetta.

That night, a November night when the winds were calm, Ronald Keable, worried about his tardy companion, heard the song of the banshee, that ominous fairy whose lamentations herald the death of a loved one— at least that's what Brodeur told me.

Keable never confided in me. Was he the kind of man who could make it all up? To have imagined it, maybe. His best known compositions revealed a great deal of sensitivity; reviewers had even criticized his penchant for pathos. That said, he was no alcoholic, not even much of a drinker. A pint lasted him an hour and, at his home, I never saw anything stronger than a few liqueur bottles. I could imagine him spending an entire evening sipping an ounce of Glayva, Drambuie or Irish Mist.

Perhaps that's why he spoke so little. How can someone who has brushed up against terror and the supernatural slip into the banality of light conversation? And how can you recount the single unique thing that haunts you when you know it probably will be repeated, with a smile, among acquaintances as soon as you've left the bar?

Moreover, Marcel Brodeur was the only real friend I knew he had.

Well, Brodeur and the druggist.

❖ ❖ ❖

I have no desire to turn him into a caricature, but Keable's head was rather well suited for his personality: it was nondescript, relatively lean, with an Adam's apple prominent enough to be noticed. Abundant grey threaded throughout the dark hair and the stubble that betrayed lax shaving habits. Bags under his eyes made him look somewhat haggard.

Probably, he was only able to sleep thanks to the pills the druggist gave him. I used to run across Keable regularly as he was doing his errands, always on foot, and a few times I was in the drug store at the same time as he was. He made no secret of it: who would have wanted to risk insomnia when the voice of your lover, dead going on six years, could reach you in the dark tunnel of the night?

For the same reasons, Keable constantly surrounded himself with music: FM radio, stereo, his own music or the less pleasant sounds of his few students. Outside, as I said before, it was the portable music player (I had already observed, amused, that he had two models, an iPod with headphones, and another MP3 player with earbuds).

As long as he erected a musical barrier between his ears and the past, he wouldn't run the risk of hearing the banshee again— whether she assumed Bernadette Dupré's voice or not.

❖ ❖ ❖

I knew no more about banshees than the common mortal did: Irish or Scottish, Celtic in any case, banshees were spirits with female voices — reportedly heart wrenching — who announced the imminent death of a loved one with their lamentation. A family matter, if you believed the legends— at least according to the explanation provided by Brodeur, from whom I got the little I did know.

And, of course, banshees could occasionally herald your own death.

❖ ❖ ❖

It's said that grieving takes a year. That, for the survivors, the worst of the distress then fades away, becomes more bearable.

That wasn't the case for Ronald Keable.

Every fall, particularly in November, he would grow more sombre, his eyes more hunted, his gestures nervous. Anyone who greeted him while coming up from behind could well make him jump. As if, week by week, the anguish gradually tightened his nerves, like the strings on a violin, until the autumn was no more than a bad memory.

That evening, the last evening anyone saw him, his mood seemed more even. Definitely not more serene. He looked as grave as a grey stone in a cemetery. But more resigned, perhaps?

I don't know if dates, anniversaries can be considered all that important. Was it that precise night, six years earlier, that Bernadette Dupré had plunged into Lake Massawippi and a tragic voice had screeched in Keable's ears in their beautiful home in North Hatley? Brodeur himself was no longer certain of the date when we spoke about it.

His *Chasse-Galerie* downed, the dregs of beer long turned warm in his mug, Keable went out into the cold night. He looked determined, as if he had finally made up his mind— and that is something I can confirm after the fact. That evening, what I

17

read in his face was more like apprehension, as if the decision he had just made would give him a bad time.

It had to have taken some time for him to walk to the Gorge, depending on whether he took a direct route or not. It was raining that evening — again — and people only went out if they really needed to, by car if possible. The police didn't find anyone who had crossed Keable's path after he left the bar.

So, no one knows exactly where he entered Gorge Park; someone who was determined could manage it without much difficulty; all it took was a minimum amount of scouting beforehand.

The Coaticook River was high that autumn; for weeks the rain had been relentless.

In the summer, Keable's body would have been found below the walk, barely much farther, among the rocks on the shore. This year, at the end of a rainy fall, the current carried the suicide victim toward the large, flat zone where the Coaticook grows calm, one hundred meters downstream from the falls.

But they only found him the next day, at noon, before his disappearance had even been reported, since the man lived alone.

No one doubted that his death was deliberate. Dark temperament, depressive mood, the two mingled easily in the lay mind.

Was it merely a moment's distraction that caused him to leave his MP3 player and his ear plugs on his chair in the bar? Brodeur and I are the only ones who know that this omission was crucial. Without music to form a rampart between his ears and the spirit world, Keable became vulnerable.

I believe that he did it on purpose, determined to finally confront his ghosts, aware that he could not spend the rest of his life plugging his ears.

Perhaps he wanted to hear the voice of his beloved one last time, even if it took on the gloomy tones of death.

As well, Brodeur and I know a few things more than the coroner who closed the file.

First, one of my students, Trottier, told me a few days after the tragedy that he had seen Keable on Child Street, running with his hands over his ears, eyes wild. Initially Trottier thought that Keable was rushing because of the rain and that he held something, possibly a clear plastic bag, over his head to keep his hair dry. But Keable had raced past the window of a shop whose neon spilled light into the night and Trottier had clearly seen that the composer's head was uncovered, that his hands shielded his ears.

"And he was talking to himself," my student added. But, since Trottier was on the other side of the street, he heard nothing. Perhaps there weren't even any words, just exclamations or confused cries. The fact is that my student was listening to rap on his music player.

Keable was scared, that much was clear. Terrorized or frightened, I would add, extrapolating with words that are not part of a sixteen-year-old's vocabulary.

Did Keable hear something only in his head or did audible keening really hound him?

Now, I'll put to paper a little more than what I actually told Brodeur. I had left the Elsewhere Bar shortly after Keable, but I didn't go straight home.

Despite the rain, dressed for the cold and the damp, I made my way to Gorge Park. To the top of the tower, to be exact, in the midst of an impenetrable night where the few rare lights from town stretched into golden or mother-of-pearl filaments. I love the shadows, the exhilaration of roaming the dark, the purple man that blooms out of me in the deep of the night...

That night I didn't see Keable at the Gorge. Even though the walkway starts barely twenty metres from the tower, shadows covered the park with an opaque mantle that even *my* eyes could not pierce.

Yet, I'm convinced that I heard something and it wasn't the cry of terror of a jumper who feels the void opening before him. And there was no wind, apart from a silken, glacial breeze.

No, what I heard that evening, distinctly although not very loud, was wailing. A long, gloomy cry, a heart-rending lament, both musical and painful, from a female voice. Obviously, I had no idea that Keable was in the park as well and that this phenomena concerned him above all. I only inferred that after the fact.

What more can I say? That shivers ran up and down my spine, shaking me to the core of my very being? That the cry passed overhead like a squall, as if some night bird carrying it had flown over the entire length of the park in an instant?

I'll never reveal why I was perched on top of the tower that night like a bird of prey. What more can I say apart from the fact that I now live in fear of once again hearing the call of the banshee and this time 'tis for me she'll wail her omen.

✢ ✢ ✢

Though less known to North American readers than some of his fellow Québécois F & SF writers, **DANIEL SERNINE** has a career spanning more than 40 years, with 39 books published. His works have repeatedly garnered prizes, including the *Grand prix de la science-fiction et du fantastique québécois* in 1992 and 1996.

The original French version was featured in *Maure à Venise,* a collection of Daniel Sernine's short stories, published by Éditions Vents d'Ouest, 2005.

❖ ❖ ❖

SHERYL CURTIS is a professional translator from Montreal, Quebec, with translated stories appearing in *Interzone; Year's Best Science Fiction 4; Year's Best Fantasy and Horror 15;* numerous *Tesseracts; The Mammoth Book of New Jules Verne Adventures;* and Sylvie Bérard's novel, *La Terre des Autres (Of Wind and Sand).*

Riding Shotgun

by Elaine Pascale

It HAD BEEN over thirty years since Angela had first seen the white wolf in the sky.

She had been a small girl when the carnivorous face in a cloud appeared, marking her as both unique and crazy. She had begun by telling no one — then followed up by telling everyone — of what she had seen.

"There is a wolf in the sky and he has the body of a man," she told her parents.

Ignored by both, she turned to her beloved brother, then to her tolerated cousins. No one knew anything about this creature, or seemed to care, yet Angela understood that she had caught a glimpse of a powerful being.

Once of age, she searched in books with topics that included: fable, mythology, deities and demons. She found information on Remus and Romulus, on Fenrir, on the Big Bad Wolf, but her wolf did not reside in any of the books. Only the sky was large enough to house him.

Her career path had been predestined and permitted by the white wolf. One night, as a teen, she saw wafts of silver smoke coming from an apartment building two streets from her home. The smoke crawled across the darkened sky, appearing to hover above the building, seeming to open its elongated snout in an attempt to snatch the building in its barbarous teeth. She and her brother, Eric, had snuck out, tightly rolled together in a big bed sheet. They had been startled by sharp, crisp thunder that sounded like a wolf's jaw snapping shut. They followed the blazing lights and sirens, and watched firefighters and paramedics pulling people from the smoke wolf, pulling people from the brink of death. While Eric had been unfazed by the experience, Angela found her true calling. This was a way to work both with and against the wolf of her imagination, the wolf that terrified and excited her. It was meant to be.

While the wolf remained elusive in his home in the clouds, occasional clues about her destiny presented themselves. Once, she found an abandoned blood pressure cuff in a field; another time, she had been unexpectedly de-registered from robotics in high school and placed into first aid. Medical training came as easily as the mythology it had replaced. In fact, at times, the two studies seemed interchangeable. Patients' stories unfolded like fables in the event of happy outcomes; allegories when served as fatal warnings. Poisoned apples, witches in ovens, girls in bears' beds — Angela had seen it all.

She even believed that her most recent partner in emergency, Gary, looked like the stock hunter in fairy tales: ordinarily handsome and modestly strong. Silent, like the hunter, and prone to an existence in the shadows until needed. Angela fancied herself in the role of the cloaked maiden— luring and out-cunning the slobbering, voracious wolf/beast.

Being an EMT felt magical: doling out miracles with the wave of a wand, or a defibrillator.

She had asked Gary how he felt about their work. His approach was more mundane.

"It's a job… my job," he answered noncommittally. "I do what I can, and there are just as many things that I can't do."

"Yeah," she agreed, "you can't save them all."

"Nope. There are rules about that."

She nodded, even though she didn't understand what that meant. "So… what do you do during your down time?" she had prodded.

"I think about it…"

"It?"

His face took on a stony look. "Death. I think about it because we're surrounded by it all day."

She smiled and tried to change the tone of the conversation, "That's depressing."

He smiled in return. "Is it?"

She realized that for her, it wasn't. She enjoyed being so close to death. The miracles she witnessed hit her like a mainlined drug. She sought that high with a compulsion equal to the strongest addictions.

❖ ❖ ❖

She rode that high with a bearded and breathless Gary, as they raced to the latest call involving a ninety-two year old male. His equally aged wife had told the dispatcher that her husband had been shot in the foot. Strangely, there was no blood, but the man was not breathing. When she peered down at his naked foot, Angela saw a scar that had seen more birthdays than she. When she opened his shirt, she was greeted by many scars; this man was as comfortable with receiving medical help as Angela was with giving it.

"He's been asleep for years," the wife called out, obviously disoriented.

"She should come, too," she whispered to Gary, as they loaded the man onto the ambulance. "She needs to be examined."

Gary nodded beneath his nonstandard black hoodie that Angela would come to identify as his signature piece, and went to take the woman's elbow, but she shooed him away.

"I always follow the trail of crumbs to find him." She smiled with satisfaction and sat on the curb, looking blankly into the back of the emergency vehicle. This made it easier for Gary to lift her and place her inside, seating her beside her husband.

Angela was able to get the man's vitals and to restart his heart. The anomalous rhythm of his assisted breathing led her to believe that his warranty had expired. Without assistance, he would stop breathing completely. Yet, the man's eyes opened confidently when breathing was restored, and he appeared aware and alert. He even winked at his wife, once.

As Angela continued working on him in the ambulance, she could not help but feel that she was being watched. She glanced at the wife, who was smiling at the roof of the vehicle, and knew it wasn't the old woman's presence that was throwing her. This felt like a hunch. Like the certainty that the coffee pot was left on when one was on route to a vacation destination. Or the need to recheck locks before going to bed. It was a tugging, deep inside, that enslaved as it distracted. It was the equivalent of being warned to stay on the path, but being tricked into a race to Grandmother's cottage by a charming canine.

When the man's eyes had opened, they focused on the front cab. Angela would have sworn that she saw Gary's face reflected in the eyes of the patient. Impossible! Gáry was driving.

"What a nice dog," the old woman casually said, and looked at the same spot on which her husband had been fixated. "I had a dog like that once, not as big, of course, but a nice dog..." She then looked at her husband, whose eyes were closed again. "Henry, I think the dog wants you to go with him."

Every time the husband's vitals ceased, the woman spoke to the dog. When his signs were restored, she stopped talking.

As they arrived at the hospital, the wife waved and called, "Bye, doggie."

❖ ❖ ❖

The feeling of forgetting something important, that nagging hunch, came to fruition later. Angela arrived home to find her front door ajar. She knew she had locked it, swore she had locked it. She always did. Besides, the television news had warned of severe gusts. Sometimes she kidded that while Eric lived in a house of stone — a formidable beach cottage that was impervious to the onslaught of ocean winds and salivating sea spray — she lived in the proverbial house made of straw: her doors blew open with such frequency and ease.

Which was why she always locked the door carefully. Which was why she always gently pushed on the outside of the door, to assure herself of its security.

The open door wouldn't matter — it would not be a stomach-dropping sight — if not for her beloved cat, Lijah, who spooked easily. He was nowhere to be found. Lijah had always been an indoor cat, so she worried about his safety. She hoped he would be on the front step, waiting for breakfast in the morning.

Her hopes were met halfway: in the morning, the cat was on the step, but he was not alive. His body looked peaceful, except for the fact that his heart had been pulled out and pulverized. Despite her training, Angéla had no idea what could cause this.

Normally, death did not startle her; she was far too accustomed to it. Besides the loss of her pet, the irony shocked Angela: she had saved one man's heart, while her companion's heart had been torn away.

Broken hearted, in a way that was neither like the saved man nor the slaughtered animal, Angela held a quick burial for Lijah and then reported to work.

When she pulled into her driveway on her way home, she had a clear view of the old oak tree under which poor Lijah lay. The stone she had placed as a temporary marker was in view, as well as a figure, clad in what appeared to be a black shroud. She could not see the face, but some intuitive part of her feared that if she saw it, it would be recognizable.

She shut her eyes for a minute to collect herself, then saw that the figure was gone.

❖ ❖ ❖

After assisting a psych transfer, a bleeding ulcer call, and a minor head wound victim, the winner of *worst case of the day* called in.

A girl had been submerged in her backyard swimming pool for an estimated fifteen minutes. She had been trying to retrieve one of her dolls which had found its way into the pool.

After arriving, they hit the *on scene* button on the rig and grabbed the defibrillators. CPR was already in progress by the police, who were using a bag. Angela began trying to get a tube into the girl's mouth, but her throat had constricted. She and Gary worked and worked; in the background the police talked to the parents and took notes for their report. Angela felt dizzy, winded. She peered at Gary's sweaty brow, shadowing his jaundiced eyes.

"God," she sighed with fatigue.

"You wanna quit? Call it *presumed*?" he whispered, reaching a hairy arm toward the tubing that Angela had struggled with.

She was shocked. They weren't supposed to quit; they couldn't quit. She shook her head, focusing on the girl. From the corner of her eye, she saw Gary's ubiquitous hood slide back, revealing feral hair much whiter than it had been before.

If his hair was an anomaly, the girl was a miracle.

Her heart began to beat again, faintly, in a lazy waltz-like time. Angela couldn't help but think about how the girl probably resembled the doll she had been trying to rescue. Her thin, golden hair was plastered to her porcelain cheeks. Her blue lips were slack and they quivered with each difficult breath.

But, miraculously, she was breathing.

Angela felt higher than the clouds where the white wolf lived.

❖ ❖ ❖

When she arrived home, her neighbors were in the street. Mrs. Taylor, who lived next door to her, was crying and talking to a police officer. Angela had been a surrogate aunt to young Lydia: had babysat her when needed, had attended her school play. They baked cookies, and shared a love of fables starring wolves. Angela had volunteered to watch the seven- year-old that night while her parents went to a concert.

Her stomach dropped as she neared the scene, overhearing the discussion between her neighbor and the officer.

"It was a horrible accident," Mrs. Taylor was saying, wiping tears with her wrist. "I had been watching her. She was in the tub, playing with a doll, washing the doll's hair." She rocked on her feet and picked at her cuticles.

"The phone rang... I thought it would be all right. I thought... when I returned, I was only gone for a minute ... no more than two ... she was under water. She's not a toddler, the water was not that deep, but she was under."

Mrs. Taylor, noticing Angela's presence, looked at her imploringly. "I tried to save her, I tried to pull her up but... but it felt as if something ... someone ... was holding her down..."

✦ ✦ ✦

Angela had been riding shotgun with Gary for some time. She confided everything, but knew little about him. She watched him from her passenger seat. She enjoyed being with him and had even imagined spending time with him off the job. She felt he knew her, understood her. And, she thought he was handsome. She liked his height and his eyes. His smile was the only thing she needed to warm up to — it could be cold and disconcerting, and his gums were purplish — the color of the inside of a dog's mouth.

Despite his cold smile, he often howled with laughter at her lame attempts at jokes. And he was very easy to get along with.

This particular shotgun ride ended at an apartment at 2 a.m. on a Saturday morning. It was a small corner nook of an old Victorian, reminding Angela of a tower that would house either a damsel with very long hair, or one with a fetish for spinning wheels. Their visit was not instigated by external witches, but from villainy within, in the form of a faulty line in the gas stove. When Angela and Gary reached the top of the stairs, she noticed claw marks on the door. Gary kicked the door open and they found a man lying on the rug, desperate for oxygen. Immediately, they tried to resuscitate him.

Just as Angela was thinking they were stabilizing him, the door to the apartment blew shut. She was reminded of her own door, blown open; both doors propelled by imperceptible winds.

"Open it," Gary growled.

Stunned, Angela couldn't help but momentarily ignore the patient.

"The door," Gary urged.

"We can get it when we load him on the stretcher."

Gary pulled away from the man and pointed to the door. Angela saw flecks of stain beneath Gary's thick nails. Flecks of color that matched the stain of the door jamb of the apartment. Flecks that matched the dense hair on Gary's knuckles.

He fixed her with phosphorescent eyes. There was a roaring in her ears, like the sound the waves made at Eric's cottage. She couldn't think, she couldn't remember why she was in this small, hot room. Her only thought was about opening the door and getting some fresh air and relief from the monotonous wailing in her ears. She was compelled, driven, to the door.

When she turned back, she found Gary still on his knees, his arms crossed, shaking his head.

"He's gone," he said, his hood forcing his face into shadows.

❖ ❖ ❖

Shotgun again, and wondering why Gary never let her drive.

Some boys had been joy riding and the ride had soon become short on joy and long on grief. According to a survivor, two cars had been racing when they came to a bend in the road. One car cleared the bend, the other slammed into the guardrail, the vehicle wedged tightly by the blood-splattered rail on either side.

Angela and Gary immediately assessed a double-fatality. The passenger had been thrown through the windshield, over the guardrail, where he slid several yards across gravel, rocks and thorny border hedges. A large portion of his internal organs had migrated outside of his body, and he gave no signs of life. The driver was still in his seat, similarly violated, and unresponsive.

The police were interviewing the riders of the other car, when one teen, obviously in shock, shouted, "Where's Will?"

"Will?" the cop asked.

"Yeah. He was in that other car, too."

All the responders looked at the car: no one else was around the vehicle. They scanned the area where the passenger had been found. Nothing. Angela tried to look, but was distracted by the fact that Gary was standing still, breathing heavily. This was the steamy exhale of a beast that could blow your house down. She examined the lit area around him— the exploring officers walked amongst the shadows their bodies made; Gary's body cast none.

One of the searching officers looked up and yelled, "Oh God, there he is!"

Will was suspended in a tree, the branches holding his neck like a makeshift noose.

"How are we supposed to get him?" Gary pulled his hood tighter. "Where's the fire trucks... the ladders?"

Angela wondered the same thing. She raced to the ambulance and got on the *walkie*. It was dead. She shouted to an officer, "Try your radio!"

The boy dangled helplessly, unconscious; his color was not good. He was not far up and, ignoring protocol, Angela scurried up the tree. Gently, she freed the boy.

"Help me!" she called.

One of the officers at the base of the tree caught Will as she lowered him, easing the boy to the ground. As Angela was getting to the ground herself, the officer called out, "He's got a pulse!"

The mainlined drug of the miracle hit Angela and she cheered. Gary, though, had turned his back to them, his interest captured by the deceased.

❖ ❖ ❖

Angela tried to sleep, but could not stop thinking about Gary's odd behavior on the scene. He had seemed disinterested, reluctant to go through with the rescue. Could she no longer trust him to help out when the chips were down? Why did he seem to lack a connection to the victims? Her phone rang, a reprieve from further worrisome thoughts.

Her mother said hello, but could manage no more.

"Mom? What is it?"

Wet gasps followed by, "It's your brother."

"Eric? What about him?"

Nothing from the other end but shattered breath. "Mom!" the acoustic equivalent to a slap across the face.

"Angela," her mother managed, "he's dead."

She remembered building forts with him and playing with flashlights beneath the tented sheets. She remembered his warmth and the way he teased her. Those are things that can't be snuffed out, that can't die. "It's not true."

"It is. Hung… he left a note."

Angela was whispering, "No, no, no…" This was not the Eric that she knew. He would not do something like this.

"There's more… he talks to you in the note."

"Oh, God!" Should she stop her; did she want to know?

"He says that you were right, all along. You were right about the wolf."

❖ ❖ ❖

All through her training and experience, Angela had been blissfully unaware of the psychological pain of death. Some of what she had seen, and had to do as part of her job had traumatized. She'd gone into a state of shock after responding to a particularly gruesome scene involving several men at a construction site. But she had never felt the hopeless despair that death leaves behind. It felt like being trapped in a wolf's mouth, all 1500 pounds of pressure per square inch, squeezing. The pressure smothered and hurt her heart.

How could life continue around her? Her brother, her oldest friend, was gone. How could *she* continue?

A few days after the funeral, Angela went to Eric's to empty the refrigerator, hoping the mundane work would empty her mind. From the window, she was surprised to see Gary standing on the beach. This Gary looked like the figure at Lijah's grave and, unlike the man with whom she rode shotgun, his face was longer, more feral.

He was not the hunter/hero. Over the years, she had confused her instant identification with him for some sort of companionable comfort. But now she knew: he was no longer in the sky; she just hadn't recognized his human form.

Enraged, she ran to him. She was furious with him and with herself. She realized what she had always known but had been unwilling to admit. "Why?" she screamed at the back of his hooded head. "Why did you have to take him?"

He turned toward her, his lupine face peeking from the folds of his hood.

29

"He wouldn't have done this… he wouldn't have killed himself. You did it and I want to know why!"

He shrugged with that aggravating disinterest. "It's my job."

He had given her this same, noncommittal answer before and it infuriated her now.

Before she could say or do anything more, he said, "Let me show you." He drew a picture of a body hanging from a tree, then another body hanging from a belt. He put an equal sign between them. "One for the other." He pointed to the tree, "*he* didn't go, so," he pointed to the belt, "*he* had to."

She felt sick. "An exchange?"

He nodded and continued drawing in the sand. The old man, the drowned girl. They were never meant to survive. Since they did, someone else had to take their place.

It was not about miracles, it was about mathematics.

Gary's demonstration began to show the fairness of it— a balance. He drew numbers in the sand, computed equations. The sand took on the appearance of a chalkboard in a master's level calculus class. He scratched out Social Security numbers, personal identifier numbers, national identity numbers, and computed those. The math worked out. There were ones who had to go when they had to go. If they didn't, another had to go in their place.

Balance.

She shook her head, angry at the simplicity of it all. "It's all an arrangement. Predestined," she muttered.

He nodded gravely, yellow eyes lowered. "Most doctors and rescuers realize that. But you, you have always been unique, the outlier. That's why you had to ride shotgun." He took on the cold smile again, the one that looks inside the picnic basket meant for Grandma and suggests the race.

"Why?"

"To learn."

She hated the lesson but knew there was no point in arguing. She also hated herself, knowing she had endangered those around her, simply because she had been too headstrong to heed the warnings. "But, how will I know the ones that aren't destined to go? We have to be able to save some, right?"

He nodded again. Then, he drew a symbol. When Angela saw the symbol, she would know: these she could save.

The wind blew sharply, toying with the loose flesh around his mouth, pulling his lips into the pantomime of a snarl.

"What about... me?" she asked.

He pointed to a number that was the same one on her tax forms and student loans. Then he reconfigured the equation around it. It needed no explanation: if she did not play fairly, the next number to be up would be hers.

❖ ❖ ❖

For some time, Angela was mindful of the symbols, or lack thereof. It was simple to 'flub' a rescue: easier than she would have imagined. But over time, something changed. Maybe a part of her missed Gary, missed riding the highs — riding shotgun — with him. Maybe she missed the miracles, which were no longer miraculous, but a revolt against Death. Or, maybe she was simply crazy. But who could have turned away from the small child swelling to three times his normal size from a bee sting? Or the newlywed, the wheels of his new SUV pinning him to the pavement, while he tried to gasp the name of his love?

Even with her own life on the line, she couldn't avoid the thrill.

As the symbols grew larger and more obvious, she made more effort to ignore them. On a day filled with another nagging *hunch*, she returned to the sandy spot where Gary had done his calculations. Despite the recent rain, she saw a number engraved on the beach, a new number, and only one: her number.

There was nowhere to hide, so she drove. Driving made her feel powerful, in control. No more passenger seat for her. She felt safe inside the familiar vehicle.

Until the passenger seat belt light began blinking. An angry chime accompanied the flashing light; a warning sent only when weight pressed on the seat.

A part of her wanted to reach out, to feel if anything, anyone, was there. The sane part of her wanted to focus on the road.

She glanced to her right: a wolfish face, cloaked in Gary's hood. Death was now riding shotgun.

As she skidded, Angela realized that she was no longer angry and not the least bit terrified. She whispered, "Hi, doggie," and she waited. Waited for the white wolf to make his move, because, contrary to rumor, to what she had always believed, when you're time came, Death played fair.

❖ ❖ ❖

ELAINE PASCALE lives on Cape Cod with her husband, son and daughter. Her writing has been published in several magazines and anthologies. She is the author of *If Nothing Else, Eve, We've Enjoyed the Fruit.* Elaine enjoys a robust full moon, chocolate, and collecting cats.

THE TWENTY SEVEN CLUB

BY J. M. FREY

LIQUID SHIVERS AT the end of the needle. It's clear, vaguely blackish in the way that the curve of the drop reflects in the low light of the dimmed pot lights, and enticing. I have no idea what it is, but I do know that it's deadly.

Terry wouldn't be offering it if it wasn't.

"No," I say. "I've… I've changed my mind." I move to get up off the edge of the tub, but Terry's hand is on my shoulder. She doesn't push, she just presses her nails lightly against my bare skin. A thrill rushes up my spine, chiming inside my brain, filling my ears with the addictive hum of songs that have yet to be written down.

Terry laughs. It's like a hundred strings being plucked together. Sometimes it's heavenly when she laughs, orgasmic joy in the *pizzicato* ripple of a sound wave, perfect, delicate harmony. Today it sounds like a toddler mashing a piano keyboard.

"You can't change your mind," she says.

"But I have. I have!"

She sighs, put-upon and patronizing and even that makes my fingers itch for a pencil and some staff paper. "Okay, fine. You can change your mind. But that won't change your fate. You signed the contract. We have a deal."

She waves the syringe at me, and the droplet splashes onto the pristine tile. The movement of her arm is a *glissando* against the air. Her toes tap beside the poisonous splatter, a barefoot drumming in perfect four-four. I spare a thought for the poor hotel maid who is going to find me. I suppose that thought should be one of charitable pity. Mostly, it's fury that some poor hotel maid is going to find me *at all*, and I can't stop it.

"I kept my end of it," Terry says. "Your turn."

"But I don't want to. Can't I just... can't you just take it back?"

"You think you're the first one to try to bargain on the precipice?" Terry snarls, anger flooding her classic features briefly before melting away, leaving her face statuary blank. "You think Kurt didn't whine? You think Dickie, and Leslie, and Alexandre didn't suddenly decide that they'd rather be has-beens?" She purses her pouting lower lip, tapping the syringe thoughtfully against her flesh, a small white indent against shiny strawberry-flavoured gloss. I want to kiss her so bad. I want to *everything* her so bad, so bad it hurts in ways that no one else can ever understand. Well, no one who hasn't had a contract with Terry would understand. No one who hasn't had her skin burn their palms. "Jimi, though. Jimi went with his pride intact, head high. Good man, that Jimi. Kept his promises."

"I was a kid!" I try. "What was ten years of fame to a teenager? I didn't realize that I'd want the rest of it, too."

"Greedy," Terry admonishes. She leans down to lick the side of my ear. Whole albums of melodies pour out of her sigh. "You've lived more in a decade than most people do in a lifetime, and you want more? More cars, more vacations, more booze, more concerts, more groupies to fuck? More designer denim and designer drugs?"

"But there'd be more for you too. wouldn't there? A hundred more—"

"Ringtones and compilation records and parody songs? No. I've sucked all the art out of you, my darling. You've got nothing left to give."

"But I do!" I should be ashamed that I'm crying. Thick, wet sobs, mucousy, desperate and disgusting, no accord between my choking coughs and the clench of my fists in the fabric of her trousers. But I've never had shame in front of Terry. She stripped it all away, all the confusion, all the self-loathing, all the awkwardness. She made me *swagger*. I gave her everything in return. All of it. Anything she asked for. *Everything* she asked for.

Except this.

"You don't have any more. You're a husk."

"I can hear it. When you touch me."

"Those aren't for you."

"You goddamned *tease*." I try to push her away, to shove past her, but Terry isn't the kind of person that you can just shove away. She is the earworm that nibbles at your brain until you go mad with it, mad for *her*. Mad for her breath against your neck, her legs around your waist, her hair, the pluck of her fingertips as she plays your spine. "Why show it to me if I can't *have* it?"

"You can have this." She holds up the needle.

"No!"

She sighs again, *adagissimo*, petulant. "Really, my darling, this tantrum is getting ugly. You made the deal. It's even signed in *blood*, you theatrical little thing, you. I've used you up."

"So just go away and *leave me alone*."

Terry laughs like a chorus of silver bells, a rolling *roulade* against the empty glass and cold ceramic that embraces us. "Oh, no. If you live, then everything else you've done up until now becomes *meaningless*. You do understand that, don't you? That's been the whole point of our little living arrangement. For your work to *feed* me it has to be respected, treasured, rare. There can't be any more. No slow slide into ignominy. No gigs at has-been clubs for lusting cougars. No embarrassing reunion tours. It all has to be gone. Completely. And in an instant. And for that to happen, you *have to be dead*."

I've been arrested for assault before, but I've never hit Terry. That's why it surprises her when I ball up my fist and crack her across the jaw. *Con Bravura.* Even the most loyal of dogs fight for their lives when they're backed into a corner. Shock gives me the opening I need to dart past her. I am out of the bathroom and slamming down the hotel corridor. I expect to hear an enraged scream, or a *crescendo* of laughter echoing after me.

All I hear is some stupid gaggle of tourists gasping. "That's—! Omigod, I can't believe it, that's really—! Did you see!?" their voices screech, *allegretto vivace*. They raise their camera phones, sway forward, catch themselves, suspended in their self-surprise for a long heartbeat, then press back against the wall. They are caught in that beautiful magnetic metronome that makes them shy away from celebrity and yet grasp for it at the same time. The three-four waltz of attraction.

I used to love that dance. The seduction, the slow smile, the gesture— plucking one of them out of the safety of their numbers for a night, making that one special among his or her peers, just by laying my hand on theirs. Transferred divinity.

I'll never do that dance again.

The slam of the fire door against the concrete wall of the staircase rattles in my ears. Blood rushes to underscore the sound of my feet as I run down the stairs, a harsh counterpoint in the arching suck of air whooshing in and out of my lungs. Music in everything I do, even as I flee.

I swerve when I hit the lobby, take the back way out, past the paparazzi parked by the valet stand. I always dive straight towards the cameras, that's my habit, living life *con force*. Breaking habits might save my life. If Terry can't anticipate what I'll do next, maybe I can...

Night air slaps my cheeks. Terry is standing by the side of the service road. Waiting. Smiling. Arms open, hands empty. No syringe. My heart splutters into a *caesura*, silent indefinitely, until it ratchets back up, pattering in cut time.

As if I could ever outrun her. Silly me.

I slow to a jog, then stop beside her. "Terry," I plead. "Please."

"If you didn't intend to keep your end of it, you should have never signed the contract."

"I was a kid. It was my first gig. You fucked me in the coatroom. How could I say no?"

"Human weakness is not my sphere of influence," Terry says with a shrug. Unfeeling bitch. "It's time, my darling." She takes my hand, and I can't fight the automatic muscle memory that makes me curl my fingers around hers.

"Please."

"It's less tragic, but this will do," Terry says. She sounds regretful. "I did so want something a bit nobler for you. You could have gone out like Jimi."

She pulls me forward, right to the edge of the sidewalk. Around us, the streetlamps spark and crack, plunging this section of the roadway into dangerous darkness. I am wearing black. I never wear anything else. Appearances are everything in this business. And no one but me can see Terry.

She cranes her head to the left. The lights of a lone delivery van bobble along the road.

"No!" I dig my heels into the edge of the kerb, struggling against the *coda*. "They O.D.ed! All of them! All the rest! That's how it's supposed to go! Not like this, Terry. Please!"

"Don't be silly," Terry breathes, her breasts hot against my arm. "Don't you use Wikipedia? If it isn't drugs or booze, it's usually an auto accident." And then she shoves.

The pain is so fleeting that I don't bother to catalogue it. The crunch is loud. I don't know if it's coming from inside my own body or if it's the sound of a windshield fracturing. Hitting the tarmac drives the air out of my lungs. It takes an inordinate amount of time to drag more back in.

Legato, dolce, a quiet slow hiss in the rest between movements.

The horn blares, the driver shouts. It's some poor stupid roadie who is probably going to sue my estate for millions for the emotional trauma. That's fine. I don't need my millions any more. I don't need anything.

Except, maybe… Yes. I think I am allowed to want *that*. One last time. It's the least she can do.

"Terry." I turn the ruin of my wrist, pulp of a hand palm up, fingers cupped, like she taught me. I reach towards her as a supplicant. Praying.

Terry smiles softly, colorless eyes sparkling. She crouches. She takes my hand.

Nothing. *Silenzio.*

The music is gone.

"No." I think I say it. Something burbles in my chest, wet and red. It might come out sounding like the word. I bet Terry understands, anyway, so I try again. "Not fair!"

Something is wrong. It's not working! For the first time in ten years, the brush of her otherworldly skin against mine makes no sound at all.

That hurts far more than getting run over ever could.

I scream.

"Happy birthday to you, happy birthday to you—" Terry warbles into my ear. *Al niente.*

✢ ✢ ✢

J. M. FREY is a actor, author, and fanthroplogist. She is the author of *Triptych* (Dragon Moon Press); *Hero Is a Four Letter Word* (Short Fuse); *The Dark Lord and the Seamstress* (CreateSpace); "Whose Doctor?" in *Doctar Who In Time And Space* (McFarland Press). This is her first horror short.

TRINITY DEATH

BY STEVE VERNON

DID YOU EVER wake up with a thirst that you couldn't quench? Two floors below me a man is opening a tin of beer. *Rolling Rock*, my favorite brand. I can hear the fizz of the cold bubbling ale. He laps at the tin, sucking at the spillage and trying not to waste a drop.

He is preoccupied.

He is easy.

I enter him while he blinks and belches.

For a moment the beer spills down his chin as his eyes glaze over.

The rotating ceiling fan whispers like the incoming tide.

And then he begins to swallow and I drink with him enjoying the heavy malt-ridden wetness filling my throat. I savor the sharp hop tang, the yeasty odor, the strong pleasing aftertaste. I empty three more tins in quick succession and then — as I feel him becoming slowly and sluggishly aware of my presence — I leave him to his empty beer tins wondering where the time slipped away.

My thirst is quenched.

I want something more and so I scan the building for sensation.

In the bedroom of the apartment above mine, a young couple is making love. They each wear rings of gold but neither is pledged to the other. Their fear adds a piquant spice to their furtive coupling. The sordid stink of danger and intrigue hangs heavily above them like a scented silk awning in a seraglio. I enter while their thoughts are scattered between passion and mutual unshared

38

guilt. It is an intriguing sensation. I am inside him, inside her. A double penetration — sharing each within each — joining with them in the sweet percussion of flesh.

I dance within their thoughts.

Their dreams belong to me.

He has a wife, young and pregnant and waiting for him to come home to the imagined sanctuary of the split-level suburbs. She, in turn, has a husband away on a business trip. I force them into harder sex, goading them, urging them into a heated frenzy. Alternately they beg for respite and plead for the other to never stop.

I want to tangle it further. Perhaps I should reach out and find their respective mates. Possibly I could lead them into their own parallel affair with each other. Perhaps I could bring them here for a foursome.

Enough.

The two illicit lovers have become aware of my presence. They feel the weight of my unseen eyes gazing upon their adultery. They blame bad nerves, they blame each other. He wilts and she dries shut. There is blood where he has torn her and the chaffing of friction burns their flesh.

I open my eyes, safe and comfortable upon the sanctuary of my living room couch. My erection tents the fabric of my trousers and begs for release. I scan their apartment for further opportunities. My search is frustrated. The young lovers have rolled to the border of their shared beds. He makes excuses for his sudden unexpected impotence. She merely wishes he were somewhere else.

Good.

I have stolen their passion.

I smile, unzip, and gently masturbate.

Images of my childhood unroll across the movie screen of my memory. I remember everything. I skim quickly, seeking the choicer memories. The juicy ones. They are far more apt for my current needs.

I see my brother exploring his puberty as he beats off in the bedroom. It is dark. The house is empty. Twenty-three years away and he thinks no one can see.

I see my sister, babysitting at the neighbors. The children are asleep. Her boyfriend has stopped by. Life becomes interesting.

I see my mother in bed with a strange pale man. I believe him to be my father yet I am uncertain. My memories begin at the gates of conception, dark and hazy. I cannot see his face no matter how hard...

And then I come— casting my seed upon the barren floorboards. Such a waste.

Perhaps I should consider luring a woman. Perhaps I should give her my child.

He could be a god.

It would be easy. I have impregnated so many women by proxy. Why not try it for real? A man should have a child of his very own. It is an immortality of a sort. That would be a thing worth having. Someday I may need it. I have lived through a thousand men's lives. I have shared countless dreams, yet someday death will come for me as it comes for every man.

Enough.

I banish thoughts of love and breeding with a wad of tissue and a shower. Who am I trying to kid? A woman would only bind me with her misguided love and weigh me down with care. She could not possibly understand the pure joy of sharing in another's thoughts and dreams. My mind would grow shackles.

I might as well be dead.

I stand on my balcony, naked to the night. Fifty floors below me is my city. My playground. I set my thoughts loose, sifting the many minds, exploring all of the countless possibilities.

I dine late at three of the city's finest restaurants— having steak with an underpaid business man, caviar with an overpriced killer and a chocolate sundae with an acned teenager. His fantasies are particularly sordid.

Tasty.

After dining, it is time for a quick check on my financial situation. My banker for this month has decided to work late. His decision was my idea. He is tired, and it is easy to nudge him into dropping a decimal point in my favor. He may catch the error three months later but by then I will have camouflaged my savings beyond the memory banks of a half a dozen separate financial institutions. I have heard that embezzlement is difficult in this computerized age but for me it is easy. The gears of finance will always turn upon the bones of men.

My landlord is happy in his ignorance. He overcharges the other tenants and never notices my own rent-free existence.

All is well with the world.

After business I find a dance club, shifting from body to body, losing myself in the rhythms of swaying flesh. It offers me a riot of sensation, frustrated yearning and egotistic showmanship.

After dancing I sleep.

It is in sleep that I enjoy the greatest of freedoms for only during sleep can I cast my mind's tendrils far into the night, mingling with the dreams of other people. I explore them. I taste them. Like a restless cable television watcher I flip through the channels and seek out fresh entertainment.

Here, a widow is dreaming about her dead husband. I lie with her briefly, enjoying his feel inside her.

His taste.

People come in so many different flavors.

A ditch digger dreams of his sleeping wife. In his dream he simultaneously throttles·her with on hand while using the other to jack off into her upturned face. She drowns in a sea of poorly planted life. I cross over, touching her dreams, seeking continuity but she is merely falling. I linger with her for a brief moment, lodging within her throat as she falls into an endless pit of trapdoors that continually open at the very last minute giving her the gift of unending vertigo.

It would be fascinating to try and exchange their dreams, each for each. Some night perhaps I will try. It is always interesting to find out just how far I can take this ability of mine. For now, though, I am quite content to fall with her for a moment longer, hoping that she might hit bottom and perhaps prove or disprove the old myth about dying when you stop falling.

Instead she awakens with a small gasp, perhaps sensing my presence. Her husband reaches for her from the depths of his slumber, and she smiles, unaware of the dark depravity of his aching dreams.

Several bedrooms later I drift into an old man's dream. These dreams are particularly fascinating in that he dreams in rare color. This alone would make him a worthwhile host for my silent vigil, but his age is also a powerful consideration. He is a former refugee and a survivor of the Holocaust. Like a fine aged wine, the dreams of the ancient Jew are always richly steeped in memory and terror. He has become a favorite of mine and he seldom disappoints me.

Tonight he is dreaming of the war. He is running and someone is chasing him through the burnt-out shells of long dead structures. Storm clouds gather, full and fat and heavy with damp promise. The wind moans of tension and strife— a nice touch, I believe. Lightning flickers and through the dim red haze I catch a glimpse of an approaching figure. The one who chases the old man through his dream walk. I strain to see the hunter's face but for some reason it is denied to me.

And then the storm hits and the buildings begin to crumble. I can see the hunter's face looming over us. Bone white and grinning, a moon-sized skull fills the entire skyscape. I see the crooked scythe and giggle softly over the sad cliché. Bloodstains spatter the skull's fleshless cheeks, dripping like tears from the skull's hollowed eyes. And then the skull falls, like a doom-bound meteor, tumbling directly towards us.

The old man tries to run but I hold him fast.

Stay, I whisper.

It is only a dream.

It cannot hurt you.

The skull strikes us in a fast swallow of thunder. For a moment I am with the skull as well as riding with the old man's graying obituary thoughts. I am inside the skull— my god I can feel such dreams and visions and power.

And then I am awake and alone in my bed.

I have been evicted and I know who it was who so unceremoniously ejected me from my seat in the old man's dreamscape.

This was no mere dream phantom.

It was Death that I touched. It was Death who usurped my place in the old man's dreams. No other being could hold such black and formless thoughts. The brief glimpse I was allowed showed me a chalky chiaroscuro, a mosaic of light and shade as cold blackling thoughts flitted over an eon-wide acreage of empty pale graves. My mind whirled with thoughts of what I had seen. I saw colors and images that ran wild. The dream faded about me like a lonely clumsy orgasm and I am alone.

I have never felt so very alone as this.

I have never been cast from anyone's dreams with such force and undeniable command. Never have I felt such violence and power. My left arm throbs and aches and my chest feels as if a sledgehammer has hit it. The old man is dead from a heart attack and I share his pain. I have fallen from my bed and my wall mirror tells me that I have bruised my face upon the floor.

I chase my breath for a full minute before I can throw off the pain. I reach out for the old man, trying futilely to catch the remnants of his dreamscape, but it is no use. That doorway has been closed.

The dead do not dream.

I slump to the floor in exhaustion as Death's hollow laughter booms in my ears like the music of thunder and kettle drums.

For three straight days my mind is celibate and alone.

I allow it to touch no one's thoughts.

I am adrift upon a sea of remorseless possibility.

What use are mere mortal minds when I have touched a God?

I touched Death and I walked with him and I danced with him for the briefest of instances.

And I hunger for more.

On the third night I set my mind free from its self-imposed fast. I allow it to wander the poorer sections of the city. The darker side, hidden from the bright lights, lost in the shadows of the skyscrapers. It doesn't take me too long to find Death's spoor down here among the ruins of poverty. Death is ever close to those who must live without hope. I find his trail in the pissy stink of a decaying alleyway lingering about the steps of two young hoodlums.

The hoodlums are arguing. They argue over a girl or a bottle or perhaps money. It does not really matter to them. All that is necessary is to strive and conquer. The apes thump their chests and the dirt yearns for blood.

Knives are flashed and young bodies tense in a grace of violence. Angry words are lobbed like flickering Molotov cocktails. I dart anxiously from mind to mind, probing the secrets of their dark-tunneled thoughts. I cannot be certain who is marked until I catch a glimpse of Death, but so far their thoughts offer nothing but the blind reflex of their switchblade dance. I can feel an aura, the whisper of Death's mocking laughter echoing in my memory. He is coming for one of them.

Their minds are so dark and murky, the only brightness the flash of anticipation as to where the next blade slash will come from. These men are evenly matched and it is impossible to predict who will be the victor. The deciding factor will undoubtedly result for something as simple as a single mistake. A blink, a cough or a fumble will tell the tale.

I dare not gamble upon steely chance. I must make certain that I am with the right one when the moment comes.

Very well.

I will force the game.

I choose one of them at random and settle into his mind a little deeper than I am accustomed to.

And then I let him know that I am here.

Our eyes open wide as we become aware of this unexpected invasion. We pause and our knife dangles limply from our hand. It is such a Gemini-moment, the two of us totally entwined as one. It is like living two complete lives in the space of A single blinking moment. We would prolong this experience but the other combatant takes full advantage of our momentary lapse of attention, as we originally intended them to do.

It is over in a single thrust. My killer's knife is keen, driving inward and upward through the amazingly porous wall of our rib cage. We feel the hungry blade like a shiny steel leech, sucking at our life's blood— and Death comes laughing, riding in on a wave of purest red. I reach for him and for just a single isolated moment I am once more one with the Death God.

Death's thoughts are clearer to me this time. I am in deeper than I was before. It is so rich and so black, a necroscape robed in sable majesty. Raven wing and tar pond, onyx, midnight, jet. Death's thoughts race past me like burning nightfall. I could swim in them; I could know his every thought and hope.

I wonder to myself if Death ever dreams?

And then all at once I am back in my home, in my own body. Death has shaken free of me as easily as a dog might shake off an unwanted rat. I can sense Death's unimaginable power, strength and intellect. I try to rise but the pain holds me fast and for a moment I am paralyzed. My insides feel like broken glass. A flash of crimson darkness passes before my eyes and I begin to sink into a sea of cold black despair. I broadcast a cry for help that ordinarily would have brought an entire city of people to my rescue. My last thoughts shout out to the entire building.

Someone must hear me.

But when I awaken I am alone. No one has come to my assistance.

I crawl to the telephone and dial 911.

In the hospital they bandage my ribs. One is cracked, the doctor tells me. There is no visible wound, but a purplish black bruise marks the spot where my assassin's knife drove home. Apparently there was some internal bleeding but no cause for alarm. I tell the doctor that I fell and I think that they might believe me. I am not certain of their belief, however. For some unfathomable reason I cannot touch their minds.

At home I notice that the bruise has grown. It stubbornly refuses to fade, growing darker with every breath I take. I try not to be concerned. I tell myself that it is nothing more than a warning. Nevertheless, I do not expect this bruise to vanish.

Death has marked me.

I spend the rest of the week in my bed. My mind obstinately refuses to travel. My thoughts are only my own and I feel so completely alone. It is devastating. By the end of the week I receive a letter from my landlord.

The letter says something about unpaid rent.

I spend the rest of that day attempting to reach his mind and remind him to mark my rent fully paid, but success evades my every attempt.

That doorway has been closed.

My sleep grows fitful as the days progress. I wake up shaking and sweating. I feel as if I have awoken from a long rest only to find myself speaking a foreign language, a tongue that is strange to my ears. I must grow used to my own dreams but they are strange to me. A staggering repetitious vision of a laughing black skull.

I feel raped.

Yet I am not ready to abandon myself to hopelessness. I tell myself that my powers have merely grown temporarily impotent, but are not completely dead. I can feel my powers, cowering like a small beaten child in the black hollow of my brain. My powers are only sleeping. All that they need is a little gentle stirring, but how long will that take?

I am losing control.

As the days pass, my situation worsens.

The grocer no longer brings me other people's groceries. The banker no longer errs in my favor.

And the landlord has sent me another notice about my unpaid rent.

And yet there is hope. I find that I am able to touch people, just barely, like a pale and fumbling ghost. Their thoughts are hazy to me, and control is not possible. I continue to struggle, hoping to reawaken my vanished power.

In the meantime my bills must be paid. I go out and try to find employment but I have so very little real experience. What an irony. I have flown intergalactic rocket ships in the dreamscape of nocturnal fantasy and yet I haven't even bothered to find myself a driver's license. So much of my waking life has been lived vicariously through others that I am nearly helpless to cope with the world.

In the end I must settle for a menial job. I am a night watchman at a downtown construction site. It is a fitting pastime. I spend my nights prowling about the darkened trench-works, playing my flashlight into the night's bleak vastness. I watch as the skeleton of steel girders grows ever higher above me. I spend entire nights standing in the shadow of steel and structure staring at a city that stares down at me.

Where are you, I wonder?

Where are you, Death?

By day I sleep. I have taken up meditation and consulted several spiritual groups in the city. I call up radio talk shows and question experts ceaselessly on soul travel, dreams and mostly Death. There is so much knowledge that I need to know before my quest can be fulfilled.

I have even consulted a psychiatrist, hoping that his ponderous dull musings might help me to reawaken my dead abilities. I carefully couch my conditions in terms of the limited reality this man understands. I talk of my growing impotence, my insecurity, my death-fixation. I find that this psychiatrist has been most helpful in helping me to understand what goes on inside my brain. Of course, I am quite handicapped in not being able to reveal my true self to him but I still feel that I have come to know this man as nearly as he knows me.

I worry about what I will do when I can no longer afford his services. He is far too expensive for a watchman's meager wages. My pay check staves off my creditors but I cannot afford my analyst. The last check I wrote him will bounce as soon as he takes it to the bank. I gave that check to him just this morning, so I probably have a day or two left before I must face my sadly unanalyzed reality alone.

I am brooding over this as I sit upon my couch sipping my last can of beer. I can picture him now, sitting in his office, talking with someone else when he should be talking to me. I can see his face and the skull beneath his face and in the shadows of his office I can see Death standing and grinning comfortably.

My mind is a clenched fist.

I feel angry.

Betrayed.

And then all at once I can really see him.

I am with him.

I feel that familiar tingle in the back of my brain.

I rise from my couch. My robe falls about my feet. I go to the balcony and stare down to the city so far below. I cannot physically see the three story brownstone where my analyst resides but that does not matter. I know where he is hiding. I can see him sitting, scribbling notes, his mind preoccupied.

And then, I enter.

It is easy.

I take him gently, easing into his thoughts. The doctor is a very precise being. For him, every cause has an effect, every path leads to an inevitable goal. His thoughts taste of crystal and ice. Every impulse in perfect lonely control.

I push deeper.

Deeply enough to let him know that I am with him.

I am here.

He sits back in his office chair, no longer listening to the long suffering matron who lays upon his couch and whines of the children who will not listen to her.

I am here!

I thrust a little harder, forcing into his secret fears and hidden dreams. I touch the darker unswept corners of his mind.

I— am— here!

I go further. Deeper than I have ever driven. I push and I feel a cold chill creeping down his spine. His senses numb. His bowels turn to jelly and the office no longer smells so sweet.

I— AM— HERE!

The uneasy grin that cracks his cheeks bleeds into a full blown howl of pain.

HERE!

I AM!

HEREHEREHERE!

Everything is darker and clouded with shimmering synaptic will-o-the-wisp sparks. I follow their glitter, probing deeper into his mind than I have ever dreamed possible. Down and down until I come to the limit. I come to the beginning, the roots of the doctor's very soul. Schist-like walls, blackened and scorched with years of suppressed regret line this area of his being. These are the walls that guard the doctor's innermost self.

The be-all.

The essence.

I pierce and shatter these self-inflicted barriers and in their fragments are reflected a multitude of my own sharded image, myself staring at myself. Clutching at the temples of our crumbling reason we scream our disbelief. The matron rises from the couch, screaming in a sharp harmony, shocked by our sudden unreasoning actions. We rise from the padded office chair.

We turn and run from our office window.

We do not want this terror but we are far beyond our own control. We try to pull away, to pull back into the safety of our own mind but we are in too deep. We keep on running. The window looms before us, growing larger by the second. We drive through the final brittle barrier, a window of shattered glass. We are flayed by the multitude of fragments, blinded by the reflected sunlight glinting from off the pane's shards.

And then, I am free.

As the analyst tumbles screaming past the first set of windows, I reach the harbor of my own body.

But I have much further to fall.

In an empathetic gesture my body has taken its own leap. However, the building in which I live is far taller than the doctor's modest three story brownstone.

I have fifty floors to fall.

In a panic I try to leave my shell, figuring to gamble on the three-story fall of the analyst. By the time I reach him he is screaming past the last set of windows.

I enter him brutally and abruptly.

We scream in renewed pain as the last set of windows blink past and we impact upon the cold grey concrete. Only three floors but far enough. We are still alive but our legs are shattered.

And our arms.

And our spine.

Our reason was shattered long ago.

And yet we are not all here.

A part of ourselves has fractured away, left behind in my own physical shell, gathering speed and falling fifty stories fast. The part of my mind that is trapped in my own shell looks down only to see a cold gray figure waiting below me.

Patiently.

It is Death.

Waiting for one last dance.

I split my mind one more time and in a last attempt at survival I leap past my own plummeting body into the mind of gray grinning Death.

"Stay," he whispers. "Stay, my son."

And so we stand together, watching as my plummeting body strikes the unyielding concrete.

Our bony cheeks are splattered with stringlets of our visceral gore.

And we smile.

We are now a trinity.

A part of us drifts above the city, the by-product of a crematorium when no one bothered claiming our remains. They burned what could be scraped up after our fifty floor fall. We drift through the eternal skies, falling and feeling forever away.

And a part of us lays in a bed in a home where some of our less fortunate patients reside. Our mind is a tumble of fragments, each shard reflecting of a pale bony grin.

We are alone.

Unable to move.

Unable to scream.

Rotated at regular intervals to avoid the unavoidable bed sores.

And a part of us lies chained within the vault-like skull of a grim gray deity. Death is our father and holds us fast and we watch his work and listen to his laughter, never daring, never dreaming to share his thoughts as the eons slip by.

✣　✣　✣

STEVE VERNON is a storyteller. He is a hybrid author with both traditionally released ghost story collections — *Haunted Harbours; Halifax Haunts; The Lunenburg Werewolf* — and independently released e-books such as *Flash Virus; Tatterdemon; Big Hairy Deal.*

What I Said to Richie Was...

by Ken Goldman

It didn't take very long. The cancer just found its way into my little brother's brain and had itself a ball. Mom and Dad knew he was dying, I knew it, everyone in the world seemed to know it. Everyone but Richie.

Terminal I heard others call his disease, probably thinking I was too young to understand, but I knew what that meant 'cause I checked it out online. His doctors and nurses managed big smiles when they visited Richie's room at the hospital, and sometimes they even made him laugh. But I saw their expressions when they turned from him. Those smiles disappeared pretty fast.

See, Richie, he just didn't understand that soon he would be no more, that everything around him would go dark and that he was going into the ground forever. At least his body was, and to be honest with you I doubt my brother's soul would be traveling to Heaven because I never much believed in that Bible stuff. I knew Richie would see no angels and he wouldn't be holding Jesus' hand either. There wouldn't be any of that eternity-with-God stuff. No, I wasn't going to kid myself. My brother's grave would have bugs, worms, probably some maggots and not much else. For sure, being dead is nothing like Reverend Lovejoy preaches in church, not that I ever paid much attention to what he had to say. For Richie, there would be only this lonely cold darkness in the dirt and lots of crawling creatures chewing his insides out and his outsides in. No angels, no God. Yeah, go tell that to a six year old and see what happens!

At least Mom and Dad were straight with me, I have to give them that. A week shy of my thirteenth birthday they came into my room and sat down on my bed. My father spoke first. I saw Mom sort of nod to him, so they probably decided ahead of time what to say.

"Adam, we just talked to Richie's doctor at the hospital. I'm afraid we have some bad news about your brother." If my father hadn't uttered another word, I would've known anyway 'cause for months Richie had been getting these really bad headaches, even had passed out a few times at school. But I just needed to hear the words, needed to know that this was something real. The look on my parents' faces pretty much told me that it was. "He's dying, isn't he?"

I guess no one expected me to say that. A long pause followed before my mother spoke. "Richie is very sick and we don't think he's going to get better. You have to be strong in front of your brother, Adam. We don't want him feeling afraid, so we have to be very— we have to—"

And then she lost it. I know she was trying not to cry, but it was too much for her and I understood that being strong about some things isn't easier just because you're a grown up. Dad looked about to break down too because his lips were quivering, but instead he held my mother. Then Mom reached for me and we all just held each other without anyone saying another word. But even with all the holding and crying and all the words my parents had said earlier to prepare me for the worst, I think that was probably the loneliest moment of my life. I think it was Mom and Dad's loneliest moment too. Even when you try to share sad feelings, you can't really. You're all alone, even when you're not. That kind of sadness, well, it's something you have to feel on your own.

Richie and me, we used to talk about all kinds of junk. You know, important stuff that brothers share about life and all its mysteries. Like, Richie wanted to know why girls sometimes made him feel all squishy inside. I knew what he meant because lately I was feeling pretty squishy about Rochelle Goldenberg whose chest suddenly took on a whole new look over the summer. So I told Richie the truth, even showed him how my Mr. Willy could do a lot more than pee. Richie said he didn't think he could make his Mr. Willy do what mine did 'cause his was so small, but I told him it would happen soon enough, and when it did then he would *really* be feeling squishy about girls. 'Course we didn't tell Mom and Dad about what I showed him. Brothers share those kinds of secrets. I never for a minute thought Richie wouldn't live long enough to experience any of that stuff.

The point is, Richie always wanted to know about the way things worked, and why things were the way they were. It's natural for little kids to want to know those things, right? Well, my little brother wanted to know about a lot of stuff way before most kids his age. Like the time we found Edgar, his turtle, on his back and all dried up on the staircase. Edgar had climbed out of his tank somehow, and for a week we looked all over for him. He must have been crawling around the upstairs, and when he found the staircase he flipped over. He was probably too tired and hungry to do much else, just lay there and die. Of course, Richie had to know why Edgar looked the way he did, and I knew it was my job to tell him the truth. Mom and Dad, sometimes they sugar-coated stuff like that, and I felt my brother should know what was what. So I held out his turtle for him and he cupped Edgar in his hand.

"Edgar is dead, Richie. He won't be here to play with you anymore."

My brother looked confused. "But he's here right now. I'm holding him."

"No, he's not here. That's his body that's here. It feels cold, doesn't it? People call it the 'remains,' because it's what you leave behind when you die. But the thing that made Edgar crawl around his tank when it was time for his breakfast, or whatever made him decide he wanted to take a swim, that's gone. Forever. Do you understand what I'm saying?"

"You mean he isn't just sleeping?"

I had to be careful with what I told him, I knew that. "Being dead is kind of like sleeping. Except you don't wake up. Not ever. We'll have to bury Edgar in the back yard. You can say a few words about him if you want, about how you'll miss him and stuff."

"Will I ever get to see him again?"

A tough question. Times like that, it's so hard to know the right thing to say. But I couldn't lie.

"I don't think so."

"You mean like when Gran'ma went away?"

"Yeah. Exactly like when Gran'ma went away."

Richie considered that. He didn't cry, not one tear. He had only one question.

"Do you think Dad will let me buy another turtle?"

That ended my lesson to Richie about the mystery of death. But now my little brother, *he* was dying, and I had to tell him what death really was about because I didn't want him leaving this world believing something that wasn't true. I knew Mom and Dad meant well and that maybe they would feel angry that I told Richie the truth, but my mind was made up. If one of Dad's lectures followed, I could take it because I knew I'd done the right thing. Isn't that what grownups are always telling their kids they should do?

A few weeks before Christmas the phone rang really late at night. I knew it had to be the hospital, so I left my bed and listened just outside my parents' bedroom. I could make out only a few bits and pieces of what Dad was saying to the doctor over the phone, but it was easy to put together the rest.

"Is he able to talk?" from Dad. A pause, then, "Well, is he in any pain?" Then the question I never wanted to hear. "How much time—?" Through the door I heard my mother begin to cry. My father muttered, "All right. We'll be there right away."

I stood frozen, not able to move, not caring if my parents found me listening to their conversation. I was still at the door when it opened. My father looked at me. He didn't seem to know what to say. But he didn't have to say anything because I spoke first.

"I want to go with you."

Mom was throwing on some clothes, and Dad looked at her for a moment before turning to me. He stood right in front of me, but somehow his voice sounded far away.

"Get dressed," he said.

✠ ✠ ✠

It was real late when we arrived at the hospital, but I was wide awake. For some reason I felt more scared than sad, although I was plenty sad too. The night nurse was just leaving Richie's room when we got there. "He's been drifting in and out," she told us. "He may be awake for a little while, but I wouldn't expect him to talk much, okay?"

He was sort of half awake when we walked in. His eyes were rolled back a little like he was there for a moment and then somewhere else. I let Mom and Dad speak to him but I stayed back near the door.

53

"Richie, we're so sorry, honey, so sorry..." Mom said, while brushing his hair from his eyes. I couldn't tell you why she was apologizing to my brother. None of this was anybody's fault. But I let my parents say what they had to say, because mostly I think what they were saying to Richie was goodbye. For me, though, I had something to share with him, and I waited until both my parents had their last words, although I wasn't sure my brother was really hearing any of it because I didn't hear anything from him. Then I stepped forward.

"Can I be alone with Richie for a little bit? There's some stuff I want to tell him."

Dad and Mom both attempted smiles that I didn't believe for a second. But they left me alone with my brother and closed the door behind them, and I was glad they did that. I kneeled as close to Richie's face as I could get and whispered, "Can you hear me, Richie? You don't have to say anything. Just open your eyes a little if you can, okay?"

Nothing happened, so I waited for a moment. But then I saw his lids flicker, and when his eyes opened for real I knew what I wanted to say. "I was wrong about what I told you, Richie. About Edgar and about dying, and all that stuff. You're going to see that little turtle again real soon. He'll be waiting for you. And Gran'ma, you'll be with her too, and she can't wait to see you. The weather where you'll be, it's always warm, like springtime. Great weather for having a catch or just laying in the sun under some really beautiful trees the way we used to do with Gran'ma. There's so many flowers, really pretty ones, and angels singing better than the choir at church. It never gets cold there. Never. I promise it's such a great place where you're going, a million times better than Reverend Lovejoy is always telling us. I just wanted you to know that, Richie, okay?"

He looked at me and just kept looking, but he didn't go to some other place this time so I knew he was taking in what I told him. And then the craziest thing. I'm not sure I really saw it happen, but— well, Richie, he smiled. It only lasted for a second or two and then it was gone, so I couldn't swear it really happened, but it sure looked like—

All right, there's more to it than that, and this part I *am* sure of. You don't have to believe me, and it's not like I plan on sharing this with anyone else. But I just had to tell someone.

I'd said what I wanted to say, and I felt good that he had heard me. I decided to leave Richie to his rest, but when I turned to leave I saw what looked like a shadow alongside my brother's bed. At first I thought maybe it was my shadow because the nightstand light was pretty low and creepy in that room. But no, it was much too big to be mine. And when I looked again I saw it wasn't a shadow at all. It was a man dressed all in black with some kind of hood around his head so it was hard to see his face. I couldn't help myself, and I jumped back a little when I saw how pale and bony that face under the hood appeared. Then I heard this voice. It spoke so low the words seemed to rumble inside his throat.

"You— you can see me?"

"Who are you? What are you doing in my brother's room?"

The dark stranger moved closer, kneeled to eye level to speak to me. Although he was close to my face, I really couldn't see much of his. He looked kind of fuzzy, like one of those grainy old black and white movies they show late night on TV that keeps going in and out of focus.

"I think you know who I am, Adam. And I think you know why I'm here."

He was right. I'm a kid. I read comic books.

"You're Death, aren't you?"

I saw the faint glimmer of teeth. I guess he must have been smiling when he said, "At your service." He leaned close to whisper, "Most can't see me — sometimes the very young or old — but maybe I'm glad you can. We wouldn't want your brother to be scared of me, would we? You're not scared of me, are you, Adam?"

He must've known I wasn't. "Can you maybe take me instead of Richie?" I asked.

That gleam of white again. "You know that's not the way this works, Adam."

Yeah, I knew. Like I told you, I read comics.

The shadowy man turned towards Richie's bed and pointed a bony finger. "It's time."

I know what I saw then. Now, you don't have to believe this next part, but I know what I saw. Richie, he was still lying in his bed, but some kind of mist or something rose from his sheets and when it came into focus I saw that was Richie too, the Richie

I remembered when he was healthy and full of life. The dark stranger reached out his hand and my brother took it like it was the most natural thing in the world to do, and he wasn't afraid, not even a little.

"These monitors will be flatlining in another few seconds. We'll be going now," the dark stranger said. "We've got a long trip, your brother and I."

Richie, he turned to me and said just three words: "I'm not scared."

I didn't know what else to say. A million things should have come to me, but only a few words did. So I said, "'Bye, Richie. Be good, okay?"

The dark stranger turned to leave but I reached out to him and said, "Wait for just a minute, will you? I want to ask you something, then you can go, all right?"

He leaned forward and I spoke low because I didn't want Richie to hear. "What I told my brother tonight. I mean about seeing his turtle and seeing our Gran'ma, and the weather always being warm. That's the way it is where you're taking him, isn't it?"

A long pause followed while I felt my mouth go dry. Maybe the guy was trying to decide if he should tell me the truth, or maybe he felt that a kid my age couldn't handle it. Then the dark stranger said, "You got the part about the weather right. Not that there's much sun. It's death, you know."

I'd hoped I was wrong about what I believed and I wanted to ask more, but in the next moment the two were gone. There was no puff of smoke like some stupid magic trick, no fading away into the dark like the phony ghosts in some special effects movie. They were just gone.

I wouldn't be seeing my little brother again. From that second, I knew it for sure. And Richie, he wouldn't be seeing Edgar or our Gran'ma either. Not ever. But he didn't have to know that, did he? Maybe it wouldn't be bugs and maggots like I once thought, but there would be no angels and clouds either.

Geez...

I know I lied to Richie, all right? I know it. I could tell Mom and Dad what I said to my brother, and they would be happy I told him all that cheery stuff about angels and sunshine in God's Heaven. I knew they wanted Richie to leave this world happy, and I think he did.

But I sure hope I did the right thing, lying to him like that. It's so hard to tell what's right when you're talking to a little kid about death, you know? I mean, it's really hard, especially when you know the truth.

Geez...

❖ ❖ ❖

KEN GOLDMAN, former English and Film Studies teacher, lives in Pennsylvania and the South Jersey shore. His stories received seven honorable mentions in The Year's Best Fantasy & Horror and appear in over 750 publications in the U.S., Canada, the UK and Australia. He has written five books, *You Had Me At ARRGH!!*, *Desiree*, *Donny Doesn't Live Here Anymore*, *Star-Crossed*, and *Of a Feather*.

To Dance, Perchance to Die

by David McDonald

VLADIMIR ZEGLOVSKY stood poised, toes bent, legs flexed, every muscle of his lean body in sharp relief. The applause crashed over him like waves surging over the beach, roses scattered like driftwood after a storm. Still lost in the dance, at first he remained oblivious to the crowd's acclaim, but as the ovation went on and on, gradually he became aware of his surroundings. With an elegant bow he acknowledged his admirers, then gracefully left the stage, body moving in such harmony that he might still have been dancing.

"Beautiful, Vladimir, beautiful." The voice, soft and slightly oily, was a familiar one. Sergei Diaghilev was the founder and manager of the *Ballets russes*, and it was he who had brought them here, to the heart of European culture, to Paris itself.

"Thank you, Sergei." Vladimir said.

Sergei's voice hardened. "But as for you, *dubiina*, how could you mess up a simple *battement développé*?"

The object of his scorn was Vaslav Nijinsky, the only dancer in the troupe who was Sergei's rival for the title *danseur noble*.

Vladimir could see Vaslav's face redden and knew if the two men started arguing, things would get very ugly. He cut in quickly, hoping to avoid any trouble.

"Sergei, it was at the end of a very difficult routine." He put a hand on Sergei's arm, hoping to placate him. "Anyway, Vaslav covered it so well that I doubt anyone noticed."

"You stay out of this, Vladimir!" There was such venom in the other dancer's voice that Vladimir took a step back. "I don't

58

need you to defend me. We all know you never make a mistake. Well, we can't all be perfect!"

With that, he turned on his heel and stalked out. Despite his dismay, Vladimir couldn't help but notice that Vaslav imbued even this simple act with drama. He shook his head. The man was worse than the prima donnas.

"Don't mind him, Vladimir."

The anger had already left Sergei's voice, and Vladimir couldn't help but smile. Despite the man's often turbulent moods, he knew that Sergei genuinely cared for his dancers. His fierce rages and his habit of slamming his cane on the ground in anger were more show than anything else.

Vladimir sighed. "I was just trying to help, Sergei. I don't know why he hates me so much."

"You may be a wonderful dancer, Vladimir, but you can be incredibly naïve. He is jealous of you."

"Jealous?" Vladimir was startled. "Why would he be jealous of me?"

"Because you are the only dancer he has met who is better than him."

Vladimir started to protest, but Sergei cut him off. "Spare me the false modesty, we both know it is true. Now, enough of this, I have someone you must meet." Sergei winked lecherously.

"Not another bored noblewoman!"

After every show, there would always be at least one woman styling herself a patron of the arts who would request an introduction to the dancers. And, more often than not, she would have her eyes on one of the *danzatore* and pursue a more... personal encounter.

Vladimir couldn't help but think that Sergei, whose proclivities were well known amongst the dancers, enjoyed arranging these meetings. Perhaps it satisfied some voyeuristic urge of the manager. Sergei had never made a pass at him, but, naïve or not, Vladimir was well aware of the way that Sergei looked at him from time to time.

"Sergei, you know that things have changed for me. I am not interested in being some noble woman's plaything."

Sergei smile was filled with genuine affection. "Ah, young love. It fills my heart with joy to see a young man's heart so filled with fidelity and love. Don't worry, Vladimir, your pretty little Nikkita has nothing to worry about. This noble woman is not like anyone you have met before."

He didn't give Vladimir a chance to argue, but pulled him through into one of the antechambers that led off from the backstage area. As they entered, a young woman looked up from the leather bound book she was reading, and Vladimir froze. Sergei had been telling the truth, she was nothing like any of the middle aged matrons who normally congregated at the ballet, elaborately made up and with diamonds encrusting bosoms that preceded them everywhere they went like the prow of a battleship.

In contrast, she was dressed simply, even austerely, in a plain white dress that flowed from the tightly fastened neck in shimmering waves to her feet. Her raven hair was pulled back severely from her forehead, and not a trace of makeup despoiled her pale, white skin. The absence of color only served to draw more attention to her eyes, which were an incredibly vivid and luminous shade of green that seemed to flicker with their own light as they looked deeply into Vladimir's own.

Sergei drew himself up proudly, as if he had invented this vision himself.

"Vladimir Ivanovich Zeglovsky, may I present Her Illustriousness, the Countess Svetlana."

Without a word, she extended a hand for Vladimir to kiss. It was as cold as ice beneath his lips and he had to force himself not to flinch.

"Leave us." Her voice betrayed no emotion, but Sergei scuttled out of the room backwards, bowing obsequiously, as if she had screamed at him.

Vladimir was used to being at ease in any situation, fully in control of a body that had been melded by years of training and practise into a flawless tool. But, as she regarded him with those eyes, he felt himself shifting from foot to foot as if he was a clumsy peasant oaf straight off the estates. The silence stretched on long enough that he could take it no longer, forcing him to speak, heedless of the protocol of waiting for her to address him first.

"How can I help your — uh — Your Illustriousness?" he asked.

"I watched you dance tonight." Her tone was still absent of any emotion, leaving Vladimir helpless to discern her opinion of his performance.

"I hope that it pleased Your Illustriousness?"

Now an emotion entered her voice and after a moment he identified it as wonder.

"It was the most beautiful thing I have ever seen. I have seen so many wonders, wonders that you could not dream of, but never before has something spoken to me like the way you moved, the way that you and the music were one."

Vladimir was used to praise, but he was taken aback by the fervor in her voice and eyes.

"Your Illustriousness is too kind."

She ignored his attempt at modesty, and placed her hands on either side of Vladimir's face. He gasped, not at the shocking intimacy of the gesture, but at the tendrils of ice that burrowed their way through his veins.

"Talent such as yours should not leave the world." Her words had a solemn intensity as if she was handing down some terrible judgment, and darkness seemed to fill the room. "I say you shall not die."

Vladimir staggered back, drawing in shallow hitching breaths. The moment passed, and once again mellow lamplight illuminated the surroundings.

He attempted to make sense of what had just happened. Had he imagined the ice and darkness? Had he had one of the spells he had heard Vaslav was subject to? He straightened up, and blanched. The room was empty, and no trace of the Countess remained.

❖ ❖ ❖

Seven years passed, and the recollection of that strange encounter had long since faded from Vladimir's memory, and if he recalled Svetlana's cryptic words, it was only as the wish that his fame would live on once he was gone, something that every dancer desired. If sometimes he woke in the middle of the night icy cold regardless of how warm his small apartment was and with the memory of a pair of green eyes peering into his own, then that was between him and his conscience and the glass of vodka he kept beside his bed. It certainly was nothing to trouble Nikkita with, especially not in her delicate condition.

Life had been very good to the Zeglovskys. Upon his return to the Motherland, Vladimir had been offered a prestigious position with the Imperial Ballet in Petrograd. Now he was able to teach, and to compose his own works, but still his passion remained with the dance itself.

Even though the Imperial title had been stripped from the academy when the Tsar abdicated, culture was too important to Russians to see it discontinued. In fact, one of the local government ministers, Anatoly Maklalov, had taken a special interest in the ballet, and in the Zeglovskys. Anxious to promote his image as a friend of the arts, Maklalov made sure that the Zeglovskys were well looked after — as much as anyone could be amidst the turmoil — and they ate well. It was Maklalov that they could thank for the meal they were sitting down to when there was a hammering at the door.

Vladimir could see the fear in Nikkita's eyes, and he gave her a reassuring smile.

"Don't worry, *milaya*. It is probably just one of the students, panicking about his upcoming examination."

He wondered if she believed him. He just wished he could believe it himself.

Petrograd was a city waiting for a spark to set it on fire, and each night there were clashes between Mensheviks and Socialist Revolutionaries on one side, and the Bolsheviks on the other. There were rumors of people disappearing in the night, just like in the days of the *Okhrana*. Vladimir worried that his position could only protect them for so long before they too were sucked into the maelstrom.

He opened the door a crack, wedging his foot underneath in the hope it might stop anyone from barging in. A vain hope, perhaps, but better than nothing.

"For God's sake, Vladimir, let me in!"

It was Maklalov! Shocked, Vladimir removed his foot, and Maklalov nearly fell through the door. He looked a far cry from his usual urbane self. His face was dirty and his expensive suit ripped and torn. Beneath his tousled hair, his eyes were wide and staring.

He clutched at Vladimir's arm. "You must help me. Please, hide me!"

"What's going on, Anatoly?" Vladimir asked, fear rising within him. "What happened to you?"

Without asking, the official sat down at the table and grabbed a glass of vodka, draining it without coming up for air.

"It's those Bolshevik scum. They have betrayed us. The rabble they call their 'Red Army' are marching through the city as we speak." Maklalov let out a stifled sob. "They are executing government officials, and I know that I am on their list. You have to hide me!"

Vladimir was torn. "Anatoly, I want to help you, you have been a good friend. But I have to think about my family. Nikkita is carrying my child; I can't risk anything happening to her. I'm sorry, I truly am, but you have to leave."

Maklalov rose unsteadily to his feet and it was obvious to Vladimir that this had not been his first glass of vodka. His face was red with fury. "You ungrateful bastard! After all I did for you, and you would throw me to the mercy of those thugs!"

As Vladimir opened his mouth to retort, several things happened at once. There was a crash as the door flew inward and three men rushed into the room. Two of them were hired muscle, big misshapen men with puffy features and broad shoulders, but it was the smaller man in the middle who caught Vladimir's eye. He had pinched rat-like features and bad teeth, and lank greasy hair combed back from a pocked and scarred forehead.

With a speed that surprised Vladimir, Maklalov knocked over the table and grabbed Nikkita by the arm, cruelly twisting it behind her back as he pulled her in front of him. She was too terrified to even scream, paralysed with fear. A stiletto had somehow appeared in Maklalov's hand and was pressed against the soft flesh of her throat, and Nikkita moaned softly as a drop of blood bloomed from her delicate flesh.

"Nobody move!" Maklalov's voice was hoarse, quivering with strong emotion.

"Please, Anatoly, don't hurt her!" Vladimir pleaded.

The rat-faced man stepped forward, an ugly gun clenched in his fist, identical to the ones his companions carried.

"Anatoly Yevseevich Maklalov, you stand accused of crimes against the Russian people. By order of the Bolshevik Central Committee you are hereby sentenced to execution, sentence to be carried out immediately."

"I'll kill her! I swear it!" Maklalov yelled. Nikkita found the strength to scream and struggle against his grip.

"Those who harbor enemies of the state are themselves traitors to the Motherland," the rat-faced man pronounced solemnly.

He pulled the trigger, the gun roaring as blood blossomed from Nikkita's dress, beneath which their unborn child lay. He fired again, the guns of his companions joining the terrible chorus as

Nikkita and Maklalov collapsed to the ground like marionettes whose strings had suddenly been cut.

"No!" Vladimir screamed, running to his wife's side. He fell to his knees and cradled her in his arms, desperately seeking some sign of life. Fire lanced through his scalp as one of the men seized his hair and rammed the barrel of a gun against his temple. Thunder roared, and then there was nothing.

✢ ✢ ✢

Vladimir slowly opened his eyes, wincing as pain stabbed through his head. His mouth tasted foul, and a rank odor filled the room. He turned his head and spat, then sat up.

"Nikkita! The latrines have backed up again. Go down and tell the landlord we are not paying our rent until he fixes the problem." There was no answer. "Nikkita?

He started, now fully awake, the events of last night rushing back.

"No, no, no…" he moaned.

He stood and looked around. The source of the smell was now apparent, flies buzzing around the bodies of Nikkita and Maklalov, pools of blood and other less wholesome fluids seeping into the carpet. Another memory struck him with merciless force, the gun against his temple, and he raised his hand to his head. He touched the wound, but even as he probed it, he could feel it closing up. Something hard pushed against his hand, and he plucked it free, gazing down at his palm in horrified wonder. He held a misshapen piece of lead surrounded by chunks of his brain.

As if the speaker was in the room, words filled his mind.

"I say you shall not die."

"No! Without her I do not want to live!" he screamed into the empty room.

There was no reply, only the sound of his sobs as he collapsed to his knees.

✢ ✢ ✢

Vladimir leaned against the mirror and watched his young class working through the exercises he had given them. His head was still pounding from the friendly drinks of the night before, and he winced as one of the boys lost his balance and fell, sending several of the girls tumbling, yelling and shrieking to the floor. That was it, he'd had enough.

"No, no, no!" he yelled. "This is not right. Get out of here. Out! Now!"

The children scattered in all directions, then ran for the door. Cursing under his breath, Vladimir looked longingly at his desk, thinking about the bottle of cheap vodka in the drawer. Instead, he walked over to the mirror. Despite the years, he still looked like the young dancer who had entranced Paris.

Slowly he began to move through the forms that his students had found so hard, gradually speeding up as he became lost in the joy of the dance. He spun and leapt, feeling the dark memories slip away, the only thing that mattered the here and now.

"Vladimir! Where are your students? The rent does not pay itself!"

He stumbled and almost fell, turning to face the voice. It should have been ridiculous, hearing such matronly scolding coming from the slight young woman standing in the doorway. Somehow, though, she always managed to cow him, making him again like a child.

"I'm sick, Tatiana, I sent them home."

She scowled at him. "Sick? You mean hung over! What will their parents say? You aren't the only ballet instructor in Munich, you know."

"Perhaps not, but I am the only one who studied at the Imperial Ballet, or toured with the *Ballets russes*. Those snobs want only the best for their darlings and will put up with anything just to say that they have a teacher from Mother Russia. The children will be back tomorrow."

It was true. The white *émigré* community in Munich was smaller than that of Berlin, but no less determined to preserve their heritage. They stuck together and observed all the customs and traditions of the home country, and would stop at nothing in their quest to create a Russia-in-Exile against the inevitable day when the Communists would fall.

Tatiana was too pragmatic to argue with him. Instead she grabbed his hat and coat and thrust them at him.

He looked at them, baffled. "What's this for?"

"We are going to buy some food. If you'd bothered to check you would have seen that the larder was bare." She cut off his protests. "You are coming, and that is final."

Grumbling, he followed down the narrow stairs and out into the busy streets. His anger was all show. He was well aware how lucky he had been to acquire Tatiana as a housekeeper. She made sure he had food and clean clothes, and even tallied the takings, meagre as they were, of his ballet school. Occasionally, she would give him a look or some other sign that she might be interested in being more than his housekeeper, which he studiously ignored by pretending to be oblivious. He was fond of the girl, but his heart was still in Petrograd.

It had been almost ten years since he had awoken to find the body of his dead wife, but even now the painful memories still seemed fresh. For months afterwards, he had simply wandered across Europe, lost and aimless, unable to find a reason to live. Countless times he had tried to end his life, only to find that death refused to take him. Poison, bullets, knives, they could all wound him and cause him pain, but none could end his suffering.

Starving and desperate, it had been through sheer luck that he had discovered the thirst for culture amongst the white *émigrés* and ever since then he had managed to eke out a reasonable living. His association with the great ballet schools had given him a degree of prestige amongst the exiles, and their money allowed him a lifestyle that, while nothing like that of Petrograd, many would be envious of. As much as he could be, he was content in Munich.

"Vladimir, are you alright?" There was concern in Tatiana's voice.

"What? Oh, I am sorry, I must have been daydreaming."

"I think we have a problem."

He followed her gaze to the end of the street. There, marching in unison and directly towards them, was a large group of brown-shirted men. They had the look of veterans about them, eyes cold and bitter, mouths drawn.

"*Sturmabteilung!*" Vladimir spat.

The Brownshirts had become a common sight on the streets of Munich, acting as muscle for the up-and-coming Nazi Party, protecting their political meetings from interference and engaging in pitched street battles with anyone who opposed their aims, whether it was socialists, communists or the authorities themselves.

All around them street vendors were hurriedly packing up their wares and trying to get off the street. That seemed a great idea to Vladimir, and he grabbed Tatiana's arm and began to drag her back the way they had come. As he turned, he froze, and began to recite half forgotten prayers from his youth. Coming from the opposite direction was another group of men. They had the same hard faces and marks of violence, but instead of brown shirts they were dressed in worker's garb as if they had come straight from the docks or warehouses. Above their heads waved a red flag, whipping in the wind.

"Oh no!" Vladimir whispered. Caught between the communists and the fascists was definitely not a safe place to be.

He was not the only one to realize this, and panic engulfed the street. Sellers and pedlars ran aimlessly, only succeeding in adding to the confusion. Vladimir and Tatiana were buffeted this way and that, and he had to struggle to keep hold of her arm. As the two groups of political thugs caught sight of each other, a guttural roar rose in the air as if some huge beast was stirring from its slumber. With cries of *"Deutschland erwacht!"* and *"Workers Unite!"* they charged at each other and all hell broke loose.

In the crush of bodies, he lost his grip on Tatiana's arm and she was swept into the crowd. Frantically he tried to fight his way through to her. "Tatiana, Tatiana!" he called urgently.

He could see her, only yards between them, but it may as well have been miles. Their eyes met, and he saw the panic in her gaze, and then she stumbled and fell and was gone, trampled under the feet of the panicked mob. With a strength he didn't know he had, Vladimir managed to force his way to her, but it was too late. Tatiana lay crumpled on the ground, her graceful neck bent at an impossible angle, her eyes lifeless and dull. Ignoring the chaos around him, he reached down and closed them.

"I am sorry, Tatiana, I wish I could have been what you wanted."

By now the two factions had met and the bodies surrounding him were no longer merchants and bystanders, but the opposing political thugs he had been bent on escaping. Instead of trying to clear the street, they were trying to kill each other. Vladimir thought quickly: perhaps they were so intent on one another that he could sneak away without being noticed. Furtively, he crept towards the mouth of an alleyway, weaving through knots of brawling men.

He was almost safe when a huge body crashed into him, sending him rolling under the hooves of a panicked carthorse. Terrified by the tumult around it, it reared and the last sight that filled Vladimir's eyes was a woman in white, standing at the corner of the square and watching him with a strange expression in her beautiful green eyes. Then the hooves came down and there was only darkness.

❖ ❖ ❖

Vladimir stared down at the newspaper headline.
Immigrant Family Burnt Alive in Firebomb Attack!
He had seen the signs, the politicians talking about those who were different, painting them as the enemy. The looks in the street, the sideway glances and the hard faces. He had seen it before, so many times, in so many different places, the hatred building and festering until finally it burst. The Jews. The imperialists. The terrorists. Always some enemy. Always someone to be made the *Other*.

Vladimir remembered the Singhs, how they had welcomed him into their homes, taking pity on a lonely foreigner like themselves. He remembered the spicy home-cooked meals and the friendly conversations. Those memories were blotted out by a mental image of the family cowering in their home as angry voices shouted and cursed outside, then the sound of breaking glass, and finally screams as the flames rose.

How many friends had he lost over the years? How many people had died while he lived on, decade after decade?

"I can't do this anymore. Why won't you just let me die?"

His cry echoed off the rafters, shocking in the silence of the house.

Rage burned incandescent in his voice. "Death! I know you are there. I can feel you, I can smell you. I can see your work in the streets outside. Show yourself!"

His voice cracked and he fell to his knees. In the far corner of the room, where the light barely reached, shadows drew into themselves, becoming inky pools of blackness, pregnant with menace. They rippled, like a stone thrown in a pond under moonlight, and she stepped forth. Svetlana was exactly as he remembered from all those years ago, the same stark white dress, the same raven hair, and most of all, the same emerald eyes. She glided across the room and stopped just before him.

"Many would envy a man who cannot die and thank me for my gift. Why is there such anger in your voice?" She seemed genuinely curious.

He stared at her, incredulously. "How can you ask that? I have had nothing but pain and suffering from your gift. Everyone I have loved is gone, every place I've called home destroyed, leaving me alone. I haven't aged a day, and I am terrified that I will never know release from this world. Please, let me die."

"Why should I?"

"I will give you a gift in return."

For the first time she smiled. "What could you, a mere mortal, offer me?"

He looked directly into her eyes. "A dance. I will dance for you."

Her eyes widened in surprise, then a look of desire filled them.

"So be it." She raised a pale hand, and soft music filled the room. It had been many years, but still he recognized it, it was the music that he had danced to the night they met.

Slowly at first, he began to move, his steps faltering and his movements rusty. But, as the music's seductive song began to work through him, sending its tendrils along his blood and bone and sinew, his body remembered its calling and once more he and the dance were one. With each moment and gesture the patterns became more and more intricate, as if he was the instrument and the music played him.

He saw that Svetlana was mesmerized, emerald eyes unable to look away. The dance brought him closer and closer to her, and with one final step he was close enough to take her in his arms.

Before she could pull away she was captured and he began to whirl her through dance after dance. As the music changed, he changed with it, spinning her through each set of movements, a waltz followed by the tango followed by a rumba as he showed her his mastery of all the dances of the world. He could see that she felt the music too, their bodies joined by its power. Her flesh was ice against his, leeching away his warmth as they moved together.

Without missing a step, he leant forward and whispered in her ear. "Release me. Please."

He felt rather than saw her nod, and a drop of moisture ran down his cheek. For a moment he was confused, and then he realized it was a tear, and that she was crying for him. The cold from her body began to rise, and he cried out as he felt it burrowing to his core, stealing the last of his warmth. The room began to dim, and as blackness fell, he smiled. This time he could dare to believe that he would not wake.

❖ ❖ ❖

DAVID MCDONALD is a professional geek from Melbourne, Australia who works for an international welfare organization. When not on a computer or reading a book, he helps run a local cricket club. He is a member of the Australian Horror Writers Association, the IAMTW and the SuperNOVA writers group.

DEATH DOLL

BY LOIS H. GRESH

DON'T FEAR ME. Don't hate me. You see, I'm not what you think I am. I'm actually a kind and gentle person, not anything like the monster in your mind. If it were up to me, you'd grow up, play with your dolls, eat chocolates and cookies, and spend your nights in dreams so pleasant you wouldn't want dawn to bleed through your window and wake you up.

I always make myself forget the ones who slip past me, but in this case, I have no choice but to remember. Those who dance around me insist that I correct my error. I can't argue with them, or they'll hound me until I go mad. They have that power, the shadows. They clutch, they shroud me with dankness and dark, their eerie howling and laughter rattles my mind. I'm a shadow as well, but only one amidst many, and I'm slim and frail, an inky thread slipped into a thick cloud.

"She was to be stillborn."

"You had your orders, and you disobeyed."

"You screwed up."

"It was her time."

For four years, they've taunted me. And for four years, I've insisted, "No, I didn't disobey orders. I did my best. She should have been ours, but the doctors interfered. They have new ways of doing things. How was I to know?"

And now...

I'm here. At your side. I won't let you down. I'll protect you from all ills. I want you to dream the most pleasant dreams.

I watch you from the crack where the walls join, and when your mother comes into the room, I slink closer, anxious to feel the warmth of breath as the two of you speak. I don't feel much warmth anymore.

I once grasped your mother's hand as she gave birth to you. Annabelle LePonte Bourbon, a beautiful and fragile woman, too delicate to carry a child to term.

You were never supposed to... *be*.

Soft breath of life and the gentle beating of her heart, I ache to be this close to your mother. When I was her age, the shadows came for me, and the air wheezed from my lungs, broken accordion, and it was painful, *so painful*, to feel my heart beat in those last few moments. Loud in my ears, reverberating, tapering off until that final beat, the sharp pain rising in my chest, my mind vivid with colors and nobody there to clutch my hand. Fluid in my skull, and my brain swelled.

It won't be so bad for you. I promise.

Your mother, Annabelle, brushes honey hair from her eyes. My hair was black as crows' wings. Her eyes look at you with such love and tenderness. They're wide and round, grey as if the color has drained out of them. My eyes were black, I painted my lips red, and I wore the Spanish skirts of my ancestors. I danced calypso and tango in the clubs, and in the audiences were women like Annabelle, pale flowers next to my rose. I was life. They were shadow.

"Beatrice dear, let's color the train red, shall we?"

You cast hollow eyes at your mother, lift the red crayon, fingers shaking as you color. A delicate sparrow, gaunt face, washed-out, the color of weathered wood. You're four going on a hundred.

Does it give me pleasure to take the wealthy, to pluck a daughter from her mother's arms? No, and why would anyone think that? I pity the wealthy. They lack a true understanding of life. They're spared the struggles, the agonies, the scrappiness. They don't have a clue what it means to do everything for themselves, to start with nothing and end up with something. But to take you, sweet Beatrice, the one gem in your mother's dull existence, hurts me almost as much as when I take a child from the poor.

The maid brings cookies. This woman is resentful, though she hides it carefully just as she hides her fat beneath the folds of her heavy black skirt and apron. When you come with me, the woman won't be as resentful. She'll reach out to Annabelle, and together, they'll cry, the poor and the wealthy joined by common human grief.

I do have some virtuous attributes. I do serve a purpose.

After cookies — chocolate chip, your favorite but you don't eat any — we get in a car with black leather seats. You wear the kind of coat I wished I had when I was a little girl. It's as soft as a teddy bear, a lush pink that reflects off your sallow face. Your hat has hearts on it, your tiny feet wiggle in patent shoes with bows on them. I huddle between you and your mother. Annabelle has her arm around your shoulders. Your faces are close. Annabelle murmurs. "What do you want for your birthday? *American Girl* doll with all the outfits *and* the book?"

You shake your head, no. For a moment, your eyes light, then flicker off again, a 20-watt bulb that's all spent.

"Some bright new clothes? Video games?"

The child who has everything…

You shake your head. No.

Annabelle switches topic, obviously trying to provoke some joy in her daughter, some positive response that will lift her own spirits. "I bet you can't wait for kindergarten in the fall, right?" I catch a whiff of her perfume, multi-layered with the scents of Mediterranean flowers, expensive. It floats in the air along with your scent, ivory soap and innocence.

The other shadows are correct to harass me, of course, because doctors can do nothing when we come for souls. What we want, we take. When it's time, there's nothing medicine can do. I suppose that I *did* disobey my orders.

I gave you these four years, Beatrice. Four years of playing with toys, of clowns and music, of everything good in life that your rich parents could provide. Annabelle won't see it this way. She'll blame me when I take you. She won't understand the beautiful gift I bestowed.

You look right through me and up at your mother. You shake your head again, and say, "I probably won't go to kindergarten, Mama."

"But, why? Of course, you'll go!"

"No, Mama, I won't," you say firmly, as if you *know*.

The car stops, the chauffeur opens our door, and we clamber out, mother, daughter, and me. The air is brisk, a few snowflakes fall, and the city is quiet. It's Sunday morning, I realize, the one day when the city lies dormant and shuttered, pretending to be at peace.

Inside the apartment of Annabelle's friend, Gretchen Pritchard Standish, direct descendent of Miles Standish of the Mayflower era, we wait for the maid to remove the coats and hats, then sit quietly in the parlor by the grand piano. This one room is larger than the house in which I grew up, and my family occupied only one room in that house. You sit on a burgundy velvet chair, kicking your pink patent shoes. You almost look happy as you gaze at the oil paintings, the flowered curtains, the gold bowls in their cabinets, the cherubs engraved all over the front of the mahogany desk.

I hope I can do it this time. It isn't easy for me when it's a child, especially one that I already spared. Even in death, with no heart beating in what was once me, I have more heart than most people.

Gretchen enters in a swish of lavish silk with her husband, William Trevor. He has a matching pocket square. Her perfume is denser than Annabelle's, and you sneeze once and squirm. Annabelle clasps your hand.

I perch on William's shoulder and marvel at the smooth skin of his face, the perfectly sheared hair, the wool of his jacket. "How are you, Beatrice? Have you been playing with the Raggedy Ann and Andy I bought for you? Have you been having tea parties with all your dollies?" His voice is lighter than I expected, almost a tenor, and his cheeks flush as he talks. His wife darts a glance at him, then looks away. I stare at her as William stoops by you and takes your hand from your mother's. Gretchen is older than her husband and beneath the makeup, old acne scars pickle her face. A bulge at her waist, she probably wears a girdle, as they called it in my time; veins like yarn beneath the skin of her legs, concealed by the gloss of silk stockings.

You snatch your hand from William and snuggle closer to your mother. "My dollies are all dead," you say.

He stands and looks down at you. "Dead? But why?" He reaches into a pocket, removes a white handkerchief, and dabs at his nose. The silk square remains perfectly folded in his jacket pocket. It's for show, I suppose.

"The dolls aren't dead. They're perfectly lovely, William," says Annabelle. She frowns at you, as if wondering what you mean.

Of course, I know what you mean. We understand each other, you and I.

"Mama, I want to go home."

The adults chuckle as if this is cute. Only I know that it's anything but cute. I can tell this is a serious matter, but I don't know why.

"We'll go home after tea and pastries," says Annabelle. "I want to catch up with Gretchen for awhile."

"We have bears' claws, cheese pockets, and blueberry muffins." Gretchen tries to sound perky but fails. She walks across the room and rings a bell for her maid, who appears with a tray, which is solid silver. The teapot and matching china centuries old. Dainty napkins. The maid doesn't look at us — it's as if she wants to disappear into the walls — and she retreats, to appear again moments later with pastries. She bows slightly, then leaves us alone again. Nobody has thanked her. Nobody has acknowledged her existence. Gretchen and Annabelle continue to chat about upcoming social events, their latest clothing purchases, and their figures. William fidgets with papers on the mahogany desk, the one with cherubs carved all over it.

I sit with you and wonder if I can go through with what I must do, and if so, when. You look through me, of course, but I look *into* you, straight through those hollow eyes to your soul.

It's against the force of nature to let something live beyond its time. Someone else went four years too early so I could give you a small space of life. But he was already old, twice Gretchen's age at least, and four more years of pain, loneliness, and senility wouldn't have brought him any pleasure.

It's hard for you to eat, even blueberry muffins which I remember from my own childhood. You nibble fragments. Gretchen eats heartily, your mother takes one pastry but doesn't eat it, and William remains at his desk, pretending to sort through mail and leaf through magazines. Perhaps the wealthy still get paper mail, but of what type I can't imagine. Investment statements?

I float, shadow that I am, from you back to William, and see that the mail is nothing more than advertisements. The magazines are unlike any I've seen, all devoted to masculine pursuits such as guns and ammo, hunting, fishing, and golf. I can picture William playing golf, but little else. Perhaps polo? If I were alive, I might think him amusing in a pathetic sort of way. I bet you'd see things the way I do, too.

Had circumstances been different, had time been aligned better, I suspect you and I would have been the best of friends.

"Gretchen's going to show mama her new curtains. Be a good girl and just wait here quietly, okay?"

You nod, eyes downcast. The air around William shifts almost imperceptibly, just a frisson of tension in his neck and shoulders.

The junk mail slips from his hands.

You fall from the burgundy chair to the rug. On your side, you look up, and he towers over you. I crouch, the rug softer than any bed I slept in while alive, and I see the dangerous flip of your tulle skirt, pink with gold flowers, and it's too high on your legs. This shouldn't matter because you're only four, but somehow, it *does* matter.

Taunts clatter around the room.

"If you'd taken her when we told you, this wouldn't be happening."

"Why didn't you obey orders?"

"If we do as we please, this is what happens."

"You're dead. Your role is to take, nothing more, simply to take."

"Is this what you want?"

No. No, and no again!

The silk square is gold with flecks of crimson. Slender fingers remove it from the jacket pocket. William wipes your tears, and the gold stains to ochre and the crimson deepens.

His skin glows. His sooty eyes widen. His wife's perfume drifts over you.

I'm not supposed to take him. It's not his time.

And what becomes of one like me, who doesn't do as told? Nothing. Yet the result ripples forward in time, causing problems such as this one. Everything is balance, you see. Give one day here, take one day there. If I take William before his time, then what becomes of his wife, Gretchen? And of their children, as yet unborn? It would be as if I'd killed those children, don't you see?

You whimper, then your tiny chin firms, your eyes still gleaming with tears. I see myself reflected in those tears. As his fingers flit through your hair and down your back, you whisper, "P-please..." and it's almost a lisp, and it's so drenched in sorrow and pain that what was once my heart can bear it no more.

William can't have you.

You're mine.

I'm to take you. Not William.

Blessings come in different forms. I lift you from his arms, and you're my pale flower, and I'm a rose. His fingers shake, and I see that he's forty going on a hundred, and do I see the tiniest of smiles upon your face, *do you know, do you?*

His time will come, and let it be soon. I won't take him. But I know they'll send something far worse than me, and it won't be pleasant.

In the brisk air of Sunday morning, two wisps dart between the snowflakes, and the dawn bleeds down.

❖ ❖ ❖

LOIS H. GRESH is the New York Times Best-Selling Author of 27 books and 60 short stories. Her books are in 22 languages and include *Eldritch Evolutions* and *Dark Fusions*. Lois has received Bram Stoker Award, Nebula Award, Theodore Sturgeon Award, and International Horror Guild Award nominations.

RESISTING EXTINCTION

THE LONG WAIT

BY R. B. PAYNE

ON THE FIFTH anniversary, Death appeared as Kurt Cobain.

Trudy knew Death had plucked a teenage crush from her memories. Even still, Kurt's messy blonde hair and shimmering blue eyes nearly seduced her.

Come with me.

It was hardly fair for Death to tempt her like that, especially when she was so helpless like this.

❖ ❖ ❖

Reaching upwards, Trudy's fingertips edged onto a ripple of stone and her body tensed as she pulled vertical another twelve inches. Raising her knee, she set her boot onto a narrow foothold and adjusted her ropes.

"How's it going down there?" Ben's voice carried on the hot summer wind. The rope above her snaked across the rough surface as it tightened and when it was taut she knew she could relax a moment.

"Good," she called, catching her breath. Looking at the route upwards she realized it would be tougher now. The rock tower known as *The Chimney* was a moderately difficult climb but the bolts were iffy and the Utah sun and wind had polished its sandstone surface to the point of slickness.

She chalked her hands.

"Ready," she shouted, and started up the narrow split laughingly referred to as *Elevator Shaft* by experienced climbers.

❖ ❖ ❖

The clatter of the Meds cart meant it was late morning. Her saliva thickened in anticipation of a dribble of apple juice. They always gave her a sip before inserting drugs into her IV.

Hands adjusted her blankets. Then came the uncomfortable tug of the PEG tube directly entering her stomach as they shifted her body to prevent bedsores.

"Here you are, Hon," said Nurse Delany.

A drip of juice slid down Trudy's throat.

Why didn't they ever notice her thickening saliva? Surely, if they paid attention, someone would figure out she was conscious.

But no one did. The doctors knew she had brain activity but not one of them thought it was enough to indicate she was aware.

Damn it, she was.

Trudy struggled to open her eyes, like she did every day. No good. She couldn't move her fingers, adjust her leg, raise an eyebrow, or utter a moan.

She was totally trapped.

✛ ✛ ✛

At the top of *Elevator Shaft*, Trudy paused on a ledge to admire the scenery. To the west were the asphalt and gravel rooftops of Moab and the endless golden and orange windswept cliffs of Canyonlands National Park.

Above her, Ben was racing up *Stardust Cowboy*, a difficult pitch, at best. Beyond lay the summit and the goal of today's climb.

On the horizon, walls of afternoon thunderheads were roiling, black and ominous.

"Hey!" Trudy called. "We've got clouds."

Ben's voice drifted back. "I saw them. Don't worry, we're almost there."

She looked up. *He* was almost there. She still had to negotiate the toughest part of the climb. Sometimes she lamented the fact that women had less testosterone than men.

"Right-o," she said, and tugging on the rope to make sure it was anchored, started up the steepest pitch she had ever climbed.

✛ ✛ ✛

Trudy heard the snap of a clipboard and Paul Drake said something to Perry or Della on the television, and she knew it was between 3 and 4 p.m.

Doctor de Roche on his rounds.

82

A gentle hand squeezed her wrist to take her pulse. She concentrated, working to make her heart race.

Please, please, go faster!

Nothing happened.

Nothing ever did.

"Any change, Nurse?" he asked.

A woman's low voice muttered. That would be Nurse Fields.

Damn it, speak up.

"Thank you, Nurse."

She heard a pen scribbling on paper and then the hollow sound of departing footsteps meant she was alone again.

❖ ❖ ❖

On the summit of *The Chimney* the air was hot and dusty, the sun intense. The thunderheads had moved closer and they agreed to rest only a few minutes.

Another time, she and Ben might have made love, but there were two other climbers smoking a joint and although she doubted they would care (and questioned the wisdom of getting high three hundred and eighty feet above the valley floor), she preferred privacy. And, anyway, her legs were complaining about the climb and she'd need every ounce of strength to get down.

Trudy swatted at a fly resting on her *Girls Rock* tattoo and watched Ben as he checked his ropes, took inventory of the gear, and swigged the last of his water. He scrambled to his feet and three-sixtied the horizon.

"God, it's beautiful."

She smiled as he ran his fingers through his hair and re-tied his ponytail before putting on his helmet.

He was ideal. Smart. Athletic. Good-looking but not taken by his own looks. He had ambition but he'd never be cruelly ambitious.

And he was totally in love with her.

"Yeah," Trudy said. "Beautiful, alright"

But she was looking at him and not the scenery as she clipped on her helmet and struggled to her feet.

❖ ❖ ❖

Ben visited the hospital only twice after she stabilized. In the beginning, he'd been there every day, but the frequency slowed until she wasn't so sure when he'd return next.

The first time was to say he was sorry. He'd already said it a hundred times sitting by her bedside, but this was somehow official. Ben was full of guilt but she had no way to console him. He sat for hours, talking to her and crying until he left without saying good-bye.

Trudy knew *why* he'd come.

He'd given up on her recovering consciousness.

She was dead to him.

It pissed her off, but it didn't last long. She'd been totally angry with him for the first year, but in the second year she'd had more than sufficient time to think through the events of that afternoon, and had reached a certain acceptance.

It takes two to tango.

Ben had made mistakes, but so had she. Climbers are responsible for their own gear. She had fucked up and paid the price.

The next time Ben appeared it was a total surprise since she had lost hope he would ever return. But one day, between meds and pulse taking, she heard the rustle of someone entering the room and a child say "Daddy, who's that?"

Ben's voice floated into her ears.

"An old friend, sweetie. Here, let me show you."

Trudy felt the pat of small feet on the blanket near her hand and the wiggling of a child vibrated the bed.

"Hey Trudy," said Ben. "I know it's been a while. I moved away and I didn't know how to tell you but I'm in town visiting my Mom so I thought I'd come by to see how you're doing."

There was an awkward silence only he could fill.

"Jeez, you look great," he said. She wondered what he saw while there was another long silence. His hand caressed her cheek.

"Is she dead, Daddy?"

"Oh no sweetie. She's just asleep. You know, like Sleeping Beauty."

"Is she waiting for a Prince to come and kiss her?"

"I suppose so."

Trudy felt warmth as Ben took her hand into his.

"You probably figured I'd get married. You know, people move on. It's, uh, been a while and her name is Heather and the two of you would really like each other. And, this squirt is Bethany. She came with the deal. You know I always shot straight with you and I... well..."

Trudy felt Ben lay her hand down and the little feet lifted away. She tried to imagine him now. Did he look the same? Was his hair long? Was he still rugged? Or had he turned corporate — a bit flabby with button-down shirts and khaki trousers? Didn't matter really, she could still remember his smile.

"...well, anyway, I just wanted you to know. So, uh, well, bye."

Trudy listened to Bethany's questions as the door swung shut and the sound of the ventilator and monitors once again became her constant companion.

Sadness flushed through her and she wished she could cry.

✤ ✤ ✤

At the top of *Elevator Shaft*, Trudy felt the first rain drop. Looking up, the sky was blue but the red rock around her was freckled with damp spots. A grey curtain of rain reached to the desert floor a mile away and the wind was carrying the rain to her. It wouldn't be long before they were drenched.

Ben dropped onto the ledge beside her and pulled down a rope from above.

"We've got to move faster," he said, looping a rope through a carabiner and attaching it to a bolt in the rock face.

A rumble of thunder immediately followed a flash of lightning.

"That was close," she said. "Maybe we should ride it out."

Ben quickly tied two ropes together.

"Go," he said. "I'm right behind you. Just stay focused, use the brake, and you'll be fine."

She looked at the knot and reached to re-tie it.

Ben stopped her. "No time." The rock surface was completely soaked now as rain pelted them and rivulets of water splashed down the rock face.

"That's a one-sided overhand bend. You know I don't use it."

A crack of thunder deafened her as Ben took the rope from her and dropped it down *Elevator Shaft*.

Trudy looked over the edge. The rope dangled a hundred and twenty feet straight down. Then, it was a ledge and forty more feet to safety.

She gave Ben a nasty look.

"Don't be so fucking stubborn," he responded.

Trudy slid into the crack as Ben stabilized her rope. Rainwater gushed in small rivers past her as she started to rappel. She was tired and wet and scared. It wouldn't be long before she was climbing down a waterfall.

"Sometimes I hate you," she called as she slid into the gaping hollow.

❖ ❖ ❖

Once it was apparent the life support systems were working, Death visited Trudy whenever her family made their annual pilgrimage.

Her folks lived in Telluride and they came to Denver where she received long-term care. They'd come frequently in the beginning, always with hope and flowers. Now, they came once a year to meet with the doctors and caregivers and have a painful discussion as to whether or not this was the year to pull the plug.

They didn't know she could hear every word.

❖ ❖ ❖

Trudy corkscrewed out of control as a roaring torrent of rainwater pushed her from the safety of the wall. She twisted and planted a foot back on solid rock.

"Ben!"

No answer.

She squinted upwards through the deluge pounding her. How far had she come? She couldn't see anything, let alone Ben. She swivelled to look down. How much farther?

A vibration in the rope sent a wave of fear through her. She'd passed the overhand knot some distance above. Then the rope slipped, letting her drop a foot or two. Suddenly she couldn't breath as she realized what was happening.

Trudy felt the knot capsize as it failed.

She had seconds.

The one-sided overhand bend was known as the European Death Knot if it had been tied too quickly or with uneven rope sizes. Maybe it was simply unable to hold in all this water.

Feet dangling, she ran her hands over the vertical wall. There had to be a bolt somewhere, if she could find it, she could attach.

Uncontrolled, she dropped another four or five feet and her scream was drowned out by the rushing water. How much more rope did she have? Her fingers flew back to the wall, searching, searching, searching.

Then, she found cold metal under the sheeting water, and her hand scrambled to locate a carabiner on her climbing harness. She slid it onto the bolt, and tied a safety rope to it.

Above her, the rappel rope went limp; the knot had completely failed. The rope tumbled by, a multi-colored snake in the murky water.

"Fuck me!" Trudy said, her heart racing out of control.

But she was safe.

Hold on tight, hold on, hold on.

And then the bolt failed, ripped from the rock by her weight, and she was tumbling earthward in a roaring cascade.

✛ ✛ ✛

Trudy lay in a field of undulating wild grass and alpine flowers, alongside a cold-looking river carving its way along the base of the Tetons. On a sandy beach, a green canoe with two oars rested, and she could smell campground smoke although she couldn't see from where it came.

A feeling of tranquility slid through her as she rose to her feet. This was her favorite place on Earth.

"May I help you, Miss?"

She turned, and there stood a ranger, his olive green uniform smartly pressed. Atop his head, the traditional park service ranger hat.

Handsome.

But something was wrong. Disoriented, she bent over and rested her palms on her knees, breathing heavily. She had the distinct feeling of falling, falling, falling.

Maybe she should sit.

The ranger checked his clipboard. "Miss Halloran? You're here for canoeing, I see. If you're ready, let's get started."

"Give me a minute," Trudy said.

"Please, come with me, Miss Halloran. It's the best thing to do." The ranger motioned toward the canoe.

"I don't feel well."

"You'll be much better once we get going." The ranger tapped his watch. "We're on a schedule, you know."

Trudy touched her hair, expecting it to be wet. Glancing at the bright blue sky, it was clearly mid-day but there was no sun.

"Where am I?" she said.

The ranger stared at her.

"Seriously, what is this place?"

"Some people say they want to know, but they really don't. It will be easier if you just come with me to the canoe. A short paddle and you'll feel much better on the other side of the river. I guarantee it."

"Tell me. I can take it."

The ranger unfolded a park map and pointed.

"In-Between Meadows."

Trudy scanned the horizon trying to get a fix on her location.

"In-Between... in-between fucking what?"

"In-between here and there. He pointed to the horizon. That's where you came from. He hooked a thumb and motioned over his shoulder to the river, "And that's where you're going. You're... in-between."

"I don't remember signing up for a canoe ride. Where, specifically, am I going?"

A perturbed look crossed his face. "Actually, I only know where you're coming from. I have no idea where you're going. It's my job to paddle you across the river."

"And what if I want to cancel my appointment?"

He consulted his clipboard. "Usually folks don't have a choice, but I see you are hanging on."

Images flashed through Trudy's mind. Red rocks. Rushing water. Her helmet splitting as she hit solid ground. She gasped and the ranger grabbed her elbow to support her.

She looked at him hopefully. "Hanging on to the bolt?"

"No," the ranger said, "to your life."

A Golden Retriever loped to the ranger. He petted the dog and pulled a tennis ball from his pocket then swished the ball in the air.

"Look at this, boy. You know you want it. Oh, yes you do."

The dog nipped at the ball. The ranger threw it to the far side of the river. Trudy was incredulous. It was an amazing throw.

"Go get it, boy." He gently urged the dog away. "Go on."

The retriever raced to the water's edge, swam the river, and climbing onto the opposite shore, and then became a golden orb of light that floated into the sky and disappeared.

Trudy took a step back from the ranger and studied him.

"I get it," she said finally. "You're Death. You're a hallucination."

"Indeed, you have identified me. But I am not a figment of your imagination." He offered his hand. "Please, come with me."

Trudy refused his hand. His skin was oddly translucent and she imagined she could see bones beneath the flesh.

"I don't want to."

"My, you are stubborn." Again, the ranger consulted his clipboard. "Well, because of your situation, I can't force you. I can let you return, but you understand I may see you again in a few minutes, hours, or days. Your vessel is gravely damaged, you know."

"I don't care," Trudy said.

"I can wait," the ranger said as he made a checkmark on a sheet of paper. "But I had to take your child. There was no choice."

In blackness, Trudy heard the rotors of a helicopter. She felt damp wind and mud drops buffet her body as the 'copter thumped onto the ground.

Why couldn't she open her eyes?

Confusing time passed.

Gentle hands lifted her.

Why couldn't she speak?

The prick of a needle. A stiff board beneath her back. A blanket over her body. An oxygen mask across her mouth. The comfort of velvet darkness approached her mind as sadness constricted her heart.

She hadn't known she was pregnant.

❖ ❖ ❖

In Trudy's world, Death was Light.

She always knew when he approached because a ribbon of luminescence brightened her peripheral vision and then she was in the In-Between.

The In-Between was always different and that pleased her. And although she hated the danger her family represented when they appeared with their conversations about her soul, her quality of life, and how much less the insurance company was willing to pay, she had grown to look forward to the brief moments where she could see and actually talk to someone.

Even if he was Death.

❖ ❖ ❖

On the first anniversary, Death said nothing, and he didn't bother to present her with the In-Between. He sat wordlessly on a molded plastic chair, a black woolen cowl covering his features. His scythe

89

leaned casually against the wall and his arms were folded across his chest.

It was all she could see in the tunnel vision that Death offered. Voices from around the bed carried to her.

"She looks so peaceful."

"I'll wait outside, I need a cigarette."

"Do you think she can hear us?"

"She's in a coma. There's always a chance she'll recover."

"It would have been so much more kind if she, well, hadn't lived. You know, I'm just saying."

"Look at all this equipment."

"C'mon, Mom, let's get a cup of coffee. I saw a machine down the hall."

Trudy checked off the voices: Dr. De Roche, Dad, Mom, her brother Bobby, and Uncle Roy and Aunt Patsy Jo from West Texas.

At the far end of her tunnel vision, Death unfolded his arms and, with an ivory-boned finger, motioned her to follow him.

Come with me.

✤ ✤ ✤

On the second anniversary of her accident, Death came as a life insurance salesman. Not a real insurance salesman, that's just how he looked to Trudy.

Grey-haired, wrinkled, wire-rimmed glasses, kindly. Leather briefcase.

"Good afternoon, Miss Halloran."

They were sitting in the reception lobby of a glass and steel office building overlooking a city she didn't recognize. Workers hurried by, but never close enough to get a true glance at their faces.

"I thought perhaps you'd be more comfortable in an urban setting while we wait," Death said.

For the moment, Trudy was speechless. It was eerily quiet, but she heard the murmur of distant voices.

"She looks so peaceful."

"I'll wait outside, I need a cigarette."

"Do you think she can hear us?"

"No, the Doctor says it's a long shot."

"Can she recover?"

"Well, there's always a chance. Did you read about that woman in Omaha?"

✤ ✤ ✤

In her third year, Trudy learned French and by the time Death visited her, she was fluent. Nurse Delany had placed a CD player next to her bed and hour after hour the lessons looped until Trudy knew them by heart.

Trudy sensed the ribbon of light. Death approached and she floated out of her body. Sight flooded into her eyes and, as they adjusted to the darkness of night, she realized she was standing on a hillside path overlooking a rustic village. The air was warm and scented with lavender.

The night sky filled with swirling clouds, the stars blazed with their own luminescence, and a bright crescent moon cast a dim light across the countryside.

Below, warm yellow light poured from distant village windows. Remembrances of her childhood flooded through Trudy as the peacefulness of the scene filled her.

"You were an art student and now you've learned French," said a voice. "I thought this place might be appropriate."

She turned to face a fiery-eyed disheveled red-headed man with a goatee.

"Starry Night. Wow," Trudy said in awe. "But Vincent Van Gogh wasn't French," she admonished.

"Close enough," said Death.

A wind kicked through the trees behind them and the sound of rising voices edged to them on the breeze.

"Well, she doesn't look any better."

"She's so thin."

"Don't they ever put lotion on her skin?"

"I'll wait outside, I need a cigarette."

"The Doctor says she seems more vegetative."

"Don't cry, Mom."

Vincent touched Trudy's shoulder.

"I thought we might have a glass of wine in the village. Despite the late hour, I happen to know a café is open and the noise of the crowd will obscure your family's deliberations. Perhaps we could wait there, Miss Halloran?"

"*Bien sur*. But promise to call me Trudy, okay?"

She took his hand and grasped it tightly. It was the most alive she'd felt in a long, long time.

Hand-in-hand, they walked down the hill to the village. Their conversation carried on the flowered breeze.

"Perhaps someday I could paint you."
Girlish laughter followed.

❖ ❖ ❖

Death was a regular visitor in the fourth year.

In the spring, Trudy's breathing became shallow and halting, her lips and mouth were scraped raw from the insertion of plastic tubes. She desperately needed to cough but couldn't. The pain in her chest felt like fire as her lungs filled with fluid. Where the tracheotomy tube entered, her neck was infected and itched relentlessly. An itch that couldn't be scratched.

Pneumonia had become a persistent companion.

Worse yet, her mind was growing dim and sometimes she didn't know where she was. Or who she was. Long periods of time passed and then she would suddenly snap back to consciousness. In moments of clarity, she knew she was wasting away.

Dying.

Becoming a vegetable.

Hold on tight, hold on, hold on.

Her life was fading.

Hold on tight, hold on, hold on.

"Trudy?"

Somewhere, a ribbon of light approached and Trudy felt the relief of the In-Between.

"Perhaps it's time for you to come with me."

"No."

An ocean wave swept onto a beach and receded. She recognized the shoreline as Malibu, a place she'd left a long time ago. Off the shore, the waves were barreling and the surfers were carving perfectly through the A-Frames.

She had grown up here, surfing and sunbathing.

Trudy watched for the longest time as the riders paddled for position and took the waves. She breathed in the salt air and curled her toes in the sand.

She turned to speak to Death and was surprised she didn't know the human form he had taken. He appeared to be some surfer dude.

"Is it really you?" she asked. "I don't recognize your form."

"Sorry," he said. "I had to come quickly, your vessel is failing, and we quickly picked something appropriate."

A perturbed look crossed her face.

"Are there more than one of you?"

"There is only one of me but many of us. Countless guides are required for such a large endeavor."

His hand swept to indicate the world.

She flopped onto the sand to rest and sat where she could talk to him and still watch the surfers.

"Then you must know what it all means. You know… life and death."

"I'm sorry, Trudy, I don't. No one knows what it means."

"So where do we go when we cross the river?"

"Existence is permanent, form is transient. That's all I know."

A beep sounded on his waterproof watch.

"It's a busy time, I have to go," he said. "But I'll be back if you need me."

"Bring me back here again and I'll teach you to surf."

Death smiled.

Then she was trapped in the hell that was her body, hoping she could stay sane until he came again.

In the summer she taught Death to *hang ten*, although the end was getting closer and closer and the Trudy in the bed hardly knew who or where she was.

❖ ❖ ❖

On the fifth anniversary, Death appeared as Kurt Cobain. They were standing in In-Between Meadows, he a blond-haired God created to guide her.

Come with me.

She took a step backward from Kurt, he was too… luscious.

High on the craggy mountainsides, the sun glinted off sheltered snow. In the grassy meadow, the air was warm and fresh with no smells of antiseptics, floor wax, or hospital sickness. It felt wonderful to be whole again and she flexed the tattoo on her arm and drew a deep breath.

Girls Rock.

"I want to see you as you really are," she said, and, after a pause, Kurt transformed to a floating golden orb.

The sounds of a lawyer reached her ears. "Pursuant to the laws of the State of Colorado…" but Trudy tuned him out. She knew what was happening. They were going to pull the plug. Other voices drifted to her.

"It's for the best."

"She's going to a better place."

"I'll wait outside, I need a cigarette."

"She'll be with Grandpa and Grandma Billings, now."

She felt the warmth of a hand on hers.

"We love you, Trudy."

Mother.

"Me too, Truds. I love you, baby."

Father.

The lawyer had finished and Doctor De Roche said, "Are we ready?"

"Yes," Trudy heard her mother whisper.

The room became quieter as the machines were powered off until all that was left was the beeping of the heart monitor.

"I'm in love with you," Trudy said to Death. "It's crazy. You're probably nothing but dying brain cells but you give me great comfort."

"I'm as real as you, Trudy."

Trudy stepped closer.

"Do you love *me*?"

The orb flickered, dimmed, then returned to brightness.

"I have grown attached to you. I enjoy our time together. I hate to see you suffer. If that's love, then yes. I'm sorry, that's all I am capable of. I wish it were more."

Trudy reached and tentatively touched the orb. His energy flowed into her.

"It could be more, couldn't it?"

"I don't know," said Death, "but I have hope."

"You know I don't want to die," Trudy said.

"You're so stubborn. I've told you death and birth are the same. There is no end."

"But there's an end for Trudy. I'm not done being Trudy. She deserves a life."

"Indeed she does," agreed Death.

"Will you wait for me?"

"Of course."

The alarm from the heart monitor wailed as Trudy flatlined.

"Well, that's it," Doctor De Roche said quietly.

Trudy could hear her mother sobbing at the edge of the bed. She felt the cold press of a stethoscope on her breast.

Her fingers twitched.
Her eyes opened.
And a tear ran down her cheek.

❖ ❖ ❖

Assembled from stolen body parts, **R. B. PAYNE** lives in the
hope of being human. Meanwhile, he writes. His stories are
in *Times of Trouble; Chiral Mad*, and a graphic dog-men novel
from Island Tales.

THAT BRIGHTNESS

BY MARY E. CHOO

IT'S THE DRESS I notice, at first.

On this bright summer day, it stands out with a creamy-white radiance. The swirls and drifts and shadowed folds fall to the woman's ankles. Her back is to me, her pale bare feet motionless on the terrace stones; her equally pallid arms are poised and still.

Her long hair almost matches the color of her garment. One hand holds a red string, attached to a blood-red balloon that bobs high above her.

She crosses the terrace, descending the steps to the park lawn on the other side. The artist in me is fascinated, and I follow. My long skirt almost trips me as I grab the railing and navigate the shallow steps three at a time. She's part way across the lawn, moving toward the dry fountain in the centre. A group of people is gathered there, and she stops, dead-still, at the edge. I approach slowly, angling to one side to see better.

"This is perhaps George's finest work," a woman facing the crowd says. "Regrettably, he assures me it's his last." She moves off to the side, gesturing at the middle of the fountain, where a large object sits veiled in a scarlet cloth.

George, a sculptor I know slightly, stands alone by the low fountain wall, looking rumpled in the heat. He isn't old; his hair is only a little grey, and his body — the shoulders and hands particularly — appears strong and fit. Still, as I look harder, I see a pain on his face that's out-of-place on such an occasion. I know that expression, the feeling it conveys. Nothing you do is ever good enough, no matter how people praise it; you have to prove yourself, over and over, and sometimes you get so tired...

He's given up, I think.

George leans across the fountain wall. He pulls the red cloth away with the air of a blind man, revealing a classical male figure in bronze, with one hand held up to the sun. The fountain springs to life, water from the upraised hand spraying both George and the figure. The cloth trails in the pooling water, turning darkly scarlet. George addresses the gathering, squinting into the sun.

"I'm grateful to you all, for your kindness," he begins. A surprising and chill gust of wind turns the fountain spray into billowing, rainbow mists.

There's a piercing cry from the woman in white. She lunges through the group, the red balloon and string trailing and her hair and garment rippling about her. Drawing the string alongside her, she doubles part of it into a cord, twining it. She reaches George, and I'm stunned when she winds the string around his neck, forming a ligature and twisting it viciously. There's a dazzling aura around the two of them. George paws and chokes, grappling with the cord as he sinks to the ground, his face contorting in terror. He starts to sway from side to side in some weird kind of rhythm, the woman moving her arms along with him, pulling. Fiery light flares from the cord, whirling about him. He shakes his head, as though denying something— people are shouting, hurrying toward them. The woman gives a final wrench, drawing blood before releasing her grip. She turns, and the face I glimpse through the shimmering hair looks terrible and hard, the dark eyes piercing. Clutching the cord, she takes several steps back, rubbing her hand on her neck and arm and leaving bloody patches.

"No!" Recovering, I rush forward to help, attracting the attention of George's assailant as I pass. She glares at me and grabs my arm, her mouth twisting, but I pull free. George lies still. Several people are trying frantically to revive him, to no avail. I ask what I can do, but they wave me off. When I glance back, the woman in white gives me one last, ferocious look, then turns and starts away. No one seems to notice her. Light shimmers all around her as she twirls the cord into a string once more, the balloon floating above. I could swear I see George's face in that bright red orb, pushing against the membrane, as if to escape.

"Did you *see* her?" I tug at a woman's arm, pointing. "My God, isn't anyone going to *stop* her?"

The woman shakes me off, looking me up and down. I'm badly dressed at the best of times — unkempt hair, worn clothes — and I can't really blame her. She's more concerned with George, and when I look for his assailant once more, I can't find her.

The park police arrive, then an ambulance. I back away in shock and confusion. It's all so appalling. Things could be over, for anyone, just like that! I don't know George well, or if he's dead or what, but I can't believe he did anything to deserve this. No one could. Still, in spite of what I think I saw, there's no blood left on him, no apparent mark, and the woman in white, well...

If I say anything, if no one else saw her — it's so hard for me to speak out, and I'm so paranoid — maybe, this time, they'll lock me away.

I turn and hurry from the park, taking a right along the sidewalk.

❖ ❖ ❖

The irony is, I'm not *on* anything just now. I won't even take medication, which makes my condition worse. It's difficult to explain how terrible, how lifeless the pills make me feel.

Several blocks from the park, I cross the street so I'll have to turn right three times to reach the studio: right and along the sidewalk on the other side, right at the main avenue and back across the road, then along the avenue and a final right into the building. What I saw in the park flickers on and off in my mind like a faded movie reel, and I make small, scared sounds of denial. I've been trying not to step on any lines or cracks, which is difficult, as the paving is old around here and laid in squares, and my legs are shaking. A man jostles me, scowling, and I land on a crack— an ominous sign.

Near the studio, the way is crowded and baking hot. The heat penetrates my sandals. A woman I've seen before sits on the sidewalk, hawking balloons, most of which are red. Today, a ragged shawl covers her head against the sun. I can't see her face, and suddenly she seems sinister. As I turn into the studio stairwell I glance back at the doorway. I could swear I see the edge of a creamy dress, a bare foot...

Francis waits for me upstairs. The huge ceiling fan turns lazily, and it's cooler. I need to tell him.

"I stepped on a crack," I begin, as if to explain why I'm late. "You know, 'step on a crack, break your mother's—'" I pause, adding lamely, "Anyway, your message said someone was coming."

"Jess," Francis greets me, nodding; he inclines his head toward the back of the studio, where I paint. A man is standing there, studying my work. I have the sense to shut up, though when I look down at my hands, they're trembling. My need to speak of what I saw is so strong, it takes all I have just to focus.

"I'm so pleased to meet you." The man, youngish, pleasant, extends his hand as I approach, and I manage to shake it. I know of him, the family— they buy a lot of art.

He's interested in one of my latest paintings — a raw explosion of color that looks like a fiery, sunset sea, scattered with hints of things — a wisp of a sail, a border of trees at the edge.

He gets to the point. It's a large canvas, but I'm still staggered by the price he names. Francis' face is all brown angles and gentleness; his mouth blossoms into a wide smile.

"Actually, she was thinking more of..."

He goes a thousand over the man's offer, and I'm shocked when the latter agrees. I'm barely concentrating. The matter is settled quickly, and before I realize it Francis has a cheque in his hand and the man is walking out the door with my painting.

Francis puts the cheque in his shirt pocket; he handles all my money affairs, which is a godsend. I look toward his work, displayed at the front of the studio. "You're a marvellous agent, Francis— an incredible artist."

"Not like you, Jess," he says, gently. I know what he's referring to, the comments: that I'm ambivalent, unfocused on my career, but that the fusion of color and light, that brightness at the core of every painting I've ever completed, has won me praise, even a mention of genius. I'd do far better if I just applied myself. I've kept my darker secrets as best I could, along with a cultivated mistrust of outsiders. "What's wrong?" he asks.

I'm shaking all over. "A sculptor in the park — George Maldern — he..." I cop out. "He collapsed. I think he's dead. That's why I'm late."

"George?" Francis is taken aback. "They were unveiling his bronze today, his fountain— we're invited to the reception. You'd have known if you'd been in this week."

"Sorry." I whisper. The memory of what I saw, improbable or not, causes bile to rise in my throat. Besides, Francis is good to me, and I don't deserve it. If I tell him — how *can* it be true? — he'd worry terribly.

"Here," I take some crumpled bills from my skirt pocket and cram them into his hand. "Part of the rent. The rest when you put the cheque through, I promise."

He puts his arms around me and I start to cry. Then I hug him fiercely and pull away. I have to force myself to stay in the studio, to try to paint. I can't just walk out. Francis works so bloody hard. He sells well, but unlike me, he's earned it, and he never gets the kind of acclaim I do.

I settle as best I can in front of an unfinished canvas, with my oils and brushes. On top of everything else, and particularly today, the familiar monster crowds in— *doubt*. Even when I do feel compelled, I paint for a few days only, then stop, paint then stop... I know, no matter what, that the work will never be quite good enough. It's a love-hate thing that consumes me.

Right now, all genesis seems stuck somewhere between my brain and my unsteady hand — it's the park thing, of course, but I won't — *can't* — sort it out yet. Thoughts about my own mortality and my sense of worthlessness are so mixed up in it all. A ray of sunlight slips through a space in the window blind, lighting up my arm. Odd, how the light seems to stay there, no matter how I move. It's so bright.

None of this is right— the colors, the mediocre composition. "Damn... useless!" I fling my brush to the floor, sending the canvas clattering after it, ruining it.

"How can you expect to realize your potential, to *really* succeed, when you only finish a few paintings a year?" Francis, stacking paintings against the wall beside me, asks calmly.

I know he's right. Even with my growing panic, I'm ashamed of my outburst. My efforts sell for decent sums, which keeps me going, but that's a shabby reason to paint.

"I *will* pay you— and you'll take your commission, of course." I pat the cheque in his shirt pocket, my voice breaking; I'm losing it. "Later..." I manage.

Francis tries to grab my hands. "Jess— Jessica! It doesn't matter—"

I'm gone, running downstairs into the street. I look nervously to the left, front and right before I start out, taking care to avoid lines or cracks.

❖ ❖ ❖

The heat builds fiercely for the next few days. By the end of the week, it's hell. I've been dreaming of the woman in white, catching glimpses of dazzling light in the corner of my eye. There've been confusing rumors about how it happened, but George did die. That confirmation shook me. Apart from what I think I saw, what if I were suddenly cut down like that, if it all just stopped? George was so gifted, I'd never measure up to a legacy like his, or anyone else's I can think of. Still...

"I didn't see that woman— I *didn't!*" If I tell myself this often enough, maybe it will make it true. Besides, I'm really scared. I've never hallucinated about anything— it just isn't part of my problem. But if this is a new symptom...

"*Check*," I mutter as I take the first of three right turns, stepping over a line. I'm not sure just when this thing with threes started, but I feel that along with avoiding cracks and the like, it saves me, that if I stick to my rituals I'll be all right. Besides, if I don't give in, the urge builds inside me until I feel I'll burst.

I'm meeting my friend Connie at Jacques— after this I go one block, another right, another block and a right into the café. From the shade of the awnings, the light beyond looks surreal. Everyone, every *thing* is different in the harsh cast of sunlight, brighter or paler, more angular...

I love Jacques, with its old-world atmosphere and rich aroma of coffee and croissants. Connie is sitting in an alcove by the far window, away from everyone. Her face looks drawn, and she has a satchel and some papers on the table in front of her.

"The ceiling fans in here sure help," I comment, sitting opposite. I take some napkins and divide them into three neat piles; wisely, Connie says nothing.

"Not going well?" I venture. I can see the papers are part of her latest novel. She's been having a rough time with it; something made all the worse, I suspect, by her considerable fame.

"What do you think?" She shoves the top pages at me. Her voice is low, coarsened by years of heavy smoking, and I know this isn't really a question. Connie loves writing. This is about pain, and I have to be careful. I read the passage, noting the change in dialogue since I last saw it, the absence of detail, which is not her style.

"I liked the first version better," I say gently, handing them back. "You revealed so much more about the characters, and the setting, the atmosphere, contributed to that."

"That isn't what *they* thought." She pushes her empty paper cup away.

They are her editor and agent, and they've been hounding her for weeks.

"My last book barely earned out its advance, Jess, and if I don't fix this— well with everything being so sensationalist, now, so plot-driven..."

Connie is dear to me, and I hate seeing her like this. She's one of those gifted artists and writers who achieve success in their lifetime, when so many don't. She's won awards and rave reviews, and has a slew of fans. But she's bound by the bottom-line mentality of all-too-many publishers, that it's all about the money now, and if you mess up, you're gone.

"This is better than your last novel Connie— it *has* a strong plot. Put back what you took out, and the story's dynamite." She hires people to vet her work. I don't know if they've seen this yet, but I can tell by her face that I haven't reassured her.

"I've tried and tried. It's no damn use." Connie hunches over her manuscript. "I haven't shown anyone the last of it. I've deleted the thing— smashed the backup." She reaches into her satchel and pulls out a wad of papers, stacking them with the others. "This is the only hard copy. I think we should take the whole thing back to my place and burn it— what do you say?" To my dismay, she leafs through some pages and starts to tear them. "Maybe I should give *everything* up!"

"No Connie, not like this." I grab at her wrists, struggling with her at first, then wresting the manuscript away. Her face contorts in anguish as she reaches after it, as though she has to commit this act before she loses her courage. It's as if she's murdering someone, and I don't even know if she wants me to stop her. The sun slips past the café awning, flooding the table.

Connie gets hold of the manuscript's edge, distraught. Nothing I say calms her. If I know one thing at this moment, it's that I have to save her book. I wrench the papers free, losing my balance, slipping off my chair and landing on my side. I still have the manuscript— there are a couple of tears. Connie drops to her knees by the table, reaching for me. Raising my head, I see a pale, bare foot next to me. Then I notice the creamy, luminous dress.

I twist back. *"You!"*

Bathed in a commanding radiance, her figure looks titanic. She steps forward, with her doubled red string and bright, trailing balloon. I feel a chill gust in the sunlight. With a keening moan, she reaches down and winds the cord around Connie's neck, starting to twist and pull.

I hear shouting, people in the background, but I see only what's before me— the light obliterates the café and patrons. It's all about us, dazzling. I scramble to my knees, reaching for the creature's hands, trying to loosen her grip. Connie's choking, grabbing at the ligature. The white menace has long fingernails, and she twists the cord with one powerful hand — right at Connie's neck — working at both of mine with the other, her nails cutting cruelly into Connie and me. Connie grapples hard, looking toward her tormentor, swaying in that same strange way that George did. The other moves with her, saying something to her, but the noise around us is louder and I can't hear that well.

"*Stop!*" I clench my teeth, putting my full weight against the woman's leg— it's immovable. Grabbing the cord with one hand, I get my other behind Connie's head, yanking her toward me. "Connie, come on, breathe, *try!*" Connie's assailant hisses at me, her dark eyes full of rage. She rips the crimson cord from my grasp, and I feel a sharp tug on that arm. My other hand loses its grip on Connie. A ragged brilliance erupts from the cord, swirling around her. I can barely see. I think Connie mouths something at her attacker, but I can't make it out— she gestures, begging...

And then it's over. The white menace and light vanish— it all happened so fast. I'm kneeling, panting, and Connie's lying on her back on the sunlit floor in front of me. There are people crowded around, and a man is crouching next to us, clutching my arm.

"I'm a doctor," he says to me. "What the hell's going on? The two of you—"

"She gets carried away," I interrupt glibly. "She's stressed, smokes constantly—" My heart sinks as Connie stops breathing. The doctor tries to rouse her, checking her pulse before beginning chest compressions. Someone holds a cell phone to his ear as he orders an ambulance. For an awful moment nothing happens; then, with a hideous gasping noise, Connie starts to breathe. She looks at me, stricken, drawing me down in a shaky embrace, and I've never been so happy to hug someone in my life.

"Jess, what was—?" Her voice sounds reedy in my ear. She can't finish. She knows. I can tell from her face. Like me, she *saw*, even if no one else did, and I'm damn sure she spoke with that thing, felt something.

"The hard copy's all right." I forestall her with a warning look. "Someone can type a new one, or maybe retrieve the file from your laptop."

There's a lot of talk around us, but no one's blaming me for anything, yet. Signs remain of an attack this time— we're both left with sinister marks and scratches. When the paramedics and ambulance come, Connie wants me along, and I climb into the front seat, glancing down the street as I reach to close the door.

The woman in white is there, hair and garment fluttering, balloon bobbing. She stands transcendent in the summer light, totally in command of the space she inhabits. She doesn't care if she attacks in broad daylight, even when there's someone like me who can see and intervene. Those terrible eyes stare right at me, her expression cruel and carved-looking, like stone. Once more I see a face in the red balloon, like some grotesque trophy— oh God no, Connie's! And then it disappears...

When we reach the hospital, I accompany Connie as they wheel her stretcher in; she plucks at my sleeve. She looks even more terrified than I feel, and she's ghastly pale.

"Jess, back there, did you see—?" Once more, she can't finish the question, and I sense she never will. Worst of all, I think I get it now— I really do.

❖ ❖ ❖

My hand is shaking so badly, there's paint all over the place and my canvas is a mess.

For days I've been looking out my window, over my shoulder, thinking I see that white dress, the red balloon. Connie's phoned me so many times, chattering frantically about the progress on her book. She's read me passages, and they're astonishing; rambling and brilliant, but I doubt they'll do for today's market. Worse, her conversations are so scattered I'm afraid she's losing it. I'm convinced her wild burst of inspiration is because of the woman in white, of some promise she made that she has no hope of keeping. She hasn't mentioned any part of that awful day, even her hospital visit, and when I press her, she hangs up. She won't see me.

I can't say I wasn't warned...

It all begins with a touch of light on my hand, my arm.

The creature's picked her time, when Francis is out. Her approach is so silent. I just turn, and she's there; no gust of air, though it's freezing. If I thought her radiance dazzling before, it was nothing compared to now. Her look has never been so direct, so cruel and angry. I see no mercy in her face, and I deserve none. I've betrayed my art. I'm a slacker, a self-pitying, pathetic loser. She starts for me, the cord ready, and all at once she speaks.

Today, it's a terrifying, banshee's-howl of a voice, full of accusation and contempt. She lists my shortcomings relentlessly, and this time her words are so loud and clear there's no mistaking them. She lunges at me and I drop my brush— I have this mad hope I can escape. We duck and weave among the easels. The way we move left and right reminds me of George and Connie, and their strange swaying.

Suddenly, she leaps, looping the dreaded cord around my neck— she twists it at my throat, playing the length out a little, toying with me. I can still breathe, perhaps speak. She's enjoying my fear and distress— I sense they're part of my punishment, and I feel an overwhelming rage.

"I'm not ready, damn you! I won't go— I *won't!* At least I'm trying!"

We begin a perverse dance of retreat and pursuit, the ligature tightening and tightening as she pulls me toward her, and me tugging on it, trying to ease it; there's jagged light all along it, and it burns. The balloon floats near. I see tiny and countless tormented faces in it, hear their high-pitched, unearthly screaming, feel their desolation and despair.

At last she corners me. I know what she wants. I've finally realized how important my painting is. I've used every kind of excuse, even my compulsions — 'poor me, I can't cope' — to avoid the challenge of my true potential. It's ironic that it's taken *her* to make me see this. The craving for perfection isn't what matters either. It's the work itself, the striving, and right now I so badly want another chance at that.

"Please." I'm still standing; I'm dizzy, and breathing horribly— I won't beg, or kneel willingly, which is a stupid kind of pride. "Just listen." I choke the promises out. It may be fear, but I mean every one of them. She smiles in disdain, finally hauling me to my knees. The light grows blinding, and there's a sharp pain around my heart before it all goes blank.

✣ ✣ ✣

My recovery is slow— like Connie, I don't talk about what happened.

Many thoughts run through my mind as I stand working. I haven't seen my nemesis yet, but I sense she's stalking me. She's always been with me, really— that source of light in my work, what others call my genius.

There is no compromise for anyone creative, only acceptance of the compelling, incessant urge to *do*. The woman in white embodies the brilliance, the force, that matrix which drives us all. She and her balloon are surreal and disturbing, like so much in literature and art, but beautiful, too. The problem lies with the darker persona that lurks in all that light, the judge and avenger, that killer Muse. She has high standards, and she doesn't like weakness.

"Jess, take a break," Francis, on his way out, urges me.

"Can't— sorry," I say gently, looking after him. He's so deserving— he should be safe from *her*. As for me, I'm in a state of both madness and growing bliss. Odd, but I feel such joy now, though I know that nagging quest for perfection will set in soon enough.

Things really do go in threes: there was George, who just quit, then poor, conflicted Connie, and now — and least worthy of all — me. My sins of omission loom large. I have to keep striving for that perfect painting. I promised.

Besides, I want — I *need* — to see what I really can do.

But somehow the colors, the focus and form required for absolute perfection elude me, and I know in this particular effort I'll fail. I've stepped on so many cracks, lately. I put it aside to finish another time, as best I can. That, too, was part of the pact— no more tantrums.

I start another canvas— my third today, and hopefully the magic number.

Is that a light I see in the corner of my eye, coming from the top of the stairs, with a bob and flicker of red? I hope she approves. She must know I don't want anything to happen, not yet— I can't succumb to her, let that force consume me...

That brightness.

✤ ✤ ✤

MARY E. CHOO's work has appeared in many publications, both print and electronic. She has been on the preliminary ballots of the Nebula and Bram Stoker awards (the latter for poetry) and is a two-time Aurora finalist.

Night Market

by Steve Rasnic Tem and Melanie Tem

CARA REALLY HAD to have a good time tonight. The way that beagle at work had looked at her, obviously knowing he was about to die...

She didn't mind assisting when animals were euthanized — in other words, killed, helped to die. The vets referred to it as "put down." People outside the profession called it "put to sleep," which made it hard to fall asleep herself when she went to bed that night. She was actually sort of drawn to that part of her job — not something she'd tell anybody, but she kept thinking she'd understand what death was if she was present often enough, touching the animal at the exact instant it passed from alive to not alive.

The vets said animals only understood they were sick, and that's why they hid sometimes — it was a self-protection instinct. But Cara loved animals more than she loved people, and she knew it was something else. People could stare death right in the face and say it wasn't there for them. But animals knew.

This morning she'd walked in, and one of the other assistants was holding the dog on the table while the vet prepared the injection, and the dog had looked right at her. When she moved, the eyes stayed on her, those brown eyes surrounded by so much white, strained into a teardrop shape. Dogs didn't cry — their tear ducts drained out to their noses, one of those vet things that were kind of fun to bring up in casual conversation and gross people out about. But dogs and other animals could still show sadness, and give their eyes that desperate shape, and stare at you, even when you moved all around the room trying to escape them, the eyes following, like a final sad dance.

Then it was done. The dog had gone limp. The owner had cried. The vet had spoken gently. Cara had stood back, waiting to clean everything up. The dog's brown eyes had stayed open.

Cara *really* wanted to forget about all that and have a good time. But this was not her idea of a good time. It was hot sitting here in the car, even though the sun had gone down behind the buildings. Her AC wasn't that great. She was tired from work. The new outfit wasn't as cool as she'd thought when she'd paid too much for it. The weed was only okay. Eli was being uncommunicative and she didn't know him well enough yet to interpret his long silences and few words; by the time she did, she wouldn't care.

Hopefully she'd get decent sex out of this before she lost interest. A kiss at least. So far, they'd barely held hands. What was up with that?

"Night market," he'd called it when he'd invited her to come. "A carnival for adults." That had sounded interesting. She liked carnivals and markets well enough.

And this new relationship with Eli wasn't very boring or irritating or demanding yet. Cara had always been better at getting into relationships than staying in them.

"There," Eli muttered.

"What?" But he didn't elaborate, leaving her to figure out for herself what he was talking about. An ordinary-looking box truck was pulling in off the street, then two more.

Fear prickled in her stomach and she took another ineffective toke, imagining her dorky little Subaru surrounded, trapped, crushed by the square, plain, sinister trucks, more of which were arriving. But they all kept going to the far end of the lot and lined up around the edges.

Eli hadn't mentioned the trucks. Even if he had, she probably wouldn't have thought until she was in their midst about the one that had almost killed her years ago. Now they were streaming into the gravel lot in this warehouse district Cara hadn't even known existed this close to downtown. Some of their headlights were eerily pale in the twilight; others didn't have theirs on at all, as if they were prowling and didn't want to be seen.

She'd been in high school and getting out of a relationship with her usual lack of finesse when she'd encountered that truck just like these. Its brights had blinded her. She'd been drunk and stoned and seventeen and angrier than the silly argument at the party had warranted. The truck hadn't hit her. It had filled her windshield and forced her off the road, totaling her car and landing her in an ICU. She'd never seen the driver. She had seen an old woman sitting in the gravel, watching her and smiling around the shadows in her face and fingering the tear-shaped buttons down the front of her shirt that had caught Cara's lopsided headlights and the flashing lights of the emergency vehicles.

That thing about the buttons had never made any sense, of course. How could she have seen the shape of something that small? For that matter, how could she have seen *any* details about the woman at all? She'd been driving so fast and she'd just noticed this figure— waiting, watching, judging her. The woman could have been any age. It could even have been a man. Whatever, it was like it had been waiting for her to have an accident. Like her parents waiting for her to screw up again, both of them when she was growing up and then just her father enough for both of them, though for all she knew her mom might be watching and waiting and sending her "I told you so" messages from beyond the grave, wherever that was.

By the time Cara had been coherent enough after the accident to try to find out who that had been by the side of the road, anybody who might have also seen the person — cops, EMTs, other motorists — had disappeared. The driver had never been found, so somebody was going on with their happy life not knowing if Cara was dead or not, maybe not even wondering.

For a while then, Cara's life had been all about recovery, physical therapy and meds and rest and exercise and her parents talking about her responsibility in the accident, by which they really meant it was all her fault. She'd just wanted to escape, to crawl off and hide like some animal waiting until death happened, or life. Only gradually had she realized just how close she'd come to dying that night.

So what was she supposed to do with that realization? It hadn't made every day more meaningful, as some people claimed a near-death experience would. It hadn't cleared her mind. If anything it had just made her more anxious about what each day might bring. Did dogs have that kind of anxiety? She didn't think so. It seemed to her they expected death eventually but they didn't know whether they'd be just sick or if they'd die at some particular moment. For sure they didn't cry over it.

Not that she'd cry over it, or tell anybody. When things got to her, she was the only one to know, so she wouldn't have to listen to how she'd brought it on herself.

She almost never drove at night anymore. Good thing Eli liked to drive. It wasn't that she trusted him-she didn't trust anybody— but so far, anyway, he was fine with driving her wherever she wanted to go. Maybe she should trust him less for that very reason. You could never tell people's real intentions. And yet you had to rely on them, you had to tangle up your life with theirs, so that if they messed up you were screwed and if you messed up they were. How many people had been killed because of violent or careless or overwhelmed or stupid other people? Probably lots.

In a way it bothered her that Eli didn't ask or even seem to notice that she didn't drive at night. Anyway, it wasn't as if she was scared of the dark— she wasn't a baby. But she also knew the world wasn't the same in the dark as it was in the daylight, no matter what her father, Mr. Rational, used to tell her. He'd say anything to calm her down, whether it was true or not, which meant she hadn't been able to trust what he said and that'd made her even more nervous.

"You just can't see all the details, so your fears fill in the blanks."

Bullshit. Cara knew that if you stared into the dark long enough you could sense the doors, giant rectangles that hadn't been there in daylight. Ever since right after Mom died, she'd tried it now and then, and she could see them. Rectangles. Doors. Big enough to let a truck through. Certainly big enough for an old lady to come in and out of. Was that what she had been— some kind of escort? She'd looked frail, but perhaps strong enough to take her father when the heart attack had silenced his constant advice.

Someday Cara herself would go through one of those doors. Maybe tonight, maybe in the next five seconds. Or maybe when she was a hundred. Maybe by herself, but maybe with an escort. But someday.

More snuffling box trucks were in the parking lot now, and more regular cars, and more people, some of whom must have walked or taken Light Rail because there weren't that many cars. And beyond that, out past the reach of the light, more rectangular patches of darker dark.

"Okay." Eli dropped his roach into an empty beer can and got out of her car.

She weighed her options: leave him here, but that would mean she'd have to drive home in the dark. Take a taxi or get somebody else to drive her home. Wait for a while and watch. Catch up with him now just to see what would happen.

Stay, she decided. Join in. Experience whatever this was. Life was too short to miss anything. And who cares if it's dangerous? You're going to die anyway. Everybody is.

As she made her way toward the line where Eli was standing at the open back of one of the trucks, odors of weed and beer and things cooking and incense washed over her even though the air was heavy and still. She really shouldn't be doing pot, with brain aneurysms running in her family; talk about tempting fate. But what difference did it make? Fate would get you when it damn well wanted to, tempted or not. She was already on borrowed time, twenty-one months more than Mom had had. And counting.

"What's going on?" she asked Eli, no doubt pointlessly. "What is this place?" That was probably the wrong word, since this "place" didn't exist without the trucks.

Eli said, "Come on," and somehow he'd already escorted her to the front of the line.

They stepped into a country diner, complete with a curved counter and high stools, Dolly Parton singing from what Cara guessed was a jukebox. The big-haired waitress plunked two bowls of mac and cheese down in front of them. Eli leaned over and whispered, "It's the only thing on the menu."

Cara didn't want to eat. Mac and cheese was fattening. And who knew what was in this stuff? Or how sanitary the kitchen was? Or who'd had their hands in it? Did the Health Department even know about this "carnival for adults"?

"It's great," Eli said with his mouth full. For him, that was practically a treatise.

Cara took a tiny bite, and it actually was good, suspiciously good. She scooped up a larger spoonful and some of the fluorescent glop spilled on her sleeve, which made her think of that morning in college over breakfast with the guy she'd spent the night with and was seriously wishing she hadn't when she'd spilled hot coffee on herself and for some reason had run out of the café.

111

Talk about making things worse for yourself. The coffee hadn't been hot enough to burn, so the only damage would've been the stain on her jeans. But she'd forgotten about the steps and fallen all the way down and cracked her head and gotten a concussion. It would have been humiliating if she'd been conscious, but she'd just lain there like road kill.

They'd kept her in the hospital for two or three days because they hadn't liked how her eyes looked or something. One of the doctors or orderlies or whatever who'd come by in the middle of the night had had tear-shaped glittery buttons on his coat. It was an odd thing to remember, or so she had thought at the time. The seven gleams of them had caught her eye as he'd leaned over to tend to her, and she'd tried to look into his face, but because of the gloom could see only the thin curve of his mouth and the pale patches that must have been his eyes.

What if he didn't know what he was doing? There was no way she could tell. People died all the time because medical professionals were incompetent, or worse, one of those "angels of mercy" you were always hearing about. They could kill and kill and nobody knew. Cara'd tried to stay awake the rest of the time in the hospital, as though that'd keep her safe, as if anything would keep her safe, but exhaustion and the meds had made her sleep a lot so who knew what had really happened?

The waitress wore a pale pink uniform. Tear-shaped buttons sparkled over her impressive chest every time she came back, to ask how everything was, to bring more napkins, to bring Eli a second chocolate malt, to ask again how everything was. Cara stared at the buttons, which was embarrassing— it must look like she was staring at the boobs.

When she forced herself to look up into the waitress's face, there was something weird about the smile. And the eyes— big and beautiful, but fixed, too perfect. Were they glass?

Cara looked down at her plate. No cheese could be that orange. And if you were a waitress, you could poison so many people. Cara was sure she'd read about cases like that. She bit her lip, and her mouth tasted like blood and fake cheese and something bitter hiding underneath like some terrible secret. She got up, excused herself, and hurried out of the truck, leaving Eli to finish his mac and cheese and hers, too, she didn't care. Leaving him to wonder what was wrong with her, except he probably wouldn't. She slipped on the ramp but managed not to fall.

The parking lot was now full of people, climbing into these dark boxes, climbing out again. In and out of these shadowed doors. People had even brought their kids. Little kids. It wasn't safe.

Eli caught up with her. "Okay, let's go."

Cara didn't know him well enough to read his expression. Pitying? Repulsed? High? "No, no, I don't want to leave," she said, even though maybe she did.

"You sick? You look pale."

"Sorry, sorry. I don't know — something about the atmosphere in there — so close. Or the food. Let's try some more— it'll be fun."

"Fun" was not exactly the word for it. The next truck had been converted into a strip club, every bit as tacky as a real one. It was packed. Once again, somebody shut the door behind them. Cara told Eli she didn't like it when the door was shut. "Effect," he explained, not explaining a thing. "But we can leave." She shook her head.

On the tiny elevated stage, a teenaged boy slowly took off his clothes to the accompaniment of canned drums and horns. He was pretty cute, in an unfinished sort of way. Then a girl wearing nothing but a bowler hat and fishnet stockings with sparkles sang a bawdy song and swung around a pole. Not wanting to draw attention to herself, Cara finally sang along with the crowd. She didn't especially want to be staring at the girl's open crotch, but Eli was probably enjoying the show, in his so-low-key-you-wondered-if-he-was-breathing way. What she could see of his face looked relaxed and expressionless.

The girl came over, swinging her hips and lowering her head. Past the sparkles that were now inches away from her face so she couldn't miss their tiny tear shapes, Cara saw eyes, but there weren't any eyes, really, just two empty holes. In the dancing girl's hand was something shiny. A knife. To cut out Cara's eyes and make her into something like the girl. What was this, some sort of especially bizarre S&M place?

But it was just a piece of jewelry. A sparkly pin. A necklace. It was just a tear-shaped necklace made of layers of tear-shaped stones, or tears turned to stone, or maybe even actual tears— the necklace appeared to fade, to dry up into wisps of hair and light as Cara reached for it. Why would she have accepted a thing like that from a girl like this anyway?

Experimentally she put her hand on Eli's thigh. When he didn't respond, she took her hand away and pretended she hadn't done that. Why had she? She was anything but turned on.

Two women were now having oral sex onstage. Then a young girl came out twirling tassels from her nipples. Something for everyone. Huge silver tears were painted on the child's dimpled cheeks. She turned her head, disgusted. Surely this was an illusion— the girl must have been a midget, or some sort of lewd puppet. There were laws.

She wanted to leave, yet couldn't make herself leave. They stayed for the whole show, which by the end involved a German shepherd and pee and a gun shooting, hopefully, blanks.

The dog had stared at her, as if asking her *what can I do about it? There's nothing I can do.*

The rowdy energy in the club — really just the back of an ordinary box truck — made the crowd seem bigger than it could possibly be in this confined space. The performers, still in their costumes or lack thereof, came around holding out containers for tips. It really looked as if none of them had eyes. Dropping a five into the pseudo-child's plastic Halloween pumpkin didn't make Cara feel any better.

Without saying anything, Eli got up and left. Maybe he'd spotted somebody he knew— it wouldn't have hurt him to introduce her. Maybe he was stealing her car. Or he was just using the restroom, most likely a porta-potty in the parking lot or some twenty-four-hour fast-food place nearby; she ought to figure out where it was before she actually needed it herself.

The crowd she was part of was moving out of the strip-club truck. Without exactly deciding to, Cara went, too. Another crowd was waiting to come in for the next show. Outside like this, uncontained by the box of the truck, it didn't look like as many people, probably no more than twenty.

Not seeing Eli or a porta-potty, she decided, since she was here and probably never would be again, why not try more of the fantasy night-market trucks, other people's special places where they shut the door and trapped you inside and made you see what they wanted you to see and share their secrets and dreams. Why not?

Maybe she'd make her own fantasy world and bring it here to the night market. That'd be cool.

There were all kinds of reasons why she wouldn't, of course— she'd have to buy or rent one of those creepy trucks, she'd have to drive it at night, and she'd have to actually come up with her own fantasy world which she had no clue about. Did she have any secrets or dreams? Not really. But it was cool to think about. Maybe she and Eli could do it together, if she could ever find him. If they kept seeing each other. She saw her car where he'd left it, so at least he hadn't stolen it and left her to figure out how to get home.

There was a "dream library" where you wrote a dream on a scroll of paper and the "librarian" rolled up your dream and slid it into one of the many pretty jars and bottles on the many shelves. The lower part of his face was blanked out and he just had tear-shaped empty holes for eyes; what a creepy, real-looking mask. People around her scribbled down their dreams enthusiastically, furiously, some of them even pulling on her arm to get her to write hers but she couldn't— she didn't have any dreams anymore. Could a person die of dreamlessness? She made up something about eyeless faces and broken glass, and the librarian nodded and hid it; she didn't even see what jar he'd put it in.

As she left, she and everybody else crunched over stuff that she hadn't noticed coming in. Down on the dark earth, she caught glimpses of droplets of glass like frozen tears.

For a while then, Cara went randomly from one truck to another, wherever she could get through the throng. There was a spaceship with aliens inside anxious to pull her apart and see what made her tick, see if they could make her cry. There was a funhouse with distorted mirrors and when she looked at herself in one she couldn't see her eyes and the smile on her face was someone else's— a waitress's or a librarian's or that of an old woman wanting nothing more than to die.

Did Cara want to die?

No, she was scared of dying.

But did she want to be dead?

Thinking about that made her stop still. People bumped into her and went around her, some of them saying sorry and some telling her to move it or worse and some not seeming to notice her at all.

She couldn't come up with the answer, so she just walked on to the next truck. Now that she'd been inside some of them, they didn't necessarily seem like threatening places anymore. She wondered whether the truck that had run her off the road and almost killed her had had somebody's fantasy world inside it, too.

The next truck she went into was a church with a stained glass window and incense and organ music and a bloody cross. Other than the performers, if that's what they were, she was alone. They told her there was nothing to fear, death was just another door and once you opened it you'd be inside God's own special dream. Cara did not find this especially reassuring.

Now the priest was tossing holy water on her, drops like God's own tears that flew and burned and would have dissolved her flesh if she hadn't shaken them off. They made a loud clatter when they hit the floor in this echoey place.

"Why don't you just take me and be done with it?" She didn't think she really meant that, but that's what came out of her mouth almost automatically, as if she'd been rehearsing the line for years. The priest just smiled, his eye holes widening and his teeth falling out, skin so thin his head was like a grinning skull. Cara left and no one tried to stop her.

The crowd had begun to thin out, and it seemed to her there weren't as many trucks now. She was surprised to realize she didn't want the Night Market to end before she'd experienced every one of these boxed fantasy worlds. She didn't see Eli. Her car was still there. The stench of weed was faint, and the aroma of beer was faded and stale in her mouth. From habit she wished for a joint or a brownie, but in a way she was glad to be doing this on her own and not high.

The disco dance truck, where the ball spun multicolored flecks of light that might look like tears if you really worked at it, didn't do much for her. The post office truck was just plain boring. A post office? Really? Somebody fantasized about a post office?

Then, somewhere between the slaughterhouse truck and the Inquisition torture chamber, the conviction came to her that if she didn't get out of the Night Market right away she would die. Now. Tonight. And if she didn't stay until it was over, she would die then, too. Maybe not right now, but she would. No matter what she did, she would die.

Well, of course. Everyone could say that. But most people wouldn't dream of speaking such a thing out loud.

Her brand-new shirt and pants were ruined, spattered by drops of blood from the slaughtered animals and the tortured people. Surely the human victims, at least, had been actors, and the blood had been fake. But with her luck it would stain anyway.

A vague despair over her ruined clothes and not particularly wanting to see Eli again and the general weirdness of the evening made her burst into tears. It had been such a long time since she'd cried it felt as if the tears were etching her skin, dissolving her eyes. Her vision became distorted. Her eyes ached. She didn't even try to stifle her sobs, didn't care much that it would ruin her make-up or what people would think if they saw her this way.

She realized she was leaning against one of the box trucks, one she thought she hadn't been in but they all looked alike from the outside and it could have moved from one parking space to another. Where were the drivers? Had they just mingled in with the crowd? Were they napping in the cabs? Did they know what they were hauling? Was there a big market for this sort of thing?

Tears were running down her face and wetting her collar. The force of her sorrow or fear or release or whatever it was bent her over, and her tears fell onto the pavement, tinkling like broken glass when they hit. Her mother used to call this, what? "Crying your eyes out." Could you really cry your eyes out? Had Mom cried like this when she'd realized she was going to die? *Had* she known? Did Dad have a premonition that his heart would break at just that instant?

"Cara."

From that blurry border between the night market's bright lights and what passed in the city for total darkness, Eli was coming toward her. She thought this might be the first time he'd actually said her name. He had a dog on a leash.

Cara crouched and held out her arms to the dog, crooning, weeping. She couldn't tell its breed or its color— mixed breed, probably; dark-colored. She couldn't tell if it was male or female, and she didn't want to think of it as "it."

He was old and sick. His slack, toothless mouth hung almost to the pavement. Both his eyes were capped by milky cataracts. He snuffled loudly, turning in her direction, her smell in his nose.

Crying now for the dog in addition to everything else, Cara murmured "Come here, pretty boy" and "Poor baby," and the dog followed her smell and the sound of her voice and made his painful way toward her, pulling Eli with surprising strength so that the leash was taut between them. Cara didn't especially want Eli to come to her, just the old dog, which paused to lick at the pavement. There was a brittle clatter as hard things struck together. *My tears*, she thought, *all my tears from my whole life,* and squinted to see the glistening glass piled like jewels in the lights of the parking lot. Eli bent and scooped them up.

The dog was determined to get to her. Some animals could sense when a person was sick. She'd seen dogs at work who could sense a seizure before it happened, and she'd read about some who could smell or in some other way detect cancer earlier than doctors could. This dog's big runny nostrils were flaring as he made his way toward her, tugging Eli along.

Eli slung the tears at her. Her own tears, sharp and hard. Cara twisted but they struck her on her back, arms, chest, belly, and everywhere they hit they drew blood.

"Stop it!" She stood up, swaying, and tried to move out of range, but he was rapidly closing the gap between them, or maybe she was inadvertently gliding closer— she wasn't sure which direction she was moving. Her intentions kept leading her the wrong way.

The three of them stepped around the parking lot, circling, dancing, a clumsy ballet. Blood and tears made her eyes sting. The dog moaned and squealed, almost a song, then in slow motion jumped up against her softly and slid down her body to collapse at her feet.

Just before Eli's arms closed around her and their open mouths joined in their only kiss, she saw the tear-shaped buttons on his shirt flowing in an endless stream.

❖ ❖ ❖

MELANIE TEM's work has received the Bram Stoker, International Horror Guild, British Fantasy, and World Fantasy Awards, as well as a nomination for the Shirley Jackson Award. She is also a published poet, an oral storyteller, and several of her plays have been produced. Stories have recently appeared in *Interzone* and *Crimewave*.

❖ ❖ ❖

2013 saw three new short story collections from **STEVE RASNIC TEM**: *Onion Songs* (Chomu); *Celestial Inventories* (ChiZine); and *Twember* (NewCon Press). This spring PS Publishing is bringing out his stand-alone novella *In the Lovecraft Museum*.

SOONER

BY MORGAN DAMBERGS

LAUREL COULD TELL the staff on the psych ward were not pleased to see her again. She couldn't blame them. Three failed suicide attempts in eight months— who wouldn't be sick of her by now? God knew she was beyond sick of herself.

She'd done everything right this time: waited for her mother to leave on a business trip, washed down her two hidden bottles of benzos with half a bottle of wine, lay down on her bed and braced herself for the awful feeling of her heart and lungs slowing to a stop. But she hadn't counted on her mother lying about the business trip. According to the nurses, her mother had been testing to see if it was safe to leave Laurel home alone for a night— and obviously, she had not passed the test. Knowing that made something twist in Laurel's stomach, but at least it explained why her mother hadn't visited once during the past week. After all, no one wanted a failure for her only child— especially a university dropout who was so pathetic she couldn't even kill herself properly.

At noon, an orderly came by to dump a lunch tray on her bedside table. He tugged open her drawer to check for anything illicit — unnecessarily, Laurel thought, since she'd had no visitors and wasn't allowed to leave her room unescorted — and on his way out, ordered her to eat. He never once made eye contact. When he was gone, she rolled onto her side, pulled the blankets up over her head and closed her eyes. She wasn't sleepy, but the smell of the egg sandwich was making her sick, and she couldn't bear the thought of her chatty roommate coming back and trying to coax her into eating, like she'd done at supper the night before.

Breathing soft and slow, Laurel focussed on her heartbeat, trying to slow it to a stop with her mind. She didn't really expect that to work, but at least it was a way to pass the endless daytime hours. When she finally felt herself drifting off to sleep, she said a silent prayer that she would never have to open her eyes again.

✤ ✤ ✤

She woke facing the window. Beyond the laminated glass, the gibbous moon hung low in the sky, illuminating the hospital room in pale silver and reflecting off the hair of the man who sat on a chair next to her bed. His face was cast in shadow. Telling herself there was no reason to be nervous, Laurel propped herself up on an elbow and flipped the switch for the light above her bed. She was relieved to see the man wearing the purple scrubs favoured by most of the psych ward nurses. She didn't think she recognized him from the ward's regular staff, but he was so nondescript it was hard to be sure— gray hair, gray eyes, neither old nor young, neither ugly nor attractive. Not someone who would turn many heads.

He held a small notebook, flipping slowly through the pages. Laurel cleared her throat softly, but he either didn't hear or ignored her. She glanced over at her roommate's bed, but the girl was fast asleep; beyond her, through the open door to their room, the hallway was dark and empty.

She turned back to the nurse, just as he pressed his fingertip against one of the pages and said, "Here. This is you."

He leaned forward, holding the notebook out towards her. Laurel instinctively pulled away, suddenly uncertain if he really was a nurse, or if one of her fellow patients had gotten hold of a pair of scrubs and wandered into her room. But she saw that her name was indeed scrawled across a line on the lower half of the notebook page: *Laurel Jane Cameron, 1990—2076*. She tried to skim the rest of the page, to see if he'd written anything else about her, but he snapped the book shut and tucked it into the breast pocket of his scrubs before she could make out another word.

He rested his elbows on his knees and looked directly into her eyes. "So why, Laurel, do you persist in trying to kill yourself when you're meant to live for decades yet?"

Laurel blinked at him for a moment, then glanced at his chest, where his nametag should have been. There was nothing there, and she realized that his scrubs had turned the same soft gray color as his eyes and hair.

She shoved her blanket aside and pushed herself up to sit cross-legged on her mattress. "But you can't… are you really…?" She glanced back at the eerily silent hallway beyond her room. "Am I dreaming?"

Death shrugged. "This is real enough to inconvenience me. You understand I've put my work on hold to come speak with you tonight? If you'll agree to stop meddling with my system, I can get back to more important matters."

Laurel bit her lip. "If you're trying to make me feel better, you're off to a great start."

"I'm not here to soothe your feelings, only to keep you from further complicating an already difficult job." Death sat back and crossed his legs. "You people seem to think it's the ones who want eternal life that get in my way. But they so rarely succeed. No, it's the suicides that cause me problems."

He gazed steadily at Laurel, and she pulled her pajama top closer against her body, trying not to shiver.

"Do you know what happens when someone ends their life before their time?" Death continued. "If I'm not there to reap your soul as you die, you disappear into nothingness— oblivion. No heaven, no reincarnation, no afterlife of any kind. You're gone forever." He steepled his fingers. "To me, it amounts to little more than frustration. I have to change my list to reflect the lost soul, shuffle dates around to fill the hole created— it's a hassle. But that is, ultimately, all it is.

"You, however… you have every reason to be frightened. Oblivion is a bleak and lonesome way to spend eternity."

Death fell silent and rested his steepled fingers under his chin, looking haughty as a king. Laurel stared at him for a moment, then let out a bark of laughter so loud she made herself jump.

"You think threatening me with oblivion is going to change my mind about killing myself? It's a long, long time since I believed there was anything good waiting for me after I die. But I know nothing could be worse than having to live like this for— God, what, six more decades?" She shook her head. "No. I'm ready to go now. I've been ready for years."

She pushed herself to the edge of the bed and dropped her feet to the floor, motioning towards his pocket. "There must be millions of people in there who're dying too young, who'd do anything for a little more time. I'm sure there are people like that right in this very hospital. If you don't want to rearrange your list after I'm gone, can't you just... switch me with someone now?"

He tilted his head to one side. "You're asking me to make a deal with you?"

Laurel shrugged. "It'd be better for everyone, wouldn't it? Whoever I trade with gets to stick around and hopefully do some good in the world. I finally get to die. You don't have your system screwed with. Seems perfect."

Death's expression hardened, and the look that came into his eyes made Laurel want to crawl back under her covers and hide. She told herself she was being silly, that the worst he could do was kill her and not reap her soul— and hadn't she just said that wouldn't be so bad? But her heart was beating too fast, each thud a reminder of what a weak, irrational, useless person she was. No wonder she couldn't even get suicide right.

"I'm not in the habit of giving in to the demands of mortals," said Death, his voice low, his words clipped. "Not even one who's idiotic enough to bargain in the wrong direction."

Laurel felt her face flush and realized with a shock that she wasn't afraid— she was angry. It felt almost foreign. It had been so long since she'd succumbed to loneliness and weariness and despair that getting angry again, getting genuinely upset... felt... good.

"It's not the wrong direction," she said, her voice just as low and clipped as Death's. "You're right. I am stupid. But I also know how much the world sucks, and that I fuck it up even worse by ruining everything I touch. That makes suicide the right choice. If I want, just once, to do something good with my life, it's the *only* choice."

Death snorted softly. "As you've pointed out, you have more than sixty years left to live— and yes, there are people who would quite literally kill for that. Yet you're certain there's nothing you can do with that time to help the world 'suck' less, besides removing yourself from it?" He shook his head. "If that's the case, Laurel, I can't believe you've tried very hard to find an alternative."

Laurel could feel wetness pooling at the corners of her eyes, and tried to blink it away. So many months had passed since she'd last been able to cry, she'd sincerely believed there were no tears left inside her, and part of her wanted to give in and let them fall. But she held on, unable to stand the thought of letting Death see how much he was getting to her. He watched her closely, his face once again unreadable. She couldn't tell if he didn't know she was almost crying, or simply didn't care.

"I've tried it all," she said. Her voice came out raspy, and she swallowed to relieve the tightness in her throat. "I've talked to therapists, taken their pills, tried to reframe my thoughts and accept myself as I am. I've been stuck with jobs and classes I hated, and forced myself to join university clubs I had no interest in to try to make friends. I've done everything people tell me I should do. *But nothing ever changes!*" She felt tears slipping down her cheeks, but didn't have the strength left to fight them. "I don't change, my life doesn't change. All I can think about is how much I want to die, and how I'd stop being a burden to my mother if I did. Nothing in this world would be worse if I died. Some things might even get a little better."

Death's eyebrows drew together. "You truly believe that?"

"I *know* it. And please don't bother *It's a Wonderful Life*ing me. There's nothing you can show me that would change my mind." Laurel smiled weakly. "Besides, I'm already working on a better plan for next time— something outside the house, so Mom can't fake me out again. With luck, I'll be dead for a while before anyone finds me. And if that includes you…" She shrugged. "I'll take oblivion over this. It cannot possibly be worse."

Death was frowning at he, and Laurel dropped her gaze to the floor, too tired to keep up eye contact. Silence stretched between them, and Laurel let her mind drift, imagining that she was already dead, and that this, this quiet, was oblivion. Eventually, she heard a sigh.

"Fine."

She snapped her head up to look at him. "Fine?"

"Yes. Fine. Clearly I'm wasting my time here, and I have souls to reap who shouldn't have to wait any longer. But in the interest of not interfering with my system… perhaps we can compromise." He spread his hands. "I will move your name partway up my list. Not to the top— but closer. I will do this if, and only if, you promise to stop trying to end your life before your time."

Laurel thought for a minute, chewing her lower lip. "How much sooner would I get to die?"

"Oh, no." Death shook his head. "It's rare that I allow a mortal to learn the exact age at which they will die. You've enjoyed that privilege once already. I will not give it to you again."

"Yeah. I guess I get that." Laurel paused. "And— someone better will take my place? Get to live longer?"

"*Someone* will take your place, yes. When you say it like that, it's hard to believe you're willing to abide by my rules, you know."

"Sorry. Okay, yes. I'll take it. It's better than nothing, right?"

"I should say so." Death reached up and extracted the notebook and a sleek black pen from his pocket. He flipped the book open to show Laurel where her name was written, then laid the book flat on one palm, crossed her name out, and wrote something else just above it— presumably someone else's name, though Laurel couldn't read his scrawl. She watched, fascinated, as his pen slid across the page, its ink glowing incandescent purple for a moment before drying to plain black.

When he was done, he flipped several pages towards the front of the book — Laurel tried and failed to count how many — crossed out another unreadable name, and wrote Laurel's in its place. He held the book up to show her, his thumb carefully positioned over her new date of death. "There. Done."

Laurel nodded. "Thank you."

Death returned the notebook to his pocket, slipped the pen in beside it and rose gracefully from his chair. "I'll see you again, Laurel," he said. Laurel watched him walk away, twisting her hands together in her lap.

He was almost out the door when she cried out, "Wait!"

He stopped and looked back at her, eyebrows raised, and Laurel wondered for an instant if a being like him could feel genuine surprise, or if he was faking it for her benefit. She made herself take one deep breath, then another.

"I just... I..." Her voice was so soft, she could barely hear it herself. "No one's come to visit. I only have my mother, and she..." She took another breath. "Would you hold me? Just for a minute? It's been so long since the last time someone... and I'm..." She clamped her mouth shut, not certain she could say 'lonely' without breaking down in front of him. She wouldn't let that happen again tonight.

She stared at her feet, afraid to look up and see that he was gone. But a moment later, she heard footsteps, and raised her eyes to see him standing at the foot of her roommate's bed. He beckoned to her with one hand.

She rose unsteadily, legs half-numb from sitting too long. As she shuffled towards him, she realized he was standing directly in a beam of moonlight, and that he cast no shadow. Goosebumps prickled along her arms. But now she was in front of him, looking up into his plain, expressionless face, and it was too late to change her mind.

She spread her arms, and then paused awkwardly, afraid it would somehow give a bad impression if she embraced him first. Before she could decide, he leaned down and wrapped his arms around her shoulders with surprising tenderness. She curled her fingers against the front of his scrubs and pressed her forehead to his chest, letting her eyes drift shut. He didn't seem to have a heartbeat, so she counted her own. It took fifty-two beats before she worked up the courage to slide her hands slowly up his chest, bringing them to rest around his neck.

Laurel almost shrieked when his hand closed around her wrist. He pushed her away, twisting her captive hand palm-up to expose the black pen she'd stolen from his pocket. Her heart hammered in her chest, and she wished she could drop the pen, but she was terrified to move in case he mistook it for an escape attempt.

Then Death laughed softly, and she jerked her head up to see him smiling at her. He released her wrist, and Laurel let her arm fall limply to her side, entirely uncertain what was happening. She raised her hand and offered the pen to him, but he shook his head and reached out to close her fingers over it.

"Keep it. I'll take its loss as a reminder why I should never trust a human."

Laurel drew her fist back and pressed it against her breastbone. "You're not angry?"

Death snorted. "Do you think I'd let you steal something I actually need?" He leaned over so she could see into his breast pocket. It was completely empty. "The pen is just a pen. It's the book that matters. And you'll need far better tricks if you ever hope to get that away from me."

He watched her for a moment, as though waiting for a reply. A thousand thoughts reeled through Laurel's mind, but she couldn't come up with a single thing to say. Eventually, he turned and strode out the door and this time, he didn't look back.

Laurel walked over to her bed and climbed onto the mattress, leaning back against the pillows. She closed her eyes and clutched her fist tightly around the pen, squeezing harder and harder until her knuckles ached and her palm stung from the pressure of her nails. The pain crawled slowly down her wrist, burning hotter and brighter until it filled her mind and blotted out every other thought.

After a while, she released her fist and opened her eyes. The pen nestled on her palm just above the angry red imprints of her fingernails. She placed it gently on the mattress, and smoothed the left leg of her pajama pants across her thigh until it was almost wrinkle free. Then she picked up the pen, wrote her name just above her knee in careful block letters, and crossed it out in two swift strokes. The ink flowed black, not glowing purple, but Laurel was still pleased with the result. She moved the pen a little further up her thigh and started again.

When she ran out of space on her left leg, she moved to her right. She knew the psych ward staff would only hate her more for this, but she didn't care. After all, she was going to die sooner now— so maybe she'd never come back here again. Her next attempt, she might finally get suicide right, or the one after that, or the next one after that. And if she happened to die too soon, at least now she knew the worst possible scenario. Which didn't sound all that bad.

She crossed out her name one more time, then wrote *1990— soon???* underneath, retracing several times so the ink began to tendril out across the cotton. After a while, the words became unreadable— just a smudge of black bleeding slowly across the fabric.

Laurel smiled a little and laid the pen on her bedside table. She reached down to touch the still-wet ink on her pyjamas, then rolled over to face the window and pulled her knees up to her chest. She closed her eyes and let her mind fall into the blackness behind them, praying, as always, that the nothingness would last forever.

❖ ❖ ❖

MORGAN DAMBERGS has had short stories published in several anthologies, including *Rock 'N' Roll is Dead* and *The Big Book of New Short Horror*. She hopes to one day publish a novel. She owns a small secondhand bookstore, where she happily spends her days reading, writing, and chatting about books.

The Great Inevitable

by Patricia Flewwelling

JULIAN AWOKE FALLING. Someone shouted a word. Julian convulsed, and he fell back against the bed like a sack of hammers. Voices male and female ping-ponged across his bed. Then there was a beat of silence.

Something nearby growled and sighed, a dry, impatient, frustrated sound.

Julian heard what sounded like a metal punch press, and again his body clenched as if his chest and knees were fingers in a fist. Every bone felt broken. He fell back against the bed, banging his head on a pillow as soft as plywood. A man's voice issued a command. Machines buzzed ominously as they charged.

All right, I'm up! Julian thought at them, and he willed his heart to beat again. *God, how long do we have to keep doing this? Come on, then. Tick-tock, leathery clock!*

Someone chuckled in the corner. As clear as day, Julian heard wood chimes rattling.

Five or six voices in the mumbling choir tentatively congratulated themselves on a job well done. Julian sighed and faded into sleep.

❖ ❖ ❖

He became aware of his sense of smell. He knew what a hospital was supposed to smell like — chemicals, cleaners and plastic — but what Julian smelled was a field of summer-baked grass and raw chicken gone bad.

A presence kept him company. For the most part, it lingered by the window; but when it came close, nurses rushed in to check tubes and wires and veins.

Do you ever get bored of this? he thought at his companion. Bone-chimes rattled as if startled by a brief quake. *Yeah, you, in the corner.* He imagined the stranger dressed in monk's robes and carrying a scythe. But instead of a bleached skull, what Julian envisioned was a warm, if impatient, smile. *So what are you really like, old man?* he thought at the figure now an arm's length from the bed. *You as boney as they make you out to be?*

The figure chuckled, but said nothing.

Dry work, this is. Day after day, here I am, making my heart pump blood around a body I can't even feel anymore. And there's you, watching me do it, as if you didn't have anywhere better to be. We make a fine pair, don't we?

Julian sensed a question, an amused inquiry that touched his heart like a radar ping. *Yeah, I know you're there,* Julian thought.

Death heaved a sigh that blew through the room like tumbleweeds.

Oh, relax. You'll have me soon enough.

For endless hours, Julian thought about all the things that keep a man awake at night: the meaning of life, unpaid cable bills, grandkids, rotten stuff he'd left in the fridge. When he caught himself thinking about bad art, Julian realized his eyes were open.

The hospital room was empty except for hideous furniture and ugly paintings. And there in the corner was Death, as visible as the sun-blanched walls, the dirty blinds and the eggplant-colored fold-out chair. Death's hood was pulled forward, so whether it concealed a warm smile or a skeletal grin, Julian couldn't see, but the overall posture seemed eager. *Expectant,* Julian thought. *Like somebody with a broom ready to smack a spider.* Death emerged from the corner.

Ever wish you could retire? Julian thought.

Death paused.

Must get sick of all the bargaining and the whining and the questions… But, everybody dies, eventually. So what's the point of fighting so hard? Even if you can postpone Death, you can't cheat him forever.

I'm sorry we're such a whiny bunch of people, he thought at Death. *Not like it's your fault we never made enough of the time we were given.*

It seemed ridiculous to Julian that Death should appear surprised. Death was as old as life itself. He'd witnessed every secret murder and every public execution. Death was there at the Holocaust. Death was the last to see Elvis alive on the toilet, eating a deep-fried Twinkie. *Nothing can surprise Death.*

Death chuckled.

Nobody ever asked how you *felt, did they?* Julian thought. He thought of Death hovering over babies' cribs. *Nobody has ever cared how Death feels. Just me.*

Julian was funny that way. He'd been a dumb kid in his day, cheating, thieving, getting a girl pregnant by the time he was fifteen... fighting, drugs, alcohol... Then Carl Larson hit him with his car in '82. Carl had felt horrified by the accident, so he paid Julian's hospital bills, supported him through physio and drug rehab, brought him into his family and treated him like a brother— like somebody worthwhile. And then Carl introduced him to volunteer work. Julian loved volunteering with the kids and the addicts, because he understood their lives better than any psychologist, priest or lawyer. The smallest glimmer of hope gave Julian a high neither drugs nor religion could. The more he gave a damn, the more he craved befriending the lost.

And maybe Death needed a friend. After all, because of Death, Julian had turned his life around. He wasn't a religious man. He never went in for that "accept Jesus or burn in Hell" stuff. But he didn't want to die knowing he'd wasted his life. He had mended his ways because he hadn't wanted people standing over his coffin telling each other how bad he'd been in life. He'd changed his heart because he didn't want to be alone at his own funeral.

In his way, Death had given Julian a reason to *live*. And in really living, he discovered life could be pretty good— if you made it that way. He'd done all right, in the end.

Elaine was doing all right too. He'd been a lousy father to her— he'd only been fifteen and strung out on meth and gasoline fumes when she was born. But in '99, long after he'd cleaned himself up, she'd contacted him, and they became friends— not as close as a father and daughter, as he hoped, but they were on very good terms. Elaine had always been fine on her own, without a father figure. She was self-sufficient. She'd do just as well when he was gone.

But when he first held his very own grand-daughter in his arms, he was a giant. Baby Janine looked at him, trusting and thoughtful. Suddenly he was invincible, and good, and he'd vowed never to let that precious little life wander down the same paths he'd taken. He'd wrestle a wild bear and suffer a thousand knives if it meant keeping her safe. These days, Elaine and her husband had three great kids: Janine, now nine years old; Eddy, four; and Isabel, only two. Julian taught them whatever he could, and when his grandkids spoke, he listened. He didn't always understand what they said, but he listened. With all his heart and soul, he listened because he was terrified of missing a single word.

But he couldn't do any of that now — no more volunteering, no more horsing around with the grandkids, no more fixing Elaine's sink when it clogged. Not in this body.

You didn't do a good job of killing me, Julian thought at Death. He wasn't bitter, just confused. *Why make us both wait so long?* And he was tired. *Do you ever get tired, Death?* Death didn't answer. Julian's eyes began to drift closed. *All right. We'll do it your way. No more bargaining. No whining. Death gets a break today.*

The edges of Death's cloak blurred and became like crawling, seeping black smoke. He leapt forward, stretching white fingers toward his face and Julian's eyes closed before he could see if they were flesh or bone.

Alarms went off. People ran in. Feet thumped. Wheels squeaked. Orders were called out and acknowledged. They threw back the sheets and dropped two clammy blocks of marble on his chest. *Damn it, here we go again.* Giant hands squeezed him from both sides like a man-sized tube of toothpaste. When they let go, he fell back as limp as ever. *Let me go!* he thought. They hit him again. The heart monitor whined. *Let me go, you bastards. Let me go.* They hit him again. The alarm blipped.

Damn it.

People said things to each other in cautious tones, hovering over him with life-dealing weapons at the ready.

Death hissed a long, heavy sigh.

Yeah, Julian thought. *I know what you mean.*

✠ ✠ ✠

He roused at the sound of someone crying.

Julian smelled grasslands and rotting meat. He also smelled Elaine's perfume.

"Why do you have to take him…?" Elaine wept. "You let serial killers go on living in luxury, but you'll take a man like my Dad…"

Her voice broke. She'd never called him that before. "All he ever wanted to do was *help* people!"

If I can just wiggle my fingers or something… give her a sign that it's going to be okay…

"It's not fair," she moaned. "He was doing so well. He was helping people."

It's going to be okay, honey.

"Dad, you have to wake up," Elaine said. "You have something to live for, remember? They ask where you are, and when I tell them, all three of them start to cry, and I… I can't keep telling them lies anymore!"

Everything will be okay.

"I just wish you would make up your mind. Either die or wake up."

Ooh-wee, you and me both, Elaine.

Enraged, Elaine said, "Death, I know you're here."

Death and Julian were equally surprised.

"I know you're here, and I'm telling you, you can't *have* him. Do you hear me? You can't have him. He's a good man!"

Heedless to her outbursts — or maybe because of them — Death approached Julian's bedside. *No, don't take me now!* Julian thought at Death. *How do you think you'll make her feel if I die as soon as she tells me to make up my mind?* A noise like a blast furnace emerged from Death's figure. Death had lost his sense of humour.

"Take someone else, if you have to," Elaine hissed, "but you leave him alone!"

Look, Julian thought, *I'll do whatever you want me to do. Just give me five minutes awake with her!*

The edges of Death's robes unravelled into smoke and flame, and he bellowed in outrage. *Even you, Julian?* Death cried. *Even you would bargain with me?* Death lifted his scythe and brought its end down upon the hospital floor with the awful finality of a judge's gavel. The sound jarred Julian in his bed.

Elaine gasped. "Dad? Oh my God— *Dad?*"

Two nurses rushed in, checking alarms and tubes and wires, and one of them stopped short. She looked back at him with an expression of mild confusion and shock. A fly-by smile swept across her hard lips, and she set to work as soon as the grin had passed.

To his left, blonde and beautiful Elaine sat in the eggplant-colored chair with her hands over her mouth, tears streaming down her face. She was torn between sobs and laughter. "Oh thank God, Dad! You're alive!"

❖ ❖ ❖

Julian awoke when someone wiped his mouth with a crusty cloth. *I smell smoke,* he thought, *only better. Salty. No... woody, with a hint of spice.* Whatever it was, it didn't smell like a hospital, and it didn't smell like Death. *Oh hallelujah, I smell a barbeque.* Barbeques meant home. *Or at least, somebody else's home.*

"Pretty strong those drugs, huh?" A man's voice.

I'm still here? It's been weeks. Months maybe. He recalled being moved around, being washed, being laid in bed, but this felt like the first lucid moment since he'd left hospital.

Little Isabel screamed as she toddled into the kitchen, holding her head. Four year old Eddy followed, protesting his innocence. Julian expected Janine to join in with all the royal omniscience of the family's firstborn, laying blame and demanding justice. But Janine didn't follow. *Must be at school,* Julian thought.

Then he frowned. Curtained behind painkillers and exhaustion, a black memory lurked.

"They have to be powerful drugs." Elaine had to raise her voice over those of her children. She picked up Isabel and held her on a hip. "He's in a lot of pain."

"He's *still* in pain?" the man asked. *Carl,* Julian thought. *Carl's here.*

"Yeah," Elaine answered, "but at least he's alive."

Something's missing. Why can't I remember? But his heart could remember; it was his mind that refused to recall the details. He could only recall a clap of thunder and a sense of sudden, terrible loss, the day Death abandoned him in the hospital.

Carl grinned. "How you feeling, old man? You ready to get up and go to work?"

Julian tried to move, but his extremities were numb and unresponsive. The kitchen was askew, because Julian couldn't centre his head on his neck.

"You hungry?" Carl asked. "It's all right, Elaine, you do what you have to do. I'll look after him."

Eddy ran out of the room heedless of the kitchen chair he'd toppled, and Isabel screamed in her mother's ear. Elaine rolled her eyes heavenward.

"Go," Carl insisted. "It'll be like old times for him and me." Carl winked encouragingly and watched Elaine leave the kitchen. "Come back to us, Julian." Carl gripped Julian's hand, squeezed it. "People at the shelter have been asking after you, wondering how you're doing... Weird, seeing you like this again. Feels like we've come full circle."

Julian was strapped into a large black chair, with cushions on either side of his head. *What do I look like to you now, Carl? Like Stephen Hawking? Or like a deformed baby in a high chair?* ·

"Do you even remember what happened?" Carl spooned orange goo out of a bowl. "You had the stuffing knocked out of you."

Julian heard the sound of a child asking a question. *Janine?* Julian turned his head enough that Carl left a smear of baby food across his cheek. But it was Eddy's impatient voice that had posed the question.

Patiently, Carl wiped Julian's face and applied the spoon where it best served its purpose. "They say when that van hit you, you flew eighteen feet and landed smack against the broadside of a cement truck." He inserted more food into Julian's mouth, and with bushy eyebrows raised, he added, "It's a miracle you're alive." He inserted one spoonful after another into Julian's mouth. At least Julian's tongue still worked.

Little Eddy returned, took command of his favorite chair, and demanded hot dogs. He didn't look twice at the disabled old man who'd taught him how to fish and how to assemble a race car track. Elaine followed, with Isabel in tow, dragging her heels. "My husband called," Elaine said. "He won't be home until late. Work."

Carl lifted an eyebrow. "He's been doing a lot of overtime."

Elaine averted her eyes. "We have a lot of hospital bills to pay."

"And like I said, Elaine, we're happy to help."

Julian watched the suntanned features of his grandson. Eddy wiggled and shouted, made his demands and sound effects and his declarations, and he made a general mess of his food. Isabel screamed two word sentences when the food was slow or dissatisfactory. Still, there was no sign of Janine.

❖ ❖ ❖

Julian had dozed off in his chair and awoke to Elaine sobbing.

Carl reached across the table and squeezed her shoulder. "It's not your fault," he said. The children had gone.

"I shouldn't have said…" She sighed. "I should have been there, Carl. Brent was already late for work, and— and those things I said—"

"Shhh," Carl whispered. "It's not your fault. It's not."

Later, the two kids were bathed and put to bed. *Where is Janine?* Julian wondered.

Then he recalled the sound of the collision as Death's scythe struck the floor.

Elaine's husband Brent arrived sometime after Carl had left. Husband and wife exchanged terse words, and Elaine went to bed early. Cursing under his breath, Brent manhandled Julian through all the rigors of bed-readiness, rushing him through the mutual indignities of bathing and changing of adult diapers. At the end of the wrestling, Brent flung Julian into bed, snapped off the light and slammed the door between them.

Brent had been driving, Julian thought, remembering the red scars across Brent's forehead, cheek and jaw. *He'd been late for work.* His feeble heart groaned. *Where's Janine?*

Overhead, Elaine pleaded with Brent, who shouted and swore back. Julian couldn't make out the words because the floorboards were too thick, but he could hear the emotions clearly enough. He heard his grandchildren crying in their beds, too. Abrupt footsteps boomed across the floor. Elaine called after her husband. Hard-soled shoes trampled stairs. She screamed Brent's name. A door swung open and slammed shut, and except for three weeping voices, all fell deafeningly quiet.

Take someone else if you have to, that's what Elaine had said. Take someone else, but don't you take my Dad. But it was Julian who'd angered Death.

❖ ❖ ❖

One morning, for the first time in Julian's foggy memory, Elaine marooned him in the living room with the TV going. Normally when she cleaned the house, she parked him in his own room out of the way. *Small mercies!* he thought. Even soap operas were a breath of fresh air.

Hanging on the wall above the TV, there was a large school portrait of Janine. She was smiling and posed with her hands folded under her chin. The portrait was framed in black, and a track and field medal hung from the upper right corner.

Janine... In exchange for the life of her daughter, Elaine had taken home a living corpse.

Elaine re-entered the living room, exhausted by her labours. With the kids in daycare, they had the house to themselves, but Julian was no more company than the umbrella stand. At least the stand had a function to fulfill.

Elaine cleared her groggy throat and tossed her hair over her shoulder. She'd been crying. "Time for your heart meds, Dad."

He opened his mouth obediently. She administered purgatory in the form of digitalis, dropping one tiny pill under his tongue. *Another drug, another day.*

"God, I can't keep doing this," Elaine muttered as she left the room with the pill bottle.

Neither can I, Elaine. With the few responsive muscles left in his body, Julian rolled the heart pill out from under his tongue and balanced it on his lip. Then, with a mighty effort, he blew the pill as far from his mouth as he could pitch it. It rolled across the hardwood floor and under the couch. *I won't be your penance any more, Elaine. I asked you to let me go. I'm going. Damned if you can stop me now.*

❖ ❖ ❖

Elaine's husband had called in the middle of dinner to tell her he wasn't coming home again that night, or any other night. She'd hung up the phone and sent the kids to bed early, then, forgetting all about her father's presence in the kitchen, she sat at the table, poured herself a generous tumbler of rum and Coke, and began to cry. When she slammed down the emptied tumbler, Julian's pill bottles jumped.

"I don't know what it is you want from me!" she screamed. "You're supposed to be so merciful, and this is what you do to my family? You kill my daughter, you drive my husband away from me, and you leave me with... with this *thing* that was my father?"

Julian turned his face away. *Soon, Elaine. Soon.* He could already sense the exasperated presence of Death. *Come on, you bastard. Let's talk face to face.*

"Mommy?" Eddy clung to the kitchen door frame.

"Eddy, I told you to go back to bed!"

"But I'm not tired!"

"Go!"

"But Mommy—"

"Fine, you know what? Do whatever the hell you want. Go in the living room and play. Do whatever you want. I don't care what you do."

Don't say that, Elaine...

Tears stood in Eddy's eyes. He returned, dejected, to the living room where his toys had been put away for the night.

Elaine poured a second drink. She muttered and prayed and groaned over the melting ice, touching her forehead with trembling fingers.

Death's stench pervaded the kitchen like forgotten garbage.

"Take this burden from me," Elaine whispered.

Come on, you son-of-a-bitch. She can't look after me and the kids at the same time.

Wood chimes clattered. Death was in the house, but he was not in the kitchen.

Oh God... where's Eddy? One moment, the boy had been banging two cars together and making siren noises. Now, the house was eerily quiet. Elaine went to the washroom and returned to a third drink, oblivious to the unaccustomed silence of the house. *Elaine, snap out of it!* He groaned. She ignored him. He grunted at her and writhed in his seat. *Elaine, wake up! Go check on Eddy!* Wordlessly, he shouted.

"Oh shut up, will you?" She poured a fourth drink as if it was a long-awaited, fatal dose.

In the other room, Death sighed, as if satisfied. *Oh God no!* Julian remembered, his heart medication had rolled under the couch, out of the sight of adult eyes, but not beyond the reach of a child's curious hands. Julian cried out and slammed his head against the rest, making his chair shake.

"Oh for God's sake, all right! Fine! You want to go to bed? I'll put you to bed." She rose and jerked the wheelchair backwards toward the door. As tipsy as she was, she had trouble with the door, the wheelchair and her own balance, so she propped the door open.

She froze, eviscerated by cold, pale horror.

No, Julian thought. *No, not this!* His toes twitched. His tingling hand fell to his lap. "Eh..." he managed to say. A seatbelt buckled him into his chair. "Ehd...!"

"Eddy!" she screamed, running into the living room.

After all, Death whispered, *she can't look after you and the children at the same time.*

Elaine rushed into the kitchen for the cordless phone. She dialled 911 and ran back to Eddy, begging for CPR instructions even before giving her name or address. She didn't notice that Julian had unbuckled his seat belt and begun to slide forward in the chair.

Baby Isabel wailed upstairs; Death was still in the house. Drunk on determination, Julian fell to his knees close to the kitchen table. *You won't cheat me again, Death.* He yanked the tablecloth. The wet tumbler of liquor fell and cracked, and after it came a cascade of rattling pill bottles.

❖ ❖ ❖

Everything was shades of grey: the dead trees surrounding the fallow field, the nodding weeds, the shadows of those who waited for Death's guidance into their final resting places. With his scythe poised, Death awaited Julian.

"Can you hear them, Julian? The people standing over your grave? They wonder why they hadn't let you die with dignity."

Julian shrugged. "They were hoping for a miracle, I guess."

"A miracle?" Death laughed. "Lazarus was raised from death to life again, but does he live still?" Death's smile hardened into a grimace. "As you said yourself: I am inevitable. I come to all, sooner or later." He growled, "I thought you understood."

Julian said, "You shouldn't have done what you did. It was my fault. I pissed you off. You should have taken *me*. Instead you took Janine, an innocent kid. Did you take Eddy, too?"

"Why shouldn't I take children as well? A child may live fully and vibrantly in only seven years, and a fool may suffer agony for a hundred— what does it matter? You all die sooner or later."

Julian touched Death's sleeve, causing the gaunt figure to hiss in disgust. "Please, did you take my grandson?" Julian asked again.

A moaning wind wove through the grey statues in Death's garden, but Death himself did not reply. "You would know, if you hadn't thrown your life away so quickly." A gleam of light flickered within the cavernous hood. "With your restored life, you could have helped Elaine save the child." Death sighed. "I had reserved a beautiful, comfortable place for you, Julian. A peaceful place." He stretched his bony fingers from his wide cuffs and touched Julian's chest, stopping him where they stood. "But *you*... First you pretended to befriend and understand me, only to insult me with your petty bargains. And then you took your second chance at life and flung it back at me like so much rubbish! As soon as your limbs had begun to invigorate, what was the first thing you did? Nothing like helping another, no. Instead, you took your own life!"

Cold spread like branching tendrils through Julian's limbs, rendering them stiff. "Do I at least get to see them again?" Julian whispered.

"No," Death rumbled. With delicate, bony fingers, he cupped the face of one of the statues. The statue rolled its stony eyes, but the mouth was twisted open in agony, and the limbs were contorted and as stiff as concrete. Countless grimacing mouths issued forth a wailing wind of regret. "I have moved them far beyond your reach."

"Not even for five minutes?" Julian asked, meaning it as a dry, if nervous, joke.

Flames smouldered within the empty eye sockets. "*They* did not spit back the gift of life." Death walked on, but Julian found he could no longer follow. "Accursed ingrate."

Julian clenched his hand over his chest as the bitter cold seeped into his immortal soul. He lifted his eyes and saw a vision of himself falling out of his electric wheelchair, crawling into the living room, administering first aid. He saw himself shouting at a seven-year-old Isabel, jolting her with his voice before she plugged a fork in an electrical outlet. He saw himself walking out with canes and braces to speak to a high school, a university, a rehab group. He saw himself a much older man, whispering encouragement to an intern, who would go on to save countless more lives.

Death swept his scythe through Julian's visions, through what could have been. Julian saw Elaine kneeling by a gravestone, screaming at all who tried to comfort her. He saw the intern stuck in a cubicle, answering calls. He saw an empty high school gym. He saw a boy injecting dirty blue fluid into his veins, then laying down to die, his mouth warped into a rictus of artificial ecstasy, his body, shrunken by decay, forgótten in the dirty snow.

He focused on Elaine again, picking up the bottle of heart medication. There were some pills left. She twisted the cap and sat down behind a tumbler of rum and Coke. "Elaine, no!" Julian reached for her image. His arm froze, turning to stone.

"You were granted a second life," Death muttered, "and you vomited it back at me." He turned his back and walked on, using his scythe as a staff. "I wait for you no longer, Julian. Time was yours, in life. Now, it is mine."

✛ ✛ ✛

PATRICIA FLEWWELLING is the author of the science fiction novel *Helix: Blight of Exiles*, the dieselpunk series *The Fog of Dockside City*, and *Judge Not*, a biography co-written with falsely-accused and imprisoned Jonathon Parker. She writes almost anything that can be labelled dark, action-packed, and ironic.

In a Moment

By Christine Steendam

THE RAIN POUNDED like a deafening drum against the wind-shield of her car. Visibility had been reduced to the small red dots of the preceding car's tail lights. Traffic still raced by as if it was a clear sunny day though, causing Carissa to grip her steering wheel even tighter, her knuckles turning white. She hated weather like this. All the idiot drivers out there that thought they were invincible in their metal death machines were more of a danger than the torrential downpour.

A car whipped by on her left, and Carissa shuddered. The next exit was hers. Once she was off this freeway she'd be okay, yet she couldn't help but think she should have taken the long way home and avoided the highway.

The truck behind her pulled out and fish-tailed slightly on the slick road. "Just slow down, buddy," she muttered as the driver pulled past her. The truck fish-tailed some more, this time just past Carissa's car and she could see that he was struggling. She tapped her brakes. What was this guy thinking? What was his hurry?

All it took was an over-correction and the truck, barely holding traction, lost what little grip the tires had and was spinning across the slick concrete. Carissa slammed on the brakes, her tires squealing but continuing in their forward motion. She pressed harder on already completely compressed brakes in a panicked attempt to stay away from the out of control truck. She kept sliding right, towards where the truck was now; it still hadn't come to a stop. All she could see was a rushing blur of red tail lights fading to the yellow glow of head light. And then the blur slowed. The drumming rain took a steadier, less frantic beat, and then stopped completely. Little spots of red tail lights and yellow head lights stood still all around her. Rain drops froze in midair. Nothing was moving. Even her car was still, the speedometer stuck at 60 Km/h.

"Hello, Carissa."

She looked around frantically, but saw no one. "Who's there?"

"A friend," the voice answered.

"Where are you?"

"Right here."

Carissa turned toward the passenger seat where the voice seemed to be coming from, and a spectral body began to take shape. A man, dressed in black, his hair jet and slicked back; he looked as though he had stepped out of the nineteen fifties. His thin lips turned slightly upward at the corners in a grim, almost mocking smile that held no comfort for Carissa, and she shuddered. However, it was his eyes that she found most disconcerting. Completely black. Not just the pupils, but the irises and the cornea, even the sclera was black. And dull, without the sparkle or shine of normal eyes. Eyes that held no life.

"Who are you?"

"Who I am doesn't matter, Carissa. What matters is you. You and your present situation."

"And that is?"

"You're going to die."

She felt the blood drain from her head and glanced around in panic. Something about this strange, dream-like man evoked fear. She didn't know whether to laugh, cry, scream, or do all three at once. All she could think was that this had to be some kind of sick joke. She had to go home and make dinner for Kalan and the kids. She couldn't die. Not now. Not yet.

"Who the hell are you?"

"I told you—"

"I know what you *told* me. Who are you really?"

"I'm known by many different names, depending on the culture. The Egyptians call me Anubis; the Greeks, Thanatos; the Romans, Pluto; the Norse, Odin; the Japanese, Shinigami; the Christians may call me an angel, for that's what they referred to me as when I wiped out 185,000 Assyrian men in one night. I supposed the Grim Reaper would be my most common name in the western world, but I don't much like that term. You may call me whatever your religion dictates.

"Then you're Death. Death incarnate."

Death scowled. "That's such an ugly way to put it."

"Well you steal lives from people, so I'd say you deserve an ugly name."

He laughed a hollow laugh. Everything about him was... lifeless. "I do not *steal* life, Carissa. I merely help souls along the way when their time has come. Don't you believe in fate?"

"I believe that everyone forges their own path."

"That's unfortunate."

She didn't bother to argue with Death. Fate or no fate, he would not have her without a fight!

"May I show you something, Carissa? May I show you your future?"

"I thought I had no future. I thought I was to die in the next few minutes."

His smile was rictus. "You will, but your children live on and are they not a part of you?"

The car, the road, the head and tail lights dissolved and Carissa found herself standing beside Death in her living room.

The sun shone through the window, it was no longer raining— not that she was surprised. This was the future. Death had told her as much.

"What are we doing here?"

"Waiting."

Keira bounced in just then and went spinning around the room, laughing. "Daddy, hurry up!"

Kalan came walking in, chuckling at his daughter's antics. She looked to be about seven now.

"Settle down, George. The movie isn't going anywhere."

George; that was what he had always called their youngest. She squealed, "I'm not George! I'm Keira!"

Kalan's face adopted a look of shock. "Not George? Then you must be an imposter!" And then father and daughter fell to the floor in fits of laughter, Kalan tickling her as she screamed in delight.

Carissa wiped away tears. Not much had changed.

"This is two years after your death. As you can see, your family is doing well. Keira and Kalan are both happy."

"What about my son Jason?"

The room dissolved and the laughter of her husband and daughter faded but continued to echo hauntingly in her memory.

A new room appeared around them. The dim lighting and lack of large windows told Carissa that it was a basement. Her son, three other boys, and two girls sat on the mismatched couches and chairs positioned around a large TV where they were playing some kind of war game.

Jason, now sixteen, had a controller in his hands and shouted animatedly at Colby, his best friend since elementary school and apparent team mate for the current game.

As the game came to a close, Jason passed the controller to the girl beside him, smiling. "Here, you give it a try. Colby's the worst. You just can't win with him as your wing man."

"Or you just suck. Should we show him how it's done, Colby?"

Carissa watched as the girl and Colby played a round and came out victorious. Jason put his arm around the girl as she smiled up at him triumphantly. "Guess it's just you, Jason," she teased.

"I lost on purpose."

"Sure you did. To make me feel better about myself, right?"

Everyone laughed, Jason included, and his laughter joined the endlessly looping laughter of his father and sister in Carissa's head.

How was she supposed to deal with this? How could she face the fact that her family didn't need her? A mere two years after her death and they were living life as if nothing had changed. Her son hadn't become some teenaged delinquent, her daughter was a happy and lively seven-year-old and her husband seemed to be managing fine without her.

"How can they be doing so well? You're just showing me what you want to," she accused.

Death shook his head. "I do not have the power to change the future or bend it to my will. I can only show you what is or what could be."

"So, you're telling me that no matter what, on this day my son will be here and my daughter will be laughing and wrestling with my husband on my living room floor?"

"Essentially, yes. If you die, this is exactly their future in two years. Would you like to see more?"

She nodded and they were once again in her living room. Keira sat by the Christmas tree, a few years older than the wrestling girl Carissa had seen just minutes ago. Snow fell softly in huge clumps outside the large picture window, adding to the Christmas-y feel in the house. Jason walked into the room, a young man now — Carissa guessed about eighteen or nineteen — no longer a boy, and sat beside Keira.

"What are you doing up?"

"I'm waiting."

"For Santa?"

She shook her head and giggled. "Don't be silly. He doesn't exist."

Carissa smiled. Keira always had been too smart for her own good.

"Then what exactly are you waiting for, miss smarty pants?" he ruffled her hair playfully.

"For morning. I want to open the present from mom."

Jason sighed. "You know Dad just buys that, right?"

"Yeah, but it makes me feel like she's spending Christmas with us up in Heaven."

Jason smiled sadly and put his arm around his little sister. Carissa thought that she even caught of glimpse of tears shimmering in his eyes.

"She's still here. Just cause she died do you think she'd leave us all alone? She's your guardian angel now."

Keira nodded. "Do you miss her? Sometimes I don't miss her anymore and I think maybe I should feel bad."

"Sometimes I miss her. Not as much now, though, but there's always an empty spot, you know? I'm not sad, though. Mom's happy where she is and I think she'd be glad to see us happy. She wouldn't want us sitting around moping over her."

Keira nodded very matter-of-factly, very adult like, and then ruined the illusion by snuggling up to her brother. She was so young, nine or ten. She had been five when Carissa had left that morning.

"Will you wait with me?"

"Sure."

The heart-warming scene disappeared too quickly for Carissa and was replaced by her kitchen, now re-modeled, where a much older Kalan stood with Jason, now in his mid-twenties. They looked so alike, both dressed in suits and drinking from whisky glasses. They could have been brothers if not for the gray sneaking its way into Kalan's hair.

"Do you think mom will be there today?"

Kalan smiled, a tinge of sadness behind his eyes. "Of course. No pearly white gates would keep her from her son's wedding."

Carissa smiled. Tears brimmed as she said, "He's handsome. Grew up well. I always thought I'd be here for his wedding, though. I thought he'd walk me down that aisle and I'd be able to hug and kiss him goodbye."

"In his mind you will be there."

She turned away. "And what about Kalan? Does he find someone else to be happy with? Does he re-marry?"

Death did not answer. The dissolving room was answer enough. What would he show her? Her husband's marriage to someone else? Their first child together? She wasn't sure this was something she wanted to see and she found herself wishing she could have taken her question back, wishing she could have died believing that she was the only one Kalan could ever love.

Sure enough, Carissa found herself sitting beside Death in the back of a church. The guest list seemed to be small. Much smaller than her own wedding had been. She recognized many of her closest friends and family along with Kalan's. A handful of people she didn't recognize sat on one side of the church, and she assumed they were the friends and family of the new woman.

Kalan stood up front with the minister, Jason stood beside him as the best man. Jason was a few years older from the last time she'd seen him. A woman stood there as well, presumably the bridesmaid, and then the music started to queue the coming of the bride. Everyone stood.

She was a simple looking woman, but pretty; the kind of pretty that didn't need makeup or jewelry to highlight it. Natural beauty, Carissa had always called it. She had a look about her that said she would be kind and loving to anyone. Looking at Kalan, Carissa's heart broke. He was giving this new woman the same look he had given her on their wedding day, the same look she got every time he told her he loved her. It was *her* look, not this woman's!

"I've seen enough."

Death nodded and they were back in the car. The world around them remained frozen.

"Are you ready to continue your journey?"

Carissa shook her head, staring out the damaged windshield. "Ready? For death? I will not give up my life so easily."

"You have seen for yourself that your family will be fine. What's holding you here?"

"I cannot allow my husband to marry some other woman, for her to be a mother to my children. I belong in their lives. I belong at my son's wedding. If they do well without me, how much better would they do *with* me?"

"You realize that you have no choice. You path has already been set, it cannot be changed."

"Then why do you even bother?"

"Because, for a soul at peace with its destiny, transition is easier than for one fighting to stay."

"What if I were to prove to you that it would be best that I remain alive? Could you change my path?"

"Potentially. But no one has been able to convince me yet that their choices are better than fate's. What makes you think you're any different?"

"You have to let me try. Take us to when Kalan is told of my death."

Almost instantly the car became a sterile hospital waiting room. Kalan burst through the doors and nearly ran to the nurse's station. "Where is she?" he asked frantically, interrupting another patient's question.

A nurse came around the counter and pulled him aside. "Who are you looking for?"

"Carissa Flemming. My wife. She was in a car accident. She was brought here. Where is she?"

"I'll be right back, Mr. Flemming. Please, take a seat."

Kalan paced anxiously near the desk, refusing to sit idly by and wait.

"Mr. Flemming?" The nurse returned and put her hand on Kalan's arm in a comforting gesture.

He stopped his pacing and looked at her, hope and worry etched on his face.

"She's in the OR. I'll take you back to where you can wait for the surgeon to finish. He'll tell you more."

"How is she doing?"

"I do not know, Mr. Flemming. Please, follow me."

Carissa and Death followed Kalan and the nurse down a maze of corridors through the hospital. They stopped at a row of seats outside a set of double doors. The quiet hall lacked the bustling activity of the rest of the hospital. Carissa shivered. This hall seemed made to bear bad news.

"You'll have to wait here, Mr. Flemming. The surgeon will come out when he is done to update you on your wife's condition."

There was no mention of Kalan seeing her after surgery and Carissa suspected the nurse knew, or at least had an idea of the seriousness of her condition and didn't want to give Kalan any false hope.

Once the nurse left, Kalan paced the hall. He tried to sit down a couple of times but seconds later he would spring back up and begin pacing again. Carissa half expected a path to wear in the floor, but these floors had held up to more than Kalan's shoe leather.

It seemed to go on for hours, but finally the doors opened. A surgeon came out, still in green scrubs splattered with blood. Carissa's blood.

"Is she alright?" Kalan nearly pounced on the surgeon but stopped short at the sight of the blood.

"You're Carissa Flemming's husband?"

"Yes. Is she okay? When will I be able to see her?"

The surgeon shook his head sadly, as if at a loss for words. "I'm afraid we lost her."

The words sounded a little hollow, rehearsed, lines delivered countless times before, but Carissa understood that he had to retain a certain distance if he was to survive his job.

"Lost her?" Kalan looked lost, unable to understand what the surgeon had just told him.

"There was internal bleeding. We couldn't stop it in time. I'm sorry. We did everything we could."

Kalan turned ghost white and leaned against the wall. Slowly, as if what the doctor had said was starting to make sense, he slid down the wall to the floor. Tears streaked his face. "No. No. No," he sobbed quietly.

The surgeon looked pained. "Is there anyone I can call for you?"

Kalan just shook his head and waved the surgeon away, unable to find words to express the pain.

It broke Carissa's heart to watch him torn apart. She walked over to him and tried to embrace him but her arms just passed through his body. They were no longer of the same world. "Can you honestly say that it is for the best to put my husband through this kind of pain? And what of my children?"

"Every transition involves pain, Carissa. He will heal." Carissa wanted to strangle Death for his lack of empathy.

"So you don't care?"

"What I care about is gathering souls for the next life. That is my purpose. You've proven nothing to me, Carissa. I have already shown you that this pain is only temporary. Kalan will heal. Your children will be happy. Is there something else you wish to show me or are you prepared to accept your fate?"

"You said before that this is the future *if* I die. Can you show other futures?"

"You wish to see what it would be like if you survive?"

"Yes."

Death frowned, but Kalan's sobbing form disappeared and was replaced by Carissa's living room. She saw herself, a few years older, sitting in a chair. She was dozing off. The clock on the mantle read 2:15 A.M. The house was quiet except for the ticking of clocks. It struck Carissa that you never realized how loud clocks were until you were in a completely silent house. If she survived she would get rid of some of them. They spoke too much of time passing, the time she had left.

The clocks were interrupted by the soft click of the front door opening and closing and Jason padded slowly past in an attempt to get up the stairs and to his room as quickly and quietly as possible.

"Jason?" Carissa had woken.

"Yeah?"

"You're late."

"Sorry, mom." He didn't look sorry. He looked annoyed at being caught.

"Where were you?"

"At Colby's."

Carissa could see the pain in her older self's eyes. Jason was lying and this was likely not the first time. What kind of trouble had he managed to get himself into?

"Your eyes are bloodshot, Jason."

"I'm just tired."

"Are you doing pot again?" There was no beating around the bush. Plain and simple. This wasn't the first time she had dealt with this. Her son was doing drugs; every mother's nightmare.

"I'm going to bed."

"Jason! You have to talk to me. You can't keep doing this to yourself. You may not realize it now, but this could ruin your life."

"I'll talk to you when you aren't throwing accusations around."

"All you have to say is no, Jason."

"If I say no, you'll call me a liar. If I say yes, you'll cry the blues. I can't win this. Goodnight, mom."

The older form of Carissa bowed her head to hide her tears and Jason took off up the stairs.

She turned to Death. "Why is he doing drugs? That isn't my boy."

"After you came home from the hospital, because you didn't escape unscathed, Jason had a hard time dealing with everything. You're paralyzed, Carissa; from the waist down. Suddenly his mother wasn't everything she was supposed to be and he was left with a cripple. It was hard for a teenage boy to deal with so he turned to marijuana. It took the edge off."

"You're saying that if I live he turns to drugs, but if I die he lives a happy life?"

"I'm saying that he had a harder time transitioning to his mother being a different person than to his mother being gone. Is there anything else you'd like to see?"

"Ten years from my accident. What is my family like?"

They walked out of the living room and into the hall where Keira, now fifteen, sat on the stairs. Voices came from the living room, Carissa and Kalan's voices, but she couldn't see either of them.

"What do you want me to say, Carissa? That I still love you? I do! I never stopped. You stopped! You became a different person after the accident; you withdrew from me, from Jason and Keira, until we were left with a shell for a mother and wife. What did you expect?"

"I expected you to stay with me, to love and cherish me through good and bad, sickness and health. That's what we vowed. *You* vowed, Kalan. An affair? That is not loving me."

"I'm sorry," Kalan's voice broke.

"But sorry is a little too late and you love her. I'm not the woman you married anymore."

No sound reached Carissa's ears but she could imagine Kalan struggling to find the words to fix what he'd broken while Carissa's stare challenged him.

"I want a divorce," Carissa's voice, broken by tears, uttered quietly, but not quietly enough for the eavesdroppers to miss.

"What?"

"Clearly you want out. I will not hold you back. Your poor, crippled wife will not stand between you and happiness with this other woman. Date her, marry her, I don't care. You can abandon me but if you ever abandon Keira or Jason, I will never forgive you."

"Jason, our drug addict son," scoffed Kalan. "He left us, Carissa."

"That doesn't mean you should give up hope. He needs us now more than ever. I'll call the lawyer tomorrow to start the process."

Carissa looked down at Keira, listening to her parent's conversation. Tears stained her cheeks and shone in her eyes. Why must her family suffer so much? Keira should never have to see her parents' divorce or her brother fall into a vicious cycle of self-destruction.

"So, I divorce Kalan because he cheats, my son becomes a drug addict and my daughter watches her family torn apart. Is there anything else I should know about?" Carissa asked bitterly.

Death's smile was a grimace again, and Carissa was getting really and truly sick of that smile. It wasn't a kind smile. It was more… condescending, as if she was an ignorant child that he was slowly, oh so slowly educating. "Do you wish to see Keira's fate?"

"Is it a kind one?"

"You already know the answer to that."

Carissa shook her head. "The divorce… She doesn't handle it well, does she?"

Death shrugged. "What child does?"

"I don't want to see it, I can't handle seeing any more, but can you just tell me?"

"She has a series of unhappy relationships in an attempt to escape Kalan and his new wife. She gets pregnant at eighteen, marries the boy and divorces him a couple of years later. She marries the next man to come into her life, divorces him and the pattern keeps going; five husbands in all, a couple of them abusers. She has three children but they don't have a great life either. She turns to alcohol to cope, but that doesn't help." Death lists off Keira's life as a checklist of facts and nothing more.

She turned and she nodded slowly, unable to say anything. She couldn't bear any more.

They were sitting in the car and Death turned to her. "I think you know that you've failed to convince me."

"I've failed to convince myself."

"Are you ready then?"

She shook her head. "How can I be ready for death? Now I'm just... torn. How can I be ready to leave this life when I don't even know what comes next?"

Death laughed, an otherworldly sound. "I cannot answer those questions for you, Carissa. You must discover the answers yourself on your journey."

"You can't even tell me who's right about the afterlife? What's waiting for me? Heaven, Hell, Purgatory, Reincarnation, nothing? What?"

Death shook his head, that smile playing at his lips. He would not answer.

"Fine, but answer me this; is anyone ever truly ready for death?"

"There are a few. The ones that take comfort in religion and think they know what comes next. There are others, like you, who are frightened and unsure. And still others that are never ready and I have to take them anyway. Their passing is often painful for the body and soul, and I'm not sure their souls ever truly adjust. You, Carissa, are ready. You're just afraid. Do not fear the unknown. Many people have died well. Look at the Christians that Nero tortured in the arena. They suffered unspeakable agonies and yet they faced their journey with open arms and I was there, with them, showing them the way. I will do the same for you."

"They were dying for a cause. I'm dying for nothing. Nothing more than fate."

"Not everyone can die a martyr. Nor would I wish that death on anyone. It's a hard path."

"Will it hurt?"

"Every transition involves pain. You have seen it for yourself in your husband's pain at your death. You have experienced it in childbirth and in growing from adolescence to adulthood. Others experience it in the transition to old age. Death is no different, but it, too, will pass."

"That isn't very reassuring."

"Sometimes you have to go through pain to get the reward on the other side. I promise you that you will hardly remember it at your journey's end."

"And you will be there with me?"

For the first time Death smiled a warm smile that could almost be described as fatherly. It was as if he had transformed from foe to friend in the moment she had given in. "I'll be with you to start you on your journey. The rest is up to you."

Carissa nodded and looked away. She stared at everything around her, this strange frozen world. There were vehicles behind and beside her. In front of her was the truck that would kill her. How long had she sat here with Death? An hour? Two? It seemed like an eternity grappling with fate but she felt oddly at easy, though not completely. She was about to die and leave her family behind. She had seen that her death was for the best, but that didn't make it easier, it just made it right, and history had shown many times over that more often than not, the right path was the hardest one to walk.

Death sat wordlessly beside her, as if sensing she needed time, but she knew that he would only wait for so long. Finally he said, "Are you ready?"

"I don't think I'll ever be ready."

"Be strong."

"You'll stay with me?" she asked again.

"Up until the moment you cross over, yes."

She smiled weakly as she held out her hand. "I need a little help."

He smiled gently as he grasped her hand. "It's time."

She nodded, squeezed his hand even tighter, like he was a lifeline when in fact he was her line to death, and then she looked fate straight in the eye.

The world slowly came alive. Rain drummed against the car, fast, then faster. Horns blared warnings. Tires squealed in distress. On impact, Carissa looked at Death and said, "Thank you."

She gasped as a flash of blinding light swallowed her. Whether it was the headlights, her mind dealing with an overload of pain, or her destination, she did not know. As the light faded, she found herself in a white landscape devoid of color, smell or texture.

"Walk," Death's voice whispered in her mind.

She wasn't completely alone. Not yet.

As she took her first hesitant steps, calmness washed over her. Her death wasn't the end, it was the beginning. Looking back, she could see her old life fading, and there stood Death, smiling. He nodded and motioned her forward.

There was still something unsettling about him, but he had helped her and for that she was thankful. Suddenly, Death's dark features faded to a wisp of smoke, and Carissa, sensing that there was nothing left for her here, walked until she was gone.

❖ ❖ ❖

CHRISTINE STEENDAM has been writing stories since she could put pen to paper and form words. Now, fifteen years later, her debut novel, *Heart Like an Ocean* is available and she is working on her second book. Christine makes her home in Manitoba with her husband, two kids, and horse.

DEATH DRIVES A CORDOBA

BY RYAN MCFADDEN

WHEN CONNIE WILKERSON received the latest text from her no-good ex, she wanted to whip the cell phone out her minivan window. He had a way of winding her up, seemingly now more than when they were married.

She read it again. 'I'm not signing off. Need second review'. She squeezed the phone so hard the seams made a popping noise and she lessened her grip. Her breath came in short gasps and tears welled in her eyes.

She glanced up, corrected her direction, and eased off the gas as she turned into the parking lot.

Don't start crying now, you twit. She had always let him get under her skin. The more she tried to unravel herself from eight years of marriage, the more he threw up obstructions, not because he wanted her back, but because he wanted to punish her for walking out on him.

He went after her personal assets, claiming he was entitled to half. Battling back in the courts was expensive. So expensive that it if she didn't win, she'd be bankrupt. With her cash tied up, she'd fallen behind in her payments and now her creditors were knocking.

She wiped her eyes with the back of her hand and began texting an appropriately acidic response.

The little girl ran from between two parked cars, green dress fluttering like a petal on a breeze. Connie reacted too late. She hit the girl, the impact registering as a sickening thud.

She slammed on the brakes and the wheels screeched.

"No, no, no!" Connie cried, jumping from the minivan. The child lay in a tiny heap several yards back.

You didn't see her because you were busy texting. How many times have you admonished him *for doing that exact thing?*

Connie's senses crystallized: the sun's brilliance reflecting off the surrounding windshields; papers blowing on the breeze; the warmth of the autumn sun even though the wind held the breath of winter. Then she focused on the fallen girl, and Connie knew she wasn't going to be all right. Nothing moved except the rustling dress.

"Tegan?" a woman called, hidden behind a row of cars.

"Over here," Connie whispered, then retrieved her voice. "Over here!" she yelled.

The woman came from between the cars, holding her sun hat on her head. When she saw Tegan, her hand fell and the hat twisted away on the currents.

Connie wanted to tell her not to touch the girl, but she knew, God, she just knew, that it didn't matter. The mother scooped Tegan's ruined body into her arms and wailed, the anguished sound sending goose bumps along Connie's skin.

Connie's phone vibrated and she glanced at it, forgetting she held it. There was a text waiting for her, and while she could see the words, they weren't registering. Instead, she hit the emergency-call button and dialled 911, told them that they were in the White Oaks Mall parking lot by the Wal-Mart.

The mother's cries drew a crowd. Connie stood in the middle of the chaos, shivering. She didn't move as people pushed by her.

Sirens wailed several blocks away.

Tegan's mom cradled and rocked the girl, ignoring pleas to release her. Connie gazed at the faces, wanting to tell them that she had done this, but that she'd make this right. Except there was no making this right.

Connie noticed a man beyond the crowd. He was tall and slender and wore a long black coat that seemed a little too heavy for the temperature. She wasn't sure why he stood out, maybe because he was calm as where everyone else was panicked. He stood partially in his idling car, one foot in the car and his hand resting on the open door.

The car was a Chrysler Cordoba, mint green. She didn't know cars very well, but she knew this one because her dad used to drive one. It was one of those large cars that no one drove anymore because they sucked down gas. Connie made eye contact with the man briefly before he looked away and slid inside. She couldn't see past the glare on the windshield. The reverse lights flashed, as if he was shifting through the gears into drive, but the car didn't move. Her phone buzzed again and she tucked it into her pocket. The Cordoba slowly pulled from its spot, the driver seemingly the one person who realized there was nothing that could be done and decided to leave. The car drove by them, and though there was no glare on the passenger windows, she didn't get a good look at the driver.

Then the car was gone, merging into traffic onto Southdale Avenue.

When the police arrived, Connie finally realized what had happened.

She had killed four-year-old Tegan.

She remembered the police asking her questions, but she couldn't remember how she answered.

A flutter of green on the wind.

The mother wailed, her cries intensifying when the Regional Coroner placed Tegan into a black body bag. The ambulance had left earlier, empty and with sirens silent, because ambulances were for the living. The Ontario Forensic Pathology Service was going to conduct an autopsy, as if the cause of death mattered. As they zipped up the black body bag, a different police officer asked Connie another round of questions. *How fast were you going? Why did you wait to call 911?* A vehicular-forensic team mapped the area, measured the skid marks, and documented the details. Connie wasn't sure if they were going to charge her, but they never asked about her cell phone, and never said she was under arrest.

You killed Tegan because you were texting.

Grief wafted from Tegan's mother in waves. Connie wanted to accept that grief, wanted to drink it in, as if it would absolve her of guilt.

She sat on the curb, hands shaking, wishing she had a cigarette even though she'd quit two years ago. Within three hours the parking lot was cleared, and all remnants of Tegan had been washed away.

Like she never existed.

❖ ❖ ❖

That first night was unbearably long. Connie wasn't accustomed to being alone yet and, in a crisis, she had no one to turn to. Days like today she wished she could call her sister Jennifer. But that hadn't been possible in ten years. Instead, she tried calling her father, but he was in Latin America on business. She didn't call any of her friends because what would she tell them? 'I killed a little girl. Ran her over and now she's dead.'

Instead of sleeping, she paced her apartment, waves of emotion overwhelming her rational mind. She wondered about Tegan: her favorite food; whether she had brothers or sisters; whether she had acted like a brat that morning, throwing her food across the table.

Connie tried self medicating with a glass of red wine to keep those images away, but the alcohol only heightened her anxiety until she felt like ants were crawling along her spine. When she finally slept, her dreams clogged with disjointed images of Tegan's body bouncing off her bumper.

In the morning, Connie considered calling in sick, but that meant she would end up home alone in her apartment. Instead, she was alone in someone else's partially renovated apartment. She sat on the unfinished floor, surrounded by hardwood samples. Dark ash, red oak, white maple. Her cell phone buzzed on the crate near the door, as it had been doing all morning. She glanced over but didn't move. Since yesterday, her ex had sent her twenty texts. She'd read some, but responded to none. It seemed all it took for her to rile him up was to simply stop responding. It was a hollow victory.

Connie wanted to throw away her cell phone, but that was how her boss Sarah stayed in contact. *The cell phone didn't kill her. You did.* Of course, Connie hadn't answered when Sarah called either.

She rearranged several pieces of hardwood without focusing on them. How was this important? How did the color of hardwood make one difference in the scheme of life?

Tegan smiled, then laughed as she darted in and out of the parked cars. Her mom chased her, her cries had become increasingly concerned as she lost sight of her daughter.

Connie dropped her head into her hands as the memories expanded. There was no way she could've known that. This was just a trick of her grief-addled mind.

The man by the Cordoba— Connie saw his face now. Rather, she didn't see his features but she thought she recognized his expression. Sympathy. Because he knew what she had done?

Around noon, Sarah came to retrieve her. Connie sat on the floor as if she had skinned her knee.

"You forgot your phone?" It vibrated again. Sarah frowned. "What the hell have you been doing?"

"I've been…" Connie gazed around her, trying to fit the pieces of her surroundings together.

What have I been doing?

"I don't have time for this, Connie. This is a simple job. You know—"

"I killed someone," Connie blurted, and then she couldn't hold it back any longer and she sobbed. Her boss was the last person she wanted to tell. Sarah watched her cry, and surprisingly, didn't fire her, or even yell. She knelt, and waited calmly. Connie told a disjointed story when she managed to choke back sobs. Recounting the events relieved some of the pressure that had built inside, not much, but a little.

Sarah put her hand on Connie's knee.

"Go home. Get some rest. Call your family." Connie nodded, wiped her nose with the back of her hand. Connie didn't have much of a family. Not anymore. But she knew what Sarah meant. *Go home and cry to your family because they know how to handle these things.*

She collected her coat, but decided to leave the phone behind.

Outside, her skin tightened from the cold air and felt refreshing against cheeks swollen from crying. Many knew her in Old South so she kept her gaze low to avoid eye contact. She wanted to disappear. She dug in her purse for her keys so she could get out of here as quickly as possible.

The autumn wind formed the crisp leaves into a mini twister. They brushed against her face and collected in her hair.

A flash of green— the tip of Tegan's dress as she ducked behind a car, giggling quietly to remain hidden.

"We're in a parking lot," Tegan's mom cried. Her voice had lost the playfulness and was taking on the stern parental tone. "This isn't a game."

Tegan's blonde hair was swept off her face and fastened with a jewelled hair clip. She peeked over a hood, saw her mom, and dashed into the parking lot. She didn't see the minivan, didn't register the pain as the grill broke her clavicle, then shattered several ribs and speared them into her heart. She died within seconds.

Connie gasped, took a step back to distance herself from the image.

She drove home to her apartment, the car windows open. She gripped the wheel tightly, afraid that if she didn't, she'd experience another of the images. She wondered if she was losing her mind— if the trauma of killing Tegan had somehow fractured her psyche.

She saw the man in the Cordoba, the windshield free of glare. He had a perfectly trimmed goatee and close-cropped hair. A heavy silver chain hung around his neck, matching the chunky bracelet on his wrist.

A car honked and Connie startled. She idled at a four-way stop, alone except for the vehicle behind her. She waved and headed the last few blocks to her home, a converted church made into a series of apartments. She didn't own the place— she couldn't afford to own anything right now. Her credit wasn't bad— worse, it was nonexistent. This place was the one piece of luck she'd had over the past six months. She was house sitting— no rent, just utilities, which she could afford with her design job.

Once inside, she peeled off her clothes and took a shower so hot that her skin reddened. She towel dried and climbed into bed and then stared at the ceiling and tried to block out the sound of Tegan hitting the bumper.

Instead of thinking about Tegan, she saw the man in the Cordoba. She tried to remember when he had arrived. Did he push through the crowd and get into his car? Or was he already there? The more she thought about it, the more she thought she knew him.

She fell asleep, and dreamed of the man. He was different this time, wearing a black overcoat with matching hat. He looked taller but that could've been because he was thinner. He watched by the woods, one foot in the car, the other firmly on the pavement, as if unsure whether he was coming or going.

She woke with a start.

That wasn't from the scene of Tegan's death!

Ten years ago, Connie and her sister had gone to their family's cottage up at Shouldice Lake. Connie had convinced her sister to go to the Singing Sands beach because their lake was infested with blood suckers. The waters at Singing Sands were calm, and the beach was shallow. But Jennifer, never a strong swimmer, disappeared beneath the surface. By the time Connie got to her, Jennifer's skin was blue and her lungs had filled with water. Connie didn't know CPR. She screamed until others came running. One of the other bathers was a nurse who performed chest compressions. Jennifer never coughed up water and never took another breath. Her blue skin turned white.

Connie replayed that day, just like she was replaying Tegan's death. What she could've done differently, how she could've saved her sister's life.

Connie's skin tingled with the realization that the man in the black overcoat had watched from the parking lot by the picnic tables. She hadn't remembered him, or rather, she hadn't attached importance to him, but now she did.

There was no reason to believe it was the same man just because he drove a Cordoba, except all her instincts screamed that it was.

Why would that man be at both incidents? What were the chances that he'd be watching, each time an impartial observer? She didn't assume that he was involved in their demises — both were random tragedies. Instead, it was almost as if the man *anticipated* the accidents, and was there waiting for them.

What type of person could anticipate a fatality?

She laughed at the absurdity. She was so wracked with guilt that she was beginning to concoct crazy stories. And yet, she couldn't let it go. She crawled from bed, her body electrified.

Connie paced, trying to recall all the details of her sister's death. That man... what had he done? Had he approached? Did she see his face? The more she concentrated, the more the memory distorted and she was unable to differentiate between the real memory, and her wish fulfillment.

She cursed, willed away the disjointed thoughts. She pushed aside the doubt as it threatened to derail her. Some things you couldn't prove, but you simply knew to be true.

That man wasn't the mythical grim reaper who brought death, cutting the living down like wheat with his black-iron scythe. Was this Death the boatman, who ferried the deceased to the afterlife? Heaven? Hell? Shangri-La? Hades? Connie didn't think it mattered. He was the collector of souls.

What if she found him? Then what? Hold him hostage? Threaten him with a gun until he agreed to release Tegan from the afterlife?

Connie knew this really wasn't about Tegan or Jennifer. This was about her, and her desire to tell Tegan how sorry she was for killing her. Then to confess to her sister how she regretted tormenting her when they were kids by setting her doll's hair on fire. How she wished that at the age of twenty-two, she hadn't whined because she was afraid of a few leeches.

Connie wanted something simple but impossible— a chance for closure.

All she needed to do was trap Death.

How would she find Death? Did he show up at every accident, every death? If so, then she assumed that she was one of the few that could see him, if death was even a *him. Because Death drives a Cordoba.* She pushed those thoughts to the side, to cling with her nails to the slim ledge of plausibility.

Hang out in the ICU? What if she threatened to kill someone? Could Death be fooled so easily, or would he know that she was never going to pull the trigger?

The more she schemed, the more she realized how crazy she sounded. There was no way to cheat Death, or to negotiate better terms. Did she plan on driving around, hoping people killed themselves in front of her, or wishing for a loose support wire on a window-washing scaffold?

She laughed bitterly.

She was losing her mind.

Bargaining was a stage of grief. Except in this case, there was no bargaining with Death.

There was no coming back from that.

❖ ❖ ❖

Connie decided to give work another try, because that was what happened in the real world.

She pulled across the street from the condos into a cafe's parking lot but then rested her head on the steering wheel, hoping that working wasn't a bad idea. Sarah had given her some leeway, but that compassion wouldn't last long, and she couldn't afford to lose this job.

She was so tired. The stress of the past two days and her sleepless nights left her exhausted, and hearing things. She leaned back and watched people meander down the sidewalks.

A woman walked a massive Rottweiler, though really the dog dragged her down the street.

An elderly couple stopped at a boutique window, never speaking, but nodding, pointing, communicating wordlessly then moving on to the next window.

An eaves-trough cleaner stretched out his wooden ten-foot step ladder. He clambered up, a length of aluminum over his shoulder. He climbed to the top step, the ladder trembling.

Connie saw it happen before it happened. *The Rottweiler spots a squirrel, then chases after it, pulling easily away from the owner. The dog sprints down the street, dragging its leash behind. It hits the ladder and the man begins to fall.*

She blinked, trying to clear her faulty vision. The woman had a firm grip on the leash and the dog wasn't free. The man on the ladder was fitting the trough into place. He teetered on the top step, the one that usually says 'not a step'.

Then the Rottweiler barked, pulled on its leash, and was free.

"No!" Connie yelled. She opened her door, desperate to warn the man.

Too late.

The dog dashed down the street, then hit the ladder. The man dropped the trough and scrambled for a handhold. The step ladder folded. The man caught a length of flashing, but it only held him momentarily. He reached for the window sill, missed, driving his arm through the window. The glass shattered, and his full weight came down on his wrist. The glass sliced through his flesh, severing tendons, ligaments, arteries. His blood squirted in an arc. His legs kicked, trying desperately to gain a traction.

Someone screamed, then the man fell backward onto the sidewalk, his head smashing against the concrete. His hand was attached by a few flimsy cords. He wasn't moving, his blood pooling on the sidewalk.

A crowd quickly gathered around him.

"He's thirty-eight-years old. He's not going to survive. He's lost too much blood and he's hit his head on the concrete. He's going to die." The thought didn't belong to her, but it didn't feel alien or obtrusive. In fact, it felt comforting, like it belonged there.

Connie wanted to rush to his side and help, but there was no helping him. The details of his life came to her in a dizzying torrent of information, but now she wondered if they had always been there and she was just remembering.

She glanced around the accident scene, at the chaos, at the people snapping pictures on their cell phones, of others turning white from seeing a man die. He wasn't dead yet, but he would be shortly.

"*It is his time.*" that voice said again. "*He is frightened and alone.*"

The woman with the dog stood motionless, shell shocked. Pale, expressionless, confused. Her gaze settled on Connie.

Connie stood at her minivan, one foot in, and one foot out. The eye contact was brief, Connie looking away. She slid back into the minivan, hands on the wheel. The woman continued to stare, but Connie could tell by her furrowed brow that she must not have been able to see past the glare on the windshield.

"*His time is over. Take him home,*" the internal voice said.

The passenger door opened and the eaves cleaner climbed in. As he'd approached, she noticed he walked with a hitch in his step from a motorcycle accident years ago, though the slight limp was out of habit as he didn't have any injuries. Not anymore. He glanced at his wrist, then at the body on the sidewalk.

They sat in silence for a long moment.

"I'm not ready," the man said, leaning back into his seat. "My wife's expecting me. I can't leave her like this. And my job..." He explained the list of goals and dreams left undone, and of commitments broken.

"*He is weighted with the burdens of the living. Soothe him so that he casts off these bonds for the world of the living is unimportant now. His time is gone,*" the voice said.

"How do I do that?" she asked the voice.

"*You have the gift to assuage his distress. He must accept that his time is gone, and yet his journey is just beginning.*"

If she concentrated hard enough, she saw the man's guilt and fear pooled at his feet like a vague shadow, the tendrils of his earthly life holding him back.

Connie put her hand on his arm. He startled, but then calmed, and the shadow receded. "She'll understand," Connie said. "They'll all understand. Your time has passed. This isn't a sad thing, but a change from one existence to another."

He visibly relaxed and said, "You're not what I expected."

"*They say that every time,*" the voice said.

He didn't seem to hear it, so she said, "Everyone says that."

"Why you?"

Why was she chosen to drive him? Why had the man in the Cordoba driven Tegan, and Jennifer? She smiled, as she realized that neither Tegan nor Jennifer had died alone and confused. Each had someone to walk the path with them.

"Because you were confused and maybe frightened, and needed someone you could trust. Because sometimes, we just need a friend."

He contemplated this for a long moment before saying, "I'm not afraid. At least, not anymore."

"There's nothing to be scared of," she said. And it was true. She didn't know what waited for him at the end of the journey—it wasn't her time yet, so like all of the living, she wouldn't be allowed into the afterlife.

"My name is Ronald."

"I know," she said.

She put the vehicle in drive. Their journey, mapped out in her mind, was a long one, and she estimated it would take several days. She wasn't scared either, but she was nervous. Because at the end of the journey, she would be granted the impossible—Tegan and Jennifer would be waiting to talk with her.

❖ ❖ ❖

RYAN MCFADDEN is a two-time Aurora winning writer from London, Ontario. His most recent writing credits are stories in the anthologies *When the Villain Comes Home* and *Blood and Water*. He is currently working on the *10th Circle Chronicles*— an ebook series.

Prison Break

by Tobin Elliott

THE FIRST TIME Scooter escaped, I was six years old.

My mom and dad had split up a year before and we'd had to move. My dad wouldn't take my dog, Scooter, and mom and I couldn't have him in the apartment we moved to. The next best thing was to give him a good home so we arranged to have him live with George and Carol Black, friends of ours with a house not too far away. I hung out with their daughter, Debbi — and yes, there were the inevitable comments about how nice it would be if we grew up and got married — that always got our eyes rolling. But at least I had a place to visit my dog. And make no mistake, no matter where Scooter lived, he was *my* dog.

We'd got him three years earlier, back when mom and dad still talked nicely to each other. Dad came home with a small, black, brown-eyed squirming bundle of joy and it was love at first sight for both of us. Though he was a black Lab, he had a small white patch over the toes of both hind legs that, in my mind, just made him even more fascinating. When my parents asked me what I wanted to name him, I picked Scooter. Don't ask why. The fog of time has eradicated whatever reason my three-year-old brain may have come up with.

Then my parents split up. We moved into an apartment, my father moved in with his sister, and Scooter went to my friends. I don't think any one of us were happy with the new status quo, but the only one that actively protested it was Scooter. Every few months, he'd slip his collar and head home. Well, what he thought of as home.

And to be honest, it was still the place I considered home as well. The place with the backyard, the small pond, the wooded area that was safe for a six-year-old to roam in... all of it now replaced by a cramped apartment with a balcony and hallways that smelled of old fried food and damp laundry. There was a park across the street now, but I couldn't play hide and seek in an area with no trees and a battered swing set. I missed my magical woods.

I guess Scooter did too. The first time he left the Black's, they phoned in a panic, but it wasn't even an hour later we got the call that Scooter was sitting in his old dog house back at our old house, now owned by someone that I felt couldn't ever understand how great the place was. They didn't have a dog. They didn't even have kids.

When we went to get Scooter that first time, he seemed quite pleased with himself that he'd been able to draw everyone back home. His thick black tail thumped the wall of the dog house as we approached, gently admonishing him. Then his big brown eyes seemed to radiate disappointment when we bundled him into my mother's sky blue '62 Pontiac and took him back to George and Carol.

A few weeks later, he did it again. I'm sure in his little doggy brain he was hoping *this* time he'd succeeded.

It happened a third and fourth and fifth time. By then, it was a routine. We smilingly referred to them as Scooter's "prison breaks". George and Carol would first call us to alert us, then call the residents of the old house to keep an eye out. By the fifth time, we just drove over and waited for him to show. When he came bounding through the woods and trotted across the yard to me as I waited by his dog house, I could almost read it in his eyes, in the way he loped across the lawn, in the set of his mouth as his tongue bobbed out making him look for all the world like he was smiling. *Finally!* I'm sure he thought. *I finally got them trained!*

We took him back to George and Carol who, as usual, apologized profusely. I never minded. I got to spent time with my dog in the back seat of mom's car. But handing him over to George and Carol... Man, it was like giving him up all over again. Every time.

I made sure that, each time I walked Scooter back to the Black's back yard and slipped the collar over his head and tightened it up, that I stroked his shiny black head, looked directly into his eyes and told him how much I loved him and how, someday, we'd be able to live together again in a nice house with a nice yard and some woods to walk in. I didn't realize until the fourth or fifth time that I also had a grip on his dog tag, the one with his name on it, and I was rubbing it between my thumb and fingers.

✤ ✤ ✤

The last time he ran away, it started the same as every other prison break. We got the call from Carol. Mom and I hopped in the Pontiac and headed over to the old place and then we waited. We'd never had to wait over an hour.

This time, we were there almost four hours before we gave up. I didn't like the lines in my mother's forehead or the set of her mouth.

We called the old place when we got back, sure that Scooter would have shown up just after we left. No, they hadn't seen him yet. They'd keep an eye out and call as soon as he showed.

The next day, I came home from school and before I could say anything, I knew mom hadn't heard anything. The lines in her forehead were etched a little deeper, the set of her mouth a little more engrained.

By the end of the week, my mom began laying down comments about Scooter maybe not coming back this time. That maybe this time he was gone. "Gone for good," was the line she used, though I could see nothing good about it.

That weekend, we stopped by George and Carol's place. By now, the apologetic refrain had been memorized, but they really stepped it up. I didn't say anything, because I knew if I did, I'd yell at how they hadn't replaced his collar with something he couldn't slip out of and escape a half-dozen times. But I also knew no one had taken it seriously, so the blame rested with all of us.

Instead, I walked to the back yard. I found his collar, still attached to the end of a length of plastic-covered wire clothes-line. And hanging from the collar, Scooter's dog tag. Without really thinking about it, I unhooked the tag and, with a quick rub between my fingers and a whispered, "Please come back, Scooter," I pocketed it.

Over the next few weeks, the drudgery of day-to-day living, work for mom, school and homework for me, crept back and did its best to pluck thoughts of my lost dog out of our minds. It mostly worked for my mother, who mentioned him less and less. But for me, I entered into a ritual that would ensure I would never forget my dog.

Each night, as I got into bed, I pulled out the dog tag from its hiding place under my bedside light and I rubbed it between thumb and forefinger and whispered, "Please come back, Scooter."

❖ ❖ ❖

Three months later, I was over at George and Carol's, having spent the afternoon playing with Debbi. It was a warm, drowsy afternoon and we were both sprawled on the couch watching an old Tarzan movie. Debbi always had a thing for Johnny Weissmuller so I guess watching him jump around in nothing but a loincloth worked for her.

My eyes were closing as I settled in for an afternoon nap when I heard a faint noise at their front door. I ignored it and shifted to get more comfortable. Then I heard it again. Scratching.

Like a dog scratching at the aluminum screen door.

"Scooter!" I yelled, and ran for the door.

My dog lay at the front door, his sides heaving. He couldn't stand, but George, hearing my excitement, came running and picked him up and brought him inside. I noticed the streak of blood on the screen.

His paws were bloody and his tongue lolled lifelessly, but he looked at me and his eyes spoke to me: *I came back to you. You believed I would and I did.*

George took off the new collar and the five feet or so of chain lead that Scooter had dragged with him from wherever he'd come from. Then he examined my dog and said that, aside from his paws, he seemed fine, just exhausted. He was going to be all right.

Tears came quickly to my eyes and I thrust my hand into my pocket and clutched at the dogtag. Squeezing my hand and eyes tight, I whispered a thank you to whatever force brought my dog back to me.

That was the last prison break.

❖ ❖ ❖

That was back in 1968. Today, over forty-five years later, I watch Scooter as he pulls his old, old bones up and makes his way over to his food dishes to listlessly lap at the water. Most of his fur is gone now, and what's left is white. His flesh hangs off him like the skin of a rotted fruit. It's pulled down from his eyes, leaving those once-clear brown eyes recessed into sagging folds that constantly run with waxy fluids. I hear his bones clicking as he walks or moves.

But by far, the worst of it is whenever he lowers his hindquarters in preparation to lie down. Every time he does it, Scooter's hips break. I hear them. I see his body jerk with the pain. But somehow, things go back to normal and, after a couple of hours or so, he's able to slowly get up again. Somehow the bones knit and the sockets are reslotted.

I know it has something to do with that dogtag.

It's something that I should have taken care of years ago. Decades ago.

I should have let go.

But Scooter's been my dog now for over forty-seven years. And it's hard to let go of the pet that taught you that miracles can happen.

He watches me as I take my coffee out to the back porch. I don't take him with me anymore as he can't make it down the three stairs to the deck, though his fleshless tail sways from side to side in a parody of its youthful exuberance. I give him a sad smile as I walk around the corner of the house and settle into the porch swing and sip my coffee.

I get myself ready. I've decided. Today's the day.

I reach into my pocket and pull out the worn dog tag. I've rubbed it so much over the years that only the *S* and the *R* are still visible.

I put down my coffee cup and look at the tag intently.

And then, before I can think about it anymore, before I can talk myself out of it yet again, I rub the tag between thumb and forefinger and I whisper, "It's time to escape, Scooter."

And this time, as the tears come once again to my eyes, I add, "I love you, Scooter."

I can only hope that will help him on his last prison break.

✤ ✤ ✤

TOBIN ELLIOTT is a Creative Writing teacher, a freelance editor and writing mentor, and a writer of horror. He has one published short story; three novellas: *Soft Kiss Hard Death*, *The Wrong* and *Vanishing Hope*; and *No Hope*, his first novel, will be published this year.

This Strange Way of Dying

By Silvia Moreno-Garcia

~ 1 ~

GEORGINA MET DEATH when she was ten. The first time she saw him she was reading by her grandmother's bedside. As Georgina tried to pronounce a difficult word, she heard her grandmother groan and she looked up. There was a bearded man in a top hat standing by the bed. He wore an orange flower in his buttonhole, the kind Georgina put on the altars on *el Dia de los Muertos*, the Day of the Dead.

The man smiled at Georgina with eyes made of coal.

Her grandmother had warned Georgina about Death and asked her to stand guard and chase it away with a pair of scissors. But Georgina had lost the scissors the day before when she made paper animals with her brother, Nuncio.

"Please, please don't take my grandmother," she said. "She'll be so angry at me if I let her die."

"We all die," Death said and smiled. "Do not be sad."

He leaned down, his long fingers close to grandmother's face.

"Wait! What can I do? What should I do?"

"There's not much you can do."

"But I don't want grandmother do die yet."

"Mmmm," said Death tapping his foot and taking out a tiny black notebook. "Very well. I'll spare your grandmother. Seven years in exchange of a promise."

"What kind of promise?"

"Any promise. Promises are like cats. A cat may have stripes, or it may be white and have blue eyes and then it is a deaf cat, or it could be a Siamese cat, but it'll always be a cat."

Georgina looked at Death and Death looked back at her, unblinking.

"I suppose... yes," she mumbled.

"Then this is a deal," he said, "Now, have a flower."

He offered her the bright, orange *cempoalxochitl*.

✤ ✤ ✤

That first encounter with Death had a profound effect on Georgina. Fearing Death's reappearance, and thinking he awaited her behind every corner, Georgina took no risks. While Nuncio broke his left arm and scraped his knees, Georgina sat in the darkened salon. When Nuncio rode wildly on his horse or jumped into an automobile, Georgina waited for him by the road. Finally, when other girls started swooning over young men and wishing one of them would sign his name on a dance card, Georgina refused to partner up and join the revelry.

What was the point? She was going to die any day soon, why should she fall in love? Death would come to collect her tomorrow, maybe the day after tomorrow.

She selected the dress that she would be buried in and asked her mother for white lilies at the funeral. She walked around the mausoleum and inspected her final resting place. Morbid scenarios of murder assaulted her. She wondered if she would die struck by a carriage, or by lightning, or in some other more remarkable fashion.

This is how seven years passed.

✤ ✤ ✤

On the seventh year grandmother died and they took her to the cemetery in the great black hearse, then gathered in the salon to drink and mourn. Georgina was standing by the piano, considering death and its many possibilities, from a bullet to an earthquake, when Catalina came over with a satisfied grin on her face.

"You'll never guess what I heard," she said. "Ignacio Navarrete is going to marry you."

"What?"

"I heard him speaking to Miguel. He's going to ask for your hand in marriage."

"But he can't!"

Georgina craned her neck, trying to spot Ignacio across the room and finally saw him in his double breasted-suit, hands covered in white silk gloves. Reptilian. Disgusting.

"I wish I *would* die," she whispered, angrily, like a bride that has been left at the altar and only now reads the clock and realizes the groom is late.

❖ ❖ ❖

When Georgina woke up, it was dark. A rustle of fabric made her sit up and a man stepped out from behind the thick velvet curtains. He wore a long coat, a burgundy vest and sported a little moustache. Though different in attire, and looking younger than she recalled, she recognized him as Death.

"I didn't really mean it," she said at once, all the scenarios of her own demise suddenly pieced together in her brain.

"Mean what?"

"Today, during the party. I didn't mean I *really* wanted to die."

"You sounded rather honest."

"But I wasn't."

"Then you want to marry that man?"

"No," she scoffed. "I don't want to die either."

"Good. I don't want you to die or marry him."

"Oh," she said.

"You sound disappointed."

"What do you want then? I mean, if you haven't come to kill me."

He produced a bouquet of orange *cempoalxochitls*, his arm stretched out towards her.

"I've come to collect a promise. Any promise, do you recall?"

"Yes," she muttered, uncertain.

"It's a promise of marriage."

Georgina stared at Death. It was the only thing she could do. She was not sure if she should laugh or cry. Probably cry and start yelling for her father. Wouldn't that be the natural reaction?

She pushed her long pigtail behind her shoulder and pressed both hands against the bed.

"I don't think I can marry you," she said cautiously.

"Why not?" he asked.

"You're Death."

"I'm one death."

"Pardon me?"

He grabbed the lilies that were next to her bed and tossed them to the floor, then placed his *cempoalxochitls* in the flower vase.

"A few hours ago you were calling for me and now you refuse me."

"I was not... even if I was... it's late," she said, reaching towards her embroidered robe. In her white cotton nightgown with the ruffles and lace trim Georgina was practically naked and she didn't think this was the best way to confront Death, or anyone else for that matter.

"Just past midnight."

"Please go," she said, quickly closing the robe, a hand at her neck.

"I cannot leave without the promise of marriage."

"I will not marry you!"

Had she yelled? Georgina pressed a hand against her mouth and immediately feared the maids would come poking their heads inside her room. And what would she say if they found a man in there?

"We have a problem. We made a deal and now I must head out empty-handed, which is impossible in my line of business."

"I'm sorry."

"Sorry," he said and smiled, white teeth flashing, "Sorry does not suffice. No, dear girl. You are indebted to me. You exchanged seven years of life for a promise"

"It isn't fair! I didn't know *what* I promised."

"A promise is a promise," he said and pulled out his black notebook. "What do you have that you can give? A cat. That is no good. A parrot. Well, they do get to live for a century but I don't think I can stand—"

"I don't want to marry a dead man."

"I'm not dead. I am Death. Particularities, details," he said scribbling in the notepad. "As you can clearly see, your hand in marriage should solve this debt of ours."

"And if I refuse?"

"Let us be reasonable. Would you like to discuss this tomorrow? Shall I meet you around noon?"

Georgina was certain she could hear her mother's sure footsteps approaching her door. Terror greater than death seized her. She wanted the stranger out of her room, out of the house before anyone realized there was a man there.

"Yes, just go!" she whispered.

Georgina went to the door, her ear pressed against it. She waited for the door to burst open. It did not. The house was quiet. Her mother slept soundly. She let out a sigh.

Georgina looked around the room. He was gone. The flowers remained, but in the morning they had turned into orange dust.

✥ ✥ ✥

Georgina's pigtail was carefully undone and her hair just as carefully swept up and decorated with jeweled pins. She descended the stairs in a tight-waisted blue dress and sat quietly at breakfast, fearing Death would knock at the door and ask to be invited in.

"Will you look at this?" her father said, brandishing the morning newspaper up. "It's deplorable. Who does this Orozco think he is? I am telling you Natalia, it is simply deplorable to see such people causing a fuss."

Georgina's mother did not reply. Her father was not asking a question, merely stating his opinion, and he expected no replies. He had been a *Porfirista* before, now he was a *Maderista* and God knew what he might become the day after. At the table, his wife and his two children were supposed to nod their heads and agree in polite silence: father was always right.

"So then, what are your plans for today?" her father asked as he tossed the paper aside.

"I want to get some new dresses made," Georgina said.

"Nuncio, will you be accompanying your sister?"

"Father, I'm heading to the Jockey Club today," Nuncio said, slipping into his childish, thin voice even though he was a year older than Georgina.

"I want to go alone. I don't need him with me," Georgina said curtly.

Everyone turned to look at her, frowning at the tone she had just used.

"Young ladies do not go out of their houses without proper escorts," her mother reminded her, each word carefully enunciated; a velvet threat.

"This is hardly going out," Georgina countered, knowing well her mother would scold her later for using such a tone with her.

But it would be worse, much worse, if Death were to show up at her home. Perhaps if he found her outside of the house she might speak to him quickly and get rid of him for good, her family never the wiser.

"I'll meet you at *El Fenix* in the afternoon," Georgina said. It wouldn't do at all if Nuncio kept an eye on her all day. "Rosario can accompany me to the seamstress."

❖ ❖ ❖

Rosario chaperoned Georgina, but she was old and tired. Most of the time she would just stay inside the carriage with the coachman, Nicanor, while Georgina hurried into a store. That day was no exception and Georgina went alone up the narrow steps that led to the seamstress. Death, his dark coat spilling behind him, appeared at her elbow.

"Good day," he said, tipping an imaginary hat towards her. "Is today a better time to talk?"

"A little better," she muttered and quickly hurried to the ground floor, where they stood beneath the stairs, hiding in the shadows.

He reached into his pocket and took out a dead dove, trying to hand it to her. Georgina shoved it away. The dove fell on the floor.

"What are you doing?" she asked, staring at the mangled corpse of the bird.

"I thought you'd like a proper engagement present."

"Engagement? You're Death. I'm alive. Isn't that a problem?"

"Of no particular importance," he shrugged.

"Wouldn't you prefer to marry someone who is dead?"

"Who do you take me for? Do you think I want to go dancing with a cadaver?"

"You don't know me."

"Easily solved. Let us go to a bar and…"

"A bar?!"

"Let us get to know each other somewhere, anywhere."

"Nowhere," she whispered, scandalized by the suggestion.

"Well, then it's back to the beginning," he said and took out of his notebook and a pencil. "I guess I'll have to take fourteen years of your life then…"

The pencil dangled in mid-air.

"Fourteen?"

"Compound interest."

"Wait," she said. "We can negotiate this."

"Marriage."

"What would you do with a wife? Have little skeletons and make me cook your meals?"

"Do you like to cook?"

"No!"

"Look, it's a simple matter. Balance and algebra. Duality and all that. Lord and lady. Do you know what I mean?"

She didn't know what to say. She had to talk to the seamstress, had to meet her brother afterwards and maybe Rosario would wake up and wander into the building.

"It would be beautiful," he told her.

Death wove a silver necklace around her neck with vines and birds. The dove fluttered back to life and landing on her hands transformed into a hundred black pearls which spilled onto the floor.

It was all wonderful.

He leaned forward, smelling faintly of incense and copal, of candles burning on the altars. His eyes were so very black, so very deep, and she thought she'd never seen eyes like that, eyes dark and quiet as the grave.

She wondered if his lips might taste like sugar skulls.

It was terrifying.

Georgina wept. She tried to hide her face, mortified.

"What is wrong?" Death asked.

"I don't want to," she said.

He frowned. With a wave of his hand the pearls melted away.

"I see. Very well Georgina, perhaps we can revisit our agreement."

Georgina rubbed her eyes and looked up at him.

"I want a day of your life. One day of your heart."

"Just one day?"

"Only one. Tomorrow morning tell everyone you are sick and do not leave your room. I will visit you."

"Yes," she said.

And then he was gone, gone into the shadows, and she ran up the stairs to the dressmaker.

✤ ✤ ✤

Georgina told the maids that she felt sick and locked the door. She went behind her painted screen and changed into a simple skirt and blouse. Death appeared early and Georgina sat down in a chair, not knowing what was supposed to happen.

"Perfect. A phonograph," he said, and ran to the other side of the room. "What kind of music do you like?"

"I don't like music. My father bought it for me."

"What about films?" Death asked, as he fiddled with her recordings, picking one.

"I don't watch films. I wouldn't be going to a *carpa*."

"Why not?"

"People are rowdy and my mother... oh, she would go insane if she heard I'd gone anywhere near that sort of place."

"I love films. I love anything that is new and exciting. The automobile, for example, is a wonderful method of transportation."

Music began to play and Georgina frowned.

"What is that?" she asked.

"You like it? It's ragtime. Come on, dance with me."

She wondered what she would do if her mother came peeking through the keyhole and saw her dancing with a stranger. What her mother would do to her.

"I don't dance."

"I'll show you."

He took her hand and pulled her up, two steps in the same direction onto the same foot, then a closing step with the other foot. It seemed simple but Georgina kept getting it wrong.

"What?" he asked.

"I didn't think Death would dance. I thought you'd be more... gloomy. And thin."

"So I'm fat, am I?"

"I mean skeleton thin, and yellow."

"Why yellow?"

"I don't know. Or maybe red. Like in Poe's story."

"My sister likes red."

"You have siblings?"

"Lots and lots of them."

Georgina, busy watching her feet, finally got it right and laughed.

❖ ❖ ❖

Georgina noticed the glass of wine, the grapes and cheese and wondered if she should drink and eat. She recalled how Persephone had been trapped with only six grains of pomegranate. What would happen to her if she ate one whole cheese?

"You're not hungry?" Death said, and lay down on the Persian rug as comfortably and nonchalantly as if he were having a picnic in a field of daisies instead of in her room. "What are you thinking about?" Georgina sat very neatly at his side, smoothing her skirt and trying to keep an air of decorum.

"What is your sister like?" she asked, not wanting to talk about Persephone.

"Which one?"

"The one that wears red."

"Oh, her. She's trouble, that one. Hot-headed and angry and crimson. She's definitely not a lady. Or maybe a lady of iron. Tough girl."

"And your brothers?"

"Well, there's one who is like water. He slips in and out of houses, liquid and shimmering, and leaves a trail of stars behind."

Georgina tried to picture this and frowned. But she couldn't really see his sister or his brother as anything but skeletons in *papel picado*, pretty decorations for November's altars.

The clock struck midnight, chiming and groaning. The twenty-four hours he had asked for would come to an end soon. Georgina wouldn't see him again. Well, hopefully not until she was a very old and wrinkled lady. Probably a married lady; Mrs. Navarrete with five children and sixteen grandchildren, bent over a cane and unable to dance to any kind of music.

"And then I'll die," she muttered.

"Pardon me?" Death asked, his hands laced behind his head.

"Nothing."

But now that the idea of old age had taken hold of her, now that she could picture herself in wedding and baptismal and anniversary pictures, grey-haired with time stamped on her face, suddenly she wasn't afraid of death. She wasn't afraid of death for the first time in years: she was afraid of life. Or at least, the life she was able to neatly see, the cards laid out with no surprises.

It was horrible.

"I hate my hair," she said and she got up, standing before the full-length mirror, and she had no idea why she said this or why the silly chignon made her so furious all of a sudden.

Her fingers tangled in the curls at the nape of her neck and she pulled them, several pins bouncing on the rug.

"I like it," he said, looking over her shoulder and at her reflection.

He smelt of flowers and incense. She thought Death would smell of damp earth and catacombs and be ice cold to the touch. But she'd been wrong about many details concerning Death. Curiously she slipped a hand up, brushing his cheek.

No, he wasn't cold at all but warm and human to the touch. In the mirror their eyes locked.

"Don't touch me," he warned her, "or something in you will die."

"I don't believe it," she replied, and kissed him on the lips, even if she half-believed it.

He tasted sweet.

Death is sweet, she thought and giggled at the thought. He smiled at her, teeth white and perfect and then his smile ebbed and he was serious. He looked at her and she thought he was seeing through the layers of skin and muscle, looking at her naked skeleton and her naked self.

"If you touch me again I'll take your heart," he whispered.

"Then take it," she said with a defiance she hadn't thought she possessed, wishing to die a little.

She slept in death's arms, naked over a rug of orange petals.

~ 2 ~

Georgina had spent the last seven years of her life thinking every day about Death. But now she did not think about him, not even for an instant; she did not think about life either. In fact, she thought and said very little.

Like a clockwork figurine she rose from her bed, ate her meals and went to mass. But she wasn't really there, instead, she lay suspended in a sleepy haze, resembling a somnambulist walking the tightrope.

Sometimes Georgina would stir, the vague sensation that she'd forgotten something of importance coursing through her body, and then she shook her head. The feeling was insignificant, a phantom limb stretching out.

❖ ❖ ❖

Georgina rode in her carriage down Plateros. Rosario snored while Georgina observed the men in top hats walking on the sidewalks and the *cargadores* shoving their way through the crowds. She'd gone to her fitting with the seamstress that morning. Her wedding gown. Now she thought about that day almost a year ago when she'd met Death underneath the stairs.

There was something she was forgetting.

There was something else.

But who cared? Wedding gown. Marriage. Life pre-written.

She was getting married in a month's time. Ignacio had bought her a necklace crammed with diamonds from *La Esmeralda* and her mother had cooed over the extravagant purchase. It would be a good marriage, her father said.

Georgina did not care.

And now she sat so very quietly, so very still, like a living-dead doll staring out the window.

Something caught her eye: a woman in scarlet, her dress so gaudy it burned even among the other prostitutes who were now starting to sneak into the streets as night fell.

Red.

Georgina had been in a trance for twelve months and she had not even realized it. In a little coffin of her own making, Georgina dreamed pleasant dreams. Now she awoke. Apple dislodged, glass crashing.

"Stop!" she ordered Nicanor, and the carriage gave a little jolt.

Georgina climbed out and went towards the woman.

"I know your brother," Georgina said when she reached her.

The prostitute smiled a crimson smile, a hand on her hips.

"Do you? Bastard son of a bitch-mother. Run along."

"No. I mean … I thought … do you know me?"

"He got a babe in you, has he? Go bother someone else dear, I've got to work."

Georgina was confused. For a moment she thought she had the wrong woman. How could she be mistaken? What could she do? What could she say?

Georgina took a deep breath.

"He is like flowers made of blackness and when he kissed me he tasted like the night."

The prostitute's face did not change. She was still grinning with her ample mouth but her eyes burrowed deeper into Georgina, measuring her.

"What do you want?" asked the red woman.

"Where is he?"

"He's not here. Not now."

"Where is he?"

"What does it matter? You don't want anything to do with him."

"I said, where is he?"

The woman, taller than Georgina, looked down at her as though she were a small dog yelping at her feet.

"You should head home and marry your rich man, little girl. Forgetting is easy and it doesn't hurt."

"I have already been forgetting."

"Forget some more."

"He has something of mine."

The red death, the woman-death, sneered.

"He'll be at *Palacio Nacional* in ten days, but then he heads north. Catch him then or you'll never catch him at all."

She walked away leaving Georgina standing by the window of a café. Nicanor squinted and gave her a weird look.

"What are you doing talking to that lady, miss Georgina?"

"I'm doing nothing," she replied and rushing back into the carriage slammed the door shut.

✤ ✤ ✤

When Georgina returned home, her father was very happy and her mother sat on the couch, pale with watery eyes.

"What is it?" she asked.

"The cadets at *Tacubaya* are up in arms," her father said.

"They're fighting at the *Zócalo*," her brother said. "They're shooting with machine guns from *Palacio National*."

And then she thought Death would be at *Palacio Nacional* in ten days. He had arrived early.

"We'll get Don Porfirio back," her father said, and as usual he was already changing his allegiances, Madero completely forgotten.

✤ ✤ ✤

It was like a party. A small and insane party. Her father talked animatedly about the events of the day, foretelling the brilliant return to the good old days, to Don Porfirio. But then the chattering grew sparse.

They said several newspaper offices had been set on fire. They said many people were dead. The roar of the cannons echoed non-stop. It got underneath their skin as they sat in the salon. Very quietly, very carefully, the doors were closed, locked with strong wooden beams from the inside.

The electricity had gone out and Georgina lay in the dark listening to the machine guns. They seemed very near.

She pressed a hand against her lips and thought Death must be there, outside, walking through the darkened city.

Her father had the carriage packed with everything he could think to carry. Even a mattress was tied to the roof.

"We're going to Veracruz in the morning," her father repeated. "We're going to Veracruz on the train."

Was there even a train left? The streets were teeming with prisoners that had escaped from Belén and they said the Imperial had been destroyed. Would there be any trains for them?

"We're going to Veracruz in the morning."

"Your hair, pull your hair up, girl," her mother ordered, but Georgina did not obey her. It seemed ridiculous to worry about hair pins.

Her mother turned around to scream at the maids. Something or the other needed to be taken. Something or the other was valuable and they would have to pack it.

It was the tenth day.

❖ ❖ ❖

On the tenth night Georgina tiptoed down the great staircase and stood at the large front door with the heavy wooden beam in place. Nicanor was sitting with his back to the door.

"What is it, miss?" he asked.

"I need to go out tonight," she said.

"You can't do that. They're fighting."

"I've got to go meet someone. And he won't wait for me," she took out the necklace. "I'll trade you this for a horse and a gun."

The necklace was worth a small fortune. That was what her father had said when he held it up and it shimmered under the chandeliers. Nicanor looked down, staring long and quiet at the jewels.

"I'll be back by dawn," she said.

"No, you won't."

"The fighting has ceased for the night. There's no noise from the cannons."

"What would you be looking for...?"

"A man," she said.

"Does he really mean that much to you?"

What a question. What did she know? How dare he ask it? How could she answer it? But there were so many things she never thought she might be able to do, and she'd done them.

"Yes," she said. "Yes, I think he does."

Nicanor took out a pistol.

~ 3 ~

The streets had transformed. The buildings had strange new shadows. It was a different city. Georgina rode through the night and the night had no stars, only the barking of dogs. She turned a street and a horse came her way, galloping with no rider on its back. The air smelled of iron and there was also another more unpleasant smell: somewhere nearby they were burning the dead.

Closer to the *Zócalo* she began to meet people, wounded men tottering by, and women. So many women. Tending to their wounded, with *cananas* across their chest and a gun at their hip. She wondered where they came from and who they were fighting for. They might be with Felipe Ángeles, called over to help Madero stall the wave of attackers. They might be anyone.

But he wasn't there and his very absence struck her as unnatural. He must be hiding.

"I am not leaving," she whispered, gripping the reins.

She rushed through streets that snaked and split and went up a hill. The city and the night had no end. She rode through them, not knowing where she was. Georgina believed she might be near Lecumberri or maybe going down Moneda. She saw a car pass her, shinning black, and kept riding.

She stumbled onto a wide street with a horse laying in the middle of it, its entrails on the ground. A group of *rurales* were walking her way. Georgina hid in the shadows, held her pistol and watched them go by.

She thought of death; a bullet lodged in her skull. She wanted to go back home.

"I'm not leaving. Show yourself, coward," she muttered.

And then she saw him, or at last he allowed her to see him, standing in an alley. He had a straw hat that shadowed his face but she recognized Death.

"What are you doing, Georgina?" he asked. "You're far from home tonight. Why are you looking for me? We've made our trade."

She dismounted, staring at his face of grey and shadows.

"It was not a fair trade."

"I was more than generous."

"You didn't warn me," she said, and she shoved him against the wall. "I've died."

"Love is dying. Or maybe it's not. It is the opposite. I forget."

"Give me my heart. It's of no use to you."

"On the contrary. It's of no use to *you*, my dear. For what will you do with this heart except let it grow stale and musty in a box?"

"It's mine."

"You couldn't have missed it that much. It's been a year and you haven't remembered it at all."

"It was not yours for the taking!"

"But you didn't want it. You wanted to die and you didn't want it anymore."

"That was before."

"Before what?"

He looked up, the shadows retreating from his face. He had shaved his moustache. He looked younger. A boy, and she a girl.

"I said a day and it was a day. What's fair is fair. You had no right to sneak out with it."

"I warned you," he replied.

"You didn't explain anything at all."

"It was given freely."

"For a day!"

"Sometimes one day is forever."

"You are a sneaky liar, a fraud…"

"Go home Georgina," he said. "My brothers are headed here. Madero dies soon and it'll be very dangerous."

"You're killing him?"

"No. Not I. I'm killing an era. But one of my siblings will. Either way, you'll want to go."

The sound of bullets hitting a wall broke the quiet of the night. Then it faded. Georgina trembled. She wanted to run but she stayed still, her eyes fixed on Death and he looked back at her with his inky gaze. It was he who blinked and turned his head away.

"Persistent, as usual. What then? Oh, fine. Here, take your heart. Bury it in the garden like some radish and see what sprouts."

He opened his hand and a flower fell upon her palm, a bright orange *cempoalxochitl*. She cupped it very carefully, afraid it might break as easily as an egg. She thought it would be difficult to walk all the way home with her hands outstretched, yet she was ready to do it. She'd put it in a box and ship it to Veracruz.

And then, unthinking, driven by impulse or instinct, Georgina crushed the flower against her mouth and it turned to dust upon her lips.

"I hate you," she whispered. "You've changed the world."

"They'll build new palaces, Georgina."

"I don't mean the palaces."

She kissed him, yellow-orange dust still clinging to her mouth. She felt a tear streak her cheek as the heart beat inside her chest once more.

The shadows shifted, turning golden and then swirling black. He rested his forehead against hers, quiet, eyes closed.

"I'm going to Chihuahua. I'm meeting with Villa after this," he said. "It'll be long. It'll be seven years."

"You'll need me."

He opened his eyes and these were golden, like the dawn.

"I do."

He motioned to her horse, which came to them quietly. He offered her a hand and she climbed in front of him, both now clad in the ink of night.

Such is the way of death.

Such is the way of love.

❖ ❖ ❖

Mexican by birth, Canadian by inclination. **SILVIA MORENO-GARCIA**'s debut novel *Signal to Noise*, about magic, music and Mexico City, is out now. Some of her stories appear in the collection *Love & Other Poisons*, and in a bunch of anthologies.

The Deaths of
Jeremiah Colverson

by George Wilhite

~ I ~

JOSHUA ROSE FROM the quagmire, blood and innards still seeping from his fresh wounds. In the next few moments, the last of his life, his recently defiled body fell away like a heavy uniform. Much lighter on his feet, he stepped away from the carnage in the jungle.

He looked down upon his corpse.

I am no longer that husk of flesh and bone. So this is what it feels like to become a ghost?

I feel no pain.

The jungle still surrounded him, but a thick mist shrouded the scene, much denser than he remembered existing *in the shit*. Grunts from his own unit, and others he didn't recognize, walked in step with him. Joshua sensed their forward motion was not of their own volition. *Some force is compelling us in this direction*, he thought.

Clenching his eyes, trying to piece together the moments before death, Joshua noticed he continued walking forward. He thought: *close your eyes — think about what happened — stop walking*, but his body rejected that final command, reinforcing his notion that some force coerced them forward.

He remembered…

Charlie was everywhere. The cacophony of rapid fire from both sides and the random screaming of orders brought the jungle to violent life. Tracers and sprays of blood in the mist the

186

only reminder this was reality, since these sporadic firefights were surreal nightmares fought against an enemy often only seen when dead. Ice Cube and Trickster trapped in that hole. Yes, that's how I earned this immortality. Saved their asses and then stepped on a land mine.

Out of the mist, a skeleton appeared. Walking toward the soldier ghosts in a kind of comic dance, it looked like a prop from a cheap horror flick. Joshua could not hold back a caustic smile. Is this a joke? Is that thing made out of plastic or papier-mâché? As this figure of mystery drew nearer, Joshua realized it was real after all. Its bones yellowed with age, creaking as it walked, jaw upturned in a precocious grin. The creature maintained a slow speed, like it had all the time in the world.

Perhaps its most ridiculous aspect was the Halloween costume it wore. Joshua thought of the outfit as a costume because it didn't seem logical Death would don the accoutrements of a soldier. Hanging on Death like a suit two sizes too large was the same uniform the grunts wore.

Why am I suddenly naming this bag of bones Death? Yet somehow, he just knew. *And what's up with that get-up?* Death reached the front of the procession, stretched out his hands, and guided the soldiers forward. Though all the others obeyed, Joshua wasn't of their accord. While he admired their stoic complacency, with each passing moment he pulled back toward the rear of the company, resisting this macabre leader.

As the soldiers followed Death, their random shuffle became a synchronized march in perfect formation. Soon, this communal exercise turned whimsical. *A dance. Yes, the fools are* dancing *to the afterlife. I can understand acceptance,* Joshua thought. *But really? Dancing with Death?* He smirked at the absurdity of those three words.

"Come on!" he yelled as they disappeared into the horizon of the dreamlike landscape. "You crazy jarheads. Fight back. Show some balls. Skank! Weasel!" He hoped their nicknames would get their attention. "Don't go so easy." But the more he screamed, the further the chasm grew between him and these submissive subjects drifting into the world of shadow.

His own defiance left Joshua behind. *But I'm not back in the shit either,* he thought. A feeling of limbo hung in the air, a region between reality and the unknown finale of Death's march.

They're headed to a river. On its shore a ferry waits. They pay the ferryman and cross that river to the Underworld.

Where did those words come from? The others were so far away he could not see such details. *Déjà vu. That's what's happening.*

"Ah, the memory crashes back, hmm?" Death stood before Joshua, devoid of the uniform now that his performance was over.

"What?" Joshua's tone did not hide his irritation.

"Of the other times. You are a stubborn boy. Now Joshua Campbell is no more. Just another statistic. This is your *fourth* time around. Three innocents lost to quell your desires. And still you refuse the *Danse Macabre*, hmm?" As Death carried on, Joshua marveled that his bones were as animated as any living being. "Yes, you feel it coming back. Stop talking and just let it happen. Again. Sit down. Close your eyes."

Joshua obeyed.

Death whispered in his ear. "It all began the first time you died. During your country's civil war..." The timbre of Death's voice produced a trance. Joshua felt bony hands on his shoulders as he drifted off.

Joshua listened, to the narrative without comment...

"Your birth name, all those years ago, was Jeremiah Colverson. You see? Always the same initials. Clever, hmm? My idea. Sorry, I digress. Nice to have your undivided attention. No, don't worry, you don't have to listen to me prattle on, telling you all this. Why tell what can be shown, I always say. I'm basically wasting time while I get this all going ... ah yes, here we are ... now it will play out like a dream for you, or one of those picture shows you people love so much. Just watch and remember. Your name is Jeremiah Colverson."

The battlefield of the Civil War South. Chaos. Blood, sweat, humidity, filth. There was Jeremiah — eighteen and eager to show those Yankees a thing or two — leading the charge, emptying his rifle, then drawing a pistol, and finally engaging in hand to hand combat. This is the day of his first death. Death arrives in much the same way as this afternoon. Jeremiah's spirit stands above his body, shocked, angry. The argument ensues. Joshua does not hear any words exchanged but intuition tells him the conversation mirrors the one he just had with Death.

"Yes and no," *Death's voice returns, like a voiceover in a movie.* "It was originally about heroism, being a good soldier. Your forefathers had always been soldiers— in England, The Revolution, and King Philip's

War. You felt like a failure. You begged me for more time. Jeremiah's time is up, I told you. But I'll see what I can do."

Death arranges a new identity for Jeremiah. A soldier in World War I on the German front lines, John Carter, is taken to the Underworld prematurely, his soul replaced by Jeremiah's. This process is repeated two more times— Jack Corelli, World War II, and Joshua Campbell, Vietnam. Each time, the soldier's argument is the same. It is too soon. I want to be a good soldier. A hero. Please send me back. Each time, he indeed performs an act of heroism leading to his death, but continues bargaining with Death, who grows spiteful now of this pretentious young man who refuses to learn the dance and follow him to the River Styx.

~ II ~

Joshua/Jeremiah awoke, leapt to his feet. Shaking his head, he looked toward Death and started to speak.

Death held up a hand to silence him. "So you see, *J. C.*," Death added snide emphasis to those initials. "You've been a thorn in my side for a long time. Now you fall back once more and refuse to join me? This senseless chaos in the jungle was still not enough for you?"

"I ... well ... I dunno," he stammered. "Why do you make me forget every time?"

"The last thing I need is some maniac spouting off about how I gave him more time. I get enough of your types as it is without encouraging it."

"I did save two buddies, but my death still seems pretty pointless."

"Joshua — no, *Jeremiah* for the remainder of this conversation — how long will you sing this song, so discordant with the *Danse Macabre*? I am running out of patience."

"But you continue honoring my request. Why?"

Death exhaled a weary sigh. "My word is my bond."

"Well, hell, that explains it! You're going to confuse a dumb grunt with riddles now. That it?"

"It is no trick. It is as simple as what I said. My word is my bond. The first time, and every time, I have ended our encounters with the same words. By now, you should recall those words?"

Joshua suddenly remembered. "A poem."

"Ah, you *do* remember. A *type* of poem, I suppose, though I don't fancy myself any sort of poet. More importantly, it is a pact:

I shall grant your request
Until you lay down your arms
We will join hands by your behest
When your last battle is done
But— *Memento Mori*."

"I still don't get it. Why can't you just tell me to stick it? You're toast. Follow my ass to Hell?"

"First of all, and I have explained this before: I do not take anyone to Hell. Our dance ends at the shores of the River Styx. Charon, The Ferryman, boats you across to the shores of the Underworld. The outskirts as you would call it. I know nothing of what happens beyond the ferry dock.

"Secondly, there is a line in the bond that states *we will join hands by your behest*. I cannot force your decision."

This gave Jeremiah an idea. "I do want another chance to serve my country. Hopefully in a more honorable conflict. But this time I want to remember everything that has happened so far."

Death appeared to think long and hard, possibly about the potential dangers of this proposition. Maybe he didn't want to get labeled a softy if the beans were spilled. "Alright. Next time around, you will remember all. *But*, you must agree that telling anyone about our … arrangement … will nullify this agreement. You will die on the spot."

It was done…

~ III ~

God, this heat is oppressive! 'Nam sucked. Tropical shit to deal with— mosquitoes, freaking wild pigs, didn't think a war zone could be more heinous. This is equally fucked, just different. Instead of eighty degrees and near a hundred percent humidity, it's just flat out breath-sucking hot. Yesterday it finally reached one hundred twenty degrees. Didn't know it was possible for humans to live at one hundred twenty fucking Fahrenheit.

Jeremiah, now Jude Colchord, laid beneath a Jeep some *raghead* decided to wire with enough C4 to fuck this neighborhood up good. Whoever the culprit was, he must really be strung out on hate.

Every time I am under one of these car bombs I have two possible ends — hero or hamburger — savior of the hour or brains and guts decorating another shitty burnt out hull of what was once a neighborhood.

Red wire. Green. Orange. White. Too many choices. The knowledge of his bargains, that he was cheating Death, and the memories of the other wars, all clouded his thoughts, making concentration on deactivating the bomb or bombs nearly impossible.

Wire cutters in hand, he honestly had no clue which one to cut.

Apparently, this Jude Colchord was some kind of stone cold stud. "Never met a bomb that could fuck with his head," he heard one of the jarheads say. Jude disarmed seventy four bombs before some *towelhead* sniper hiding on a roof emptied an assault rifle into his chest. Even though he was wearing a vest, a couple of the bullets penetrated the material, one pierced his heart.

Jude's spirit caught a break, was allowed to leave this world of grief, and Jeremiah's entered his body. His unit gasped when he rose from the earth; they had been certain he was dead.

When Jeremiah made his last bargain, Death had warned him. *If you really want me to change the rules, leave your memories intact, there will be complications. You have continued to be a good soldier, and fit in each time we have done this, because I have always erased your previous lives. You knew the rules of engagement and the battlefields because your primary conscience, at least while awake, was that of the dead solider whose body you took over.*

Jeremiah had cut him off. "Stop talking and do it already."

Death had obliged.

Now, he was here, mind on overdrive, just as Death prophesied, Jude's expertise failing in the detritus of Jeremiah's worried thoughts.

Jeremiah/Jude cut the green wire. The payload of the detonation was beyond comprehension. How could that destructive force be packed into a rusty old Jeep? There would not be a body to bury. His organic material was spread over the two blocks. The six soldiers who escorted him here died instantly.

It happened again, just like in the jungle...

The devastation still spread before them, fire and smoke rising, chaos in full bloom as survivors raced about. But the seven dead soldiers stood in the street, surrounded by dozens of civilian casualties, all their bodies intact. Some moments passed before most of the others in this confused assembly realized they were ghosts.

Jeremiah knew immediately. He took several steps backward. Death was coming to perform his hideous dance. *No fucking way. This is entirely my fault. I don't deserve to dance to the Styx.*

Death found him hours later, hiding in a burnt out office building.

"What are you doing?" The bone man wore a Kevlar helmet and vest. On his left breast a button read: *Born to Kill.* "You thought you could hide from me? I am like that shepherd Jesus mentions in your Bible. Ninety nine sheep don't cut it. I must account for all."

"Not ready to dance, old friend. This is bullshit. I just got here."

"You are the one who wanted to change the conditions. I told you—"

"Yeah, yeah. You're so fucking *smart.*"

Death shrugged.

"First car I get under fucking blows. This was not a legit shot. Tell you what. One more go, and I promise it'll be the last."

"The next war might really break you, young soldier. It won't be pretty."

"War never is. But at least give me one more shot at valor."

Death threw up his hands. "I suppose you'll have to find out for yourself. There is no valor in the next war."

"Just do it. One last time."

And one last time, it was done...

~ IV ~

He was transported to a battleground of eerie familiarity. Its terrain was much like South Carolina during the Civil War that set this whole crazy return-from-the-dead thing into motion. *Impossible. Wars are not fought on our own soil anymore. It must just* look like *America.*

"Get yer ass over here, boy!" A disembodied voice called out from the confusion.

Jeremiah obeyed, running in the direction of the order.

He reached a trench and leapt inside. The same voice that drew him in scoffed: "'fuck you doing? Get your virgin ass down here."

The trench held about a dozen men of various ages and ethnicities. Of all the militaries Jeremiah had served in, this most resembled the first. Again, an eerie feeling of the Civil War days, even though he could see that the technology was modern.

"Answer me or I'll throw you to the Separatist dogs, you prick. I oughta rape and roll ya myself for runnin' off like that. What'dya think this is? Fucking VR video game? This is where we fight for our nation. Do *NOT* run off like that again or I'll do ya myself."

"Yes, sir."

The man guffawed. His breath reeked. He looked like he hadn't bathed or shaved in a month. *This guy's in charge?*

"Sir? Listen to the fuckin' new dick. What'rya callin' me sir, for, kid? Shit. Ain't nobody actually in charge here. You know that. Just tryin' to keep these Sodomites off our land's all." He laughed again, showing a mouth of rotten teeth.

Jeremiah peered at the men in the trench. No standard uniforms for this lot. They wore civvies— the only common elements in their wardrobe were navy blue caps and black T-shirts bearing an emblem he did not recognize.

Jeremiah didn't say anything, trying to take this all in. Death appeared, hunkering next to him. This was a first. Death never showed up while he was still alive. The skeleton wore one of the black shirts. Grinning, he pointed to the patch. It read: *The Southern Civilian Commonwealth.*

Fuck! The truth struck him the moment he read the moniker. *Things have come full circle, then?* Death nodded, having heard his thoughts. "Son of a bitch, a *civil war*?" he said the words aloud without thinking.

The rotten man laughed again. "Who you talkin' to now, tender dick? Hey, guys. We got ourselves some kind of psycho fuck here." Laughter all around him. "'course, it's a civil war! Nothin' but the third one in the last three years. Where you from? Fucking Mars? Maybe you oughta get some sleep, boy."

No valor. Jeremiah had to admit. Death had warned him. *There won't be any hero's death for me here. I should have stopped long ago. All the sacrifices we soldiers made over the decades for this? To be back where we started?*

Jeremiah pulled the pistol from the would-be leader's holster and placed the barrel on his temple.

~ V ~

The line of dead soldiers from the Fourth Civil War of the United States of America was tragic in length and scope. In all his previous deaths, Jeremiah had never joined such a long procession. While women were added to the ranks the last time around, the dead here included many more women, and child soldiers.

Jeremiah was still reeling from the revelation that his country had slid into this decay; his heart felt broken by the return of the in-fighting. Deep inside, he wanted to resist Death once more, but he held firm. This was the final straw and he, like Death, kept his word.

Now that Jeremiah was compliant and falling in line, Death was nowhere in sight, presumably at the front of the line, leading the way.

Jeremiah nodded and smiled. "You got me," he whispered. "I will follow." Death's pact resounded in his mind. This time, he remembered every word without assistance:

I shall grant your request
Until you lay down your arms
We will join hands by your behest
When your last battle is done
But Memento Mori.

"*Memento Mori*," he said aloud. Never any kind of scholar, especially crap like Latin, he had not known what those two words meant and didn't ask Death to explain. "Remember your mortality. That's what it means," he said. He didn't care that he talked aloud now. The others must be in their own worlds anyway. "I have no idea how I know that. I just do."

The procession moved in step now, right feet then left, in a rhythm, a dance, that dance of death Jeremiah had resisted for nearly two centuries. The final dance steps led to the edge of the River Styx.

A chant began, first among the dead up front, then slowly working its way back— five syllables in sync with their marching, the last one drawn out to the meter of two steps.

Memento Mori-ii.
Memento Mori-ii.
Memento Mori-ii.

Jeremiah remained in sync with his fellow pilgrims but increased his stride with each step. He wanted to move closer to the front to see Death. Once there, the familiar mist surrounding them had turned into a dense fog, but he could make out the banks of the river. He realized this was the furthest he had ever traveled towards the afterlife.

Seeing Jeremiah approaching, Death grinned in a fashion more akin to a Halloween cardboard cutout than a fearsome figure in charge of expiration.

"So you are ready, dear boy?"

Jeremiah nodded, half-smiled, at a loss for words for the first time in his exchanges with Death.

"You didn't know before, did you? *Memento Mori.*"

"Not a clue." He laughed. The relief of laughter, the overall sense of a lightness he felt in that moment made him more confident; it was time to let Death have his way.

Jeremiah reached out his hand. Death clasped it firmly.

All the time Jeremiah had bargained for, his quest for valor in battle, a heroic finish to his military career— it all seemed pointless now. Far more courage was needed for this acceptance of the end of life and the confidence to march forward.

✧ ✧ ✧

GEORGE WILHITE is the author of the horror collections *On the Verge of Madness* and *Silhouette of Darkness,* as well as nearly one hundred stories and poems in print or online.

BEST BEFORE/
BEST AFTER

THE SHADOW OF DEATH

BY PAUL KANE

YOU KNOW ME... or you think you do.

Nobody knows — or understands — who I really am. How could you? It would blow your tiny little minds. But I'm the shadow that passes over all of you at some point, obliterating life. That's why you *think* you can relate to me, but it's an illusion. Something you tell yourselves to stay sane.

Death comes for us all eventually, you say — like it's a shared experience. But you enter this world alone, and you go out of it the same way.

It's a process.

And I take no great pleasure in what I do — it is, simply, my duty. There is no enjoyment. I witness some of you out there 'taking' lives deliberately, although how can you, really? Only one of us can truly *take* life. But the look of satisfaction on your faces, the glee in the eyes as you shoot, stab, bludgeon each other until your hearts beat no more. You think you're compelled, but you don't know what real compulsion is. You're addicted to the high, that's all. The paltry release of chemicals in your brain.

But to *have* to do this. That's what it truly feels like to be me. Yet still there is no appreciation of what I do. Only scorn. You even try to ward me off ... creams and surgery to defy ageing, scientific breakthroughs, cloning... None of it will ever work. It... *I* am inevitability, pure and simple.

Don't you idiots understand? What I do gives your life meaning. You should be praising, not berating me. Oh, what do I care anyway? I gave up worrying about what you humans think a long time ago, when I was still young. Yes, I had a childhood; not in the way you imagine, but I did. A very lonely one... And it taught me a lot about the world. How it all works, what must be done in order to maintain balance. It's very complex, you see. Or you probably don't. Even the most intelligent, those who claim to understand how everything ticks, don't get it.

The young, the old, the clever and the stupid. Good or evil, I make no distinction. Some I take in batches, others individually. It's just the way it works.

For example, that apartment block fire a few months ago. I claimed thirty of you that day. Knew each and every one by name, knew their histories: where they worked, or went to school; what they liked to eat; their hobbies. My knowledge goes far beyond that of those boffins I was just talking about. And it's matched only by my power.

Take young Cheryl and her family (*I* certainly did). They were sleeping when the flames reached them on the eleventh floor. A single mother, she'd worked long and hard to look after her children— little Harry, five, and his sister Maggie, just three. Cheryl liked to take them to the park on weekends, when she wasn't working shifts at the café. Liked to push them on the swings. So much hope for the future as she looked on.

Gone now, all of them. Sad but necessary.

The elderly couple on the second floor — Albert and Rita Finnegan, both into their seventies — among the first to pass over, consumed by the fire. Albert was devoted to Rita, and had been looking after her since the first stroke seven years before. But it was growing harder for Albert to cope, with his arthritis. If you'd asked them, they would have said it was a blessing that they went, and that they'd gone *together*. Because they'd hardly ever spent any time apart since Albert asked for her hand in marriage so long ago.

You see? Balance.

But still you don't understand. I witness only confusion, fear and — in some cases — anger over what I do. Sometimes I despair. You pray to deities to help you, keep you safe. More fantasies, dreamed up by those who can't face the truth.

There *is* only me. I'm the constant. Waiting for the moment I'll be called on to act. Far from being frightened, you should be glad of this reminder. Yet you vilify me. There are artists' representations that look nothing like me, *intended* to shock. They get so much wrong. Some say I'm an angel (just told you, no religion) with wings, some that I'm a skeleton. A knight wearing black armor, riding a dark horse, wielding a sword and cleaving people in two. But am I male, female? Neither? Some even speculate I'm a monster, a giant spider-creature weaving my web of death. No. I am none of these. As I say, you couldn't possibly comprehend what I am. None of your computers can give you the answer.

And the names! My favorite, I think, is The Reaper. That's a classic. With my scythe, harvesting souls... Harvesting for what? I don't particularly want souls and wouldn't know what to do with them anyway. And I'm not helping to transport them somewhere! For some of you that's good news (the murderers, preying on the weak), for others that knowledge brings sorrow. But I'm not here to ferry you to paradise, or anywhere else.

Ever looked up the meaning in a dictionary? Reaper? Reaping? It also states 'to reap the benefit of one's exertions'. What *fucking* benefit do you think I get out of all this?

But you could say just as you don't really understand me, I don't understand you. Not as such, not anymore. I wouldn't be able to do this if I did. I must remain impartial, be neither right nor wrong, neither virtuous nor wicked. I'm pure and I'm forever.

Once upon a time, I admit, I *thought* I was in love with one of you. A girl called Lily, like the flower. Her hair was the color of sunlight, lips like rubies. If I was ever to figure out humanity it would have been through her. She could have been my Rita; I might have been her Albert. But this isn't a fairy tale, or the movies. I'm not Brad Pitt— she wasn't fucking Claire Forlani. I knew, deep down, it couldn't work. For one thing, she didn't see me. None of you do until it's too late. I actually allowed her... *wanted* her to see me. But still she didn't.

She fell in love with a boy called Thomas who, coincidentally, did look a bit like Pitt.

They're both long since gone. Not that I took any pleasure from that, either. I'm not allowed the luxury of revenge. Did she even see me at the end of her life? Maybe... it was hard to tell. She was screaming too much.

Lily... like the flower. Like the flower you send to funerals... or is that orchids? Or both? Doesn't matter. Funerals are usually connected with religion, and that doesn't factor into the equation.

No God, no Heaven, no Angels. Just me. What I do isn't pleasant; I make no apologies for that. Why should I— and who should I apologize to? Definitely not you! If you could only see yourselves.

No, I shouldn't— *can't* feel emotion. It was talking about *her* that did it. Remembering.

Remain neutral. No wavering. Not even when I look into the eyes of someone I take. Not even when I looked into hers...

Oh, you insects make me sick! You've no idea of my reach, my abilities. I may not have the luxury of enjoying it, but to snuff out that spark in you so completely — so irretrievably — takes a degree of skill. I am *all* in that moment, I am everything.

They were blue, her eyes. Like cornflowers.

Why remember that? Why did I start telling you about it? I've held my memories in check for so long...

They say that, at the end, your life flashes before your eyes. It doesn't. Only the important bits. Only the regrets, mistakes and tragedies. The kind of things you people dwell on. The misery.

You really *are* stunningly ignorant. The number of times I've tried to get you to wake up. Like a few days ago, that millionaire injury lawyer, Stoddard. All he's ever cared about is making money, mainly out of other people's misfortune. Ever hear the phrase: 'You can't take it with you?' All the stuff you can buy, but you can't buy more *time*. Can't write me a cheque and hope I'll leave you alone. I tried to explain this as he breathed his last, but he was more worried about his precious fortune in that safe.

"You're dying," I said, "and that's your major concern? Maybe you should be thinking about all you could have done with it to help your fellow man." Not that I'm the ghost of Jacob Marley or anything. I care even less about his fellow man than he did. It was the principle. All that cash and it hadn't delivered one day of real delight. He must have known I was coming sometime, but did he enjoy his life more? No. I rest my case, your honour.

Not one precious day, out having a picnic with a loved one. Wasn't even married. Nobody to hold hands with, to... to...

Memories again. Of the way her dress swished on a summer's day when she walked. Out in the countryside, laughing. Thomas holding her hand, not me.

Just the important bits. The regrets.

The blood as it splashed on that dress. Red like rubies; like her lips.

You enjoy the way that it feels to end someone's life. I don't. I can't... *ever*. But it's what I must do. What I've always done. I am the shadow that passes over all of you at some point, obliterating life.

A shadow... like the one I can see right now, moving towards me. But how... how can this—

Red like her lips. Like my hands, back then— and today.

The shadow draws closer. And, unlike you, it *does* know the truth. It knows who — what — I am. I can't help laughing, but promptly shut up.

But I'm forever. I am—

No more games, no more charades.

—the withdrawn orphan who dreamed of being something *more...*

The darkness crosses the room, sweeping the floor of this abandoned warehouse I've been forced to flee to. The place *they* will eventually find me, much later. Not that they'll be able to judge me then. No, that's happening now, by a much higher power.

It's appeared like this because that's what I believe it to be. It's how I've always described *myself...* metaphorically. But it is so much more than that. Only metres away and I can feel the iciness of its touch: black tendrils spreading out from the main body, entering my mind.

I see it suddenly as everything you people think it is. Flashing in front of my eyes, the images changing as I blink: the angel, face blank, wings unfurled and flapping; then the knight on horseback, brandishing his sword; next the monster, the spider-creature with red eyes (red like rubies, like her lips, like the blood on her dress... like the blood on my hands back then). There's blood on them now, too: as I clutch at my stomach in an attempt to hold it in— the bullets having done their worst.

All of these representations I see, and so many more:

A young boy (looks like Cheryl's son) also winged, but the wings are the color of cream. I know his name is Thanatos. *Blink.* Now an old, ugly woman, gnarled and twisted (like Rita after the stroke), with a long blue nose (cornflower blue), and a poisonous tongue. This is Giltinė. *Blink.* Suddenly a thing with three eyes and leathery skin, and skulls in its headdress— it has a snout and fanged teeth. It holds court (just as Stoddard once did) to decide my fate. This is Yama. *Blink.* Something with a bone-like head, eyes gazing out of it, all teeth, wearing a necklace of human eyeballs. Mictlantecuhtli. *Blink*. A pitch-black crow, morphing into an eel, a wolf, then a cow... then a beautiful naked woman with hair like sunshine. This is Lil... no, Morrigan the Phantom Queen. *Blink*. A toga-clad figure with tanned skin, holding a thin rod with a hook on the end... He has a jackal's head. Anubis. *Blink*. A figure in rags, standing in a boat on a smoky river, holding out a hand, waiting for payment. Charon, the Ferryman. *Blink*. A short man, wearing a tall hat, smoking a cigar, holding an apple in his left hand. Papa Ghede, the corpse of the first man who *ever* died.

Faster now, image upon image. A hooded man in a cloak, face pale, head totally bald, playing chess... *Blink*. A woman, also pale, but with black eyeliner and spiky hair— a goth, wearing a silver ankh on a chain around her neck and sporting an Eye *of Horus* tattoo below her right eye... *Blink*. A man standing next to a white sports car, dressed in a sharp designer suit, looking a bit like Samuel L. Jackson... *Blink*. A dragon-headed thing, with razor-sharp talons... *Blink*. Something that is little more than streams of crackling electricity... *Blink*. A figure made of fire, like the one that raged in the apartment block where thirty people lost their lives...

They died at my hands. Because I was pretending to be something I'm not.

And the last one, finally. The smooth, bleached skeleton holding a scythe, cloak wrapped around it like an extension of itself. Like a shadow. The (Grim) Reaper. The entity after which I was named... by those who'd been waiting for me at my last assignment, who'd been tracking me even as I tracked my next target— my research meticulous. It has been their job to try and put an end to my spree.

'The Reaper' they called me. And I am... was. Have been ever since—

Since my heart stopped.

Red as rubies; red as the blood on her dress; on my hands. Lily lying at my feet, Thomas running from the picnic, though he wouldn't escape. It was his time, just as it had been hers. I made that decision; for them, and those who followed (but I *didn't* enjoy it, honestly, not even the first. I'm not like you people out there murdering, savoring it; not like you at all!).

Only... it hadn't really been my decision to make, had it? Truth is, I've been doing this for so long, I think I'd actually convinced myself. But I can't fool him ... her ... it. The thing in front of me. The one I was emulating.

All those people had more time left, I can see that now, I'm being shown, it's passing before my eyes. All those futures: Cheryl going on to run for the local council, her son becoming a pilot, her daughter a model; Albert and Rita dying together still, but in their sleep, in their bed, not roasting alive in what must have felt like the fires of Hell (no religion, remember? there's nothing... but, oh Christ, I really hope there's *something* afterwards now). A fire *I* started with a bottle of vodka and a lit rag. Even the lawyer, Stoddard, who might not have realized the error of his ways, but whose money would pay the medical bills to keep him around 'till he was a hundred. (If he'd only told me the combination of his safe, I might even have let him live... I only needed a few thousand to keep my work going.)

I'd always assumed Death was detached. Calm, unemotional. Neutral. Impartial, neither right nor wrong, neither virtuous nor wicked. Not today. Today Death has come for me— might even have engineered this whole thing, sick to the stomach of this insect's capers.

And today Death is angry.

Now I understand what *true* power is. (And I can finally feel my heart pounding in my chest again— though not for much longer, I suspect.) The being that stands before me *is* forever, older than time itself, while time is running out for me. That's why it's been forcing me to recall every single face. How I've wasted all my allotted time; all the people I've ever wrongly taken. No, not taken, because only one of us can do that. And it isn't me... God almighty (oh please be listening now!). It. Isn't. Me.

The skeleton with the scythe is gone. That was just for effect, like all the others. To prove a point. That Death is everything we think it is, just different things to different people. Or all things to all people. I was wrong; just as it knows me, we don't just *think* we know it. We *do*, in all its forms.

The shadow is back, looming large. No, not a shadow— *I* was the shadow. At least I got that part right. I was the shadow of something much more remarkable than myself. A laughable imitation.

Time to be punished for my presumptuous behavior.

It consumes me, sliding over my body like liquid flame and burning just as harshly. I've lost so much blood from my wounds, but that isn't what's going to end me. It takes such a degree of skill to snuff out a spark so completely, molecule by painstaking molecule, and fuck does it hurt!

Now I know the secret of it all. I know who — what — Death truly is. And that knowledge finally and efficiently blows my tiny little mind.

Death comes for us all eventually. But you enter this world alone.

And you go out of it the same way.

It's a process.

> Between the idea
> And the reality
> Between the motion
> And the act
> Falls the Shadow

> *The Hollow Men*, T. S. Eliot

✣ ✣ ✣

PAUL KANE is the award-winning, bestselling author and editor of over fifty books, including: the *Arrowhead* trilogy; *The Butterfly Man and Other Stories; Hellbound Hearts;* and *The Mammoth Book of Body Horror*. His work has been optioned and adapted for the big and small screen.

AN INSPECTOR CALLS

BY REBECCA BRADLEY

HE ARRIVED ON a cross-Nile ferry jammed with customers—
with bereaved families, I mean, each bearing a shrouded corpse
on a board, and wailing fit to draw the notice of Osiris himself
through many cubits of solid sand. My new employee was easy
to spot, being the one who was not weeping, tearing at his garb,
or liberally besmirched with ashes and dust.

He was different in other ways, too, ways that did not at first
dispose me well towards him. Priests take some pride in being
a soft lot, pasty from spending their days in dark sanctuaries
and shaded temple courtyards, spreading easily into prestigious
paunches by their middle years. Apart from his spotless linen kilt,
this one looked more like a field hand or professional warrior,
tall, broad, flat-bellied, muscled like a statue, his skin almost
Nubian-dark. Over a long, well-shaped nose, he was absorbed
in watching the swarms of mourners offloading their dearly
deceased onto the shore.

"I suppose that's the new lector priest. Not bad." Nofret was
at her post on the quay, ready to direct the mourners towards the
tent of purification set up between the canal and the necropolis. She is the kite-mistress, the headwoman of the professional
mourners, twenty years in the business and very good at her
job; she is also my beloved wife and the mother of several of my
junior embalmers and my dear little daughter, Merbeset. Nobody
does grief as well as my Nofret, nor has a better eye for what
the market will bear when it comes to negotiating fees with the

bereaved. As the last corpse came ashore, she assumed a mien of warm sympathy, and waddled off to round up our new clients, with Merbeset at her heels. I left her to it and dodged through the crowd towards the lector priest.

He was just stepping onto the bank, moving with a stately grace that I was forced to admire. Perhaps, I began to think, it was no bad thing that he looked so unpriestlike. I could see him going down very well in funeral processions, well enough to add a few grains to the profits of the house. Slap a mask of Anubis over his head, and he might play the god's part far better than our current wine-soaked Overseer of the Secrets, and save us a bit on the subcontracting as well. His hands were empty. I looked past him for a porter staggering under baggage, but the priest was alone, and the last off the ferry. No matter, I thought, we could provide him with robes and a sash out of our stocks of linen until his gear arrived.

"You must be Hormaat," I said as I reached him. "I am Anubis, proprietor of this benighted necropolis."

He looked down at me over that slightly too-long nose, not into my eyes but at a spot that was roughly at the centre of my forehead. Amun bless me, he really was the tallest priest I'd ever met. After a moment of silence, he shifted his gaze downward to meet my eyes.

"You call yourself *Anubis*?" he said. "You dare to take the name of the great god himself, he who fetches the dead to the Hall of the Two Truths?"

Self-righteous pious turd, I said to myself; but *what* a resonant voice! I could imagine the effect of such sonorous tones on our living clientele, that wonderful voice booming funerary spells across an echoing necropolis. But I had to laugh at his gravity. "Anubis is not the name I was born with, my friend, but it's a damned good name for the owner of a mummy factory, wouldn't you say? Come along, Hormaat, I'll—"

He stopped me with a heavy hand on my shoulder. "I am not Hormaat."

"What do you mean?" I cried. "The guild promised he'd arrive this morning. We've got a stack of stiffs to deal with in the Cutting House, plus three or four new ones to wash from this boatload, plus two funerals tomorrow, and I'm seriously short-handed. Why isn't he coming?"

"The one that was called Hormaat in this life cannot come," said the newcomer in his rich voice. "He cannot come because he has begun his own long journey to the Hall of the Two Truths."

Now I was irritated. "You mean he's *dead*?"

"I was with him when his journey began. His flesh now lies in a tent of purification on the west bank at Thebes, while his *ka* waits for guidance at the gates of—"

"Save it for the paying customers," I broke in. "Well, may Set take him and Amemit devour his *ka*, but I suppose it can't be helped. You'll do just as well. What was your name again?"

"My name is— Saweser." He had paused for a beat before speaking his name, almost as if trying to think up a good one, and I felt a brief touch of suspicion. Was he truly a priest? Had the guild really sent him? But contemplating his grave, impassive face, I decided he just had a naturally measured way of phrasing himself, which would not come amiss when he was reading the spells.

"Saweser?" I repeated. "Son of Osiris? Well, that's another grand name for a necro priest. Have you worked with embalmers before?"

"With embalmers, no," he said, "but I have worked with the dead." He looked into my eyes so strangely that I felt my suspicions stir again. I was, however, extremely short on lector priests.

"Good, so you know some of the basics, and I guess you're not squeamish. Come along, I'll give you the tour and then get you started."

❖ ❖ ❖

Our first stop was the washhouse, as we embalmers call it amongst ourselves. To the rest of the world, it is more formally and respectfully known as the tent of purification. Mine is a professional yet decorative structure of carven poles hung with rather fine patterned matting, all inwoven with repeating friezes of life, prosperity and health. I noticed Saweser nodding with approval at the bright matting, the tall jars of lotus flowers that flanked the opening, the large barrels of Nile water and palm wine for the ritual bathing of the deceased.

"In my experience," I whispered to him, "spending a little extra on this part of the setup is never a waste. Remember, this is just about all the customers ever see." He gave me that strange look again, but made no comment.

Just inside the entrance, my dear Nofret was dickering with a pair of principal mourners, an ash-covered farmer in a ritually torn loincloth and his equally disheveled wife. Our sweet Merbeset crouched not far away, the darling, observing but keeping her mouth shut, like a good little apprentice mourner. Nofret was using the wooden models, three little corpse-dolls depicting the likely results of different levels of expenditure. They graded from lifelike, through somewhat disturbing, to a bony horror with bared teeth: a reminder to the customer that you get what you pay for when it comes to embalming. Nofret had them talked up to the second model already. The deceased, a handsome boy of about ten, lay naked on one of the pallets, ready to be washed once the price was settled. Saweser surprised me by kneeling beside the dead child and gently patting its hand.

"Sentimental, are you?" I whispered to him. "I thought you'd worked with stiffs before." He rose to follow me out, but he did not look at me this time.

❖ ❖ ❖

We followed the same path the corpses take after their bath, to the large courtyard enclosing the Houses of Purification and Beauty— or the Cutting House and the Stuffing House, as we like to say. Unlike some necro bosses, I prefer to keep a little distance between the mourners and the processing department. Therefore, my main operation is in a separate compound on the desert edge of the necropolis proper, a good long walk from the washhouse, surrounded by a shoulder-high mud wall topped with acacia thorns. The thorns are not to keep *people* out; the smell, I've always thought, makes a more effective barrier in that regard, rot and incense, sewage and resin, like a combination latrine, abattoir, and perfumery. No, the thorns are placed in hopes of keeping out desert scavengers, who seem to *like* the smell.

I pointed out the sights to Saweser. Just inside the gate were the huge dumps of natron, glistening like powdered silver. Ahead of us was the House of Beauty, a large flat-roofed mudbrick structure with few windows; to the right of that was the smaller, and much smellier, House of Purification. And all over the extensive courtyard lay the dead, ranged in tidy rows, each one visible only as a natron-covered mound with a wooden toe tag at one end. This is where our deceased clients spend up to forty days, slowly pickling and drying in the natron salt and the sun, until they're ready for wrapping and planting. I took Saweser's arm and strolled over to the far corner of the courtyard, in front of the House of Purification, where some very junior embalmers were at work.

"We had a little trouble with the jackals last night," I said.

His head jerked up. "Jackals? What kind of trouble?"

"The usual kind. A pack broke in and made a meal of some of our customers. We're dealing with it."

In truth, it was a very minor attack. The jackals had come over the wall at the corner, thorns or no thorns; they had disinterred no more than a dozen corpses, and not eaten much of any of them. My juniors were collecting the strewn body parts into large baskets, pawing through the scattered natron with salt-inflamed hands to retrieve the toe tags.

"Whatever will you do? How will you make sure that each departed one is correctly assembled?"

This time, it was I who gave him a strange look. What an idiot. "Why bother? We've got the toe tags. Everything gets wrapped up nicely anyway."

"I understand," Saweser said, so coldly that I began to be irritated. Who in the names of all the Ennead did he think he was? All the customers needed to see was the correct name on a bandaged mummy of roughly the right shape and size. Trying not to show my annoyance, I took his arm and led him towards the House of Purification— then changed tracks toward the House of Beauty. Foolish, perhaps, but I did not want this long-nosed disapproving bastard son of Set to see how we were cutting corners in the Cutting House this week, being so short-handed and all. Normally I like my cutting crews to do a reasonably professional job — the careful slit in the abdomen, a hand slipped inside to draw out guts and other innards for separate processing — but not when we've got a backlog. Faster to stick a funnel up the arse, flood the gut with cedar oil, and move on to the next stiff; after a week you pull the plug out and just pour the innards away, with the families none the wiser.

Since the Stuffing House also holds our storerooms of linen and spices, of incense, cassia and myrrh, it is the best-smelling corner of my little empire. I led Saweser through the front doors, which are flung wide during the day to keep a good draft blowing through, and down the central hallway, flanked on both sides by the fragrant storerooms. From a workshop at the end floated the competing voices of several lector priests attending on different corpses, and the effect was, I thought, pleasantly busy and professional. I looked up at Saweser — gracious Isis, was he even taller than before? — and saw that this place, at least, had managed to impress him more favorably. We stopped on the threshold of the workroom.

The embalming crews, which included three of my sons, were doing not a bad job. With Saweser at my heels, I walked around inspecting the several mummies currently in process: two adults and a child recently pulled from the natron piles, four or five adults at various stages of bandaging, two adult-sized packages of linen ready to be boxed up for burial. Several lector priests were hurrying from table to table as needed, mumbling from their scripts or supervising the placement of amulets within the linen. The half-drunk Overseer of the Mysteries was not present; this, I thought, was probably just as well.

We stopped at the worktable where Penanap, my second son, was stuffing the dead child's belly cavity with balled-up linen scraps and handfuls of sand, along with some token sprinkles of myrrh. I saw the disapproving look begin to creep back onto Saweser's face. What, did he think other mummy factories did not make similar economies? My son greeted me cheerfully, with a curious glance at my companion.

"Another funeral for Merbeset to shine in," he said to me, indicating the blackened mummy of the child— a little girl, I saw, of about Merbeset's age. Yes, our precious Merbeset was much in demand as a mourner at kiddy funerals. Natural talent, I was proud to say, though there was also Nofret's excellent training in weeping, writhing, and tearing at the hair without doing actual damage. Someday, I hoped, Merbeset might be kite-mistress here in her mother's place. I clapped my son on his shoulder and turned to introduce him to the new priest.

But Saweser was paying us no attention. He was examining the dead girl-child with a little smile on his face, like a fond uncle, and he reached out to brush her tough, blackened cheek with his fingertips. Penanap rolled his eyes.

"Are you quite sure," I asked Saweser, "you've worked with stiffs before?"

He looked down at me with his brows drawn together, but then his gaze slid right over my head. I whirled to see what he was looking at, because I fervently hoped the instant fury flooding his face had a target that was not me. And it did.

Khaemwese had just staggered through the door to join an invocation in progress: our resident Overseer of the Mysteries, the living incarnation of the great god Anubis while he wore the jackal mask. Seeing him for a moment through a newcomer's eyes, I could halfway understand Saweser's rage. The mask was overdue for replacement, worn and scabbed where gold leaf and lapis-blue paint had flaked away; the tips of both ears were broken. When set on Khaemwese's fat shoulders, balanced over his wobbling belly and breasts, the mask was actually pretty comical. And the Overseer was drunk as usual, swaying between two young sweepers, slurring the invocation shamefully when his turn came to speak. I gave him a filthy glare myself.

"Is *that*," Saweser hissed, "what you consider to be a fitting incarnation of the great Son of Osiris?"

"Well, not really," I said, "but he works on a very small commission. You know how things are in the business."

Saweser growled — yes, actually growled like a dog — deep in his throat, and swung his furious eyes and great snout of a nose around to me. The crews were watching us, the lector priests had fallen silent and were standing there with their silly mouths hanging open, even that damned Khaemwese was paying a vague and dribbling attention. Very bad for discipline, I thought, as well as for our tight schedule. Time to put the snotty bugger in his place.

"Priest," I said coldly, drawing myself up, "remember who is boss around here. *I* am, and *you* are my employee. So either you take your big nose and your oily hide back to the east bank on the very next boat— or you grab a script and start gabbling over the stiffs, along with the others. But I warn you, I am sick to death of your attitude."

An odd change came over his face. He looked almost amused. "Sick to death? Not yet."

"What do you mean? I gave you an order!"

But he was already heading for the workroom door, reaching it in three paces of his very long legs, pausing to look back at me. "I serve a different master," he said, "and came to this place on other business. But I will remember you," he added, "when your heart is weighed in the court of my father Osiris, in the Hall of the Two Truths." And he was gone.

Damn it, I thought, a spy! Most likely (and my heart misgave me, as we say) an inspector for some dratted nosy commission from the Great House, checking into business practices in the mummy factories. As if any of the other necroyard bosses did things any differently! As if Osiris himself would care! But I could not risk letting that lying conniver report back to his masters.

"Catch him!" I cried. "He can't have gone far!"

But he was not in the corridor when we flooded out of the workroom to give chase, and even those long legs could not have reached the outer doors in that short a time. "Check the storerooms!" And so we did, all of us, embalmers, lector priests, sweepers, right down to fat Khaemwese puffing along under the Anubis mask. Saweser was nowhere.

I left the others doing a frantic second search, sweeping bales of linen off the shelves, checking inside the coffins, thrusting lamps into the darkest corners. Meantime, sweating and quaking with disquiet — no, of course I was not feeling guilty — I took myself to the gate of the compound and surveyed the track that led along the edge of the necropolis, back towards the tent of purification and the riverside.

There was no sign of Saweser, unless he was hiding himself among the heaps of natron, or skulking among the tombs in the necropolis. But then my dear Nofret appeared far off along the track in a cloud of her own dust, cradling a bundle in her arms. Even at that great distance, I could hear her wailing in that wonderfully-trained voice of hers. As I've said, nobody does grief like my Nofret.

It seemed, though, like an odd time for a rehearsal, and if it was a demonstration for Merbeset's benefit, it was wasted. Where was the child, anyway? I took a few steps along the track beyond the gate, intending to meet Nofret and warn her about the false lector priest. Then I saw what she carrying, and began to run.

❖ ❖ ❖

REBECCA BRADLEY, author of the *Gil* Trilogy and numerous short stories, has fond memories of working as an archaeologist in Egypt and the Sudan, and once shared a dighouse with a crowd of millennia-dead Nubians. She now lives in the West Kootenays of British Columbia, with some very lively cats.

What Would Lizzie Do?

by Sèphera Girón

NICOLE JERKED AWAKE, the morning sun burning her eyes as she sat up. Someone had been there, right there beside the bed; looming over her.

But no one was there now.

She pushed long dark strands of sweat-soaked hair back from her face and took a deep breath, aware of how fast her heart was still pounding. It hadn't stopped pounding erratically since she had entered the tiny old house the previous afternoon. She stared at the portrait of Andrew Borden hanging on the wall on the other side of the room as she breathed in the thick, dense New England air.

"You again," she said sternly and flopped back onto the pillows, staring at the ceiling.

Ghosts, just ghosts. She knew almost all of them now.

And despite the secrets they shared, she still didn't know the truth about the one ghost she had yet to meet.

Lizzie Borden.

For the past six years, Nicole had been drawn to the Lizzie Borden house. She had joined up with a ghost-hunting group in Toronto and the team had actually spent the weekend travelling to Salem and then to the haunted *bed and breakfast* in Fall River. Nicole also frequently visited the Borden graveyard and Maplecroft, the home where Lizzie moved to after the trials.

Nicole's first night at Lizzie's had been terrifying. Unexplainable noises and shadows, touches and whispers, brief wafting smells of rotten meat, rancid urine and coppery blood. When she sat on a couch, the sensation of a cat brushing by her legs kept causing her to look down yet there were no living cats to be seen. She hadn't slept all night as the team investigated the floors with their K2 meters and cameras, recording voices that weren't there and pictures that would later turn up orbs and smoky blurs.

She had returned several times since, sometimes with a group, sometimes on her own.

She rarely slept, of course. Fear and excitement kept her adrenaline racing all night as she attempted communication with the spirits rumored to be haunting the murder house.

Over the years, she had mostly encountered Andrew Borden, the stern frugal father who had been rumored to take far too much of an interest in his adult daughters and not enough in his second wife. His indignation at being axed in the head a century ago was still thick in the air most nights, his essence terrifyingly aggressive, his presence keenly felt should anyone attempt to speak ill of him.

Nicole always chose his bedroom as her own when she slept over. She knew who he was and what he was. She wasn't so sure about *some* of the other house ghosts.

For instance, on the third floor, there was a room where children played. Children who had been drowned by their mother in the well next door. The sound of a ball rolling across the wooden floors could be heard all night long as well as ethereal snatches of children's laughter.

There were the wandering ghosts of vagrants and a few of the clients that the Bordens had "dressed" in their makeshift morgue basement in the late 1800s, caught in the portals and timeslips that the house allegedly possessed. They were spotted on the stairs, skulking in bathrooms, slipping around corners before Nicole could fully see them, their voices murmuring on tape recorders punctuated with mournful screams of angst and pain, their images reduced to glowing circles or murky mists in photographs.

A more recent addition to the roaming cast of spirits over the decades was the handyman Michael, who had worked many years for the *bed and breakfast* and then died in a mysterious fire shortly after he retired, sometime in the 2000s.

But no matter how she inspected the orbs in pictures, listened to the wailings on the recordings, sat with her psychic energy tuned up high to "feel" whoever might be present, there was never a sense that the Lady of the Hour, the High Priestess of Ax Murderers, was in the meekest wisp of wind that blew doors shut in the stifling August heat.

She wasn't here.

Nicole got up from Andrew Borden's bed and stretched. Glancing at her cell phone, she saw that she had slept an amazing hour and a half, and yet had mountains of time before the first breakfast service was to begin. Still clothed in her "What Would Lizzie Do?" tank top and jean shorts, she walked through the doorway to Lizzie's room. The usual mishmash of emotions that were not her own swirled around her, so dense and urgent that she could almost see them, but not quite.

She left Lizzie's room and went into what was known as the John Morse room which was already musty and musky as the morning heat slowly engulfed the space. John Morse had stayed in this room when he came to visit. Nicole stood in Abby's murder spot between the dresser and the bed, facing the wall. She planted her feet firmly into the rug, although the original murder rug had been removed and a vintage rug installed. However, there were rumors that the blood from Abby's smashed skull could still be seen in the floorboards beneath the rug.

Nicole closed her eyes, imaging the axe coming down on her head, the sudden shock, the realization that her skull is broken and her brains are leaking out as the axe comes down again and again...

Did Abby see who held the axe? Was Abby ever able to catch a glimpse of the coward who bashed in her head while she made beds in the oppressive August heat? And why was she making the bed when she had little Bridgette Sullivan to do her work? Or was she helping out the Irish maid by making the beds herself? They had already had a huge row about Bridgette washing the windows in the sticky heat after suffering food poisoning from the rotten mutton the family had been forced by thrifty dad to eat for days in a row.

Nicole left Abby's murder room. Hushed whispers from the other half a dozen sleepless ghost hunters echoed through the little house. She made her way carefully down the front stairs. There had been several incidents over the last century of people being pushed by unseen hands and she wasn't eager to join the list.

She walked through the front hallway, avoiding the front parlour and continued into the living room.

Nicole sat on the murder couch. Of course, it wasn't the real murder couch, just a replica, but the vibrations from that day of horror still coursed through her bones. The couch was where Andrew Borden had been axed in the head, likely while he slept, while rotten mutton gurgled in his belly. She stared across the small room at the wooden rocking chair by the window. She had taken pictures of the chair over the years and there were always strange orbs surrounding it.

Gently, the chair began to rock.

She shook her head, deciding it was the vibrations from the other ghost hunters creeping around the house with their dvrs and K2 meters.

The clock on the mantle whirred and stuttered. It had always tick-tocked irregularly and today was no different. It had the annoying habit of chiming way too many times an hour, which always startled whoever was in this room.

She closed her eyes and thought of Mr. Borden. Where had he gone that day? Who had his enemies really been? Were the whispers of deviance between father and daughter part of the catalyst for the gruesome spectacle that unfolded over a century ago?

She imaged the man from the portrait, stern with an unfixing stare, doing his "business rounds" as they called them. Walking around to the tellers, checking books, counting money, his stomach still roiling from the spate of food poisoning that had stricken the family the previous day. No doubt the oppressive summer heat had sent him home to his couch, where he sat in deep thought until the hatchet hit his head.

Was he sleeping when the axe fell? Was he thinking? Did anyone say anything to him before the blade hit the bone? She asked questions of the spirits, eagerly waiting for the answers. Her arms and legs felt weighed down with some unseen oppressive force. Her stomach rumbled, the hair on her arms stood on end.

Sweat dripped down her forehead, her body sinking, sinking into the couch as she visualized the events that might have happened that day.

Her head ached then shards of pain shot through her body. Shock and disbelief were a faint ebbing in the distant mists but soon they spun into focus in her mind's eye. There was a sickening crunch as her skull splintered into pieces with the blows.

No time to turn her neck, no time to see as an unseen person grunted with every swing of the axe. Over and over the instrument fell, brains leaking out, an unseeing eyeball split in two.

She lay on the couch, intact in a sleep paralysis state, her body frozen as she waited for yet another blow that didn't come.

Her body twitched and she sat up, eyes still shut as she stretched her arms out in front of her and jiggled each of her fingers; visions and paralysis gone.

Nicole opened her eyes in time to see a whirl of grey and black mist rise from the couch and float towards the kitchen. The mist hovered at the frame of the kitchen door for a moment, almost as if hesitant, and then proceeded. Nicole stood up to follow it but it was gone. Vanished into nothingness.

In the kitchen, Kim and Jenny were comparing pictures on their digital cameras. Nicole nuzzled into their twosome to inspect the evidence. The staff was busy preparing the traditional "morning of the murders" breakfast so the girls had to squeeze nearly into the bathroom to stay out of the way.

"Did you see anything come in here just now?" Nicole asked as she looked at the viewfinder of the camera. It wasn't the kitchen, just orbs clustering outside of the house in the darkness of the night before.

"No," said Kim, shaking her head. "You mean just now?"

"Damn, was hoping you caught it on camera," Nicole said. "It was the grey mist that floats from the couch to the kitchen. It was even on one of those ghost hunting shows."

"You saw it?" All three turned to look at the door frame, Jenny holding her camera up as if it would still be hanging there, waiting for its Kodak moment.

"Just now. I lay on the murder couch and thought about the murder and then when I sat up, a grey mist floated up and into the kitchen."

"How cool is that?" Kim said. Jenny nodded. "So much cool stuff happens here. Even after all these years."

"Have you ever seen Lizzie? I thought you channelled her at a séance once."

"I've felt her or the essence of something of her, I'm sure of it," Kim said. "I asked with the tarot cards and all that, but I'm never sure if it's her or something playing with me, imitating her."

"I know what you mean," said Jenny. "I've never been sure I've connected with Lizzie in the eight times I've slept here. Everyone else, I sure have. I have stories about everyone but her."

"I wonder why that is?" Nicole mused. She pulled her attention from the doorframe and focused on the basement door. She sighed deeply. "I guess we'd better check the downstairs," she said. "You guys in?".

"Why not? I never tire of the basement creepiness," Kim said with a grin.

The ladies all pulled out their flashlights and turned on the light to the basement. Piles of boxes and other items were all over the cellar. The storage area for the *bed and breakfast* ranged from supplies to office files to laundered linens. The flickering light added a spook-house thrill to the dank dingy basement.

"It's going again," Jenny said looking up at the light bulb. "I've changed it six times since we got here last night."

"You'd think they'd fix the wiring," Kim said.

"What? And ruin a perfectly good haunted house?" laughed Jenny. "No way."

"The owner told me last night that she's had the electrician in three times since January and over a dozen times since she bought the place. No one has an answer about this light."

"Lizzie," Kim said with a smirk. "She's here in the blood room."

They walked over to one corner of the basement that was its own room. There was a hole in the wall where a large washing bucket had been placed, a re-enactment of times gone by. Nicole wandered along the racks of the *bed and breakfast* linens, all folded away.

She touched them, her eyes shut; the linens are filthy piles of soiled rags. The stench of blood and urine stung her nostrils as she envisioned a tired, sweaty Lizzie hand-scrubbing each and every rag.

"She had to wash them," Jenny said, her voice sounding distant in Nicole's ears. "Her father made her take a job and she handled the ladies' monthly rags. So gross."

"I'm still not sure I believe that part of the story," Kim scoffed. "I never have. I thought this room was bloody from the corpses they used to dress when this was a funeral home."

"That's a fairytale too. The only corpses dressed here were upstairs on the dining room table; Mr. and Mrs. Borden."

"The truth is so lost in a hundred years of bullshit. Who knows anything anymore," Jenny sighed. "I personally believe she washed the period rags and that's where she hid the axe."

"I do believe the axe was hidden in laundry or something. For sure. And she burned that dress, remember?"

Nicole's head swam, her nose plugged with the acrid smell of ammonia and rotting blood, the mustiness of the basement, the idea of the bloody axe with pieces of dad still stuck on it, tucked away in one of the filthy piles.

No DNA back then. Blood was blood.

The air grew thick and she opened her eyes. She watched Jenny and Kim stare at each other then at Nicole.

"Did you feel that?" Jenny asked with wide eyes. "Something touched me."

"Something is squeezing me," Kim said. "Like I'm a rag doll in King Kong's hand. Let's go." Jenny and Kim hurried back up the creaking stairs while the light bulb sputtered and sparked.

Nicole went to a pile of laundry, holding her little maglight with one hand while picking through the bloody linens with the other. At last she found it and held it in her hand.

The head of the axe. The splintered handle fell to the floor. Bits of hair still clung to the sharp blade and Nicole fought the urge to vomit.

She closed her eyes and when she opened them, she was standing in the lobby at Maplecroft. She knew it was Maplecroft and hurried back to the front door to peer out the broken window to check. Yes, the bushes were overgrown and the "for sale" sign still hung out front.

In her hand Nicole held the axe. The intact axe, bloody with clumps of hair stuck to it, blood smeared down the handle. She stared at the glass on the floor below the broken window. She shook her head, trying to remember how she came to be here. She didn't remember driving or more importantly, parking. She didn't remember leaving the *bed and breakfast* and running down the street. The fact that she was dripping with sweat and with blood streaked across her clothes and legs along with newly forming bruises didn't give her any clues as to what had happened. She had been in the basement at the Borden home and now she was here. At Maplecroft. The home Lizzie and her sister Emma purchased after the trial. The home where Lizzie lived until she died, entertaining theatre folk and carrying on torrid love affairs with pretty little actresses.

Maplecroft had been abandoned the past few years while the current owners tried to sell it in the recession in the sleepy little town where time had stood still.

A door slammed from the upstairs level followed by a crash like the sound of a vase smashing to the floor.

"Lizzie? Anyone? Who is here?" Nicole quickly ran up the stairs, gripping her flashlight in one hand, carrying the axe in her other. She paused at the top of the stairs and looked down the hallway at several doors.

She walked down the hallway, her heart pounding. A door slammed shut as she walked by it. Another creaked a little bit open and she glanced inside to the empty bedroom. She continued on until she reached the last room. The door was closed.

It sounded like there were voices whispering behind the door. Nicole jiggled the handle.

She opened the door. Immediately she recognized that this would be Lizzie's room. The style was similar to what was Lizzie's room at the *bed and breakfast*.

A woman wearing an old-fashioned black dress stood staring out the window, her back to Nicole.

"Lizzie?" Nicole asked. "Did you do it? Did you?"

The figure vanished without so much as a flinch.

Nicole left the room. She returned to the top of the stairs. The sense of the house had changed.

As Nicole went back down the stairs, her ears rang with the sounds of laughter and the scratchy, tinny tone of a phonograph record playing a happy tune like "Buttons and Bows" or some other old-fashioned song. Now that she was standing here, really seeing the place, she was stunned. She had expected an abandoned dust-ridden cloth-draped home but instead found a lively spectacle of working lights and old fashioned but obviously used furniture.

She stood staring down the hallway to where the grand ballroom must be. As she was about to walk towards the ballroom and the voices and the music, she was startled to see Lizzie Borden herself standing in front of her. Lizzie, not as the stern matronly manly figure with a round face and glassy eyes, but a middle aged Lizzie with overly dramatic make-up, a short pin curled hair-do and a bright red form-fitting dress. Her figure was alluring, round and hourglass with the ample paddings particular to her era. Her bright red lips pouted at Nicole.

"Welcome to my party," she said in a low, sultry voice. Nicole stared at her, speechless despite the thousand of questions she needed to ask.

Lizzie hurried her towards an immense walk-in closet full of dresses and shoes. "Quickly, choose something fun and naughty."

Dancing and spinning, snatches of faces in the blurs, being passed from man to man, the scratchy record repeating over and over. Nicole laughed as she danced, sweat dripping from her face as the old-fashioned black and grey dress pinched her unbearably, the old shoes slipping on the wooden floor, her ankles aching, her toes cramped.

Lizzie laughed and took her hand, pulling her from the dance floor.

"You're fitting right in," Lizzie smiled. Nicole swallowed and nodded; thirsty, exhilarated, thrilled to finally meet Lizzie but exhausted from the oppressive heat.

"It's time to meet my distinguished guests," Lizzie boasted as she led Nicole to a receiving line of characters that looked like they had been lifted from the pages of different eras in a history book.

Nicole gasped as she shook hands with Ted Bundy, Jeffrey Dahmer, Elizabeth Bathory, Vlad Tepes, and so many others who had performed despicable deeds in their lives. She briefly experienced a sense of *déjà vu*, a moment taken from *The Rocky Horror Picture Show* and "the master's parties."

No sooner had Nicole shaken hands with the last of the special guests, she was stricken to the ground, her head hacked again and again with an axe by Lizzie Borden herself. Nicole's blood splashed Lizzie's dress, the stains barely noticeable as they were absorbed the instant they hit the fabric. Nicole screamed and reached up to stop the blows, but it was pointless. The party guests, the hoards, descended on Nicole, slurping up her fresh blood, squabbling and shoving each other as they tore at her body for the meat. Distinguished guests reduced to ravenous animals with gnashing teeth and clawing hands.

Nicole ran down the winding stone streets of Fall River. She returned to the *bed and breakfast*. Relieved she saw the three ghost hunter trucks still in the driveway. She hurried inside the house and found Kim lying on the murder couch.

"You'll never guess..." Nicole said, panting as she tried to catch her breath. She shook her friend who was lying in the Andrew Borden pose. Then she saw the blood pool on the floor, leaking brains, tufts of hair all around.

Nicole stood up and screamed. She realized she still held the axe and threw it at the rocking chair that rocked rapidly.

"Help!" she screamed. Her voice echoed eerie. Then, the house was weirdly quiet. Wasn't it time for breakfast? But the table wasn't set, there were no cooks, no voices from the other guests. But the trucks and cars were in the driveway. They hadn't hit the road yet.

What time was it anyway?

The clock was still tick-tocking its staccato beat, whirring and humming. The gears grinding, how old was that clock? Was it the original clock?

Nicole wiped sweat and blood from her forehead.

The clock chimed at her.

The rocking chair rocked.

The body on the couch was still dead.

"Nicole," a voice said from behind her. Nicole turned to see Lizzie standing before her. A frumpy Lizzie as in the famous portraits. Hair pulled back, eyes glazed and unhappy, her mouth set in frown. She wore a shapeless dress and an apron spattered with blood. In her hand, she held the bloody axe.

"What's going on?" Nicole asked; she was cornered and could only move forwards towards the dining room.

"That's right," Lizzie said as she led Nicole into the dining room. "Come sit down and have your breakfast."

Nicole reached to pull out the chair nearest to her, nodding at her ghost hunter pals already seated around the table. She screamed.

Her friends, the other six ghost hunters, were propped in their chairs, their faces dripping with blood from their bashed in skulls.

Lizzie placed a steaming bowl of stew in front of Nicole.

"Stop your screaming," she said sternly. Nicole stared at Lizzie, her screams turning to burbling sobs. She gulped and sniffed as Lizzie sat down in front of her own bowl of stew.

"Eat your mutton," Lizzie commanded, and lowered her head to slurp at her own raised spoonful. "Do you want to be part of the family or not?"

Nicole stopped sobbing and lowered her gaze to her stew. The odor of rotten meat mixed with the musky smell of New England in the summer heat made her stomach roll.

"Eat it," Lizzie said again.

Nicole's lips quivered. Lizzie stood up, her hand reaching for the nearby axe. Nicole quickly reached for her spoon and scooped it into stew. Lizzie sat back down and continued to eat and stare at Nicole. Nicole took a tentative taste, barely licking the stringy meat and nearly vomited from the putrid smell and taste.

"Eat your mutton," a strong male voice boomed. Nicole looked over to see Andrew Borden now sitting at the head of the table, Abby by his side. Both still suffered the bloody wounds of their deaths. Bridgette, Emma, John Morse and Michael the handyman sat around the table too. The ghost hunters were gone.

"Eat your mutton," Lizzie coaxed. "And I will share with you the secrets about Lizzie Borden."

Nicole stared at Andrew Borden. He now looked like the portrait that hung in the bedroom. A stern, glowering man who stared at her with the intensity of a shark's black eyes.

Nicole glanced at Abby, a mirror of the glum woman she'd seen in the portraits. What a miserable family they were. And what were the real secrets?

She wondered what Emma knew?

What would Lizzie tell her? What would Lizzie do?

Nicole ate the mutton.

✠ ✠ ✠

SÈPHERA GIRÓN is about halfway to her expiration date and still has loads to say. The author of a dozen published books, she's also penned hundreds of short stories, blogs, articles and horoscopes.

Ashes to Ashes

by Amy Grech

JACK HAD BEEN dead for less than a year when his widow spotted something gray in a corner of the cellar that resembled a heap of dust but throbbed like the heart of a dying man.

A sudden heart attack had claimed Jack nine short months ago...

She'd had his body cremated.

Ashes to ashes, dust to dust.

Sara passed the heap of dust whenever she brought her dirty clothes over to the washing machine. She couldn't avoid it. The first time the heap moved, Sara bit her lip and shrugged it off, along with a sudden chill that crept through the open cellar door.

Hastily, she dumped her dirty dresses into the washer — all of them were black — and closed the lid. She passed the heap again on her way upstairs, and shuddered. She didn't stop shaking until she bolted the cellar door. In a half-hour she would have to go back down to put her dresses in the dryer. She dreaded the thought.

Sara wore her wedding dress, which she had dyed black for Jack's funeral.

Until death do us part.

His final resting place, a black urn with JACK etched in gold letters, sat on the mantle, right next to their wedding photo. Two feet taller than she was, he resembled a gentle giant. His enormous arms held Sara tightly. Gingerly, she lifted the cold, gold frame and remembered the splendor of their wedding day two decades ago, immaculately preserved for all the days of her life.

As she cradled the photo against her chest, Sara closed her eyes and pictured herself hugging Jack. She held her new husband. He held her as tightly in his strong arms as he did on their wedding day, and whispered words she would never forget: *"I will always love you. I will never leave you. I want to make love to you forever."*

She inhaled and smiled, seizing the moment, yearning for his tender touch. In her mind, Jack still smelled as fragrant as an orchard full of oranges. His eyes were as light as the sky, his hair as bright as the sun, and his ashes gray as the heap of dust in the cellar. Sara's eyes snapped open as the fond memory faded to black.

Jack's ashes and this photo were the only tangible mementos she had left to cherish. She set the picture down. Carefully, she lifted the lid of the urn and peered inside, seeking that familiar, fine powder that always greeted her; black emptiness greeted her where grayness should have been. She winced, remembering the heap of dust in a corner of the cellar.

How did his ashes end up in the cellar?

The lid slipped through her trembling fingers and shattered on the floor.

Sara shuffled over to the couch and collapsed. She had never thought that keeping Jack's ashes in the house would be such a burden.

❖ ❖ ❖

Did I meet him when we were college sophomores or juniors?

Jack and Sara strolled across campus somewhere… she tried to remember where but couldn't. It didn't matter though, because he wore a University of Michigan sweatshirt. They paused in front of a sign that read: *Psychology Laboratories*. He practically lived in that building junior year.

Jack waved. Sara waved back.

❖ ❖ ❖

Did he ask me out on our first date, or did I ask him?

They sat on a bed in a small but neat apartment. Jack's place had always been a mess, so Sara knew right away that it had been her apartment, her bed.

"I'm glad you came over." She smiled and moved closer.

He took his leather jacket off and tossed it in a corner. "I never mind spending quality time with pretty girls."

Sara blushed. "Do you spend a lot of your time with pretty girls?"

"None of them are as pretty as you." Jack took her hand in his and squeezed it hard enough to let her know he cared.

She brushed black locks away from her face. "I don't believe you."

He kissed her for a long time to prove his point.

The image lingered deep within her mind, like their first kiss, but it didn't last nearly as long.

✣ ✣ ✣

Did we make love the first time in his apartment or mine?

They were at her place again. The lights were off. Candles bathed the room in an effervescent glow. Jack kissed her deeply. She held him tight. Their shirts, jeans, and underwear were scattered throughout the room.

Jack loomed, trembling above her. "I love you."

"Then show me." She pulled him on top of her and guided him in.

Their movements were awkward and unsteady at first, but neither of them minded much; desire bound them together. Sara wrapped her legs around his. Jack wrapped his arms around hers and squeezed tight.

✣ ✣ ✣

Sara started to cry.

Did Jack get down on one knee when he proposed?

They stood in front of a blue, two-story house, his arm draped over shoulders; her arm wrapped around his waist. Sara's mother looked on from the front stoop while her father snapped pictures of the happy couple. They smiled for the camera and tried not to blink.

Jack and Sara walked to the restaurant holding hands. He always squeezed harder than she did.

Joe's Bistro was right down the street. Their usual table, in a secluded, dark corner, made the candle between them romantic because it was the only source of light. Jack ordered a bottle of the finest red wine and a plate of spaghetti with meatballs for them to share.

After dinner he got down on one knee, opened a small, black box, slipped a diamond ring on her finger and said: "Marry me, Sara."

She admired the ring. "Oh, Jack, I thought you'd never ask!"

Suddenly, the moment was snuffed out in her mind as if it were the candle wick that had burned so brightly between them dying.

❖ ❖ ❖

She headed for the cellar again. The stairs looked forbidding, even though the cellar light was on. She grabbed the sides of her dress and held them up so she wouldn't fall and end up sprawled out on the floor next to the — harmless? — heap of dust, Jack's last hurrah.

When she neared it on her way back to the washer, Sara clenched her fists and stared at the dust. As she passed, the heap began to beat faster and faster.

Sara lifted the washer's lid and then tossed her wet, black dresses into the dryer. Her hasty attempt to make it upstairs without looking back was hindered by the sudden aroma of oranges.

Sara looked behind her.

The dust had vanished!

She went over to the spot where it had been and touched the cold concrete; not a speck remained. She ran upstairs, without looking back, and bolted the cellar door.

She found herself hovering over the topless urn on the mantle, glancing inside once more. Grayness prevailed where black emptiness used to be; Jack was back.

Sara held the urn in her sweaty, trembling hands and shut her eyes. Jack danced with her again, but he kept stepping on her toes. That didn't happen on their wedding day. Sara was sure of it!

Cautiously, she opened her eyes, startled to see her husband standing next to her. She placed her hand on his shoulder. This time it rested there, instead of passing through thin air.

She cringed at the gentle touch of a warm hand that smelled like oranges touching her hand; she screamed. Suddenly, the hand squeezed hers hard— so hard her hand began to ache until the pain led to numbness.

Jack let go of Sara's hand long enough to hug her harder than he had ever hugged her before. He whispered words in her ear as he had done before, over and over, but the words were different now: "*I have always loved you; I will always love you. I have never left you; I will never leave you. I want to make love to you forever; I will make love to you forever.*"

He squeezed so hard that Sara's whole body throbbed so fast that her heart could hardly keep pace.

And the harmless heap of grey dust in the corner was the only thing, the last thing she remembered.

✤ ✤ ✤

AMY GRECH has sold over one hundred stories and three poems to various anthologies and magazines including: *Dead Harvest*, and *Shrieks and Shivers from the Horror Zine.* Amy is an Active Member of the Horror Writers Association.

THE GREYNESS

BY KATHRYN PTACEK

ANGELA GAZED DOWN at her husband's body in the hospital bed and wondered what it was like to be dead.

This isn't what I should be thinking, she told herself, and yet it was. She reached out and placed her fingertips on his arm. Warm. Her fingers trembled as she watched his chest, waiting for him to draw in that next breath, waiting to hear the exhalation, waiting, waiting, waiting.

They were all waiting out in the hall for her, too… Waiting ever so politely before they bustled in, before they intruded upon her last time with her husband.

They told me to take as long as I wanted. She put her other hand up to her mouth to stifle a giggle. As long as I wanted— an hour, a day, a week? How long was too long? Too short? What if she swept out of the room right now? Would they think less of her? Think she wasn't a very good wife?

She rubbed her fingers across his skin. It still felt like him. She bent down and kissed him and closed her eyes and remembered all the times they had embraced and explored each other with their lips and tongues.

❖ ❖ ❖

Her husband hadn't been old, hadn't been young, hadn't been sick. Apparently something was going on inside Ben, something that she hadn't noticed, something no one realized. Had *he known?* she wondered. If so, he hadn't said anything, but then he wouldn't have. He would not have wanted to worry her, to make her wonder what was going to happen.

She inhaled deeply. All she smelled was the antiseptic tang of the hospital room, but beneath it lay a faint odor. Death? She opened her eyes, but didn't see the grim reaper or anything remotely like it lurking in the corner. Again, she almost laughed. Why would she see that now when her husband died an hour before? His spirit or soul or anima or whatever was gone— it had slipped away into the night, and left his shell, had left her behind.

She traced the curling hair on his forearm, smoothed a rough patch of skin — hadn't she suggested he have his doctor check it out? — intertwined her fingers with his…

Beneath her palm resting on the top of his hand she felt a brief warmness, and for a wild moment she thought he was alive, that he was moving. But she opened her eyes and all the joy that had surged through her in that instant drained, and there lay his body. Dead. Dead is dead.

Only then did she laugh, loud and long, not even stopping when the two nurses and administrator with all the pesky paperwork stepped into the room and gaped at her. She laughed even harder— papers to fill out when her love was dead. She laughed until the tears washed down her cheeks.

❖ ❖ ❖

Days blurred by… all the little things, all the big things she had to do. All the things she and Ben hadn't thought about, because, surely, death was a long way away.

That's what he always said, but every so often she saw something in those yellow-brown eyes — those wolf eyes — that said otherwise. But she had thought he was just fearful, as she was, and so they never talked about what had to be done. More papers to fill out; the meetings with the lawyer; arrangements, arrangements, arrangements. She was self-employed, so there was no boss to call to say she wouldn't be returning to work for a while.

In the old days, she thought as she stared into the closet to pick out clothes for him to wear in the casket, *he would have died at home, and his sister and I and maybe another woman would have washed the body carefully, with respect, and we would have dressed him in his finest suit, and he would have laid in the coffin in our parlor.*

Except we don't have a parlor, she thought, her lips twisting into a bit of a smile as she thought of the two-bedroom apartment. No, far from it. A chuckle threatened to escape, and she wondered why she thought it was funny. Nothing was funny now; yet everything was funny.

She found the charcoal grey suit he wore on business trips, the pale grey shirt he liked, the tie adorned with red koalas that she had given him one birthday, the black socks and shoes. Belt? Of course. What about underwear? Once more she found herself laughing aloud. She did that a lot lately. People stared at her, too. She laughed sometimes in the middle of the grocery store. Just stopped pushing the cart and stood there, veggies on one side of the aisle, pasta on the other, and laughed and laughed, like seeing a can of corn was the most amusing thing. Sometimes, the laugh started out as a chuckle; sometimes it bloomed into a full-blown guffaw, and she would find her shoulders shaking, and she'd realize she had tears in her eyes.

Carefully, she folded his clothing and placed it into the large shopping bag. Then she grabbed the handle of the bag, locked the apartment, and headed to the funeral home. She walked because it was only a few blocks away — Ben used to joke that it was certainly convenient to have a mortuary nearby! — and because it was a warm autumn day, the kind of day they both enjoyed so much, the kind of day they would have gone walking with the dog. Her hand holding the bag trembled, and then she was there and up the steps to ring the doorbell. Again, she felt that bit of warmth on her palm, and she rubbed her hand against her jeans. *Oh, good*, she thought, *I'm getting hot flashes now*.

"Come in, Mrs. Martinson," the undertaker said as he opened the door. Joseph Whyte reached out to take her hand, and once more she felt the warmth. She looked past his shoulder because she couldn't bear to meet his too-kind eyes and saw a number in his office just off the parlor. 57. She blinked, and the number shimmered, then disappeared gradually, leaving an after-image in her mind.

"Are you all right?" Whyte asked, then said quickly, "I'm sorry... of course, you're not. Come this way." He led her into his office, and she sat, the bag at her feet.

As he talked, he showed her catalogs, and she marveled that there was such an industry built up around death. In the end she handed over the shopping bag when he said he would see to it himself. For that, she was glad. Whyte had a cousin who worked with him, and she didn't like the man; the first day she had gone to the funeral parlor the cousin had swept her up into a hug. She had pulled away and had seen unshed tears in his eyes, and for some reason that bothered her.

Now that she was in the office, she studied the furnishings. She didn't see that number at all, and that worried her. She was seeing things, feeling things... did grief cause hallucinations? She didn't know.

Could she have been thinking of something else and then thought she saw the number? But what? *Heinz 57* ketchup? *Too absurd, even for me*, she told herself. She rose and thanked the man, but she did not shake his hand again.

✢ ✢ ✢

Angela got through the funeral at the church, with its solemn music and the too-sweet scent of dead lilies, and she nodded when people she knew and didn't know approached and told her how sorry they were. She kept her hands clasped lightly around her clutch purse, as if holding onto that would keep her anchored somehow. She found she didn't want to touch anyone, didn't want anyone to touch her. She'd built up this little cocoon of ... whatever ... around herself like an invisible force field, and she didn't want it breached. She knew that if anyone put a hand on hers or slipped an arm around her shoulder she would break down and laugh and cry and howl until they took her away and sedated her. She couldn't take it... not now, not yet.

So she nodded and nodded and nodded, and all she could think about was going home and laying down for a nap, retreating from the greyness that shrouded her.

She rode in the car behind the hearse, and she endured the rest of the ceremony beside the open grave. It started to rain, but the funeral director had anticipated the bad weather, so canopies protected her and the others seated there. Then it was over. She wanted to get home, get into bed, not think, not do anything, not—

Someone called her name, and she turned and saw it was Tommy. Without thinking, she reached out because, after all, this was Ben's dear friend from college, and the warmth blossomed beneath her palm, and past him, on a gravestone in the next row over, she saw a black numeral: 1. She blinked— and he gave her the look, the one that always made her cry, and now she began weeping uncontrollably.

"I'll take you home," Tommy said, and she nodded against his shoulder.

There were more pats on her back from other friends and neighbors now as they crowded around her, tapping and touching, and she felt like the world was shrinking in on her, like she couldn't breathe. Tommy saw the desperation in her eyes, pulled her away, and escorted her to his car.

He didn't talk on the drive back to the apartment, nor did she. She thanked him as she got out, then he followed her inside and made coffee and sat down in the kitchen and said nothing. She changed into comfortable clothes and once more in the kitchen, she sat and sipped her coffee, and still they didn't talk.

Tommy just gazed out the window, while she continued staring down into her coffee mug. How could her husband have died so quickly? Didn't he know they had so many things left to do? They hadn't finished all the trips they planned, and she hadn't given him the present for his birthday next month, and... and... and... She tried to stop thinking.

Tommy made dinner for them both that night, and she pushed the food from one side of the plate to the other. She suspected that he had talked to the other friends, and they had decided to stay with her for the next few days. Tonight would be his tour of duty, as it were. She wondered briefly who would show up tomorrow...

She went to bed an hour or so later, while he bunked out on the couch, and in the morning he fixed them breakfast. She nibbled on the toast, then he kissed her cheek and said he had to leave. She nodded and thanked him. She listened to him leave the apartment, and she went to the window. She saw him get into the car and pull out of the parking lot, and she watched as the dump truck barreled along the street and smacked into the convertible.

She screamed and flung herself out the door and ran down the stairs... but it was too late. Her husband's best friend was dead.

❖ ❖ ❖

Another funeral. Angela stayed in the back, spoke to no one, and left before everyone drove to the cemetery. At home, she made herself some coffee, then stood at the window while the coffee cooled.

If he hadn't come back here... if he had stayed for another hour... if, if, if.

If.

Hours became days, and days became weeks. The grey still enveloped her, still made her numb at times. She did things out of rote. She got up, went to the store, walked the dog, made a meal now and then, watched TV without seeing it, walked the dog again, went to bed. The next day was just a repeat of the day before....and the day before that.

Friends dropped in, bringing casseroles that she dutifully stored in the freezer, and they told her about all the things she was missing, and she nodded.

"And isn't it just weird?" Leslie said on the first day of winter as they sat in the kitchen. "Mr. Whyte and all."

The greyness shifted a bit. Angela frowned. "What are you talking about?"

Her friend glanced over. "Oh, I guess you're not keeping up with the papers."

She shook her head. "No. I get them, then don't read them. Maybe one of these days I will."

"Then I guess you didn't hear about Mr. Whyte."

"The funeral director?"

"Yeah, he died. Some rare fast-growing tumor. And isn't it just so weird... Ben hasn't been gone for even two months, and then Tommy, and now this guy."

"Yeah." Two months... "He didn't seem sick when I saw him."

"Well, he was kind of old."

"Not that old, I thought."

Two months. "This was in the paper, right?" Leslie nodded. Angela went to the stack of papers and flipped through them until she found the right issue... and yes, there was his obituary. She checked the date of his death, and it had been almost two months since she had taken her husband's clothes to him. Almost two months, but not quite. Just a few days under.

Fifty-seven days, to be precise.

Abruptly, she sat down.

❖ ❖ ❖

Her friend left shortly after that, and Angela was glad. She needed to think, not talk...

She had shaken Mr. Whyte's hand at the funeral home. She saw the number 57. He had died that many days later.

She had shaken Tommy's hand at the graveside ceremony. One... the number she had seen on a gravestone. 1. And he had died the next day.

What the hell? What is this? And she remembered that both times she had felt a warmth on the palm of her hand. And she remembered that day when she'd sat by Ben as he lay in the hospital bed, with her hand atop his... and the warmth had been there, even though it wasn't possible. His skin was already cooling off; there should have been no warmth, and yet, she knew that's what she felt.

She put her face in her hands and closed her eyes, and told herself it couldn't be. *But it was. Wasn't it?*

Somehow this ... thing ... this ability had transferred from her dead husband to her. She stared at her hands. They appeared no different than before, and slowly she traced the life line across her palm and thought about all the times as a kid when friends had "read" her palm and said she would live a long life and have a loving husband and four kids or more. They had all giggled because at that point they weren't even that interested in boys.

She felt a wet nose against her leg and glanced down to see the mutt there. He wanted his walk. She stared at him and remembered that Ben had taught the dog to shake hands. No, she thought; I won't do it. She retrieved the leash, snapped it to his collar, and headed out to the park.

How do I prove this? she wondered. *Not everyone I shake hands with will die in the next week or month or year or two. Will I meet someone and then see a number that's so huge that it indicates years or even decades?*

There was only one way to find out.

Angela saw someone at the park whom she'd seen before, and she stopped to chat, and before she walked away, she extended her hand and shook with the other woman. 14. She saw the shimmering number on the wall of the building across the street.

Now to keep track, and she wondered that she could think about this so coldly, so objectively. She rushed home and found a pocket-sized notebook and made a note of the day and the shimmering number. She knew the woman's name, so that could be verified.

Every day for two weeks Angela chatted with the woman while their dogs sniffed each other, and when she went home that night, she thought that perhaps she had been wrong. But when she saw the headlines in the newspaper the next morning, she knew she wasn't. Her park acquaintance had gone home the night before, drowned her little child, then killed herself.

Angela put the paper down and squeezed her eyes shut. How could this woman have done something like that? She didn't seem like she was unraveling. Each time Angela had seen the woman in the park, she had been friendly and had talked about her daughter and the plans she had for the four-year-old in the spring. In the spring. She had been looking forward to the new year, and now she was dead.

❖ ❖ ❖

For several days Angela didn't budge from the apartment. She took the dog out for a quick walk twice a day, then she raced home. She didn't want to see anyone, she didn't want to talk to anyone. She ignored phone calls; she refused to come to the door when someone pounded there. She just called out that she was fine.

Except she wasn't fine, and she realized she couldn't hide any longer. What must her friends think? They were already worried, but now they left messages for her. Don't give into the grief! they said. You have to move on! they counseled. Don't become a hermit! Think of yourself; you're still young! Go out and try not to think!

In the morning, when it wasn't quite as grey as it had been, Angela showered, dressed, and left the apartment.

She greeted everyone she met warmly, and she shook hands with the shopkeepers and their customers and the deliveryman and mail carrier, and after each instance, she saw a number. She had her notebook with her, so each time she jotted down the number and the occasion of the meeting. She did that all day long, walking along the streets, greeting people she knew — after all, she and Ben had lived there a long time and had come to know a lot of people, if just even by sight — and then she headed home.

She kept tabs on the obits in the newspapers, and each time someone she'd shaken hands with died, she put a little check mark by the notebook item.

There were, she thought some three months later, *a lot of obits, a lot of dead people*. And even the newspaper reporters had started to notice the high incidents of death in that area of the city. It was odd, these clusters of death, authorities said, because the deaths weren't all murders or suicides. *Bummer about the stats not working out*, she thought, and almost laughed aloud.

She watched from her window and wondered how long the people out there had to live. What about the people in the apartment building? Wasn't there supposed to be an association meeting that night? She imagined she would have to shake a lot of hands; it was the courteous thing to do, after all.

She laughed, this time long and hard, and the dog raised his head and whined softly.

She couldn't stay in. She had to find out about more numbers. Wasn't there someone who didn't have a number?

She went back out again, and headed in a different direction. *Time to skew the stats some more.*

She shook hand after hand all along her walk. She was the epitome of a friendly person. She smiled. She laughed when she chatted with acquaintances. *3. 17. 41. 65.* The numbers shimmered and flew by her, and once she reached out to touch the numeral, but there was nothing there, of course.

She paused when she saw a patrol car cruise by, and thought the two cops inside must be searching for something, anything!

But they won't find anything, she told herself, *because who would believe it?* She paused in front of a shop window and wondered who the haggard woman staring at her was. She grimaced and realized it was her own reflection. *I look like hell*, she thought. *I have to work on myself. I have to eat better; I have to get some sleep. I have to remember to comb my hair before leaving the apartment.* But as she stared at the circles under her eyes and at the hollows in her cheeks, she wondered if it was worth it.

Should I shake my own hand? she thought, trying not to giggle. *Will I see a number? Did Ben do this?* How long had he had this ability? And why hadn't he said anything to her? Did he think she wouldn't believe him? Well, maybe she wouldn't have. But maybe she would have. He should have warned her!

And as she stared at her gaunt face — like death warmed over, her dad always said — she wondered something else.

What if ... she took a deep breath ... what if she wasn't just seeing the number of days left in someone's life? What if this whole thing was something more, something like— No. It couldn't be, but yet... What if she was the one who caused these people to die? After all, there had been a lot of deaths in the area since Ben's death. Surely, not all those people had been about to die. What if, somehow, she helped them along? Maybe it was like a roulette wheel, and when she held someone's hand, the spinning wheel stopped, and the little death ball jumped and bounced and the number that came up was the number of days left in that person's life.

So, if she didn't shake someone's hand, she wouldn't know, and they wouldn't know, and maybe they would live forever and ever. Or at least for another decade or two.

Interesting. She chuckled, and she watched as a man walking behind her glanced over at her, then looked sharply away. *Don't like what you see, eh? Me, either.*

She spun away from the shop window and thrust her hands into her pockets. What now? Home to the greyness and the dog and staring out the window, or... or something else.

Only one way to find out, she told herself, and she walked down the street, heading to the hospital. She had to see the doctors and nurses who had worked on her husband, who had failed to save his life. She wanted to shake their hands and tell them she knew they had done all they could. Except they hadn't. She knew that somehow they had messed up... or Ben would still be alive today!

And maybe when she got to the hospital, she'd find the ambulance crew there, too... She'd shake their hands as well, and thank them, all the while thinking they could have worked on Ben faster, could have made better time to the hospital.

And when she was done there, perhaps she would stroll to some other wards to pay a few visits. Maybe the maternity ward. She glanced down at the lifeline on her hand... *No loving husband and no four kids, and if I can't have them*, she thought, her dried lips quirking into a smile, *maybe others shouldn't, either.*

She started whistling as she walked into the greyness.

❖ ❖ ❖

KATHRYN PTACEK's novels (in various genres) are being reissued as ebooks from Crossroad Press and Necon Ebooks. Check out her Facebook page for updates. She lives in the beautiful northwest corner of New Jersey where she keeps a lively garden. She collects teapots and beads.

things in jars

BY JUDITH & GARFIELD REEVES-STEVENS

CHICK DIDN'T KNOW how long he'd been driving, or exactly where he was, only that the Jeep was overheating, the tank was bumping on empty, the hundred grand was safe in the blood-splattered gym bag, and he wasn't dead yet. That was a good feeling. Not being dead. He wanted to keep it that way.

The knife wound hurt like hell, though. Bleeding seemed to have stopped some miles back. Another good sign. Fat Ernie hadn't had good aim or much strength after his shattered teeth got shoved down his throat. His dying slash against Chick's ribs hadn't done all that much damage. Certainly nothing punctured. Nothing time couldn't heal. Gas was another thing. And water. Hot as the desert was, the Jeep's temperature gauge was register-ing hotter, the little white needle deep in the red. It made Chick think of his own knife, deep in Fat Ernie, blood everywhere. The knife was wrapped in a sweaty workout towel stuffed in with the cash. The weapon would be the second thing he'd bury in the desert. Fat Ernie had been the first, one long day and two stolen cars ago.

"Next time steal a car with GPS, a-hole," Chick said. Talking to himself, he'd managed to stay awake and drive all night. So he kept talking to himself, now through the blinding day, along the endless road stretching out to a vanishing point lost in the silver shimmer of a mirage at the smeared horizon.

The engine missed, the Jeep lurched, the gas needle below empty now. Chick swore, just as he had when Fat Ernie had slashed the knife down his side, ruined his new jacket, his best shirt. His eyes moved to the rear-view mirror. Still nothing. His gaze shifted back, ahead.

That's when he saw it. Something in the middle of nothing, nowhere. A weathered wooden sign stuck in roadside scrub and gravel. Sand-scoured letters spelling out:

last chance

gas

food

things in jars

Just beyond, a ramshackle old shed of a building with a faded Coca-Cola sign on the side, a single gas pump out front.

Of course he pulled in, coasted in more like it. The Jeep dying just as he reached the pump. His luck was holding.

Chick got out, squinting in the glare of the desert day, legs stiff, side of his chest prickly with dried blood. He checked under the dirty blue windbreaker he'd lifted from the first car he'd stolen. The long cut had scabbed over. No big deal.

"Yo!" he shouted. "A little service!" His voice didn't even echo, the air was that still. All he heard was something creaking. Gentle. A slow creak, silence, another creak. It was coming from around the side. He pictured some old geezer in a rocking chair. That'd be about right for a dump like this. He started for the side of the shed, then remembered.

He turned back to the Jeep. No sense lugging the gym bag around, calling too much attention to it. So he took it off the passenger seat, pushed it deeper under the dash, locked the doors, laughing at himself because probably the only living soul within fifty miles was the old geezer in the creaky rocking chair and he was round the corner.

But it wasn't a rocking chair. It was another sign. This one hanging from a metal rod off a post. For a moment, Chick didn't register whatever it was the sign said because of what he saw behind it, twenty feet farther on.

A big old tent. Striped red and white, or used to be before the sun got at it. Like the circus had come to town about a hundred years ago and never left. How'd he miss seeing something that size from the road?

Creak.

The sign was swinging, slow and gentle. Chick didn't even register that there was no breeze. He was too distracted by what this sign said.

things in jars
admission 25¢

Twenty-five cents? Nothing cost twenty-five cents these days. He looked at the tent. It had an entrance, though whatever was on the inside was lost in black shadow.

He glanced back over his shoulder to—

He jumped, choked, breath held.

"Heard ya callin'," the attendant said, standing right behind Chick. He wore oil-stained overalls, the name *Harry* embroidered on the filthy oval nametag. He wiped his hands on an oil-slicked rag. He squinted and his face creased up in deep furrows like parched land and made Chick think he was as old as the tent.

"Make some noise would ya, a-hole." Chick hadn't heard his approach.

The attendant, Harry, ignored the comment. "Need some gas, huh?"

"Whaddya think?" The guy was an idiot.

"Water, too?"

Chick stared at him. "It's the desert."

"Take a while."

"To fill a gas tank?"

The attendant didn't seem to notice that Chick's responses were coming shriller and sharper, too much like a man in a hurry, trying to outrace panic. Which he was.

"Gotta start the pump," Harry said. "Get it primed. Don't get a lot of call to use it so I keep it shut off." His face contorted in what Chick thought was supposed to be a grin. "Good for the environment."

"Yeah, yeah, whatever, man. Just do it fast."

The attendant nodded sagely, as if Chick had made a wise, out-of-the-box suggestion. He wiped his hands again. Chick noticed a reddish tinge to the stains. Had a sudden doubt that it *was* oil.

"Feel free," Harry said. He gave a nod, looked past Chick. Chick knew he meant the tent.

"What's in there?"

"What the sign says."

Chick glanced back to the dark entrance. It did look cool. Shady. Relief and respite from the sun. "Well, what kinda—" But he didn't finish the question because the attendant was already rounding the corner of the shed, out of earshot, then out of sight.

As enticing as the promise of shade was, Chick took off after Harry. His future was under the dash in the front passenger side and he wasn't about to risk it.

The attendant was starting up some kind of machinery in the shed and Chick heard the muffled grind of a pump rev into life, smelled the acrid stench of diesel fuel. Harry had him pop the hood so he could get at the radiator, used the rag to twist off the cap, then stepped back with no great hurry as scalding water geysered and sputtering vapor spewed. "Take a while," the attendant said once more. "Gotta let it cool." He took a long time to say that last word.

Chick swore as he locked the Jeep again. He hated the desert. Hated the sun. Hated being stuck here waiting on a doddering old fart. He thought of the shade.

He made his way back to the tent. Stood at the entrance, smelled the difference in the air that issued from its dark depths. Inside was cool, not musty. Surprising. The scent of whatever the tent held was somehow electric, plastic, in the way new electronics smelled coming out of their packaging. He took another breath, inhaled deeply, trying to puzzle out why the scent seemed so familiar. He stepped inside.

Not as dark as he'd thought. Out of the glare of the sun, the impenetrable shadows of the tent's interior were lightened by daylight glowing through the canvas.

And everywhere, there were jars.

Sweeping toward him, towering over him, a frozen tidal wave of glass. Large jars, small jars. Jars stacked on shelves and tables and each other. Some were clear, some were dark, some had ordinary twist-off metal caps, others were held in wooden crates or cages or rope or chains and sealed with wax or padlocks and one huge one held sideways in a vise clamped to an antique metal bracket.

He saw a bell jar upended on a plank of wood, covering a square of what looked like toffee with a bite mark taken out of one side, a child's tooth embedded in the other.

Chuck didn't get it.

He looked at another jar. Floating inside, a knotted ball of two-headed snakes. In another, a baby's finger. In another, a milky liquid that maybe had something *moving* in it.

"No way." Chick's voice sounded like a whisper in a room cloaked with heavy curtains, swallowed instantly. The silence was physical.

He shook off his unease and moved on to another row of jars. Saw an old baseball card on a stand in one jar, but didn't recognize the player or his uniform. Another had maybe something like stewed tomatoes, all red and wet and wrinkled? Pig knuckles in another? A spider's web. A dried heart. Another empty except for what looked like tiny handprints pressed on the glass from the inside.

"Okay. This is stupid."

He turned to leave, but the entrance wasn't where he thought it was, only more shelves, more tables.

More jars.

"Hey!" he shouted. But his voice went nowhere.

He spun around, tried to get his bearings, and failed because the tent seemed larger than he'd expected, a lot larger on the inside than the outside.

"Got to be two tents."

He walked ahead, turned a corner, stopped to find a jar crammed with floating eyeballs, and all of them staring at him.

"Stop it," he muttered.

He turned another corner, looked for scuffmarks in the dirt floor, anything that might point a way to an exit.

And then he saw it.

A hole in the canvas high overhead had let in one long, dust-filled spike of sunlight and it shone down on one jar among the multitude, sparkling off the curved glass and making the object inside gleam with a pure blue metallic gloss like molten desert sky.

Chick didn't want to be distracted. He wanted his Jeep filled with gas and water and one hundred grand of untraceable cash and he wanted out of here and on with his life. But it was a very unusual blue, deeply compelling in its way, so a moment or two longer in here wouldn't really matter.

He went closer to the jar, bent down to get a better look at what was inside.

Something the size and shape of the kind of hefty pens Fat Ernie always used to write his coded entries in his notebook. A Montcalm or Cross or something fancy like that. But there was a subtle indentation along one side that made Chick's fingers twitch as if they *had* to hold it. And that color. The sculptural balance of the pen itself. It looked for all the world as if someone had conceived of and then made the *perfect* object to be held in a human hand in order to... to what? Chick couldn't tell. The object was standing up on one end, leaning against the inside of the glass jar, and the bottom tip where he'd expect to see a nib was obscured by something thick and dark and crusted. For a moment, he thought of the scabbed-over knife wound striping his ribs. Dried blood? What would dried blood be doing on something like that?

"Good question," the attendant whispered in his ear.

Chick jumped the proverbial mile, spun around. Harry stood ten feet away, far out of whisper range.

"Screw you old man, you scared me!"

The attendant shrugged it off, nodded at the jar. "You like it."

Chick's heart was thundering. He felt his hands tremble and he folded his arms to still them. "What is it?"

"Take it out."

Chick looked back at the jar, at the object inside. For a moment, he felt as if all the other jars in the tent were empty, that only this jar held something. He wanted it.

"Go ahead," the attendant said. "It's calling you."

Chick didn't bother asking what the crazy coot meant by that, just picked up the jar. The object clattered inside as it shifted around. A series of glowing white dots lit up on one side, then faded. He put his hand on the twist-off cap, hesitated.

"Seriously, what is it?"

"It'll tell you."

"Tell me what?"

The attendant took a moment to look around at all the jars, almost as if he was counting them. "Every jar has a story." He looked back at Chick. "This one's yours."

Chick was tired of the geezer. He twisted off the cap, pulled out the object, and just as he had suspected, it *was* perfectly balanced.

"I know this. It was Andrugene's."

Even as he said the words, Chick had no idea who Andrugene was, and then he did. "The rock star." He paused a moment as the details came to him. "What a schmuck. The guy had everything, and then…"

"Go on," the attendant murmured.

And as if he were there, Chick remembered—

✣ ✣ ✣

—the doctor's office. Not like any Chick had seen. Everything was new and crisp and expensive, as if it was made tomorrow, not today. And Andrugene was there. Tall, slim, head shaved, diamond earring, tattoos everywhere, peace, love, respect, the cheering crowds, the women, the men, the private jet, the parties, the most Grammies, the biggest sales, everything— Andrugene's life engulfing Chick as if he were living it not just observing. As if *he* were Andrugene.

The doctor, subdued and respectful, looked at the MRI images on the desktop screen she had angled for him. Slice after slice of the brain that had given birth to so many songs, created such beauty, and such wealth. "As we feared," she said.

Andrugene could barely say the word, but knew he had to. "Inoperable."

The word hung there in the silence. But the doctor drew herself up, unwilling to let it stay there alone. "Today," she said. "Today. But microsurgery techniques are constantly improving. The instruments become smaller, the targeting more precise..."

"When?" the superstar asked.

The doctor was reluctant to go on the record. She adjusted her glasses. "Five years? Ten? It is difficult to say with certainty."

"Not for me," Andrugene said. He was twenty-six and already worth billions. And yet a handful of cells in his skull was threatening to take it all away. "How much time do I have?"

The doctor glanced at the MRIs again. "Six months." Then she met his eyes directly. "But you understand, you could have more."

Andrugene understood. "Let's do it."

❖ ❖ ❖

"I don't understand," Chick said. He stared at the blue metal object in his hand.

"Sure you do," Harry said. But where Harry was now, Chick couldn't be sure. Somewhere off to the side, behind a wall of jars? Chick turned to see if—

❖ ❖ ❖

Andrugene lay on the yielding plastic surface of the cooling platform. The needles in his arms still stung, and he could hear the whirr of the heart-lung machine as it siphoned his blood, drew heat from it, one carefully calibrated degree at a time, mixed it with the doctor's potions, and pumped it back.

The light in the prep room was low and amber, like sunlight filtered through old canvas. The doctor a wraith in white, hair and face swathed, moving silently, checking, rechecking, then standing at his side.

"I'm cold…," Andrugene breathed. His voice sounded distant even to himself.

"You'll get colder." The doctor seemed sad, though he couldn't see her face, only dark eyes behind glasses behind the plastic visor, already receding behind reflection after shimmering reflection. "But not for long."

Andrugene sighed as the prep room began to fade, swirls of darkness rising from the edges of his vision as if a spotlight on his stage were blinding him with a single point of—

He gasped when an even brighter light flared so intensely that he tried to turn away but his muscles burned as if they were being gouged from his body with a knife.

✣ ✣ ✣

In the tent, Chick stumbled back, sputtering with pain. "What the f—"

"Shh," the attendant said as he clamped his oil-slicked hand around Chick's. "You don't want to drop it."

Chick looked down at Harry's hand, wrapping his, holding the object. So blue, so—

✣ ✣ ✣

"Is that better?" the doctor asked.

At least, Andrugene assumed his questioner was a doctor. Difficult to be sure because his vision was still washed out by the bright light, growing dimmer now, thankfully, though his eyes still throbbed as if he'd been in the dark too long. His arms ached, too. And his legs. He tried to shake his head, to shake himself awake, but couldn't.

"Is something wrong?"

"Can't move," Andrugene said. Even his throat hurt.

"Just restraints. Coming out of suspension, movements can be awkward, erratic. Can't let you hurt yourself."

"Coming out…" Andrugene smiled despite the pain. "Then the tumor…?"

"I don't know about that," the doctor said. Andrugene saw him move to a white wall and begin to sit down. For a moment, there was no chair, and then one seemed to balloon from the wall to meet him. It was so fast, and so odd, that Andrugene wasn't certain that he'd actually seen it.

"But I've had the procedure, right? That's why you woke me up?"

"Ah," the doctor said. He looked at his forearm, brushed his finger through the air. Something glowed up at him. "This is your first time."

"I don't understand."

"That's all right. My questions will only take a few moments of your time."

Andrugene struggled, managed to move enough that he felt the sting of needles in his arms. He was still hooked up to equipment, plastic tubes filled with who-knew-what snaking over the edge of the bed. That's why he was restrained. That made sense. He settled back. "Ask away." He had time to spare now.

"Good, good." The doctor made motions over his forearm again and light flickered up from something Andrugene couldn't see. Probably an iPad or phone or something. "I'm interested in the recording industry's reaction to President Ortega's crackdown on stimloads."

"Say what?" The doctor's words had been garbled.

"Illegal stimloads."

"What's a... stimload?"

The doctor looked away from his forearm. "Understandable. Sometimes memory can be affected by revival. We can start slow. Go back. Say to... when Ortega was elected for his first term."

"You mean Obama. President Obama."

"No, no. That's fifty years too..." The doctor stopped, checked his forearm again. "Oh for... When you were suspended, *Obama* was president?"

"Right. Who's Ortega?"

The doctor stood and the chair slurped back into the wall and Andrugene could see that his questioner had no iPad or phone— it was the skin of his forearm that glowed like a computer screen.

"I'm terribly sorry," the doctor said. "There'll be a technician here soon." He walked toward another wall and a door was suddenly there, opened, and closed behind him.

"Wait!" Andrugene cried out, then coughed because his throat burned. "I need to—" Something cold flooded up through his arms and took his breath away and the light in the strange room dimmed and darkened into a single vanishing point and—

❖ ❖ ❖

Chick turned to Harry and Harry was suddenly a dozen attendants fractured by reflections in a dozen jars, then a hundred Harrys, a hundred jars, all trapped in a diamond of light.

"What're you doing to me?" Chick cried out.

"Not me," a hundred Harrys answered. "Out of gas, out of time, too hot… It isn't me."

Chick spun, furious, hand raised, ready to throw the object he held. The object that was… so beautiful. So perfect. So meant for him. His upheld hand trembled, unsure, uncertain.

"You don't want to do that," all the Harrys said. "Not 'till the story's finished."

❖ ❖ ❖

Andrugene snapped alert, sat up, eyesight perfect, muscles feeling… surprisingly good. It was as if he had just awakened after drifting off during a fantastically good massage. He felt like standing up from the warm seat he was sitting on, stretching, running a mile or two then—

He couldn't stand.

He looked down. Saw a seatbelt. More straps across his chest. He looked for a clasp or connector.

"They don't like you doing that, dear."

The soft voice came from an older woman he didn't recognize. Her hair was short and white, her face lined, but her eyes were bright. Her pale blue hospital gown was decorated with what looked to be three-fingered hands and starbursts.

"I'm Ann," she said. Like him, she was seatbelted and chest-strapped into a small chair that reminded him of something from an airplane. Both chairs were mounted against a white wall and flanked by more chairs running the length of it. Each one past Ann was occupied by a man or woman, all ages but mostly old, all races but mostly Asian, all of them except Ann looking stunned, eyes open, but not responsive, though the man immediately beside her seemed to be coming around. Andrugene looked to the other side. He was first in line. Looking down, he saw the chairs were on a track that ran along the floor by the wall. He realized then they were moving, slowly and silently, along it.

"What's your name, dear?"

"Andrugene."

She smiled. "Of course. Andrugene comes before Ann. Some of the facilities still go by the old ways."

"What facilities? Where are we?"

"Oh, could be anywhere by now." She looked at him more closely, her expression sympathetic. "Is this your first time, dear?"

"First time what?"

"Extracted from storage."

"Storage?"

"Well, there are so many of us. No place to put us. But they are humane." She made a comical face. "Won't pull the plug, I mean."

Andrugene stared at her in confusion, not wanting — not *daring* — to believe what she was saying.

Ann smiled brightly. "I like to think we're like books in a library." Again, the narrowed eyes, the expression of concern. "You do remember books, dear? What year were you born?"

Andrugene told her.

Ann's eyes widened, impressed. "Oh my goddess. You *are* an oldtimer." She looked down the row behind them. "I've met some of these others before. I think the researchers want to ask most of us about the Nomii riots. I get asked about that every generation or so." She looked back at him. "But you were born a century before the Nomii were even invented." She leaned forward, whispered, "I believe you've been misfiled, dear."

Quite understandably, Andrugene screamed then, but somehow, he suddenly felt a surge of wellbeing as if his brain had been flooded with endorphins from a really great workout and he felt so good that he couldn't even remember why he had screamed and—

✥ ✥ ✥

Chick sat on the dirt floor of the tent surrounded by walls of jars through which no path gave exit.

As good as he felt, as rested and as calm as his body was, his mind was a gibbering fool, sobbing with fear. He had to get out of here, back to the Jeep, full of gas, cooled with fresh water, the money in the gym bag his ticket to a brand new life free from Fat Ernie and the collections and the squalid emptiness his life had become to the point at which he could imagine taking someone else's in order to escape his own.

It had seemed like such a good idea at the time.

Getting up seemed like such a good idea right now.

Never stopping here. Never entering the tent. Never looking in the jar.

All such good ideas.

All too late.

"Shh," all the Harrys whispered. "The story's almost over. Listen to it."

Chick sat on the dirt floor, wanting to scream, wanting to run, but all he could do was look down at the oh-so-beautiful blue object in his hand, with its dry crusted residue that might have been blood, with the little dots of light that now glowed and flickered along one side of it, that in its perfection spoke to him, and to him alone—

❖ ❖ ❖

Andrugene next woke in an office.

He had no reason to think that's what it was, but that was what it felt like. A small cubicle. Walls a bit grimy. Plastic? Metal? Glass? No way to tell. This time he was sitting in a chair, with no straps and no padding. He glanced down and saw he was wearing a one-piece gray overall with no buttons, zippers, or pockets. The sleeves were long so he couldn't see his bare arms, but he was certain no needles were stuck into them.

Across from him was a desk, or something desklike. A block of the same material the walls were made from. Behind it sat a man, Asian again, though his skin was darker than Andrugene would expect, heavily creased and wrinkled, with deep furrows like parched land. He was bald, as well, not even eyebrows.

The man was writing, wielding a distinctive blue pen with a smooth metallic finish. Lights flickered along the shaft of the pen, synchronized with the movements the man was making as he wrote.

Andrugene's fingers knew exactly how that pen would feel.

❖ ❖ ❖

Chick's fingers knew exactly how that pen would feel. He was holding it after all.

❖ ❖ ❖

Though the bald man's motions suggested writing, he wasn't actually writing on anything. Instead, a stream of glowing letters formed inches above the surface of the desk, scrolling from side to side. Andrugene didn't recognize the letters. Their shapes were nothing he had seen before.

The man seemed to become aware of Andrugene studying him. He looked up. "Greetings. I am Aarl." He moved the pen over the desktop and new streams of glowing letters appeared. Now Andrugene saw an image of himself mixed in among the unreadable text. "You are, Andrew Michael Gennaro. Sino Pax Epoch." Aarl had a thick accent. Andrugene couldn't place it.

"Where am I?"

Aarl made a coughing sound, moved his pen, read new unreadable letters. "Just a few questions, first." The last word sounded like "fust."

"I don't think so," Andrugene said. He stood up, hiding his surprise at being able to do so. He waited for something to happen, for restraints to shoot from the wall, for his brain to be flooded with drugs. Nothing happened.

Aarl didn't seem concerned, didn't react. "Fust question," he said.

"No questions," Andrugene told him. "Not 'till you answer mine. What is this place? What year is it?"

Aarl wrote, read, looked up at Andrugene, held out the pen as if inviting him to sign something.

"You asking for my autograph?" Andrugene wanted to laugh. But he knew he couldn't waste time. What if he had been taken out of suspension by mistake again? What if they were going to put him back on the shelf?

"Screw that," Andrugene said. He'd given up everything for another chance at life. He wasn't about to let some useless clerk or librarian or whatever Aarl was cost another second of lost time.

Andrugene took the pen from Aarl's hand, no resistance.

Aarl bared his teeth in some twisted form of a smile, as if it was something he'd never done. He mumbled a few syllables, waved his hand at the glowing letters above his desk, the glowing image of Andrugene.

The smooth hard surface of the pen felt perfect in Andrugene's hand. As balanced as the finest throwing knife.

Nothing was worth another lost second of his life.

He drove the pen up under Aarl's jaw, felt the pop of membranes and the soft parting of flesh as the perfect instrument slid perfectly through muscle and bone and into brain.

Aarl blinked once, his eyelids fluttered, and then he slumped back in his chair, blood dribbling down past the pen embedded in his jaw.

Andrugene waited. But still nothing happened.

There was a door on the far side of the room.

Andrugene pulled the pen from the dead man's jaw, held it as a weapon, walked toward the door.

Finally, his life was about to begin again.

The door opened as if it had been expecting him.

✣ ✣ ✣

"No, no, no!" Chick said. He shook his hand violently, as if he'd been burned, desperate to throw the blue object onto the dirt floor of the tent. But it was as if the thick dark material had crusted to his skin, like the dried blood across his ribs.

He could not let go.

✣ ✣ ✣

Andrugene stepped out onto a metal floor in a dark corridor. He shivered in a draft of cold air, puzzled by the crisp scent of plastic and electronics.

He became aware of the deep vibration of some vast unseen machinery at work somewhere nearby. Far down the corridor, a solitary point of light gleamed and shimmered. He walked toward it, bloody pen in hand.

The corridor opened into an atrium. Immense. The full scope and size of it hidden by shadows. The machinery thrummed and echoed. The air was colder. The walls of the place were lined with large cylinders, glass-walled, frosted, stacked like jars.

His hand shook as he scraped at the closest cylinder.

Inside, a person. Sleeping. Suspended.

He scraped at another, and another. Eventually, he even found Ann, though her face was no longer wrinkled and her hair no longer white, her bright eyes unseen behind serene, closed lids.

He stood back, confused, upset, and called out. To rouse anyone outside the cylinders who could hear him.

But no one answered. Totally alone.

With the spur of growing panic, he began running, through the atrium, heading for the far side where, in the dim light, it seemed the towering walls of glass cylinders ended.

Halfway, there, lungs burning in the frigid air, he could tell the source of the illumination was starlight. He saw the Milky Way before him, thankful at least to be at ground level and not buried inside some long lost underground storage chamber.

Then he arrived at the edge of the atrium and saw that the Milky Way and the endless stars were behind an enormous window that stretched hundreds of feet side to side and overhead.

That's where he found the dedication plaques. Dozens of them, in languages known and unknown, and eventually the one written in English.

The one that apologized to the four million resurrectees aboard the *Fair Wind*, held too long against their will. The one that explained they had been genetically restored to live healthily and happily on the new world that awaited them at the end of their journey.

The dedication plaque had a small icon of what was apparently a communications device at the bottom. The pen. Andrugene touched his murder weapon to it.

Glowing letters and numbers appeared over the plaque then, along with lines and circles showing the great journey now underway between Earth and the new world, only four hundred more years to go. Please report to Mr. Aarl, the letters said, to resume suspension...

❖ ❖ ❖

Chick gasped as the pen escaped his hand and flew through the close air of the tent, gleaming end over blood-encrusted end until it clattered inside the jar he'd found it in.

He didn't know how long he stood there, trying to separate himself from the story, until he began to suspect that maybe he never would.

That's when he became aware of Harry standing behind him, taking a step even closer as he whispered into Chick's ear, "That'll be twenty-five cents."

❖ ❖ ❖

Chick staggered from the tent and into harsh desert sunlight. His eyes stung and his muscles hurt as if he'd been held motionless for days, for untold time.

He looked for the attendant but mercifully didn't see him. Maybe his luck was back. About time.

He walked as quickly as he could to the front of the shed.

His Jeep wasn't by the gas pump. Instead, a cherry red 1958 El Dorado Cadillac purred there, freshly polished, top down, ready to go.

Harry emerged from the shed, overalls gone, clad in a sharp plaid sports coat that Chick was vaguely aware would've been all the rage half a century ago.

"Jeep's around back," Harry said. He spoke quickly, a man in a hurry. He jingled a set of car keys on a rabbit's foot chain. He cocked a thumb in the direction of the shed. "Hung yours up by your working duds."

Chick's eyes were caught by the sparkle of sunlight dancing on the metal key ring hanging on a small hook just inside the shed. Beside it, a set of brand-new overalls. He could guess the name embroidered in the oval.

"How long?" Chick asked.

Harry was already behind the big white wheel of his El Dorado. "That's up to the jars." He slammed the car into gear. "It won't be forever."

Then gravel sprayed and dust billowed and as Harry shot toward the shimmering horizon, his last words trailed off in the dry, still air. "But sure as hell they'll make it feel that way."

✛ ✛ ✛

JUDITH & GARFIELD REEVES-STEVENS are *New York* and *Los Angeles Times* bestselling novelists. Stephen King praised their thriller, *Icefire*, as "the best suspense novel of its type since *The Hunt for Red October*." Their newest novel of supernatural horror and suspense is *Wraith*, from Thomas Dunne Books, an imprint of St. Martin's Press. Recent projects include consulting with the Disney Imagineers as writers for the new Shanghai Disneyland, and creating the horror series, *Incarnate*, based on one of Garfield's novels, for HBO Canada.

Right of Survivorship

by Nancy Holder and Erin Underwood

THAT'S GOTTA HURT, Michael thought, as he spared a glance at a streaming BBC news report on his laptop. On the screen, grainy security footage showed three men breaking into the Old Map, the pub down the street from his uncle's antiquarian bookshop. One skinhead shattered the window with a tire iron and the other two barreled on in. Michael pursed his lips together in a grim half-smile. No, he didn't think he'd be flying to London anytime soon.

He was about to resume work on the merger when Mr. Hartner, one of the senior partners, rapped on the doorjamb. Michael kept his door open. International corporate law was like a war, and he did everything necessary to maintain his position on the front lines. Drawbridge down, no moat in sight.

He half-stood as his boss walked in— and forced himself not to grimace as Asha Sen followed after, very chummy with the old man, smiling in triumph at Michael. She didn't have an appointment, and he'd refused to see her.

The British attorney was as beautiful in person as she was on Skype. She wore her long, straight black hair tied back with a golden pin and a black suit that complemented her lovely dark complexion and almond-shaped eyes. There were shadows under those eyes and her cheeks were gaunt. When she saw him, she sucked in her breath just a little and blinked. The O'Dare genes were strong. He knew he looked like his uncle, only younger, with his coal black hair and silver eyes.

"Look who I found in the waiting room," Mr. Hartner declared, the traces of his British accent more pronounced than usual. "Why didn't you tell me you had family business with Morris and Fletcher? You know we have a longstanding relationship with them." He smiled at Ms. Sen, and she smiled pleasantly back. "The timing is providential as we have a London client who's been sitting on her proxies. Michael, you can hold her hand and get your uncle's papers in order at the same time."

"I have the merger," Michael protested. It was the plum assignment of the quarter, and he had fought tooth and nail to get it.

"You'll only be gone a few days, yes? If anything comes up, I'll put Brian on it," Mr. Hartner said, and Michael tried to flash Ms. Sen a killing look. Brian Glick was his bitterest rival. Michael had given up what was left of his social life in order to score this assignment and he would be damned before he let Glick touch it. But Ms. Sen stood firmly in the elderly attorney's line of sight, and hence, protected from Michael's glare.

"There are two flights out tonight," Ms. Sen informed Michael and Mr. Hartner at the same time.

"Our staff keep suitcases packed and ready," Mr. Hartner told her. "We have an in-house travel agent who can book the tickets. Got your passport, Michael?" His voice was amiable, but Michael heard the warning in it: he'd better be ready. He knew better than to disappoint a partner.

He'd better go.

"Of course, sir," he said.

Mr. Hartner left, and Ms. Sen stayed behind. Maybe she was used to swaying men with her beauty, but it wasn't working on him.

"Congratulations," he snapped at her.

"I wouldn't have done it if it weren't absolutely necessary," she replied, unruffled. "As you know, you stand to inherit everything, if you agree to sign the lease in our London office by ten o'clock this Thursday."

"A lease that you neglected to FedEx along with every other piece of paper in my uncle's file cabinet," he said pointedly. "All of which I've already signed and had notarized, and returned to you."

"I was unable to include it," she replied.

"Because it's *enchanted*."

She dipped her head in assent, and he made a point of returning his attention to his laptop. "My uncle never once mentioned any of this... insanity."

"Your cousin was next in line, but when Sean died, you became Daniel's sole heir. By then..." She stopped speaking and despite himself, he took the bait and looked up at her. He and Sean had been like brothers. Sean had come to visit, they went out drinking, and Michael should never have let him drive. After that, he'd stopped going to London.

"By then you had cut your uncle out of your life, and broken his heart," she said.

He blinked, shocked that she would say such a thing straight to his face, and masked his emotion by muttering "I'm busy" and turning his attention back to his work.

❖ ❖ ❖

It was bucketing rain. Enroute to JFK, the cabbie listened to the news; the violence in London was escalating from a local skirmish to full-blown riots throughout the city. Economic uncertainty, hostility toward immigrants, the fading middle-class, and "keeping English jobs for the English." Michael was even angrier with Ms. Sen, both for dragging him to London and for her cutting remark about how he had neglected his poor, dying uncle. It was unprofessional and untrue. He had even sent Uncle Daniel a birthday card not two weeks ago.

No, he hadn't. He saw it in his briefcase now, as he double-checked to make sure he had his passport— and still in need of an international postage stamp. A frisson of guilt tickled his spine, and he snapped his briefcase shut.

She paid the fare; they stepped out of the taxi and headed inside the terminal. At the airline kiosk, he printed out his ticket while she stabbed her finger at the next touchscreen over, her expression growing darker with each error message that lit the screen.

"Something wrong?" Michael asked, peering over her shoulder.

"My reservation's gone," she said double-checking the itinerary that Michael's assistant had printed out for them. She lightly smacked the screen. "And the flight is full."

"Pity." His voice dripped with insincerity.

"I'll take the later flight." She tapped the screen again. "Faeries," she swore.

"I beg your pardon?"

"Bloody hell! The later flight's been delayed."

"Thanks to you, I have to take this flight. Mr. Hartner has already arranged for me to see our client tomorrow morning," Michael said, savoring his reprieve.

"I know."

And it was only then that he realized that what she had said was "faeries." Which could mean that she believed in the mystical lease he was supposed to sign— a longstanding compact, centuries old, made between the O'Dares and Mab, Queen of the Fair Folk, perpetuating the human race's lease on the planet. According to Ms. Sen, it was due to expire, and if he, Michael O'Dare, didn't renew it, the world would fall under the control of the *Sidhe*, the fae realm that Queen Mab ruled.

"So you're telling me that the faeries screwed up your reservation," he said, smirking, but her cheeks colored as she made her reservation for the following morning on the kiosk screen. When she didn't answer, he pushed a little harder. "I'm the one who has to sign the lease. Why didn't they screw up mine?"

"They can't interfere directly with the Leaseholder," she bit off.

"They interfered with you."

"I'm not the Leaseholder, Michael. I'm just your attorney. "You should head to the security check now," she said, nodding in the direction of the winding TSA lines. "My colleague will be waiting for you at Heathrow after you clear customs. He'll have a sign with your name on it. Do *not* leave the airport unless you're with someone from my firm."

He raised his brows. "Don't tell me. Faeries?"

She was typing her passport number on a keypad on the screen. "They can't stop you directly, but they'll try to waylay you by stopping those you are with. So, no talking to anyone. No trusting anyone except *us*."

That means no trusting anyone, he thought. Which was already how he lived, so no problem there. He hadn't forgiven her for her "you broke his heart" comment and she hadn't seen fit to apologize for it. He couldn't get away from her fast enough, no matter how attractive she was or how nice she smelled. He tried to recall the last time he'd had sex. Or even gone out to dinner with a woman who wasn't a corporate client.

"See you in London," Michael replied coolly, and turned his back on her. He didn't appreciate having his hand forced, and he didn't like to lose.

On the plane, he was informed he'd been upgraded from business to first class— not the usual protocol, but he wouldn't turn down more legroom and champagne, especially on a red-eye flight. But as he was directed to his spacious seat, the large, welcoming grin on the face of the passenger abutting his side table made him cringe. He needed to go over their London client's file, and he would prefer to be given his privacy rather than having to handle a chatty stranger.

"Evening," the other man said in a booming Australian accent. He was drinking a beer. "I'm Broomfield. Matthew Anthony Broomfield."

"Listen—" Michael began.

"Heard there's going to be some turbulence." He glanced at the aircraft's door. "Missus not coming?"

Michael blinked, taken aback. "She's not my missus." He sat down with the file folder already in his lap. "I'm sorry, but I have a lot of work to do."

The Australian smiled. "Of course you do, successful man such as yourself. No worries. I've got a good book and a bad movie to entertain myself."

Michael nodded. If the man had taken offense, he had the grace to keep it to himself.

❖ ❖ ❖

You're so shut down. So closed off.

Now he recalled the last time he'd had sex. Toni. It had all gone downhill so fast. She wasn't the first woman to say that, and she probably wouldn't be the last. Personal relationships created weaknesses that he couldn't afford while clawing his way to the top of the firm. He had actually caught himself surreptitiously checking the time while she'd broken up with him. It was a little shocking, even to him. But wearisome, too.

Maybe when he was older, he'd do the relationship thing.

The next thing he knew, the plane was touching down on the London tarmac. He put away his work, frustrated that his mind had wandered. Broomfield took off his headphones and started talking about his movie. The trip through the airport went smoothly, except for the Australian's constant chatter as they waded through the line of travelers clearing customs before stepping out into the public area of Heathrow Airport.

Michael looked at the horde of chauffeurs bearing placards with people's names written in neat black ink, but none of them bore his name. He reached into his pocket for his phone. It wasn't there.

"Shit," he muttered.

He dropped his bags and dug through his pockets. As he began a second round of searching, a meaty hand appeared, bearing his cellphone like a pearl in the palm.

"Looking for this?" the Australian said. "I found it in my bag. Must have fallen out of your pocket on the plane."

"Thank you," Michael said, relieved.

He took it and switched it on. Nothing happened. The battery had been fully charged before he'd boarded, but still it didn't power up.

The Australian looked at him. "Need a ride?"

"No, thanks. I'm expected," Michael said. "They'll be here."

"I'll shove off, then." The man gave him a little wave, which Michael half-heartedly returned, and he resumed the search for his ride.

No one.

He waited another fifteen minutes, sighing and shifting. Finally he darted over to a cart and bought a phone charger, then found a place to plug in so that he could retrieve and send messages. It wouldn't charge. Something was definitely wrong with it.

She'd said to stay put, but he'd been to London enough times to get himself a cab. He was due at Lady Davis's in a couple of hours; if he left now, he had just enough time to stop off at their London office to finish reading her paperwork, say hello to his London counterparts, and freshen up. He jumped into a cab.

❖ ❖ ❖

Lady Davis was waffling on her proxies because she didn't trust anyone to run the companies in which she held investments. She was worried about the future of Britain, and no wonder. The ride from her beautiful row house to his uncle's flat was unnerving, to say the least. Windows boarded up, more "for let" signs than businesses, it seemed, and armed British soldiers in the streets. At the Hartner & Lowe London office, the staff had made anxious jokes about the state of the nation and the barbarians at the gates. "I mean," a colleague had said, "it makes one hesitant to suggest any sort of long-term strategic planning."

The cab dropped him off at Charing Cross Road outside Ogham Antiquarian Bookshop, in front of the unassuming blue door that led upstairs to his uncle's flat above the store.

As he walked up the interior stairway and into the flat, he smelled dust, tobacco smoke, and licorice, and he stopped for a moment, half-expecting to hear his uncle softly singing as he cooked up some beans and chips for dinner. Uncle Daniel had stepped in as the father he'd lost, but he wasn't at all like Michael's father. Could two brothers be any less alike? Uncle Daniel sang old Celtic songs and told old stories— fairy tales and poems about moons and galleons. Michael's father had been into tennis. Then again, that was what Michael had loved about Daniel.

"Hello, Uncle," Michael murmured, as he opened the door and flicked on a light. The birthday card sat heavy in his briefcase.

Daniel's apartment had always been filled with the oddest assortment of antiques and one-of-a-kind objects— ivory Chinese fans and lanterns, ebony elephants and windup monkeys complete with brass cymbals. A painting of Oscar Wilde whose eyes followed you everywhere, Michael swore.

Then there were what appeared to be journals with yellow covers, dozens of them. Michael vaguely remembered seeing a few in a box beneath Uncle Daniel's bed, back when he was a boy and he had thought he'd heard a strange, metallic laugh echoing through the rooms before Daniel had come upstairs from the shop. Michael had had no interest in them back then, but now?

Now Michael was alone in a dead man's home, and he tried to remember the last time he'd phoned or even emailed him.

Daniel had known Michael was busy; at least, Michael tried to tell himself that. He made himself a cup of tea and sat on the couch, surrounded by the journals, and opened one at random.

They taunt me that we're almost out of time. They say we're done for. They say that when the world is theirs again, they'll make the valleys green and the waters blue. But their Queen is cruel. Icy. Asha promises me that Michael will come.

Asha. Asha Sen.

Mab came for dinner. She had strawberries and sugar. I spilled the milk and she cooed over it as if it were a lamb. She counted it precious. She brought me whiskey and once she thought I was good and pissed, she tried to trick me out of the Lease. Asha arrived in the nick of time and she knew what to do. Salt and needles and Mab was out the door!

Then I sang Irish songs — you know what they say, the Irish sing sadly of love and merrily of battle — and I cried on Asha's shoulder because I'm alone in the world and must hang on for a fortnight to sign the Lease. Asha reminds me that we must expect more tricks from the Fair Folk until it is all taken care of. She's been reading her Yeats and all the old stories for clues about what they'll try. When I speak of Michael, she frowns, and then she softens and says that he is coming.

"So is Christmas," I told her, "and that's one thing we can count on."

"We can count on the faeries," she said, "to make it go hard with us."

Asha. There she was over and over again, encouraging Daniel. Affirming him. Deluding him. Michael shut the journal and threw it down on the stack on the coffee table. The freakishly, obsessively towering stack.

He had failed Daniel miserably by not being here during the last days, and because of that, Asha had stepped in and taken advantage. Daniel's mental condition was clearly fragile, allowing him to be preyed upon. Now she was trying to play Michael for the same kind of fool, but to what end? Whatever she wanted, she wasn't going to get it from him. He owed his uncle that much. He would never sign that lease.

As if on cue, he heard high heels clicking on the stairs. A key turned in the lock; then Asha stepped through the front door in her rumpled navy suit. When she saw him, the fear on her face hardened into anger.

"Where have you been? Why aren't you answering your phone?" she asked, jabbing the old brass skeleton key at him. "I was worried!"

"There was no one there to meet me. So I took care of my business. Besides my phone is broken."

She caught her lower lip between her teeth and set down her bag. "I thought *they* might have—"

"They? Oh, right. The faeries that are set to inherit the Earth, if I don't sign some piece of paper. You sure had my uncle convinced about that *faerie tale*. Why? What's in it for you?"

She jerked. Then she saw all the journals. "Where did you get these? I've been looking for them everywhere." She began to gather them up.

"I believe those are mine," he said. "Evidence if I decide to sue you."

She froze. "For what?"

"Preying on an old man. Warping his mind so that he couldn't tell fantasy from reality. Encouraging his delusions. Scaring him when he was old and sick." His voice cracked.

She glowered at him. "I beg your pardon. Your uncle was my friend. I was the one who took care of him when he was sick and dying. Not some nurse. Not you."

"Don't forget Queen Mab. Looks like she checked in on him pretty often. They were old chums." He opened a journal. "You brainwashed him. You told him what to believe."

"You used to believe, too," she said. "Don't you remember? He told me about when you were little. You saw the faeries everywhere. Because you're an O'Dare."

"I didn't, I'm not—"

"And as for what I told him to believe, I also told him that you would come before he died."

She let the remark hang in the air. Then she grabbed her bag and left the flat, shutting the door with exaggerated care.

"Screw you," he said quietly.

He picked up another journal and flipped through it, but he was tired and, he realized, hungry. There was nothing in his uncle's fridge, and only a jar of blackberry jam and some spices in the pantry. The jam was for when Queen Mab came by, he supposed. He hoped that when she came, she would bring him some whiskey.

He went downstairs and onto the street. Asha Sen was not there, pouting and waiting. She was gone. Good. Night was falling, darkness puddling around the buildings that had once housed ethnic grocers and tiny takeout places. He smelled cumin, lemons, and garlic.

Then he thought of the Old Map, recently vandalized, and decided to go there. He walked down the street, made a couple of turns, and swung inside. No one greeted him as he was seated and given a menu; years ago, he'd known everyone who worked there by name.

"Well, now, this is downright uncanny," said a familiar voice. Michael looked up to find the Australian standing next to his table.

Michael felt foolishly relieved to see a familiar face that was not Asha's. He strained to smile and said, "What are the odds?"

"It's a small world. What can I say?" said the Australian, smiling. "Join you?"

They spent the next hour talking politics, science, and movies—anything but faeries. They drank beer and then the Australian bought a couple rounds of whiskey. Michael got a little too drunk, then way too drunk, and he didn't care. The world, such as it was, was back to normal, whatever normal was. Faeries, his ass.

They both watched as one of the waiters drew back a curtain and showed another waiter the plywood sheet covering the window that Michael had seen broken on the news video. The second waiter nervously patted the piece of wood and whispered something under his breath as if to assure himself that it would stand up to further violence.

"I saw that happen on TV," Michael said. "Skinheads tried to loot the till."

"Crikey," the Australian murmured. "Humanity! You'd think by now we'd have solved everyone's problems."

"Maybe we *should* just give it back," Michael muttered. "We're doing a real bang-up job with the place." He put both his hands on the table as the pub spun around him like a falling autumn leaf. "I'm going home."

"Walk you?" said the other man.

"I mean New York."

"Missing that bird who's not your missus?" the Australian said, and snorted a laugh. "Poetry."

Michael couldn't make himself smile. "Not in the least. She's what you'd call an unmissed miss. A real PIA, if you get my meaning."

"Women," the Australian agreed.

They grinned at each other and Michael drained the very last drops of his whiskey.

"And on that note, it's late and I have a morning appointment. No rest for the wicked, don't they say?" the Australian said. "What's on your agenda tomorrow?"

Tomorrow was Thursday. Michael felt a fierce joy at the thought of blowing off Asha's magical deadline.

"Not a thing besides catching a flight back home," Michael replied. As he put cash on the table, he re-remembered the man's name, which he had forgotten and remembered several times already. "Matthew. Great to run into you."

"The same." The man picked up his coat.

They parted at the pub's front door. The evening air was cool and fresh. Michael remembered books and stories and old Irish songs about lost battles and the evil English. O'Dare was an Irish name, and although his uncle said they'd lived in London for generations, Uncle Daniel had still spoken with a wee bit o' lilt.

"Too late, me boyo," Michael murmured. "You'll never hear that voice again."

A commotion in the opposite direction caught his attention. The end of the street was surprisingly crowded; a young man in jeans and a T-shirt threw something at the plate glass window of an electronics shop. The man yelled something about taxes and another young man, this one holding a baseball bat, took a swing at the same window. The crowd transformed into a mob that howled and smashed away the remaining glass before swarming into the store. Sirens blared in the background while people re-emerged carrying cartons, boxes.

Michael was stunned. They were looting.

Michael's waiter poked his head out of the door, then called back over his shoulder, "Call the coppers, Wills! It's starting up again." He looked at Michael and added, "Best come back inside, sir."

"My place is close," Michael said, pointing away from the chaos.

"Then best get going," the waiter said.

But Michael knew a mob could turn on a dime, so he hurried the rest of the way back to the bookstore. A sense of ownership came over him— this was his family's store. It belonged to the O'Dares. To him. He needed to protect it.

Through the bookshop's front window, a dim light left on from earlier in the day reflected from the back room. Given the turmoil, Michael stopped to turn off the light before heading upstairs to the flat.

The aged book smell was like a calming shot of whiskey after the shock of the riot. He'd always loved that smell. He'd spent some of his happiest times here with his uncle, shelving old leather-bound books, and listening to tall tales about faeries and the tricks they played on humans. When he was a kid, those old stories had felt so real. He had even imagined seeing the occasional faerie as he walked through Hyde Park with his uncle, but after Sean's death, life in New York and the daily legal grind had worn away the magic, turning those stories into what they really were— fanciful tales told by a sweet old man. Yet, somehow, standing there in the bookshop, he remembered what it felt like to believe.

Then he heard the gentle sound of breathing punctuated by soft crying from the back room. He tiptoed forward, avoiding the floorboards that creaked when you walked on them and he hovered on the threshold. Light spilled over his shoulder to reveal Asha Sen, sitting cross-legged on the floor with photos of Daniel spread around her. Mascara-stained tears streaked her cheeks.

. She looked up and pursed her lips when she saw him standing in the doorway.

"I won't be long. I was just looking for a picture."

"I think you found one," Michael said. Asha uttered a startled laugh through her tears and nodded.

"I guess I did." She heaved a sigh and looked back down at the photos. "I used to stop by every night to check on him, even before he got sick. I'd sit next to his bed, reading to him for hours. We had just finished *Robinson Crusoe*." She pointed to a stack of leather-bound classics whose spines and covers were marked by years of wear. She wiped her cheeks. "I miss him."

Michael knelt next to her. Outside, the angry crowd was surging down his street. Anger, mistrust, frustration. Fear. He felt all that, boiling inside; but Asha's grief smashed a different wall within him, a wall of his own: after his father's death, he had clung to his dotty old uncle, a man who lived on fairy stories and whiskey, and somehow when he was little, Michael had believed that faeries could bring his father back. But of course that hadn't been true. Faeries weren't real.

I couldn't let myself believe Uncle Daniel was dying, too, he thought. *That he would leave me. I couldn't go through it again.*

If it hadn't been for Asha, his uncle really would have died alone. Maybe she wasn't the evil lawyer he'd made her out to be.

Maybe that role was his.

"I'm so sorry." He touched her shoulder and used his other hand to dab at the tears on his cheeks.

"I didn't think you'd come back," she said.

He sighed. "I was planning to go home tomorrow morning, but... do I have to believe to sign the lease?"

"No. You just need to sign."

Michael thought for a moment and then nodded. A few extra hours' delay to honor the old man; it wasn't much, but it was the least he could do.

"Then I'll sign it. For him. And for you," Michael said looking at the picture in Asha's hands. Then he looked at some of the others on the floor, and still more hanging on the walls, softly lit by moonlight.

There were dozens of images that included Asha at different ages. A young girl in a frilly sundress, a young woman wearing a university gown, and one that could have been taken last week as she stood beneath the bookshop sign, shielding her eyes from the sun. There were photos of Sean, too, and of him and Sean. And then, after that, there were only two of him that his mother must have sent.

Asha had spent more of her life with Uncle Daniel than Michael. While he had focused on his career and hadn't visited in years, Asha had been there all along.

"I'll sign it," he said again.

"Thank you." Asha reached up to touch his cheek. The space between them collapsed; their lips touched, and he wrapped his arms around her. Responding, she pressed against him and they held each other gently. Then, after a time, the gentleness vanished and something different came over him. Something very new, as Asha kissed his closed eyes, his forehead, and his lips.

He caught his breath. *This* was what magic felt like.

✤ ✤ ✤

Magic.

In the dawn, Michael woke to find Asha breathing gently beside him. Her hair was mussed and her mascara tears had dried beneath her eyes, and she was still beautiful. Lying there with her next to him felt like home. Instead of rousing her, he watched her sleep, enjoying the comfort of having her close.

When she finally opened her eyes, he grinned, feeling foolish for watching her. She pulled him close for a kiss.

Half an hour later, they were pulling on their clothes. Then Asha reached for the black leather briefcase she had brought with her.

"This is a copy of the lease," she said, handing him a large sealed envelope. "I was going to give it to you last night. Now that you're in England, you can take possession of it. But I have to warn you that I haven't read it."

He stopped tying his tie and stared at her, thunderstruck. That was an unbelievable admission for an attorney to make under any circumstances, but in this case, when they had discussed and debated a legal document on two continents and she had insisted that he had to come to London to sign it, he simply didn't believe her.

"He did try to read it to me," she said, "but the words became gibberish as soon as they left his mouth."

The walls crashed back down around his heart. She wasn't devious or manipulative, she was utterly mad. She must have seen the change in his feelings; she paled and reached out a hand and said, "Please, Michael. Please trust me."

"I need to look it over," he said. He opened the envelope.

"I should have ordered a car from our firm," she said apologetically. "We'll take a taxi and you can read it on the way, all right?"

He blew air out of his cheeks and nodded very unhappily. What was the saying, in for a penny?

She led the way downstairs; as they pushed through the front door, they were surrounded by a sea of angry people. He saw bats in their hands, bricks. The mob pressed them against the wall and Michael caught himself saying, "Look out," putting himself in front of her. Shielding her.

Michael locked the door, hoping it would be enough to keep the crowds away if things got worse. Asha grabbed his hand with a crushing grip and pulled him.

"Come on. We have to get off this street," she yelled over her shoulder as she bulldozed her way through the swarming mass of people.

They threaded their way down the lanes and streets. There were rioters everywhere. He heard the crash of breaking glass, angry shouts, a siren. At last they reached Trafalgar Square, heading toward Pall Mall.

Asha hailed a black cab and they climbed in. Michael pulled out the lease; it was in English, and written in contemporary legalese. The professional habits of years of training compelled his slow, deliberate read as they inched along the Mall toward Earl's Court. Traffic came to a stop a dozen blocks from Asha's office. Horns blared as cars tangled together, trying to push their way into the street, which had become little more than a parking lot.

"Oh, my God. We're not going to make it!" she cried, looking at her watch.

"Where's your office?" Michael said, looking up from the last page.

"There. With the flags." She pointed toward a white building with colorful pennants hanging above the entry. It was at least ten blocks away. "Pull over," she told the driver.

The lease was quite specific about the timing of his signature. If they were late and he didn't make it, it would be finished. Done. He thought it over. And then he thought of how he had felt when he and Asha had made love. As if there was more to the world than he knew or believed.

"No. Keep going," he told the cabbie. He turned to Asha and said, "I'll meet you there."

She started to say something, and then she quickly kissed him and nodded.

He threw open the door, wishing he'd brought his track shoes. He ran, dodging around cars that packed the intersection and sliding across hoods in his best Bruce Willis imitation when there was no space for a pedestrian to cross.

Less than a block from the office Big Ben chimed, echoing all around him and signaling that ten o'clock had come...

...and gone, even as he dashed up a flight of marble stairs toward the doors of Asha's firm.

Standing outside the door, blocking his entry, was the Australian. He gave Michael a toothy smile.

"Matthew? Excuse me. I need to get inside," Michael said.

The older man crossed his arms over his large belly without moving aside.

"You're late. It's expired."

Michael gaped at him. "What did you say?"

"Your lease is up."

"You're kidding, right?"

"Mortal, I never 'kid.'" The Australian grinned triumphantly, raising his hands in a diva-like pose, which made his protruding belly stick out even further.

The tips of Matthew's fingers caught the sunlight, which slithered down his hands like liquid gold, covering his arms and body before catching fire. Molten flames raged momentarily before dying out.

In his place stood the most beautiful woman Michael had ever seen, with flaming red hair caught up in an emerald crown. Her age was impossible to tell. Her dress was a mix of flowing green silk, covered with emeralds and diamonds that held the sunlight. Her eyes were icy, her smile even more so.

"You have lost, O'Dare," she declared, her smile turning cruel and barbaric. "Fine day for rioting, wouldn't you say?"

"My God," Michael said, stumbling away.

Asha, heaving with exertion, arrived in time to keep him from tumbling backwards down the stairs.

"Please. Call me Mab. 'God' is so yesterday. Now, if you'll excuse me. I have a lease to sign. Ms. Sen," Mab said dismissively.

"Mab, no, please," Asha murmured.

The two watched as Mab entered the building. The door began to swing shut behind her. Asha buried her face in her hands and Michael fought to pull himself together. It was true. All of it.

"I don't lose cases," he said slowly. "Damn it, I do *not* lose."

He gripped the copy of his lease and caught the closing door with his other hand.

"Not so fast, faerie," he said, dashing inside. They were in a long hall decorated with oil portraits. His shoes echoed on a marble black-and-white checkerboard floor.

"Your time has come and gone, mortal. Be gracious in defeat, and I'll grant favor upon you as the former Leaseholder." Mab's words trailed behind her.

A door opened before she reached it. With Michael on her heels, she glided into a large conference room dominated by an enormous ebony desk. Humans and strangely-glowing people in elaborate gowns — faeries? — stood around a large round table. Some of the humans were crying in each other's arms. The faeries were smiling and, at the arrival of Queen Mab, bowed low, then straightened and began to applaud and cheer.

Panting, Michael raised his arms for silence. Mab tipped her head indulgently and signaled everyone to give him their attention.

"The name is O'Dare," he announced, "and you might think you know me because of those who have come before me to write their names on this lease." He held up the document.

"I know all I need to know," Mab said.

A quill pen in a golden inkwell was perched beside an ancient scroll of parchment. The letters were indecipherable until Michael strode up beside Mab. Then they obligingly changed into English characters.

He blocked her hand before she could sign beneath the blank that read REVOKED.

"Not so fast. We are not in breach," he said.

There was murmuring around the room. Mab rolled her eyes. She reached for the lease again, but her hand recoiled as if hitting an invisible wall.

"Article five, section three B states that the signing deadline is based upon the realm of origin of the document," Michael said.

Mab dipped her head. "Yes. And it's after ten o'clock here."

Michael grinned. "Except I'm not a citizen of the British Realm."

Mab narrowed her eyes. "What?"

One of the faeries rose. "Your Majesty, this mortal is stalling. His argument is specious. Please feel free to sign."

"No. I demand my say," Michael said, and a thrill shot through him as he saw that Mab was unable to follow through, even though she tried again to sign the document.

"Your problem, Mab, is that you're stuck in the past. You need to modernize your thinking. Article eight, section nine A clearly states that definitions are adaptable to the correct time of the realms in which the parties dwell, and the State of New York, where I dwell, is no longer subject to British rule. Therefore, we're on East Coast Standard Time, which would make it about four o'clock in the morning, giving me plenty of time to sign."

"You're a British citizen, born and bred," Mab insisted.

"To an American mother, making me a dual citizen. The lease reverts to my time zone as a resident of New York. And you're out of ploys." Michael set his U.S. passport on the table next to the lease, and plucked the feather pen from her fingers. He signed his name with flare and watched the ink glow red for a moment before fading to black.

Now it was time for the mortals in the room to cheer. Asha threw her arms around Michael's neck and kissed him. He kissed her and held her and then he started laughing. He felt positively *impish*, besting the queen of the faeries.

"Well, you can't blame a girl for trying. I almost had you, O'Dare," Mab said once the room had quieted back down.

"Almost is only good enough in horseshoes and hand grenades," Michael said putting down the pen.

Mab shrugged. "What is time to a faerie? I have infinite patience and one day this world will be mine again."

"Not today," Michael said, matching her toothy grin.

The faerie queen glowered, her eyes burning like embers, and then she vanished. The rest of the room emptied of the fae, leaving only a handful of humans behind. They rose and rushed Michael, patting him on the back. Champagne corks popped.

Asha introduced him to Sir Christopher Wright, her boss, as she said, "You know that in twenty-five years, you'll have to sign again."

"Be easier if you were already in London. We certainly have a place for you here at the firm," Sir Christopher said. He cocked a brow. "And as you're the last of the O'Dares — and believe me, on that subject we are positive — it would be prudent for you to start having children as quickly as possible."

"That's very generous of you, sir, but I think I've put the law behind me," Michael said. "I own a rather lovely bookshop now."

Asha beamed at him. "You do. And I think, Sir Christopher, that I'll have to help him run it."

"I think you will," Michael replied.

The scroll rolled up of its own accord and Sir Christopher reverently cradled it against his chest. "This goes back in the vault, then. For twenty-five years."

"I'll be here," Michael said. "With time to spare."

❖ ❖ ❖

New York Times bestselling author **NANCY HOLDER** has received five Bram Stoker Awards. She is currently writing a series of novels based on the TV show *Beauty and the Beast*. *Vendetta* and *Some Grave All* are out now. This is her second short story written with Erin Underwood.

❖ ❖ ❖

ERIN UNDERWOOD is a writer and editor as well as the publisher at Underwords Press. She is the co-editor of *Futuredaze 2: Reprise* with Nancy Holder and is also the co-editor of *Geek Theater: 15 Plays by Science Fiction and Fantasy Writers*. This is her second story with Nancy Holder.